More praise for

SKIN DEEP

"Murder, mayhem, and multiple identities merge in this electric series opener . . . Del Franco does a commendable job of blending each of Laura's different personas into the addictively fast-paced narrative and fully believable setting."—*Publishers Weekly*

"Think *Alias*'s Sydney Bristow with magical powers . . . clever and out of the ordinary. Fans of Jim Butcher's Dresden Files and Rob Thurman's Cal Leandros series will enjoy."
—*Library Journal*

"The uber-talented Del Franco . . . presents a story where menace and treachery ensure these players are put through the literal wringer. It's terrific stuff!" —*Romantic Times*

"Mr. Del Franco does a rather impressive job of rolling three characters into one and keeping readers at the edge of their seats anticipating the next move. *Skin Deep* is fast-moving, written with great detail, and introduces readers to a series that urban fantasy readers are sure to enjoy." —*Darque Reviews*

Raves for Mark Del Franco's Connor Grey novels

UNQUIET DREAMS

"Connor Grey is rapidly becoming one of my favorite fantasy detectives." —*Locus*

"A tale filled with magic, mystery, and suspense . . . a well-written story with characters that will charm readers back for another visit to the Weird." —*Darque Reviews*

"An urban fantasy wrapped around a police procedural that makes for a fast-paced, action-packed novel . . . This looks to be a great new urban fantasy series, judging by the first two books in the series." —*Gumshoe*

"Readers who like a mystery as the prime plot of an outstanding fantasy will be thoroughly entertained and challenged. This is a great new series with the potential to be a long-lasting one."
—*Genre Go Round Reviews*

continued . . .

UNSHAPELY THINGS

"It will pull you along a corkscrew of twists and turns to a final, cataclysmic battle that could literally remake the world."
—Rob Thurman, national bestselling author of *Chimera*

"[An] entertaining contemporary fantasy mystery with a hard-boiled druid detective . . . a promising start to a new series."
—*Locus*

"An engaging urban fantasy . . . a bravura finale."
—SF Reviews.net

"Masterfully blends detective thriller with fantasy . . . a fast-paced thrill ride . . . Del Franco never pauses the action . . . and Connor Grey is a very likable protagonist. The twisting action and engaging lead make *Unshapely Things* hard to put down."
—*BookLoons*

"The intriguing cast of characters keeps the readers involved with the mystery wrapped up in the fantasy . . . I look forward to spending more time with Connor in the future and learning more about him and his world."
—*Gumshoe*

"A wonderfully written, richly detailed, and complex fantasy novel with twists and turns that make it unputdownable . . . Mr. Del Franco's take on magic and paranormal elements is fresh and intriguing. Connor Grey's an appealing hero bound to delight fantasy and paranormal romance fans alike."
—*The Romance Readers Connection*

"Compelling and fast paced . . . The world-building is superb . . . Fans of urban fantasy should get a kick out of book one in this new series."
—*Romantic Times*

"A very impressive start. The characters were engaging and believable, and the plot was intriguing. I found myself unable to put it down until I had devoured it completely, and I'm eagerly looking forward to the sequel."
—*BookFetish*

"A wonderful, smart, and action-packed mystery involving dead fairies, political intrigue, and maybe a plot to destroy humanity . . . *Unshapely Things* has everything it takes to launch a long-running series, and I'm very excited to see what Del Franco has in store next for Connor Grey and his friends."
—*Bookslut*

FACE OFF

Mark Del Franco

ACE BOOKS, NEW YORK

THE BERKLEY PUBLISHING GROUP
Published by the Penguin Group
Penguin Group (USA) Inc.
375 Hudson Street, New York, New York 10014, USA
Penguin Group (Canada), 90 Eglinton Avenue East, Suite 700, Toronto, Ontario M4P 2Y3, Canada
(a division of Pearson Penguin Canada Inc.)
Penguin Books Ltd., 80 Strand, London WC2R 0RL, England
Penguin Group Ireland, 25 St. Stephen's Green, Dublin 2, Ireland (a division of Penguin Books Ltd.)
Penguin Group (Australia), 250 Camberwell Road, Camberwell, Victoria 3124, Australia
(a division of Pearson Australia Group Pty. Ltd.)
Penguin Books India Pvt. Ltd., 11 Community Centre, Panchsheel Park, New Delhi—110 017, India
Penguin Group (NZ), 67 Apollo Drive, Rosedale, North Shore 0632, New Zealand
(a division of Pearson New Zealand Ltd.)
Penguin Books (South Africa) (Pty.) Ltd., 24 Sturdee Avenue, Rosebank, Johannesburg 2196,
South Africa

Penguin Books Ltd., Registered Offices: 80 Strand, London WC2R 0RL, England

This is a work of fiction. Names, characters, places, and incidents either are the product of the author's imagination or are used fictitiously, and any resemblance to actual persons, living or dead, business establishments, events, or locales is entirely coincidental. The publisher does not have any control over and does not assume any responsibility for author or third-party websites or their content.

FACE OFF

An Ace Book / published by arrangement with the author

PRINTING HISTORY
Ace mass-market edition / August 2010

Copyright © 2010 by Mark Del Franco.
Cover art by Chris Cocozza.
Cover design by Annette Fiore DeFex.
Interior text design by Laura K. Corless.

All rights reserved.
No part of this book may be reproduced, scanned, or distributed in any printed or electronic form without permission. Please do not participate in or encourage piracy of copyrighted materials in violation of the author's rights. Purchase only authorized editions.
For information, address: The Berkley Publishing Group,
a division of Penguin Group (USA) Inc.,
375 Hudson Street, New York, New York 10014.

ISBN: 978-0-441-01903-8

ACE
Ace Books are published by The Berkley Publishing Group,
a division of Penguin Group (USA) Inc.,
375 Hudson Street, New York, New York 10014.
ACE and the "A" design are trademarks of Penguin Group (USA) Inc.

PRINTED IN THE UNITED STATES OF AMERICA

10 9 8 7 6 5 4 3 2 1

If you purchased this book without a cover, you should be aware that this book is stolen property. It was reported as "unsold and destroyed" to the publisher, and neither the author nor the publisher has received any payment for this "stripped book."

For my mom, who will always be there

ACKNOWLEDGMENTS

Thanks to Anne Sowards, my editor, for her much-appreciated patience and support, and to Sara and Bob Schwager, copy editors extraordinaire, who always make me look good. I would also like to thank John Liguori, Paul Carroll, and Andrew Schieffelin, who patiently listen to my rants and still return my calls knowing one's coming. And special thanks to Jack, who gave me the time and space to write.

1
CHAPTER

THE DESOLATE ROAD stretched off into the darkness
like a black scar through the woods. In the predawn light, the
trees leaned forward, their leaves dull gray, void of true
color, their trunks shadows among shadows. Laura Blackstone shifted in her car seat, the engine a soft rumble behind
the classical music whispering from the speakers. Watching the
road, she sipped her coffee. Other cars sat hidden among
the trees, a bit of chrome here and there gleaming beneath
the waning moon, the glow of cell phones dancing like orange fireflies as others waited with her.

To outward appearances, Laura was calm and relaxed. She
had spent years learning to control her emotions and reactions.
Herself. Learned not to show fear or anger or stress. Those
emotions all happened inside now.

Of course, to outward appearances, she didn't look like
Laura Blackstone at all. People who knew Laura Blackstone
knew the woman who worked as the public-relations director
at the Fey Guild. They saw a fit woman, her face of an inde-
terminate young age, who spent her time spinning the fey
agenda for the media. They saw a druid, one of the fey who

had the ability to manipulate essence. She didn't look different from humans. She fit in.

Trying to convince humans that the power of the fey was simply an expression of who and what they were and not dangerous was important to her. It wasn't magic, what she did. It was inherent in the nature of the fey, an expression of someone who came from Faerie. Some fey had better skill in manipulating essence than others. Some had none at all. Essence could be dangerous. So could a knife or a gun. Or a fist. Having the potential to use essence as a weapon didn't mean every fey would use it that way. They didn't wake up in the morning and decide they were going to hurt someone. Some did. Laura wasn't naïve. Some humans made the conscious choice to cause pain, too. But to Laura, singling out the fey as the sole source of danger and worry in the world was wrong.

Which brought her to the dark car on a dark road, masked to look like someone else. Glamours were one of her skills, and she made them better than anyone else. With the right manipulation of essence, she could alter her appearance. The transformation was complete in every sense—visual, auditory, and tactile.

If a colleague from the Guild walked up to her and asked for directions, he would have no clue that the thin, dark-haired woman in the car was the blond public-relations director he worked with. If she were to introduce herself, the soft Irish lilt in her voice would sound nothing like Laura's strictly American speech pattern. Her clear blue eyes would stare at him with no indication they were truly green. The mask was complete. He would believe she was someone named Mariel Tate.

That was what attracted the notice of the International Global Security Agency. InterSec first tapped Laura as a policy advisor. By treaty, it worked with governments around the globe as a police force for the fey that extended beyond the borders of nations. When the agency realized she had skills beyond the diplomatic, it recruited her for the special-operations division. Laura Blackstone disappeared from their roster, and Mariel Tate was born.

Five miles out, Sinclair sent.

The phrase reverberated in her mind. The fey called it a sending, the wrapping of thoughts in a tangle of essence to send messages to each other's minds. Sinclair was descended from a jotunn, a fire giant of the Teutonic fey, but he was more human than not. He didn't have the abilities of someone who was fully fey, but he could do sendings. They were difficult for him, which was why he sounded so rough in her mind, and he used them only sparingly.

Laura had met Sinclair on her last major mission. Through a series of mistakes and compromises, he ended up working for InterSec on a probationary basis for reasons that gave her a keen sense of responsibility. He was where he was because of her. She wanted him to succeed. It didn't escape her that her worry about him was more than professional concern, but she wasn't going to dwell on that in the middle of a job.

A political organization called the Legacy Foundation was showing signs of going radical. Sinclair had inserted himself into the lower rungs of the power structure, where people were more likely to trust a newcomer. After a few weeks, the decision had paid off with information that Legacy was moving a shipment of weapons into D.C. InterSec had decided to intercept the delivery and, with luck, solidify Sinclair's undercover status.

Laura had been waiting hours for Sinclair's signal. She made her own sendings to give the others notice that it was showtime.

Against the pale ash sky, arc lights blazed to life. The metallic blue strobe of police lights flashed from the tops of three cars parked along the breakdown lane. People exited their cars, men and women in law-enforcement uniforms. They moved cones into the road, then lit flares to reveal a large traffic sign propped up against sawhorses. In a matter of moments, a drunk-driver checkpoint was in place in the middle of the Virginia back road.

Laura drank the remains of her cold coffee and dropped the empty cup on the floor as she left the car. She moved into the trees across from the checkpoint, sensing other InterSec agents taking their posts nearby. Even in the dark, their body signatures—their personal essences—whirled with color in Laura's sensing ability. Druids were adept at sensing body signatures, but the same quirk of fate that gave Laura the ability to create flawless glamours seemed to have limited her ability to sense essence unless she was close to it. Farther along the road, she knew Danann fairies hid in the trees although she couldn't see them. One by one, they exchanged sendings confirming they were in position.

Two miles, Sinclair sent.

An engine made a hollow sound in the far distance. Where the road met the horizon, a dim glow grew until it resolved into headlights.

Got you. Good luck, Laura sent.

The engine throttled louder as a panel truck approached. One of the uniformed officers strolled into the road and waved a flashlight with an orange cone attached to the end. As the truck neared, it slowed and pulled into the breakdown lane. A white man, rough-skinned and dark-haired, leaned out the driver's side window as another officer approached. "Is there a problem?" he asked.

The officer flashed his flashlight in the driver's eyes. "This is a DWI checkpoint. Have you been drinking this evening, sir?"

"No," he said.

The officer swept his beam along the side of the truck as two more officers took up position several feet to the rear of the vehicle. "Where are you going this morning, sir?"

"Arlington," the driver replied.

The officer pointed the flashlight inside the cab, illuminating a rider in the passenger seat. "Can I see your license, registration, and insurance please?"

The driver's head moved out of sight as he leaned toward the glove compartment. The officer took the moment to make eye contact with his backup. The driver handed out folded papers. The officer stepped back. "I'll be back in a moment, sir."

He walked in front of the truck and got into the police car. Seconds stretched into minutes.

They're getting antsy. Guns are coming out, Sinclair sent. Laura relayed his message to the surrounding agents.

The police officer returned from his car, this time with his partner strolling along the passenger side of the truck. He handed the papers to the driver. "Can you step out of the car, please?"

"Is there something wrong, officer?" the driver asked.

"This is a random roadside sobriety check. It'll only take a minute."

Laura tensed as the driver didn't move. She knew the agents posing as the police officers and knew they were ready for anything. The driver's door opened. The officer on the opposite of the truck pointed his hand at the cab. "Close your door and stay in the car."

Laura couldn't see the other side of the truck, but by the lack of any further talk or action, she assumed the passenger had started to open the door, then complied with the order to close it. The driver stepped out and was put through the standard field tests. He touched his nose without any problem.

"Follow me, sir," the officer said as he led him to the back of the truck. They moved far enough away that Laura couldn't hear them. The officer had the driver walk the painted line marking the breakdown lane.

When the driver finished, the officer moved closer to the truck again. "What's in the back?" he asked.

"Tools," said the driver.

"Let's open 'er up," said the officer.

The driver hesitated. "Can you do that?"

"Do what, sir?"

"Search my truck without a warrant?"

The officer cocked his head. "Who said anything about a search? Are you saying I should get a warrant?"

The driver shrugged. "I'm just asking."

"So, are you going to open it up?" the officer said.

The driver shook his head. "Not without a warrant, I ain't."

The officer grasped the handle. "Well, you go ahead and find yourself a warrant while I take a look inside."

The driver took a step forward. "Hey!"

Another officer pulled his gun and pointed it at him. "Get back and keep your hands out."

The driver froze as the first officer turned the handle. Before he had the chance to open the door, someone inside kicked it. Gunfire erupted, and the driver fell to the ground as the two officers dropped back to the sides of the truck. More gunfire sounded from the passenger side.

Two men jumped out of the van, their AK-47s sparking yellow flashes as they fired into the open air. Sinclair appeared behind them, his height making him easy to recognize. While the first two men swept the ground with more gunfire, Sinclair leaned away from the van, firing into the distant empty road. InterSec agents swept out from the tree line, bolts of essence springing like white lightning from their hands.

Laura primed her own essence and ran toward the truck. She fired at the back of the closest man, and he fell over. The second man stepped between her and Sinclair. Sinclair trained his weapon on her.

Head shot, she sent.

Sinclair fired. She reacted to the flash, snapping her head back and throwing her body onto the pavement. As she landed, she rolled to a still position, facing the van. She watched Sinclair grab his companion by the back of his vest and pull him away. As they ran for the tree line, Sinclair fired another barrage as they disappeared into the shadows of the trees, forcing the InterSec agents to back off.

Laura waited until the sound of gunshots moved into the

distance. She stood, brushing off debris. Although she had been far enough away from the propellant gases from Sinclair's blanks, the odor of gunpowder had settled on her. She joined two of her fellow agents by the prone body of the driver. A druid she didn't know looked up, unimpressed. "The idiots killed one of their own, Tate. It doesn't look like this bunch is going to be tough to handle."

Her lip curled down in annoyance as she stared at the body. "What's the status of the guy in the passenger seat?"

"Dead," someone called out.

Laura sighed as she crouched by the guy she had shot. He was alive, but unconscious. She wouldn't know if his brain was scrambled until he woke up. With no ability to shield themselves, humans didn't take essence shots well.

You doing okay? she sent to Sinclair.

Almost clear. Get the air cover to move west. They're too close, he replied.

She did as he asked, then watched the essence-fire flashing in the distance shift away. She stood out of the way at the rear of the truck as the team brought lights in closer. The heavy-duty crates inside the truck appeared innocuous. Someone flipped one open. She snorted in mild despair. Rocket launchers. Legacy must have changed or added to the weapon manifest at the last minute because Sinclair had reported the shipment would be guns and ammunition.

From the far side of the van, EMTs pushed a gurney with the sheet-draped body of the front-seat passenger. Another group wheeled up to the driver's body. Two dead. One foolishly had stood in the wrong place at the wrong time, and the other stupidly had fired a gun that gave licensed law enforcement the right to return fire. She wondered whose lives were being saved by confiscating the weapons. She wondered if two dead—even two of the bad guys—justified their mission. She wondered if their goal would be achieved with blood on their hands. For a moment, she wondered what the goal was but pushed the thought aside. That wasn't her job.

"I'm heading in," she said. The nearby agents would han-

dle the cleanup. That was their job. As she approached her
car, she noticed a few bullet holes in the front fender. She
hadn't realized she had been close to being shot. She slid
back into the driver's seat and switched the classical music
to something heavier—industrial rock filled with crashes and
static and angst. It felt more appropriate under the circumstances.

You okay? she sent to Sinclair.

It's all good, he said. The reply was soft and slow, which
meant he was a fair distance away.

See you when you can, she sent. He didn't respond, probably saving energy. All the sendings he had done tonight were
going to give him a headache by morning.

The lights of the checkpoint vanished into the darkness
behind her. She let the weight of the evening slip away and
released the tension of the operation. Another day, another
success. Two dead, but they weren't her dead, and they
weren't InterSec.

It's all good, she thought. The thought settled heavily in
her mind.

CHAPTER 2

ORRIN AP RHYS stared out the large round office window, his wings undulating in the subtle current from the air-conditioning. The purple- and red-veined wing layers glanced off each other with gentle nudges, faint flickers of white shimmering in the bright light of the office. In the near distance beyond him, the top of the Washington Monument pierced the bright blue sky. The ornate trim around the window framed the view like a photograph. "How can a *leanansidhe* be in my Guildhouse and I not know about it?"

Laura straightened in her chair at the Guildmaster's change in conversation. She had been thinking about the dawn mission, mulling whether the deaths could have been prevented. The public-relations implications of Rhys's latest projects slipped from her thoughts as she remembered the van driver falling from shots fired by his accomplices. The mention of the *leanansidhe* brought her focus back to the conversation.

She avoided looking at Resha Dunne, who sat beside her in front of the Guildmaster's long ebony desk. Resha was the Guild board director who represented solitaries, small groups and individual fey—like a *leanansidhe*—who didn't fit into the major fey species categories. The *leanansidhe* survived by absorbing essence from living beings. People died when that happened.

Resha crossed his legs, the hem of his pants riding up to reveal a strip of blue-gray skin. On a day-to-day basis, Laura tended not to notice Resha's appearance. As a merrow, his pale skin was normal for one of the sea folk, and Laura was used to working with fey whose appearance did not fit into mainstream sensibilities.

"Well?" asked Rhys.

Resha fidgeted. "InterSec is not obligated to inform me about its staff, Orrin."

Rhys turned, anger glinting in his eye. "Not obligated? We're talking about a *leanansidhe*, Dunne. Not some inconsequential water sprite."

Cress, thought Laura. They were talking about Cress, her InterSec colleague. Not some dangerous being with no moral qualms about killing people. Cress had rejected that role for herself, finding alternative means to survive. They weren't talking about one of the most feared fey in existence. They were talking about her friend.

"This *leanansidhe* seems different," Laura said.

Rhys stalked to his desk, his gossamer-thin wings sweeping back with the motion of his body. "It's dangerous. We can't trust it."

With a nervous flick of his short-clawed fingers, Resha brushed at his knee, not looking up at Rhys. "She saved our lives, Orrin."

Many lives, thought Laura. Cress had thwarted a major terrorist attack at the National Archives and almost died in the process. Even Rhys had a personal debt to her. Not that it mattered, apparently.

"Are you two defending it?" Rhys asked.

Laura wet her lips. Rhys didn't know about her undercover work for InterSec. Part of the delicate balance of her life was maintaining that secrecy. "I think, sir, that things may not be as they appear. Perhaps we need more information."

Rhys startled them with a slap of his hand on the desk. "I need no more information. I know what this thing is, and I want it out of my Guildhouse."

Even sitting, Resha appeared to cower. "I will look into it."

Frustration burned within Laura. As the Guild's public-relations director, it was not her place to argue with him about it. Worse, she couldn't argue without revealing why she knew what she was talking about. It chafed to watch Resha capitulate despite the fact that he had a duty to stand up for the rights of the solitary fey. Even if it was a *leanan-sidhe*.

Rhys leaned back in his chair. "Now, what has been the response to our donation toward the rebuilding of the National Archives?"

Grateful for the change in subject, Laura placed her hand on the folder with the information. As a druid, she didn't need to read from her notes. Her innate memory retention filed away data for instant recall later. All she had to do was focus on whatever she wanted to recall, and the information would start to flow. "It moved public perception of the Guild slightly upward, but has had no impact on the overall negative impression of the fey. Do you want specific numbers?"

Rhys grunted. "Not now."

"Was the money not enough?" Resha asked.

Laura didn't answer. If Resha weren't so prone to clue-lessness in front of everyone, including the Guildmaster, she would have been embarrassed for him. But Resha was Resha, and his naïveté came with the territory. Over the years, Laura had taken to pretending to be fixed on her files or notes when Resha made his off comments.

Ever since the fey folk from Faerie appeared in the modern world a century earlier, the majority of humans feared them and their power. Someone like Laura, a druid with no discernible physical characteristics to distinguish her from humans, enjoyed the benefit of social acceptance. Someone like Resha, with his skin tone and forehead peak and sharp, predatory teeth, had no hope of blending in. Yet, despite having told her once of his personal discomfort with prejudice, he didn't understand that money did not always buy acceptance.

Rhys made a dismissive gesture. "The important point is humans are making a distinction between the Guild and the fey as a whole. That works to our political advantage. The human politicians can safely support our initiatives without undermining their voter bases."

Resha repositioned his chair to face Rhys. "In some quarters, there are calls for the Guild to fund the entire renovation."

Rhys frowned. "I've heard the rumblings. Who are these Legacy people?"

Laura masked any reaction that might indicate she knew about Legacy. The Legacy Foundation sought an end to the fey monarchies in Ireland and Germany. Until recently, they acted primarily as a think tank, better funded than most, whose primary focus was to convince the U.S. government to sever diplomatic ties with the monarchies. Recent information indicated they might be radicalizing, which was why she and Sinclair had started infiltrating it for firsthand data. She wasn't aware of any specific news items or press releases from Legacy regarding the incident at the National Archives. "They're a coalition of fey and humans who think the monarchies are dangerous. They do a lot of humanitarian work for people affected by the fey. For instance, I know they run medical clinics for humans who have essence-related injuries."

Rhys smiled. "Perhaps we should offer our support."

With a serious and considering look, Resha bobbed his head. "Perhaps funding for one of those clinics would show them we care about such things, too."

Laura met Rhys's eyes for the briefest of moments. Resha had a tendency to be either dense or clueless. Rhys smirked back. "That's an excellent idea, Resha. In fact, I think it would look less heavy-handed if you made the call."

Pleased, he bowed his head. "I'd be happy to."

A satisfied smile flashed across Rhys's face. Having a joke at Resha's expense felt petty. Rhys underestimated Resha and, although often justified, the merrow was astute enough to take advantage of the perception. "I'll send you what information I can find, Resha. When you're ready, we can pull a press release together," she said.

Rhys waved a dismissive hand toward Resha. "Laura and I need to work out some details on the Draigen macCullen reception, Resha. Send me a budget recommendation and let me know as soon as Legacy catches wind of things."

Resha stood and bowed his head. "I will keep you apprised, sir."

Laura shuffled the files on her lap as Resha left the room.

"He's useful occasionally," Rhys said.

Laura's smile was practiced detachment. She wondered what Rhys said when she left a room. She sensed he liked her, liked her work; but she had irritated him on more than one occasion. He made no effort to hide his displeasure then, but he didn't seem to hold a grudge. Still, he was her boss, and she played things carefully with him—distant enough to keep things professional, familiar enough for him to view her as an ally. "With all the strong personalities in the Guildhouse, he can be quite a disarming advantage for you."

Rhys grunted. "We're going to need all the strong personalities we can get in the next few weeks."

Laura retrieved a folder and pulled out several papers stapled together. "Senator Hornbeck wants to speak last at the Archive memorial service."

She handed him the schedule. The terrorist attack at the National Archives had resulted in the deaths of twenty-nine people and millions of dollars in damage. The Guild had plenty of cash to fix the building. The loss of life wasn't a problem solvable with money. Rhys skimmed the schedule. "That's fine. I'll take whatever criticism he wants to throw at us after I speak. We can spin it later in the media outlets."

He dropped the schedule. "Speaking of which, from now

on I want every document relating to the attack to refer to 'Inverni terrorists.'"

Laura folded her hands on top of the folders and pursed her lips. The fey were, in truth, refugees in the world. Faerie existed, or at least had at one time, and was ruled by fairies of the Danann clan. In the early 1900s, the event known as Convergence occurred, the puncturing of the veil between Faerie and the modern era, and the fey found themselves trapped. Their common struggle to find acceptance among the human populace did not mean that the fey forgot their own internal animosities.

"You want to argue with me again," Rhys said.

Laura let out a tired chuckle. Rhys was a Danann, as was High Queen Maeve. The Danann had a long-standing rivalry with the Inverni, who were the only clan strong enough to challenge Maeve's rule. When Convergence happened, Maeve made a secret deal with the United States and Great Britain. In return for her aid in time of war, the two human governments agreed to defend Maeve against any threat to her sovereignty. Including the Inverni. Specifically the Inverni.

"I don't argue, Orrin. I advise. You decide your course of action." She used his first name purposely to indicate her comment was more personal and off-the-record. It was a conversational trick she used often with Rhys, a way of gaining his confidence by showing him she was comfortable being honest with him.

He smiled. "We have to deflect blame for the attack from the High Queen."

"It's a mistake to imply all Inverni are terrorists, Orrin. You will end up protecting Maeve's standing with the human government at the expense of unity among the Celtic fey."

His smile became more predatory. "You say that like it's a bad thing."

With amused disbelief, Laura leaned her head back and ran her hand through her blond hair. "Guildmaster, you were the target of an assassination attempt, and that was *before* the world knew your part in the drafting of the Treaty of London. Unless you have a death wish, I do not see the benefit of this course of action."

Laura had always thought the Treaty of London was the greatest political accomplishment the fey folk had achieved when they arrived from Faerie. The Danann clan had ruled the Seelie Court securely ever since. She had no idea that success had come at a steep price. What no one knew for a century was that the Treaty contained a secret clause in which the U.S. and Great Britain agreed to defend Maeve against any challenge to her rule. Only the Inverni clan, which was currently led by Draigen macCullen, had the power to make that challenge. By default, the clause made the Inverni instant criminals subject to imprisonment if they protested Maeve's rule in any way.

"I am in contact with the High Queen," he said, which meant, in effect, the end of the conversation. If Rhys was acting on Maeve's authority, nothing Laura said would have an impact.

"Am I to draw any inference between the use of 'Inverni terrorists' and the visit from Draigen macCullen?" she asked. Draigen was the leader of the Inverni clan in Ireland and, by coincidence, sister to Terryn macCullen, Laura's supervisor at InterSec. When the Treaty clause had been made public for the first time, Draigen announced she would be visiting the U.S. to discuss business relationships with the president of the United States. Everyone knew that was a cover. Draigen was coming to put pressure on the U.S. to denounce the century-old Treaty.

Rhys closed one eye. "An unfortunate intersection of events, Laura, let me assure you."

He was lying, she knew. The expression on his face told her so as much as her truth-sensing ability. Laura didn't mind working the politics between humans and fey. Politics between fey and fey were another matter. Deep, centuries-long animosities simmered between the various races. Some of the issues made no sense post-Convergence. Laura sighed. "Where will the reception for Draigen be held?"

"Here. In the ballroom," he said.

High Queen Maeve couldn't forbid Draigen's visit without making the situation between the Inverni and the Dananns worse, and the U.S. president couldn't appear to snub one of the most important fey leaders in the world. "We're covering for the president, aren't we?" Laura asked.

Rhys shrugged. "We can't let it appear that the president is endorsing Draigen. He'll meet with her privately, but a White House reception is out of the question."

Laura chuckled again. "And Draigen cornered you into the Guildhouse venue instead at the risk of inflaming the situation by refusing her."

"I don't think it's funny," he said.

"No, it's not. It's deft, though. You'll have to tread carefully with her, Orrin. She doesn't sound like a pushover," Laura said.

He opened a folder on the desk. "Now, that is advice I can take. I'm going to put Resha on this, but I don't want the solitaries getting too cozy with the Inverni. I want you to watch him."

Laura stood. "As you like. Do you need anything else?"

He cocked an eyebrow. "If you can think of a way to make Draigen disappear, I would appreciate it."

She let herself out the door. "You'll be the first to hear it."

As she waited for the elevator, anger pressed against her chest. As director of public relations for the Guild, she had a job to do. That meant doing as she was told. But Rhys was playing a dangerous game with the Inverni. It was wrong, and he knew it. The world had changed in a hundred years. The Inverni were not the rulers of the Celtic fey, but they had become powerful political players. Labeling them terrorists simply because they disagreed with Maeve wasn't something the human governments would approve. By slandering the Inverni, Rhys might very well provoke them.

What made it all the worse was that she had to decide whether to share what she knew with InterSec.

"How angry is he?" Resha asked her.

Between her limited sensing ability and the essence-dampening wards in the hallway, Laura hadn't sensed him come up behind her. "It'll pass, Resha. I think he's more annoyed that he didn't know a *leanansidhe* works for InterSec. If he can feel like he is doing something about it, he'll let it go."

Resha agreed, his peaked forehead looming toward Laura with a disconcerting movement. "I should warn Cress."

"Cress? You know her?"

Resha's sharp teeth slashed in a smile. "I know every solitary in this building."

"You lied to Rhys?" Laura asked. And to her. She hadn't sensed it at all.

Resha shook his head. "Not at all. I said InterSec isn't obligated to tell me anything. That's not the same thing as knowing something regardless."

It was moments like this that made Laura admire Resha. Although she often found him irritating, he had flashes of cunning that made her cautious around him. Because Rhys underestimated him didn't mean she should lull herself into doing the same. "One of these days, Resha, Orrin is going to catch on to you."

He blinked several times, obviously affecting confusion. "Not if I can help it."

As she boarded the elevator, she thought she knew exactly what he meant.

3
CHAPTER

THE MORNING INTERSEC operation, like so many others, had left Laura keyed up and jangled. Getting shot at—even on purpose—did that to her. The afternoon volume of work in public relations had slowed to a trickle. She was used to shifting gears between jobs, but sometimes coming off an adrenaline rush needed more transition. She needed to clear her mind, and the best way to do that was exercise. As she gathered her gym bag, the cell phone she used for Inter-Sec contact vibrated. She confirmed with a glance that her office door was closed before she answered the phone.

"Do you miss me?" Sinclair asked.

The sound of his voice relieved and pleased her. Despite Sinclair's tendency to make light of, well, everything, she doubted he would joke if he was in trouble. She kept her tone purposefully neutral, teasing him with indifference. "I haven't thought about you at all since you shot me in the head. Busy day."

He chuckled. "Yeah, mine, too. Spent the morning running away from InterSec agents only to end up in a bunker to answer lots of questions from Legacy."

"They bought your story?" she asked.

"I had a witness to my heroics. Thanks for leaving at least one of them alive, by the way." His voice went dry on the last comment.

"Not my fault. They spooked. Our guys spooked. I wasn't happy about it," she said.

"Well, they're cutting me loose for the night. Want to get together?"

"Sure, I'll meet you in Stafford," she said.

He made an audible groan on the other end. "Do we have to?"

"I can use a workout," she said.

"How about in an hour?" he asked.

"Perfect. See you there." She closed the phone.

InterSec's training academy and research facility in Stafford, Virginia, was an easy ride south of Washington on I-95. Easy, as long as it wasn't rush hour or something wasn't going on at Quantico. Once she was able to replace her shot-up car from the morning mission, Laura made it within normal drive time before the end-of-day commute started. Sinclair was there before her, leaning against a beat-up Silverado truck. He had a few minor scratches on his face from his run through the woods, but other than that didn't seem any the worse for wear.

Despite his strenuous day, Laura cut him no slack in the exercise rooms. White lightning streaked in a fan pattern as Laura scattered a burst of essence from her fingers. Sinclair ducked, one leg bent, the other thrown sideways, almost flat to the floor. He grunted as a finger of essence skimmed over his back, the glass particles embedded in the fabric of his safety vest dissipating the force of the hit. The instant the barrage passed, he was on his feet in a defensive posture. He grinned as they circled each other in the glass-lined training room.

Laura didn't change her expression but continued analyzing his moves, forcing him to react as quickly as possible. Essence could kill. She could restrain only so much of its intensity. Despite Sinclair's safety clothing, a slight hit in an unprotected area carried the risk of crippling him. Which was why they were in the box of glass, one of many rooms like it at the training facility. Thick sheets of glass lined every surface. Glass dissipated essence, rendering it inert, so no one outside the room was endangered.

She had avoided talking about the morning operation, preferring to lose herself in the workout. They had been at it for two hours before she brought up the subject. "They didn't find your escape suspicious?"

He shook his head but remained focused on her movements. "Not with an eyewitness to my killing an InterSec agent."

Still not registering any visible reaction, Laura noted with satisfaction that Sinclair was finally sweating and breathing heavier. His stamina didn't surprise her, considering his grandfather was a jotunn, one of the Teutonic fire giants. His speed and agility, however, impressed her. His giant heritage showed in his height, not so tall to be mistaken for fey but well over six feet. To see someone that size twist, leap, and turn to avoid essence strikes impressed her.

"Do you know what the rocket launchers were for? I thought we were expecting guns," she asked.

They circled each other, Sinclair not letting his guard down because she was speaking. "No, but they're pissed about losing them. The guns were picked up by another team."

She shot a burst of essence at him, which he easily avoided. She was getting tired, too. "Have you gotten any more names?"

"They're using a pretty tight organizational cell structure. I've only met my team unit of ten. We're down a few guys after this morning. I got a promotion, though. I'm hoping it'll get me closer to the people in charge."

When Sinclair had worked for the D.C. SWAT team, he discovered Laura was working as an undercover InterSec agent. Terryn macCullen, Laura's superior, forced him to make a choice—join InterSec or face incarceration to protect the agency. The fact that Sinclair joined willingly didn't

make it a fair choice. Laura felt an obligation to give him
whatever skills she could to protect himself. It was only fair.
His joining the agency had been forced in order to protect
her as well.

"Well, don't be so proud of yourself. They're the bad
guys." She decided to hit him with essence, one high shot,
one low, to see how he would handle it. In midthought, she
changed her mind and shot a spray of essence across the
floor. Sinclair leaped sideways, pulling his arms in as he spun
in the air, then landed in a push-up position. Laura paused. It
seemed like an unusual move for a ground-level attack. She
narrowed her eyes. But it was a perfect move if she had hit
him high and low.

Still propped on his hands and toes, Sinclair cocked his
head at her. "What?"

She shrugged. "Nothing. Let's go again."

He hopped to his feet and tensed his body, ready to shift
in any direction. Laura lifted her hands, starting to fire at his
left shoulder but going for his feet again. Sinclair moved to
his right and jumped, the jagged streak of white light passing
beneath him again. Laura put her hands on her hips.

Sinclair landed on his feet. "Something's going through
that mind of yours. What's up?"

"Let me try one more thing," she said.

A head shot, she decided, shifting to his chest at the last
moment. She fired. Sinclair ducked again, but this time kept
going until he was crouched with his knees almost to his ears
and his arms thrown to the sides for balance. He stood.
"Okay, that was one more thing. What's going on?"

"Describe how you react to my shots," she said.

He rocked his head from side to side. "I watch the shape
of your body signature. Before you release essence, it . . . I
don't know . . . sort of dimples."

Everyone had essence signatures—even humans. Most
fey sensed essence in one way or another. Druids had more
sensitivity than most and could determine species with a sec-
ondary vision that registered essence as vibrant colors in their

minds. Fairies sensed body signatures, too, but they had to physically touch the person or an object the person had come in contact with in order to read the energy. Sinclair did neither of those things. He sensed the shape of a body signature, which he claimed was like a fingerprint, unique to the individual. Neither Laura nor anyone else had ever encountered that type of ability. But what Sinclair described had to be true. It was how he had discovered Laura—by sensing her shape under its various glamoured disguises, something no other fey could do. "And that's how you know how to anticipate the direction of the strike?"

"Yes."

Laura's talent for creating glamours so detailed and tangible made her invaluable as an undercover agent for Inter-Sec. Her skill was so high, she had never been discovered. Until Jonathan Sinclair met three of Laura's personas and recognized the same shape in each one. With her secret exposed, Terryn threatened to detain Sinclair indefinitely.

Sinclair had a secret of his own. The one species Laura—or any fey—could not create a glamour for was human. Humans had weak body signatures because they weren't from Faerie. Laura's glamours hid her druid essence under those of other species, obscuring one powerful body signature for another. A fey body signature, though, shone through a human glamour persona like a bonfire. For everyone except Sinclair, the grandson of a fire giant, registered as completely human. His fey essence was so subtle, Laura's sharp skill didn't see it unless she concentrated and knew what to look for. Sinclair wiped his forehead with a towel.

She backed away, setting herself into position to resume the practice. "Pay attention specifically to the change you see in the shape of my body signature this time. Try to focus on the whole thing, not just the dimple."

She spread her hands, planning to wedge him between two fans of essence, then changed her direction to his feet. Sinclair spun sideways and jumped up, avoiding the strike. "Why did you turn sideways?"

Catching his breath, he placed his hands on his hips and looked down in thought. "Before you let loose, I thought you were going to squeeze me between two strikes, but when the dimple formed, it was aimed at my feet."

"Why did you think that?" she asked.

A smile crept onto his face. "There was a change in the shape that looked like it was about to dimple, but it didn't. Wow."

His pleasure at the thought pleased her. "You can sense at such an acute level that you react subconsciously."

His smile turned into a grin. "And you thought I had no abilities."

Amused, she twisted her lips. "I never said that. You did."

"Yeah, I guess I lied."

Laura folded her arms and leaned against the wall. With her truth sensing, Laura knew he meant he hadn't known, not that he had hidden the ability. Sinclair was an enigma to her—confident, assertive, yet cautious. He had spent his life hiding his fey nature. Humans and fey did not interbreed success-fully. Sinclair's grandfather knew that his grandson would be the subject of intense scrutiny, so he gave Sinclair a spell to hide the small hint of his feyness. The spell was bound to a medallion that Sinclair always wore. It hid excess essence, which for Sinclair meant his fey nature. He read human to her senses—and everyone else's.

Sinclair lied about himself. So did Laura. Having that par-ticular character trait in common was not the best basis for a relationship. She knew she could be trusted. She didn't know if Sinclair could. More and more lately, though, she thought he was worth the risk. "You didn't know."

"You don't know that," he said. She watched and listened as he spoke, testing the nuances of his speech. His words and tone indicated truth. Laura had limitations on certain of her abilities, a fact that she had shared only with Terryn macCul-len and Cress. For one thing, the field range of her sensing ability was limited for someone with her power. The more important secret, though, was that that limitation seemed to result in a huge advantage. Instead of a wide-ranging sensing ability, her short-range skill included truth sensing. Sinclair was telling her the truth; he hadn't known about his own acuity.

Or so she hoped. He had managed to hide his fey nature from her, something that was hard to do. She took no solace in the fact that he had hidden it from everyone. Not for the first time in the last few weeks did she wonder, If he could do that, could he evade her truth sensing? Could he lie to her?

Terryn assured her no one else knew about her skill, so theoretically no one would know to counter it. She had never realized how much she had taken for granted knowing when someone spoke truth. Until she trusted Sinclair enough to believe him, she had to assume he was lying. She felt deaf or blind around Sinclair and wondered how people functioned without truth sensing. She didn't like it.

"You would be surprised what I know," she said. It was a bluff, but only she knew there was something to bluff about. Sinclair couldn't know about her ability. She thought. Hoped.

He sauntered up to her, crossed his arms, and smiled playfully down at her. "Surprise me."

She looked away with her own smile. He couldn't have been more physically appealing to her with his dark blond hair and warm honey skin. The unusual lightness of his brown eyes made them look like rich caramel or amber. Warm eyes that said, Trust me. She liked his height, almost a full head taller than she, another thing she wasn't used to. She wished he wasn't so appealing. His attraction sparked something in her, made her realize how shut off from a personal life she had become. He made her think about things that made her afraid. If he had been less appealing, she would have felt safer.

Sinclair stepped closer, close enough for the body heat he radiated to touch her skin. He had that look on his face that said he was going to kiss her. He knew it would annoy her if he did. Not because of the kiss, but because someone might be watching. She didn't want people to know they were becoming involved, not yet, not until she knew what it meant.

A chime sounded, breaking the moment. They stared at her duffel in the corner of the room. Laura retrieved her PDA and read the message.

"Time to go. Terryn's got a job for us in town. He wants us to shake up the police at a crime scene," she said.

Terryn had been tracking a recent series of attacks against the fey and fey businesses. In the previous weeks, fey entrepreneurs around the city had been mugged and assaulted, and their businesses vandalized. The incidents were too frequent to be random. He wasn't liking what he was seeing—particularly since his sister Draigen would be arriving soon and there was a lack of any concrete investigation from either the Washington, D.C., police or the Guild. His text message had passed word that another fey business had been attacked. The new attack had resulted in deaths.

Sinclair pushed his lower lip out. "He's got bad timing."

Laura smirked as she lifted the duffel. "Or very good."

4
CHAPTER

AS SINCLAIR EXITED the freeway into downtown D.C., Laura toyed with her necklace, an emerald on a gold chain. She wore it always, both as a memento of the person who had given it to her and as a tool for creating glamours. Light glamours—like enhancing her skin tone or adding a glow to her hair—she produced with a simple manipulation of her body signature. More complex ones, ones that changed her appearance to someone entirely different, required a talisman to hold a template for the persona. Gemstones were ideal to use because their crystalline structure retained templates better than anything else. Once the template was set, her body signature powered it with no additional effort.

As they drove the local streets, she allowed her body essence to interact with the stone. The essence activated the template embedded within—the characteristics of Mariel Tate, her InterSec persona. As Mariel, she was a well-known InterSec agent, distinct and unconnected to Laura Blackstone. Physically, they bore little resemblance to each other, Mariel's willowy figure and long dark hair a stark contrast to Laura's more toned shape and wheat blond hair that fell to her shoulders. As the essence field activated, a soft tickle of static swept over her as the glamour settled. Her InterSec uniform remained since she had changed into it at Stafford.

Sinclair cast curious glances at her as he maneuvered their car toward the northeast of the city. "Why Mariel?" he asked.

"Why not Mariel?" she asked.

He grinned. "We're about to pull rank on D.C. cops at a crime scene. I seriously doubt that after you took over a police station, held a captain hostage, then flipped everyone off when you left, they'll be happy to see Mariel Tate again."

Mariel had power and was not afraid to use it. Laura had designed her for brains, looks, and ability. Over the years, she had established Mariel as a force to be reckoned with, and the persona had become her default InterSec player. Laura enjoyed the persona because she was able to use her fey abilities without restraint—something that wasn't appropriate in public relations. "I did not hold him hostage. I simply didn't let anyone else in the room while we talked."

Sinclair chuckled. "Same difference."

Laura shrugged. "I got the job done. That's all that Terryn asks. Terryn said to rattle some cages. Mariel rattles cages."

They passed through Logan Circle, a section of the city due north of the Guildhouse. "Isn't this a local crime incident? Why didn't he ask the Guild to send someone over?"

Laura pursed her lips. "He probably did and got nowhere. Internal politics." InterSec's local authority in D.C. was tenuous at best—based on the fact that at least one of the victims in the new case was not a U.S. citizen. Not quite the explicit intervention protocol that InterSec's international mandate demanded, but Terryn didn't like the D.C. police dragging their heels.

Traffic slowed as emergency lights flashed into view ahead. Sinclair double-parked near a paramedic van. They left the car, pausing to survey the scene. "I'll tell you one thing for sure, Jono. After the Guild hears we were here, they'll get involved. If there's one thing Guildmaster Rhys doesn't like, it's being embarrassed in public."

A gaping hole puckered the front of the building up on the U Street corridor of cafés and boutiques. Wrapped bars of soap and lotion bottles in bright yellow-and-orange packaging lay scattered on the ground amid fractured-building char and debris. Odors tweaked Laura's nose as soon as she left the car. Heavy soot, burnt herbs, crisped wood, and a touch of C-4 explosive.

A plainclothes officer came toward her. "Agent Tate?"

She stepped under the crime-scene tape with Sinclair beside her. "Yes."

"Mariel Tate?" he asked. She sensed annoyance from him, particularly directed at her. Someone wasn't happy his case was being looked at by another agency.

She cocked her head, letting him see her eyes, which glittered with the preternatural light of an Old One, a fey who had lived in Faerie. "Are you expecting more than one Agent Tate?"

The look had the intended effect. The officer's mouth closed as he paused. "Yes. Well, I mean no. We got word a few minutes ago that InterSec was sending someone."

She paced across the front of the building, not looking at the officer as she perused the damage. *Follow my lead, Jono,* she sent. "They have. This is Officer Sinclair. He's consulting with us."

The policeman narrowed his eyes as he pulled out a memory. "Out of Anacostia?"

Anacostia was Sinclair's last posting with D.C. SWAT, where he was when he met Laura on a case. The entire D.C. police force knew that Sinclair was the only survivor of his squad. Rather than keep him in Anacostia with a new crew, he was officially on leave, an administrative lie that Terryn had put in place.

"That's right," he said.

"Surprised you'd be working with . . ." The officer glanced at Mariel and stopped speaking.

Mariel tilted her head at him. "I didn't get your name, officer."

"Willis. Detective Willis," he said.

She turned her attention back to the building. "Well, Willis Detective Willis, maybe we can skip the biographies, and you can fill us in."

Her sarcasm had the desired effect. Willis's body signature glowed with anger. Good, Laura thought. He'll grouse about her, and word will get back to the Guild that much quicker.

"Bomb thrown through the window. Two bodies inside. The owner and a customer. An Inverni fairy and a normal."

He said the word without a hint of embarrassment, a feeble attempt to get a rise out of her. "Normal" was a mild dig. It meant human, as opposed to the "abnormal" fey. The fey used the same word, only their meaning was intending to convey someone, a human in particular, was nothing special. Laura didn't like either sense of the word, but she didn't rise to his bait. "This is the eighth fey business to be attacked in the last two months, Detective. Dead bodies mean this one is an escalation, don't you think?"

He frowned. "We've been looking at several leads."

Laura gave the shattered storefront a significant look. "Just looking doesn't seem to be going anywhere."

"You got something to say?" Willis asked.

Laura gave him a bored glance. The Mariel persona had a stop-in-your-tracks attractiveness that prompted people to resent her or fall over themselves helping her. She used both reactions to her advantage. Willis was falling into the former category.

Sinclair stepped between them with a feigned obliviousness. "Maybe we can take a look inside?"

Willis hesitated, shooting one more glare at Mariel before leading them through the remains of the door. A uniform theme ran through the store design and product packaging, bright colors in a brightly lit space. The small shop sold skincare products and beauty aids. Laura didn't recognize the brand. The owner probably marketed his own skin-care line. Lots of fey with herbal expertise did. The scented air was an unlikely mix of burnt chemicals, flower oils, and blood.

The apparent owner lay partially visible halfway down the room, crushed behind an overturned and destroyed counter. Against the wall on the opposite side of the shop, the mangled body of the customer slumped against the base of a shattered display case. Laura squatted to examine the line of scatter from the explosion. Pivoting on the ball of one foot, she peered toward the street, then back along the floor of the store.

"Any witnesses?" Sinclair asked.

"Not yet. We're canvassing and checking for store-security footage," said Willis.

Laura pointed at the floor. "I don't see any glass on the floor near the window. All the scatter is outside. The bomb wasn't thrown in. It was brought in and detonated inside."

Willis slid his hands in his pockets. "I'm sure crime scene would have picked that up."

Yeah, but you didn't, Laura thought. She was getting a sense of why Terryn wanted InterSec to push the case along. If the officer in charge had such a bad attitude, she wasn't surprised that the broader investigation into attacks against the fey wasn't progressing much. She stared at the customer, the emotional part of her mind clicking off as she registered the extent of the damage. The bomb had savaged the lower half of his body until it was unrecognizable. She stepped around a fallen shelving unit for a closer look at the body.

"The scene hasn't been cleared yet," Willis said.

Ignoring him because she knew he was the type that hated being ignored, she crouched next to the body and slipped on latex gloves. With a professional detachment, she examined the destroyed body. Major damage. She pulled his torso away from the wall to peer behind him. Her senses picked up chemicals on his undamaged side that shouldn't have been there if the bomb went off in front of him.

"You're disrupting a crime scene," Willis said.

"I think I know what I'm doing," Laura said with enough inflection to imply Willis didn't.

More anger clouded his body signature. "Is this my case or not?"

"Relax. We're here to help," Sinclair said.

Willis shoved his hands in his pockets. "I didn't ask for your help."

Sinclair gestured with resignation. "We didn't ask to come. We're all doing our jobs here."

Laura released the body, letting it fall back against the wall. Resting her elbows on her thighs so that her hands dangled, she pressed her sensing ability against the man's skin and found traces of industrial oils.

"This isn't a customer. It's the bomber," she said.

Surprised, the officer stared at the dead man. "You can tell that by looking?"

She stood, removing the gloves. "Something like that. I'm picking up C-4 in the air, and this guy"—she gestured at the body—"has chemical traces on his skin that are in line with bomb-making materials. Given the body damage and the extreme coincidence of the chemicals, I'm comfortable with my assessment."

She pulled an evidence envelope out of a pouch in her jumpsuit and slipped the gloves inside. She handed Willis her business card. "Call me when you have an ID."

Before he could respond, she walked out. Sweeping her gaze over the gathered crowd, she checked for anyone or anything unusual. Nothing jumped out. A typical rubberneck crowd. She glanced back at the store. Sinclair emerged with Willis, who glared at her again.

"That's it? You came down here to yank my chain?" he asked.

"I gave you a lead, Detective Willis. Would you like us to hang around some more?" Laura asked.

He didn't answer. Sinclair stuck his hand out. "It was nice meeting you."

Laura didn't wait to see if they shook. Let Willis resent her. C-4 didn't happen to end up here. It wasn't like someone could purchase it from the local drugstore. Terryn had sent case details on the earlier fey attacks. They were being given low priority by the police department. Nothing they could be truly called out on, but anyone in law enforcement would know. Maybe if they had pushed a little, they would have seen more organizational intent behind whatever was happening.

Sinclair walked beside her to the car. "That was bitchy."

Laura smiled. "Thanks. That was the point. You watch. Terryn will get a call from the Guild's Community Liaison Department before we get back. They'll take the case now."

"It was kind of hot, too," Sinclair said, as they got in the car.

"Feel free to turn up the air-conditioning," she said. She enjoyed teasing him. He did, too. She knew she might be pushing it too far, though. Despite his persistence, even Sinclair had limits to his patience. She had almost invited him on vacation with her but panicked at the last moment, pretending to have miscommunicated. They had dinner before she left and a few times after she returned. Terryn decided to try Sinclair undercover with Legacy, and they didn't have time to see each other then.

Sinclair chuckled as she tossed the evidence envelope on the dashboard. It was an honest chuckle. He was still patient.

5
CHAPTER

BACK AT THE Guildhouse, they rode an elevator up to the InterSec unit. Laura caught curious stares from the other passengers. Although she and Sinclair hadn't been at the crime scene long, enough airborne particulate had settled on their clothing that a fey with mild sensitivity could sense smoke, maybe the C-4. If she could smell it on Sinclair, other fey could smell it on her. If they hadn't been wearing InterSec jumpsuits, no doubt someone would have called security.

Reaching their floor, Sinclair went off to the conference room while Laura trailed down the hallway in the opposite direction. She found Cress sorting through labeled glass jars filled with what looked like dried herbs. Laura paused in the door and watched her work.

She marveled at how such a small person could be so dangerous. Essence manipulation was not dictated by a person's size, but the frail Cress hardly seemed like anyone's worst nightmare. *Leanansidhe* were rare among the solitary fey, but not so obscure that people didn't know what they looked like. And they all looked similar. On the occasion when Cress talked about the *leanansidhe*, she referred to them as her sisters, which made sense from a physical standpoint. They did have a familial resemblance, at least among the ones in the archive pictures Laura had seen. Cress was the only one she had met in person, but they were all short, with thick black hair falling in rippled waves to their shoulders. Their heart-shaped faces, with their delicate features, had lured more than one person to their deaths. Their eyes truly set them apart, though. Deepest black with no whites. Laura found that aspect disconcerting at times.

Cress smiled without looking up from her work. "If you're spying on me, you're not doing a very good job."

Laura chuckled as she stepped into the room. "I'm sorry. I was woolgathering. What are you working on?"

Cress held up a vial with something green floating in a clear fluid. "Today, I am a botanist. We're trying to figure out where that panel truck from your morning mission has been, so I'm looking at the junk in the tire treads."

Cress worked a dual-function job with InterSec. Her primary role as a forensic investigator drew on decades of knowledge. In fact, it was her species that made her particularly adept when dealing with fey crime. Her acute sensitivity to essence allowed her to see things a druid might miss. But that responsibility had evolved out of an earlier fascination: medicine. As she made her way in the Convergent world, Cress had focused her attention on healing and became a doctor, one of the first fey to have been graduated from an American medical school. Her achievement caused a sensation in both the human and fey worlds. Humans feared the fey, and Cress's securing a spot in a human program caused all kinds of xenophobic reactions. As she was a *leanansidhe*, one of the most feared beings of Faerie, the fey treated her no better.

As Laura drew closer, Cress wrinkled her nose. "C-4?" she said.

If there was one thing Laura had learned about *leanansidhe*, it was that their abilities made them more sensitive to everything, not only essence. She dropped the evidence envelope on the desk. "Exactly what I thought. I tried to get some sample without the D.C.P.D. realizing it. Can you run these gloves and see if it has any taggant?"

Legal manufacturers of C-4 embedded idiosyncratic chemicals that served as identification markers. The taggants provided clues as to who manufactured a particular explosive as well as who the intended customer was. From there, following the chain of custody to determine where it got loose in the world would be a matter of running down paperwork. If they were lucky. Making C-4 wasn't a mystery. It could be done illegally if someone had the right connections to buy the materials. That would be a lead since the raw materials were tracked, too.

Cress moved the envelope to a tray. "Of course. Is this from the bomb that went off this evening?"

"Yes. Terryn's not happy at how it's being handled."

"Are you taking the case?" Cress asked.

She shook her head. "Not directly. We're looking at all the attacks from a broader perspective. A number of small connections to the Legacy case we're working on have cropped up, but we're not running the investigations on the individual crimes. I'm not thrilled that there's C-4 floating around out there. If Terryn doesn't push them, I'm going to make Com-Lie take it whether they want it or not."

The Community Liaison Department was the Guildhouse's local law-enforcement arm, notorious for ignoring crimes that had no political benefit to the Seelie Court. "I'm sure they'll do the right thing," Cress said, a smile threatening the corner of her mouth.

Her words dripped with doubt, and she knew Laura would sense it. Laura responded with equal insincerity. "Now, now, Cress, we're all allies here."

The abrupt vanishing of the smile surprised Laura. "Yes, well, so we all hope," Cress said.

The nuances of truth were muddled, something that happened when Laura couldn't sort the difference between hope and belief—both of which someone might hold as true. She wondered if Cress had heard about Rhys's displeasure about her but hesitated starting what might be a larger conversation than a simple how-are-you.

"Everything okay?" Laura asked.

With no whites in Cress's eyes, Laura found it hard to read her expression, but there was no mistaking the sadness that came over her. "Did you hear the news about Ian Whiting?"

Ian Whiting's car had been found on the Key Bridge that morning. All his personal effects were piled neatly on the passenger seat. He'd left his shoes and a note on the railing of the bridge. The scholar from the Druidic College had apparently committed suicide. "Yes, I saw. I had a class with him a long time ago. Did you know him?"

She closed her eyes. "He saved my life. No, that's not true. He gave me a life. Before I met Terryn, Ian helped stabilize my abilities. I can't imagine the man I remember killing himself."

Laura rested a comforting hand on her shoulder. "That was a long time ago, Cress. People change. Not always for the good."

She shook her head. "I don't think he's dead. I think he walked away from his life. Too many people wanted too many things from him. That was true back when I met him. The man lived for research. He valued life. Until they find his body, that's what I think."

Laura hugged her. Cress didn't respond—she wasn't physically comfortable with people—but she did allow herself to hold Laura's arm. "I'm sorry."

"Me, too," she said softly.

On the counter behind Cress, Laura caught sight of a clear evidence bag with a handheld stun gun inside. She held the bag up for a closer look. "What's this?"

Cress returned her attention to her test tubes. "A fortunately malfunctioning liquid stun gun. I was almost mugged this morning."

Laura gaped. "Mugged? Are you all right?"

Cress looked more amused than anything. "I'm fine. Two guys came at me. One of them fired the stunner, but the liquid didn't release correctly, and he ended up stunning himself. The other guy ran off. It was rather amusing, actually."

"Did you report it?"

She shook her head. "I didn't have time. Too much to do here, and I didn't want to lose half a day making the report. I left him there looking stupid, but I took the gun."

Laura placed the bag back on the counter. Liquid stun guns were the weapon of choice for humans who preyed on the fey. They shot a stream of liquid that carried the electrical current to the target—highly beneficial when the target didn't need any gadget to shock someone. The trick was to take a fey unawares and fire before he returned an essence-bolt.

"You need to be more careful, Cress. The fey aren't the most popular right now, and you make an easy target."

Cress grinned. "Yes, well, I have my own defenses. People may not like them, but they keep me out of trouble."

Laura pushed away from the counter. "Terryn's debriefing Jono and me. Any chance we can catch up later?"

She didn't answer right away, and again Laura sensed turmoil. "I'd like that, Laura."

Laura touched her on the arm. "You okay?"

Cress smiled, but Laura thought it looked feigned. "I'm fine. We can talk later."

Whatever was bothering her, her expression seemed to indicate it wasn't the mugging. Since Cress was willing to let it wait, Laura gave her arm an affectionate squeeze.

The conference room held an oval table with chairs facing a wall of television and video screens. The dim glow of a flat-screen computer monitor illuminated the surface of the table-top in front of each seat. Local, national, and world news played on the television screens. Laura scrolled through the messages on her PDA while Sinclair leaned back and watched a basketball game.

Terryn macCullen entered with a firm gait that caused his long wings to arc sharply behind him. Inverni fairies' wings tended to pale shades of blue and green and rose into points high above their heads. The wings moved of their own accord, shifting and separating as fairies sat or lay down, and their energy fields came in contact with objects. Laura had glamoured herself as a fairy in the past, but the wings she displayed were an illusion. Terryn explained once that they acted like opposing magnetic fields, automatically sensing physical surfaces and barriers and moving accordingly. The closest he could describe their sensitivity was somewhere between the acute touch of skin and the dull sensation of hair.

Terryn dropped data drives on the table and plugged one in. Laura adjusted the monitor in front of her, its privacy screen rising out of the tabletop. Financial spreadsheets popped open. "The financial data we pulled after the Archives incident connects the Legacy Foundation to the Triad terrorist group," he said without preamble.

Laura recognized the earlier data. Triad was the organization responsible for the terrorist attack on the National Archives.

Despite a century of integration, the fey engendered suspicion and fear among some human populations. No one—fey or human—understood how parts of Faerie and its people appeared in the modern world. Beings of myth and legend—fairies and elves, druids and dwarves and a host of other fey—walked the world trying to find their place in a strange new reality. Their innate ability to manipulate essence set them apart. The elusive form of energy that allowed the fey to perform tasks perceived as magic scared the hell out of most humans. It didn't help that there were, in fact, fey groups like Triad that were taking more aggressive means to further their political agendas.

Laura looked at Terryn from beneath her brow. "Rhys brought them up this morning. They're making noise about the National Archives. If they're connected with Triad, are you saying they're interested in more than harassing loyalists to the fey monarchies?"

Sinclair cleared his throat. "We were at a murder scene, Laura. That's a bit more than harassment."

She winced as she skimmed through documents. "Right, Jono. Of course. I meant I was surprised about their connection to Triad. That makes them more sophisticated than we've thought. This looks like major money-laundering."

Terryn shifted some documents on their screens. "Legal, or as legal as it gets. Several of Legacy's benefactors contribute checks and anonymous cash donations. Again, all legal, but the quantity raised suspicions that federal rules were being circumvented, which triggered a review. It's the source of those funds we were able to match up with other intelligence. Genda Boone has pulled together a framework of the players involved."

As Mariel Tate, Laura shared an office suite with Genda, a Danann fairy who specialized in financial analysis. The two had formed an easy friendship although Genda wasn't aware that Mariel was a glamoured persona.

"So, in addition to weapons-smuggling, we're looking at an organization that has a political motivation to use the weapons," said Sinclair.

Terryn shifted new documents to the front of the displays. An organizational chart appeared. "Their professed goal is unity among human and fey without a monarchy."

Laura scanned the chart, recognizing a few high-profile politicians and businessmen. "Odd goals for a place with so many anti-fey people on its board."

The organization chart shrank as Terryn expanded the template to include more people. "We've found connections to a sort of shadow board of directors. Peeling back the corporate layers, we start to see interesting contradictions and oddities."

Laura recognized several names either from high public profiles or internal research—a group of unsurprising businesspeople, some politicians, and a few notable military personnel. Then things got interesting.

"Is this right? These look like fey names now," said Laura.

Terryn nodded. "They're separated by several layers, but that's right."

"That would fit the unity thing," said Sinclair.

Laura examined the names. She recognized some, including Tylo Blume, an important businessman among the elven tribes. He was also a legal arms merchant and sometime philanthropist. "Blume's showing up bothers me."

"Maybe not so surprising, considering that our corresponding intelligence is from his Triad corporation," said Terryn.

Blume had had a falling-out with a former Triad partner named Simon Alfrey, an Inverni fairy—and political rival to Terryn—who had been responsible for the recent terrorist attack at the National Archives. Despite claims of innocence, Laura was deeply suspicious of how much Blume knew about Alfrey's plans.

"The Archives incident would be precisely the kind of thing this group fights against, wouldn't it?" asked Sinclair. "If Blume's in this group, then he's been telling the truth that he had no idea Triad was involved at the Archives."

Laura rocked her head from side to side. "It could be a blind to cover his activities. Or he could have staged the event to drum up support for Legacy."

Sinclair snorted. "Wow. That's pretty cynical."

Terryn didn't change his expression as he reviewed the documents in front of him. "At InterSec, we examine every angle. We don't have the luxury of trust."

Sinclair frowned. "So people are guilty until proved innocent?"

Terryn did not look up. "Circumstances are evaluated for all contingencies. InterSec discards them as it discredits them, Agent Sinclair. If you can't be thorough, I can find you a desk job."

Sinclair rocked back on his chair. "Hey, we're buds. Call me Jono. Maybe later we can go hang out and have a few beers."

Laura didn't look up as she felt the flash of anger from Terryn. She was going to have to talk Sinclair. Terryn was the wrong person to taunt. "I think what Terryn's saying is that we try to be as objective and analytical as possible."

Terryn shifted more documents onto the screen. "I think Terryn said exactly what he meant."

Startled, Laura did look then. Terryn maintained his focus on the information in front of him. He was never short with her. In fact, it was so out of character, it took her a moment to realize her jaw had dropped in reaction—an emotional display that was out of character for her. She closed her mouth and glanced at Sinclair. He shifted his eyes away before they made contact. Embarrassed, Laura cleared her throat. "Of course."

Terryn wasn't known for his sense of humor. His expression was subtle, but his message was clear. Laura's decision to bring Sinclair into the agency did not sit well with him. He tapped his screen. "We're getting some chatter that Legacy may be connected to the recent attacks on fey businesses. There are also indications that they are going to target Draigen for some type of political action when she arrives. I want inside information."

Laura sensed the emotion beneath the way he said her name. Terryn was heir to the rule of the Inverni clan. Because of political intricacies she didn't fully understand, he had refused the underKing title to spite High Queen Maeve and appointed his sister Draigen as regent. Her arrival in Washington had to be causing all kinds of conflicts for him, both personal and professional.

She assessed the workup in front of her. "Draigen's going to be here soon. We've got Jono in with Legacy's weapons people, but that's not the part of the hierarchy responsible for strategic planning. We should have done an infiltration higher up in the organization sooner than this."

Terryn seemed distracted as he reviewed the files. "We need to go in now. With the connections between Legacy and the fey attacks, I'm concerned Draigen might be in their sights. We're going to go with a hard insertion."

Sinclair arched an eyebrow. "I'm not sure what you mean, but it sounds fun."

Laura bit back a smile while Terryn shot him an annoyed look. A woman's picture popped onto their screens. "This is Allison Forth. She's in the U.S. illegally, using Fallon Moor as an assumed name. She is wanted in Ireland for participating in a Dublin bombing. As Fallon Moor, she has a nebulous administrative title at Legacy."

"Okay, I'll bite. What's a hard insertion?" Sinclair asked.

Laura examined the image. Moor was a brownie, a race of fey that usually allied with the Seelie Court. Brownies tended to prefer lives of orderliness and cooperation. When something happened to disrupt their plans, they transformed into boggarts, the maniacal version of their normal selves that could be dangerous. The transformation was a mania in which their rationality slipped away until they could restore balance in their lives again. Moor's pleasant face belied the list of crimes that scrolled up next to it. Laura was already thinking of ways to create a persona template of the woman. "We bring Moor in, get her to cooperate, and I take her place at Legacy."

"Sounds like that could go bad very easily," he said.

"That's why we call it hard," she said.

Sinclair leaned back in his chair again and crossed his arms. "What's our authorization for all this?"

"I'm authorizing it," said Terryn.

Sinclair tilted his head, a curious expression on his face. "Look, I'm undercover on your word only, macCullen. Some of this stuff sounds against the law. I don't know how you did things in Ireland, but people have rights here, including to their political opinions."

Without a word, Terryn pulled up more documents—police reports, individual criminal records, Web site snapshots. Sinclair became quiet. "Not if they cross the line into subversion. When that happens, it falls within InterSec's jurisdiction. I believe, Agent Sinclair, you will note the connections between Legacy rank and file and the recent attacks on fey businesses."

Sinclair grunted in reluctant acknowledgment. Terryn lifted his gaze and settled his deep green eyes on Sinclair. Terryn was an Old One and could turn his deep gaze into a formidable weapon of intimidation. Facing someone who had seen centuries pass, kingdoms rise and fall, and deaths uncounted was a humbling experience.

Laura's second surprise of the meeting was watching Sinclair meet that look without flinching. For a moment, she thought Sinclair was going to argue with him, but instead he wrinkled his brow and returned to the screen in front of him.

"The documents are on your email, Agent Sinclair. Feel free to review them and see if they meet your legal concerns. We can discuss any questions you have later. You're dismissed," Terryn said.

Sinclair stood, not quite smirking, and muttered as he left the room. "Maybe in your mind."

His parting glance at Laura told her there was probably going to be more than one discussion later. Laura stared down at the table, gloom settling over her.

"He's going to be a problem," Terryn said.

She didn't look up. "It's all new to him, Terryn. I'll talk to him."

"If he can't get on board with the job, we'll have to find another solution," he said.

She didn't want to think about another solution. Despite Terryn's initial threats of incarceration, there were worse situations than a cell. InterSec had outposts in some of the most desolate places in the world. "I know. Give me some time."

Terryn gathered his folders. "Things are moving quickly, Laura. Time isn't something we have."

He left. Perplexed at his uncharacteristic abruptness, Laura slowly spun her chair around and stared down the empty hallway.

6

CHAPTER

A BALL OF paper flew across the room as Laura entered Sinclair's office. It hit the wall next to her head and landed beside the wastebasket. Sinclair crumpled another piece of paper and tossed it. And missed. Laura watched as he balled up more paper. Neither spoke as she leaned against the door-jamb, and he continued throwing and missing. Laura poked her foot at the growing pile of paper. "Have you never done this before, or do you just stink at it?"

He glowered at her and missed another shot.

She blinked her eyes at him, affecting an overly enthusi-astic attitude. "Maybe your aim will improve if you picture the wastebasket as Terryn's head."

He paused, then threw a paper ball at her head. She batted it away, and it landed in the wastebasket. "See what you can accomplish with teamwork?" she asked.

He gave her grudging smile, leaned back, and began toss-ing a small green stress ball straight up and catching it. Laura let out an exaggerated sigh. "If you're going to play with your-self, I can leave you to it."

"Ha-ha," he said.

"He speaks," she said.

He dropped forward and tossed the ball from hand to hand. "I don't think this is going to work out."

"It has to," she said.

He stared at the ball as he passed it back and forth. "And what if it doesn't?"

She moved up to his desk. "Jono, listen to me. You can make this hard, or you can make this easy. What you can't do is make it impossible."

"Impossible? He forced me to join InterSec because I figured out your real identity, Laura. I didn't ask to be here. Plus, he treats me like an idiot," he said.

"And you do the same. Like it or not, he's the boss. Terryn will let you disagree with him. He won't let you insult him. You have to earn his trust. That's what this whole situation is about," she said.

Annoyed, he glared. "I do not kiss ass."

She spread her hands out. "No one's asking you to. Just respect the fact that he knows what he's talking about. Because he does. Believe me. If I didn't trust Terryn macCullen, I'd be dead ten times over."

He tossed the ball up. "I don't know if I like the politics around here."

She crossed her arms. "I think you need to learn them before you decide that. The fey are complicated, but despite what you were raised to believe, we're not evil, Jono. There are reasons Terryn thinks the way he does. You two probably have a lot more in common than you realize."

Sinclair snorted. "Yeah, right. I'm sure the uncrowned heir to a throne can get down with my issues."

She considered his point. As a fey/human hybrid, Sinclair was unique. That was why his grandfather created the spelled medallion for him—to hide his true nature. The jotunn knew enough about the fey and humans in the Convergent world to know that his grandson would have been poked, prodded, and tested. Social integration moved slowly in most parts of the world. Biological interbreeding would speed things up considerably, and that was something many people would find appealing—and others horrifying. "He's got a target on his back simply because of who he is, Jono. Sound familiar?" she asked.

He glanced at her with lowered eyes. "It's different."

Exasperated, Laura slumped into the guest chair. "Jono, give me one week of no conflict. Do the job we both know you can do."

He grinned. "Was that a compliment?"

She pursed her lips. "If I say yes, can we drop the subject?"

He spun in his chair, then leaned on the desk. "If I say yes, can we go out for dinner?"

She rolled her eyes. "Yes."

He frowned. "Wait, I lost track. Is that 'yes, that was a compliment' or 'yes, we can have dinner'?"

She stood. "It was 'yes, this conversation is over.'"

His frown deepened into playful confusion. "I think I'm a yes behind."

She leaned toward him with a smug, playful smile. "That's because I'm one step ahead of you."

He threw another ball of paper at her. She snatched it out of the air and threw it back. "Do you want to review your strategy with Legacy?"

He shrugged. "What's to review? Show up. Act like I don't like the fey—which won't be tough—take notes, and leave."

"Where were you born?" she asked.

"Philadelphia."

She shook her head. "Wrong. Never use your own data for a persona."

"Persona? You're going to make me a glamour?" he asked.

"No, but you're still undercover. That's as much a persona as a glamoured persona. You need to be convincing. You are going to get to know these guys like friends. You don't know how long you're going to be there. You need to create a credible life for yourself that has no connection to who you really are. When it's all over, you don't want to leave anything behind that might lead to the real you."

"The real me," he said.

"The real you," she said.

He cocked his head at her. "Is this the real you I'm talking to right now?"

She blinked. Not the question she was expecting. In the brief pause, a cascade of thoughts and emotions sped through her mind. *Yes. No. What? Of course. But . . . He's baiting me. No, it's fair given the context. Ouch. Talk about pushing a button. How dare he? Is he serious or playing with me? Again.* "Ha-ha," she said. It was the best she could come up with, and she felt stupid for it.

Sinclair's measured look said he wasn't sure how to interpret the response. With a subtle flick of his eyebrows, he decided to let it pass. "Okay, so I need a better cover than a name."

"Cress can help you build a legal framework in case someone decides to look into your history. She's good. Excellent, in fact. Your job is to build the personality—who you loved or hated, your favorite books and movies, what you like to eat. Drill it into your memory and stick to it. The slightest lapse can be trouble, so keep it simple but keep it . . ."

"Real," he finished.

"Yes."

A faint smile creased his face. "This is what you do every day?"

She shook her head. "Not every day. Most jobs only require an occasional appearance. Only deep cover takes over your life."

He laughed. "I've been driving limos every day for two months."

She smiled. "But you didn't need a persona for it, just a name. As Bill Burrell, limo driver, you've been interacting with low-level Legacy staff briefly. The job doesn't require that you interject yourself into the workings of someone's life. You get to be Bill Burrell and go home at night. It's different now that they're letting you in deeper. You become someone else. Start by creating a job history. What did you do before you drove limos?"

He pursed his lips. "Circus performer."

She didn't laugh. "Too contrived."

"It was a joke," he said.

She compressed her lips. "I know you think it was, Jono, but you need to understand something. I take this seriously, and you need to take this seriously. When you've proved you can do the job, then you can joke."

It was his turn to get annoyed. "I'm getting tired of all this 'proving myself' bullshit."

"It's hard. I know. But it's that way because the stakes are high. A mistake can cost lives. Look what happened on the road this morning. You have to show you won't get yourself killed. That's the first step. Then you have to show that you can be relied on not to get a teammate killed."

"I didn't ask for this. You screwed up, not me," he said.

She winced at the truth of it. "You're right. You exposed me. I didn't know my body signature had a shape that doesn't change because I'm wearing a glamour. I never anticipated that someone could sense that shape like you can. But I didn't let those mistakes get me killed. Now I'm trying to show Terryn and Cress and whoever else cares that those mistakes aren't going to get them killed. And the only way I can do that is to help you succeed at this. If you're telling me you don't want to do it, then you need to decide whether you like your hell hot or cold because Terryn will send you somewhere extremely unpleasant whether you like it or not."

"And you're okay with that," he said.

Sighing, she shook her head. "Not in the least, and I will do whatever it takes to make it not happen."

He smirked. "So you'll have dinner with me?"

"Yes, as long as you understand it has nothing to do with anything else."

He smiled. "Night watchman."

She smiled back and settled into his guest chair. "Better. Now, let's bring Bill Burrell to life."

7
CHAPTER

WITH SINCLAIR SLUMPED half-asleep in the passenger seat the next morning, Laura pulled her SUV into a parking space a half block away from Fallon Moor's apartment building. She turned off the engine, let the seat back to make more leg room, and picked up her coffee from the console. The pale dawnlight revealed a flat-front, nondescript building in a muted shade of brick in a line of similar row houses. It had no distinct architectural character, but the location near Logan Circle was pricey enough to warrant its appeal.

The morning commute coasted past the SUV on the left, traffic moving at the speed limit at the early hour. Within a few minutes of parking, it started to slow, as the traffic began its gradual build for the day. Early risers made their way along the sidewalks, coffee cups and briefcases in hand, their faces neutral except for the occasional avid cell-phone talker. Another typical day in a typical city neighborhood with the noted exception of its being home to an international terrorist.

Sinclair slouched in the passenger seat. That a grown man with rugged good looks seemed like a little boy when asleep amused her. She wanted to smooth the worry line off his forehead but resisted the urge. They were working. "Am I going to handle this myself, or are you going to wake up?" she asked.

Sinclair shifted sideways in his seat, his eyes open to slits. "It's so nice to wake up next to you."

She chuckled into her coffee. "Yeah, if you actually, you know, woke up."

He reached for his coffee. "You drilled me half the night. Even I think I'm Bill Burrell now."

She smirked. "Be glad you only had to do a history. It's worse when you have to bring some kind of expertise to the job."

He snorted. "Well, I think I'm bringing some expertise to the job."

A motion near Moor's building caught Laura's eye, and she cocked her head for a clearer line of sight. A man in a maintenance uniform stepped out and swept the sidewalk. She leaned back. "I've had to learn languages for missions. I became a qualified English professor for one. I've been on archaeological digs, and no one questioned my knowledge. There's a difference, Jono, between behaving like someone and becoming that person. You're using existing skills and memorizing a life history you can create on the fly. You can't do that every time."

Even as Sinclair complained about the hour, his gaze was on the street. "Boast much, Cuddles?"

She flushed with anger and embarrassment, at the nickname, at his tone, and at the dig. Several cutting responses flew through her mind. As the silence lengthened, she caught herself short and laughed. "Sorry. You totally have a point there."

He smiled. "Thanks. You do, too, but it would go down better with doughnuts."

"I'll try to remember that next time you're snoring when I'm going through the drive-through. And I'm going to pretend you didn't call me Cuddles," she said.

They fell into a comfortable silence. Laura was tempted

to quiz him on his undercover persona but resisted the urge. She had to acknowledge to herself he knew it. In fact, she had quizzed him far longer the previous night than she needed to. He had it down, but her own anxiety kept her at him. On several points, he had become so comfortable with the constructed history that his voice resonated near truth when he spoke. Now, that impressed her. As she had gone to sleep, she allowed herself to hope everything would work out for him.

As the caffeine kicked in, Sinclair eased straighter in his seat. He tapped his fingers to the beat of a song playing on the satellite radio. "Do you like to dance?"

"Sometimes," Laura said.

He glanced at her. "That's kind of a yes-or-no question."

She pulled her hair back and flipped it up from where she was leaning on it. "Not really. There have been times when I've liked current music enough to dance to it and time periods when I didn't. I liked the stuff in the seventies and some of the eighties."

Sinclair cocked an eyebrow. "Time periods? How old are you anyway?"

Laura pursed her lips. "Umm . . . right now, Mariel is twenty-eight."

Amused, he grunted. "Okay. How old was Janice Crawford?"

Laura lifted her eyes in thought. "Well, I wanted to create a SWAT persona who was old enough to have some experience but not too old to be considered a washout. She was twenty-eight."

"Uh-huh. And Laura Blackstone?"

"Oh, Laura Blackstone is older. Twenty-eight and a half."

He tilted his head at her. "I like younger women."

She smirked back at him. "Oh? And how old are you?"

He rubbed his chin. "I'm going to go with thirty."

She let a smile linger on her lips to hide a sudden sense of unease. Her truth-sensing ability detected a fluctuation. His statement should have registered as an outright lie, but it didn't. Granted, he had been joking, but humor didn't hide underlying responses. "That's not what your birth certificate says."

He arched his eyebrows with a playful look. "Really, Mariel Tate? My birth certificate might be altered?"

She pressed her lips into a thin line to hide her annoyance. She hadn't considered that his biographical details might have been altered. Cress wasn't the only person in the world who was good at constructing fake life histories. "Thirty, is it, then? It must depress you to be so old."

He laughed as he shook his head. "Nah. It works out 'cause, like I said, I like younger women."

"Then maybe you should—" Laura began.

"There she is," Sinclair interrupted.

Fallon Moor had emerged from the entrance of her building and turned up the sidewalk. Laura mentally chastised herself for being distracted. She had not seen the brownie leave the building. Moor stopped at her car, parked a few spaces up, and unlocked the door. Sinclair started to open his door. "Not here. She's sufficiently high-profile that Legacy might have security watching her," she said.

He closed the door. "I didn't notice anyone."

"Me, either. That doesn't mean they don't have someone in one of these buildings." Laura started the SUV. When Moor pulled out of her space, Laura merged with the traffic behind her. She watched her mirrors for several blocks, but no one appeared to be following. Moor cut across the lane, parked her car on the corner of a side street, and turned on the emergency lights. Laura pulled into the space in front of a fire hydrant a few car lengths away while Moor entered a small tea shop.

"What's she doing?" Laura asked.

Sinclair narrowed his eyes. "She's getting tea . . . and . . . wait . . . a croissant. It's definitely a croissant. I'm thinking she's secretly French."

Laura pretended to be impressed. "You're good."

He grinned. "Want to know how good?"

She rolled her eyes and got out of the car. "Let's go."

They both slipped on sunglasses as they strolled up to the shop. The glasses were clichéd government-agent intimidation, but they looked good. Moor shouldered her way slowly out of the shop with her cup of tea in one hand and the croissant in the other.

Laura held up her badge. "Fallon Moor? Agent Tate, InterSec. This is Agent Sinclair. We'd like to talk to you."

Moor froze, her expression hard-edged for a second before slipping into puzzled confusion. "InterSec? What's that?"

Laura didn't need her sensing ability to pick up the obvious subterfuge. "Let's not play games, Moor. We're enforcing a Homeland Security warrant. You've overstayed your visa."

Moor's eyes began to bulge. Cornering a brownie like this was breaking with routine, especially since Moor was on the run from the law. Laura recognized the first stages of a boggart mania as the panic at being confronted set in. Laura took a casual step to her left to increase the distance between herself and Sinclair. "Let's keep this calm, Moor."

"You must be mistaking me for someone else. It happens to brownies all the time," she said.

"Let's talk about that back at the station," Sinclair said.

Moor stepped back with indecision. "You're making a mistake."

"No, you are," said Laura. Before Moor could react, Laura held her hand out and muttered in Gaelic. A small tangle of essence shot from her palm and settled over Moor. The brownie's body flexed and pulsed as the boggart mania tried to kick in, then went still as the spell activated. Moor's eyes glazed dully with sleep.

"That was simple," Sinclair said.

Laura removed the tea and croissant from Moor's still hands and placed them on the window ledge of the tea shop. "There was no point in prolonging it. She knew the warrant was an excuse."

"So, to be clear, we have a legal right to kidnap people, right?" he asked.

She shot him a mildly exasperated look. "It's an arrest, Jono. The warrant is real."

He splayed his hand against his chest. "That's a relief. I was afraid without a warrant, we'd get in trouble for spelling the woman into a stupor."

She ignored him and muttered in Gaelic again. Moor rose an inch or so off the ground. Laura gestured to Sinclair. "Care to do the honors?"

Sinclair took Moor's elbow and coasted her toward the SUV. "This reminds me of our first date."

Laura fell into step on the opposite side. "It wasn't a date."

"We had drinks."

"We had a fight. Threats were involved," she said.

He sighed. "Yeah, it was pretty hot."

She shook her head. "You are incorrigible."

Sinclair brightened with faux excitement. "Encourageable? I knew you couldn't resist me."

"*And* you're hard of hearing. Another flaw."

She opened the rear passenger door of the SUV and helped Sinclair lift Moor onto the backseat. Sinclair leaned inside and buckled Moor in. He pulled out and grinned down at Laura. "Maybe we can talk about me over dinner?"

She gave him a sweet smile. "That will double your usual audience."

He chuckled as they resumed their seats. "Then we can go dancing. I bet you'll like new music. I can show you some pretty good moves."

She rolled her head toward him, then back toward the road ahead. She hated to admit it, but he did amuse her. "I think I've seen enough of your moves for one day."

8
CHAPTER

STILL GLAMOURED AS Mariel Tate, Laura entered a small, narrow anteroom deep within the Guildhouse. Light from a large window into the next room illuminated Terryn where he stood in the half dark. Without expression, he stared into the other room at Fallon Moor sitting immobile, Laura's sleep spell intact.

"Sorry I'm late. I was trying to process her in, but everyone suddenly became scarce," she said.

Terryn handed her a folder. "We can process her later. I want to keep this out of channels for now, which is why I'm delivering the paperwork to you personally."

Laura took the folder with a moment of unease. She could argue with Sinclair all she wanted that his not being an official employee of InterSec was irrelevant since the secrecy protected him. She could argue that he wanted the job, and his paperwork was a mere formality that would be cleared up once Terryn felt comfortable. She could even argue that some of their mission protocols allowed them to bend the rules other agencies had to follow.

Given all that, she wondered how to justify to him that a

woman named Fallon Moor sat in a glass-enclosed chamber under arrest, and no one knew she was there. Not the public. Not her family. Not her lawyer. If InterSec—no, dammit, if Terryn—decided not to process her into the system, no one would ever know. Except her. And Sinclair.

She trusted Terryn. She believed he would do the right thing. Eventually. That thought gave her pause. It was the eventually part that bothered Sinclair. How long was it before eventually became inexcusable?

She pushed her thoughts aside and opened the folder. The first set of documents was an expedited deportation order for Moor from the Department of Homeland Security that would send her to Tara without court delays. The second set was a plea deal with an offer of asylum in the U.S. with a prison term in exchange for cooperation. Both documents had been drawn in anticipation of Moor's arrest. They gave no indication that she, in fact, had been arrested. So Homeland Security did not have explicit knowledge of her presence either.

Laura closed the folder. "If she refuses to cooperate, we're stuck."

Terryn gave her a thin smile. "Not really. It will make going undercover more difficult for you, though."

She wanted to laugh, but it wasn't funny. If Terryn had decided she was going undercover at Legacy, she was going undercover at Legacy. He had put her in such situations before, and she hadn't questioned Terryn's methods until Sinclair began to make an issue of some of them. She stared at the sleeping woman. "But what about her?"

"What about her?" Terryn asked.

Laura licked her lips as she weighed a response. His tone registered indifferent, even callous. She knew Terryn could be single-minded, but she wondered if he cared about the ramifications of his actions beyond his own point of view. It was true that Fallon Moor was a criminal who was creating an obstacle to their plans. She was a person, too, though. "Never mind. We can talk about it later."

She had a job to do. As she placed her hand on the doorknob to the room, she boosted the essence charge in the emerald stone on the chain around her neck. She entered the room, dropped the folder on the table, and took the seat opposite Moor. With a casual gesture, she released the sleep spell with a burst of essence. Disoriented, Moor caught herself as she swayed toward the table. She glanced around the room without surprise. Her gaze settled on Laura. "I want a lawyer," she said.

The hard truth resonating in her voice did not surprise Laura. "Lawyers may be involved eventually. What's your name?"

"Fallon Moor."

This time, the lie rang through clearly. Laura pulled the deportation papers out and pushed them across the table. "Try again."

Moor glanced at the paperwork and pushed it back. "It's like I said to you earlier. You're mistaking me for someone else. I never heard of Allison Forth."

Laura stood and slid the paperwork back in the folder. "Okay. Sorry. That's not my problem. You can sort it out with the Seelie Court."

"I will fight extradition," Moor said.

Laura pulled a lazy smile. "That won't be necessary. You are already on sovereign territory of the Seelie Court. Your transfer is a matter of a plane ticket."

Moor's eyes bulged. With a few breaths, she fought the rise of her boggart mania, and her face relaxed. Laura was impressed with the level of control and noted it for the future.

"I demand a lawyer," Moor said.

"For which? Your deportation or your acceptance of asylum?"

"I have rights," Moor said.

"So did the people who died in the bombing you participated in at the Dublin airport. I'm sure you can clarify that with the Seelie Court when you get back to Ireland."

Moor set her jaw. "What do you want?"

Laura took her seat again and slid the asylum documents out. "Your cooperation."

Moor's eyes became hooded. "For what?"

"Legacy," Laura said.

"I work there. It was a convenient place to hide," she said.

Laura leaned back, tapping her pen on the table. "Legacy claims they want unity among the fey and humans. They think abolishing monarchies is the way to achieve that. You have a career of antimonarchial activities that involves violence. I get your excuse for being there. What I want to know is why they want someone like you."

Moor smiled. "I'm very good at keeping people on message."

Laura arched an eyebrow. "So what's the message this time? Extortion? Murder? Another bomb?"

"I don't know what you're talking about," she said.

"We've got a dead shopkeeper and a dead suicide bomber, Moor. It's only a matter of time before we connect them to the other acts of anti-fey violence, then to Legacy. We're almost there already."

She sneered. "Then what do you need me for?"

Laura released some essence into her eyes, letting it shimmer in the manner of an Old One. Moor didn't try to hold the gaze but looked away, easily cowed by the power in front of her. "I want to know what's being planned, Moor. Whatever your goals are, they won't be accomplished with murder. I'm going to stop it with you or without you."

"Go ahead, then. You can't connect me to anything," she said.

Laura nudged the folder. "I don't have to. Whatever is going to happen, you're out of the game. For good. The Dublin case against you is open-and-shut. You want the justice of the Seelie Court, I will be more than happy to accommodate you." She pushed the folder closer. "You want to live, I can accommodate that, too."

"I want time to think about it. And I want a lawyer," she said.

Laura placed a pen on the folder. "Fine. I'll give you time. You have thirty seconds. After that, the deal is permanently off the table, and you go to Ireland. I'll pay for your lawyer's flight myself. I don't have more time than that, I'm afraid."

Moor stared at the documents in front her. Laura weighed the options herself—humane treatment in a U.S. jail in exchange for the betrayal of her associates or certain death at the hands of Maeve's justice. The Seelie Court was not a kind and gentle judge. It didn't take Moor long to decide.

"Where do I sign?" she asked.

Laura spread the documents out and handed her a pen. "I'll walk you through it."

9
CHAPTER

LAURA HAD PLANNED the detention of Fallon Moor for early in the morning in order to free up time for the rest of the day. She was glad she did, since between the initial interview of Moor and the subsequent paperwork, she didn't get upstairs to the public-relations department until noon.

The chaos on her desk did its best to depress her, but she retaliated by remaining focused. The reception for Draigen macCullen produced layers of pressure that she hadn't anticipated. Working for Guildmaster Orrin ap Rhys as his public-relations director and for Terryn macCullen as his top undercover agent created conflicts that were becoming harder to ignore. At this point, she recognized that Rhys was no fan of the Inverni—neither past nor present—and enjoyed fanning the flames of their disagreements. As a diplomatic extension of High Queen Maeve's court, the Washington Guildhouse was playing a major role in discrediting the Inverni position—and Laura was finding her job as public-relations director bumping up against her moral and personal ethics as a friend and colleague of Terryn.

Regardless of her job title on the Guildhouse letterhead,

Laura's public-relations position had expanded over the years by a slow accretion of tasks and favors that had nothing to do with her primary job. Her inherent drive to get things done had clouded the fact that she had let things get out of control. Hiring Saffin Corrill as her assistant helped manage the unwieldy numbers of responsibilities, with the added benefit of finding someone she could trust. Where Laura didn't want to say no to people, Saffin had no problem booting them to the curb.

To complicate things more, Rhys didn't know she worked for InterSec. Terryn, of course, knew about her Guild work but made it a point never to ask her for inside information. Which made things harder, since the decision to reveal or not reveal was hers. Depending on the situation, she sometimes was forced to make a choice between Terryn and Rhys, something that did not always sit well depending on which job hat she wore.

Which all came down to why she had become more involved in Draigen macCullen's reception than she would have otherwise. Rhys had assigned the lead responsibility to Resha Dunne, but Laura wanted Draigen's meeting with the president of the United States to succeed. If Draigen succeeded, Laura wouldn't have to draw a line in the sand with Rhys regarding how far she would go to discredit Terryn's clan. If Draigen succeeded, Laura's personal feelings for Terryn wouldn't make her feel obligated to disclose Guild strategies against the Inverni to him. She didn't want Draigen to succeed. She *needed* her to.

Saffin arrived with a stack of folders, which she laid out along the front edge of Laura's desk. "This folder contains top-priority issues. This one has potential issues. This one has issues I don't think are issues. And this one has issues that I know aren't issues. Some people need to find better things to do with their time."

Her efficiency amused and gratified Laura. She and Saffin had worked together for years, knew each other's rhythms, and helped each other get their jobs done. Without Saffin,

Laura's double life would have been impossible. She had saved Laura's reputation several times—once literally saved her life.

Brownies by nature were skilled organizational personalities with a knack for order and efficiency. Those talents came at a price. Stressed by an obstacle in their path to successful completion of a job, they transformed into boggarts—a manic version of their normal selves. She had seen the effect recently with Fallon Moor. The physical transformation was exhausting for brownies—and dangerous to the people around them. "Going boggie" had a range of behaviors from an annoying relentlessness to outright violent acts.

Without comment, Laura observed the healing cuts on Saffin's face and arms. Saffin had been caught in the recent terrorist attack at the Archives and gone full boggart. Her body became a killing machine to save her life and the lives of others. While Laura knew it was a matter of being in the wrong place at the wrong time, she couldn't help feeling responsible for what Saffin had done, especially since Laura had had to encourage it to save them. If Laura had prevented the attack in the first place, Saffin wouldn't have been hurt—or hurt others. Saffin hadn't blamed Laura. She didn't dwell on what she had done but accepted it as the inevitable outcome of her nature. Laura wished she could be so comfortable in her own skin.

"How about I take the office complaint folder, and you take the reception one?" she asked.

Saffin flipped her wispy blond hair over her shoulders. "Sure. Of course, that means the reception hors d'oeuvres will be vegetarian, people will have to get their own, the music will be rockabilly, and I might consider some kind of role-playing party game to loosen everyone up."

Laura shook her head. "You do not like rockabilly."

Saffin smirked. "Neither do fairies. Everyone will leave early, and I'll have enough leftovers to not cook for a week."

"You convinced me. I'll take the first folder," Laura said.

Saffin sighed. "Have it your way. A Stray Cats reunion would have been awesome."

Laura pulled the folder closer and flipped it open. "I won't be in tomorrow, but text me if you need anything."

"No problem." Laura picked up a slight pause before the reply. Saffin was the only person outside InterSec who knew about Laura's double life. She had figured it out on her own years ago. That she kept it to herself—not even discussing it with Laura until recent events exposed her knowledge— assured Laura that she could rely on Saffin to keep it a secret. From experience, she had no doubt that Saffin would have no problem running the office without her.

Saffin picked up the papers in the desk out-box. "I'm going for a mani and a pedi. Be back in an hour."

"Should you be telling me you're running personal errands on company time?" Laura said.

Saffin grinned as she walked out the door. "It's for the reception. That makes it work-related *and* a tax write-off. Is this a groovy country or isn't it?"

Laura chuckled. If there was one thing she could count on, it was Saffin Corrill not missing a detail. She spent a few minutes reviewing the folders and making notes. She checked her watch. She wanted to be gone before Saffin returned because she wasn't, in reality, going to be gone. Despite Saffin's knowing about her InterSec life, she didn't want to become nonchalant about it.

She retrieved her handbag from under the desk and opened the closet door behind her. Pushing aside the coat and spare outfits, a warding spell keyed to Laura's body signature made the back of the closet appear to be solid. Laura stepped through the wall and disappeared from her office.

10
CHAPTER

ON THE OPPOSITE side of the closet from her office, Laura dropped her bag on the bed of her private room. A work space occupied one wall. Ranks of storage boxes lined the surfaces of two tables. Jewelry-making tools were scattered over the work spaces, everything she needed to make a glamour. Over the years, the wall above the tables had become covered with photographs—some of herself under glamour, some as reference for creating new ones. Her unmade bed filled most of the room, the remaining space crammed with a bewildering array of outfits, hats, and footwear. Throughout the city, various apartments held the clothes only for individual personas—like the nearby corporate suite for Mariel Tate or her condo in Alexandria.

The hidden room, though, was a refuge. No one else entered. Terryn had arranged for the office behind her own to "disappear" from the building's floor plan. The only other person who knew about it was Cress, and that was on the off chance Laura had an emergency. Not even Saffin knew, or at least Laura thought she didn't. But Saffin always surprised her with the things she picked up on.

Laura slipped into the chair at the worktable and opened a drawer in a small storage container. A collection of rubies shifted against each other, some polished enough to catch the light with a deep red wink, some dulled by long disuse. The storage container held dozens of gems, mostly rubies, diamonds, and emeralds. They worked well for persona templates and were common enough gemstones that they didn't attract curiosity when she wore them. The dollar value of the collection was not something she thought about. InterSec had paid for some, but others, like the emerald for Mariel Tate, were her own. As with most fey, money became less of an issue as time went on.

She trailed her finger through the pile of rubies, pushing most to the back of the drawer before deciding on a quarter-carat stone. She dropped it on the tabletop, then retrieved it with tweezers to examine it through a jeweler's loupe. Minor blemishing marked the stone, and the soft shapes of trapped air bubbles marred it here and there. She recognized the patterning from having used the stone years ago. She liked it, not too flawed and small enough in size not to raise eyebrows if someone noticed it. The advantage of her skill was that she did not always need large stones to make realistic glamours but stones that enhanced what she intended.

From another drawer, she sorted through empty pendant bezels. Resetting the stone in the same bezel it had been in once before would save time. Pleased at her luck, she found the piece and placed it next to the ruby on the table. Lowering the ruby into the bezel, she used her stone pliers to crimp the prongs into place little by little, turning the setting with each pass. Retrieving the loupe, she examined the gem again, checking for any gaps. She gave a prong another firm press for good measure, then threaded the bezel onto a thin gold chain. Sliding her hands beneath her hair, she clasped the necklace around her neck.

From a small plastic envelope, she retrieved a few strands of wheat blond hair. Cress had collected them from Fallon Moor's cell while Laura had been interrogating her. Holding them up to the light, she coiled the strands around her fingers. She pictured Fallon Moor as she scanned the hair for the faint traces of her body signature.

Everyone and everything generated essence. Body signatures were unique to individuals, with an underlying resonance of their species type. Brownies—like Saffin or Moor—were Celtic fey, who moved in and out of stories like far-flung cousins stopping by for a visit. No one disliked brownies in particular. They weren't powerful like the Danann or Inverni fairies. They didn't have ancient political rivalries with other species. They had little interest in politics and less patience for class distinctions. What they were, thought Laura, were brilliant organizers with a touch of obsessive-compulsive disorder who had no patience with sloth. When brownies became interested in something, they absorbed everything they could about the subject.

She found the hint of Moor's signature, too subtle for most druids to trace. With practiced skill, she infused a mental image of the brownie's face with her own essence, bound it to Moor's body signature, and pushed the result into the ruby. The essence bonded to the structure of the stone, forming a template to build an entire persona upon. In the mirror over the worktable, Laura's reflection shimmered and settled into a rudimentary version of Moor. Her skin tone darkened to a warm fawn color, hair shifted to a warm blond, and her features flattened. With the framework in place, she turned to the real work of building the glamour.

The first order of business was the eyes. Laura's natural green eyes blazed against the dark skin, but with a few nudges in the essence pattern, the color darkened to a hazelnut with a touch of red. She rounded her cheekbones and chin, turned the nose up a bit, and pushed the eyebrows higher on her forehead. The process worked liked sculpting, refining the essence here and there to bring out a natural form that would fool the sharpest eye. With a slight dampening, she softened her voice. Moor wasn't a loud talker. With the image complete, she added the final touch—dropping almost a foot off her frame. Watching the effect amused her, as if she were a character in some child's story caught in a spell. She leaned back and appraised the result. For all intents and purposes, Fallon Moor, a moderately attractive brownie, looked back at her.

The time she spent creating a glamour always surprised her. Hours flew like minutes while she threw herself into the process, focused on producing the perfect image. She took a break with some fruit juice, staring at the reflection with a critical eye. She liked the Moor image—self-assured without being aggressive, competent without being arrogant. Thinner than her usual preferences, but most brownies were. With a few tweaks to disguise the original source, she thought she might be able to use this particular glamour again.

With a final swig of her drink, she set out on the final level of imaging. She needed a boggart version of Moor in case a stressful situation arose, and she had to play the role. Since she had observed considerable self-control in Moor, she decided to create a more measured boggart, one that didn't devolve into complete savagery. Weaving in among the essence pattern in the stone, she layered aspects of Moor's physical characteristics that she could activate if necessary. Like an inventory of spare parts, she added alternatives to bulge her eye ridges, widen her mouth, sharpen her teeth, and elongate her limbs. With luck, she would need only to project the threat of going boggart to get her point across. If she needed to produce a full transformation, having the full template at hand would save her time and energy.

With a final infusion, Laura finished the template and slipped off the necklace. She left an essence reserve in the stone, enough to power the glamour on its own by wearing it. She could always reabsorb it if she needed the energy, but given her schedule, she didn't think that necessary. She had plenty of time to sleep and recharge her body essence naturally.

Tired, she stretched up and out of the chair. She checked her watch. After midnight. Driving to the Laura Blackstone condo in Alexandria didn't appeal to her. It wasn't like she needed anything there. Her workroom served her needs more than any of her apartments, and she had plenty of clothes to choose from. She propped pillows against the wall, curled up on the bed, and turned on the television.

She wasn't a big fan of TV. Given her day-to-day life, dramas didn't interest her, and the humor of sitcoms was often lost on her. She liked to watch with the sound off, trying to parse the emotions from the visuals. After a while, her attention wandered, and she thought of Sinclair.

He intrigued her. Working through her interest in him seemed a lot like the way she watched TV, as if she were her own voyeur. She didn't have daily interactions with people and didn't seek them out. At some point, she had stopped having any, pushing a personal life onto a dusty back shelf while she committed herself full-time to work. Then Sinclair showed up, tangled in her work and life. At first she felt obligated to help him succeed at InterSec because he had ended up there because of her. Now, though, she wanted to help because she . . . because she wanted to, she admitted. On gut instinct, she felt a level of trust in him she hadn't felt with anyone in a long time.

He said he liked her. The cautious side of her, the side she had spent most of her recent life cultivating, was always suspicious of someone taking too much interest in her. Someone taking interest was someone who might expose her. That was her work brain thinking. Her attraction to him worried her. Laura Blackstone didn't trust anyone, she thought.

That was a lie right there. She trusted Terryn macCullen. She had meant it when she said that to Sinclair. She trusted Cress, no matter her nature. Maybe a few others.

She pursed her lips. More lies.

She trusted those people to do their jobs. Trusted them to be there when she needed them to protect her. Trusted them to do the right thing—or even the wrong thing—for the right reason. What she didn't do was trust them with Laura Blackstone—the real Laura Blackstone. The person. The soul behind the image.

She murmured a laugh to herself. Laura Blackstone wasn't even her birth name. It was the best name she had for who she was today. She had become so proficient at protecting herself, she had nothing to protect anymore. Who was Laura Blackstone? Who was she when she left the Guildhouse or InterSec or this hidden room?

An agent. A cipher for a human being. No one.

She didn't think she had given him a reason to pursue her, but he had. At least, she thought she hadn't encouraged him. Maybe that was it. Maybe Sinclair was interpreting her joking and dismissiveness differently than she intended. Maybe Sinclair took it all as a playful challenge.

She sighed. More lies.

Trying to convince herself that what she was doing was something other than signaling to Sinclair that she was interested was another example of denying who she was. Lately, she wanted more out of her life than her work. She needed something more. She knew that. The constant forward motion of her jobs chafed at her, and her recent vacation in the Caribbean hadn't alleviated it. Sinclair was opening her eyes to the fact that there was more to life than hiding behind a mask.

Her gaze wandered to the worktable, trailed over the neat boxes of gemstones, the reference photographs tacked to the wall, the tools she used to create glamours. From where she stood, she couldn't see her reflection in the mirror, only the empty space of the room aglow from the silent television. That space, that small space in a hidden room, was the definition of who she had become.

Her chest felt heavy as she realized that it was a problem. Sinclair made her want to let it go. She rolled onto her side—away from the empty mirror—and settled herself. She smiled at the memory of Sinclair sleeping in the seat next to her in the car and the impulse she had to touch him. He was making her care again, and that wasn't a bad thing.

11
CHAPTER

EARLY THE NEXT afternoon, Laura entered the small restaurant a few blocks from the Guildhouse. She paused near the hostess station, letting her eyes adjust to the dark room after the bright light outside. Given the circumstances, she had decided to appear as Mariel. Since she was going to make her first foray into the Legacy offices later, she decided to wear a physical outfit for Moor's appearance and produce a glamoured one for Mariel, a warm taupe woven business suit over a cream blouse. A little softer than what Mariel usually wore, but the lunch was not business.

She spotted Cress near the back of the room and left the vestibule without waiting for the hostess to return. Sensing Laura's arrival, Cress looked up, and brief disappointment flitted across her face. The expression made Laura curious as she slipped into her chair. "Hi, were you waiting long?"

Cress forced a smile. "Not long. A few minutes."

"What's wrong? I thought you had an odd look on your face when I came in."

She shrugged. "For some reason, I was expecting you to look like yourself."

"Don't be silly. We're in public." Cress's face fell, and Laura immediately regretted what she'd said. "Cress, that sounded so wrong. You know what I meant."

Leaning back, Cress focused on the surface of the table. "I know. I understand that Laura Blackstone can't be seen talking to the demon fey over breadsticks and butter."

"Okay, not fair. You know I don't think that about you."

Cress sighed. "On a day-to-day basis, sure. But when I healed you, Laura, I felt what you felt."

Weeks earlier, Laura's body essence had been poisoned. The only way to save her life was to let Cress merge their body essences. The process Cress used to absorb the poison was raw and intimate, and not only on a physical level. For a moment, Cress and Laura had been aware of each other's thoughts. Laura wasn't proud that Cress learned of her fears about the *leanansidhe*, a fear that was ingrained in all the fey. A *leanansidhe* was difficult to fight since its ability was to drain essence—which was what the fey used to protect themselves. An attack by a *leanansidhe* meant death for all but the most powerful fey, and even those powerful enough had a challenge confronting them. Even given that, Laura felt that Cress had to recognize her determination to confront those fears. "Still not fair, Cress. I didn't know what was happening. I most certainly didn't think you were a demon fey. My essence was being invaded. I was panicked. I think anybody would have been."

Cress played with the wrapper from her straw. "You're right. I'm sorry."

They sat in awkward silence as a busser filled their water glasses. Laura shifted her chair closer to the table. "This got real heavy, real fast. I asked to have lunch with you because I thought you were upset about something and needed to talk. Is it me, or is it something else?"

Cress pressed her lips together. "It's not you. I'm hearing rumblings that the Guildmaster is trying to boot me out of InterSec."

"He can't. InterSec is a multinational agency. It's not under Guild authority," Laura said.

Cress wasn't convinced. "True, but he does control the Guildhouse. If he bans me from the Guild property, it amounts to the same thing."

She had a point. A Guildhouse was sovereign territory of the High Queen, which allowed a Guildmaster to do what he or she wanted in the name of security. "The only reason he'd have for doing that is because you're a *leanansidhe*, Cress. That's racist, and everyone would recognize it."

A cynical smirk curled on her face. "Just because I'm fey doesn't mean I'm the right kind of fey. The fey are probably more racist than humans."

"Maybe. But Rhys would still have to prove there's something fundamentally dangerous about you, and that he can't do. Not after your years of service, and especially not after the Archives."

That few people talked about Cress's success against the terrorist attack at the National Archives frustrated Laura. Cress had been largely responsible for minimizing the number of lives lost. She used her ability to absorb an explosion of lethal essence that could have killed several hundred people. Instead, fewer than thirty died, and that was because of damage that the bomb caused. The effort almost cost Cress her life, yet the only thing people talked about was whether she was dangerous to be around.

Cress smiled, not convinced, perhaps, but she saw a glimmer of hope. "The fact that I might have to defend myself is galling, though. It's the last thing I need right now."

Laura paused as the server placed their lunches on the table. "What do you mean? Are you okay?"

"I'm fine. Completely recovered."

Laura arched an eyebrow. "Completely? You almost died, Cress."

She speared a shrimp off her salad. "I've been able to replenish what I lost."

Despite her defense of Cress, Laura resisted the urge to shudder. *Leanansidhe* survived by absorbing essence, the basic life force of everything. What made them such feared beings was their preferred source of nourishment: people. When a *leanansidhe* absorbed essence from someone, that person wasn't likely to survive the experience. Cress had made a choice not to absorb essence from anyone without invitation. As far as Laura knew, Terryn was the only one who trusted her enough to allow it.

Laura wondered if that aspect of their relationship was the cause of Cress's turmoil. Cress and Terryn weren't simply work colleagues. They were lovers—a relationship that predated Laura's life at InterSec. Despite their different natures, Laura saw a relationship of deep commitment. It baffled her, in a way. She had enough trouble trying to figure out if she should allow herself a personal life without complicating matters by being worried that a significant other might accidentally kill her. "Terryn seems—distracted."

Cress tilted her head. Her whiteless eyes appeared to stare and made people feel self-conscious. They bothered Laura, too, but she felt it had nothing to do with her being a *leanansidhe* but with normal social interaction. "He's under pressure."

Laura thought about Terryn's unusual abruptness and anger at her debriefing. "I noticed. Is there anything I can do to help?"

Cress stared. "You know Terryn. He deals with things in his own way."

The answer didn't surprise her. Terryn held his emotions close—which was why his obvious level of annoyance at Sinclair surprised her. Cress was the same way, which ironically was what probably drew her and Terryn together. They were friends, but Laura never socialized with them outside the office except for an occasional dinner at their apartment. The dinners tended to be quiet and, frankly, dull. The three of them came together through work, and while they depended on each other more than most colleagues, they all maintained a personal distance that prevented a more intimate friendship

Cress compressed her lips. "Have you ever met Draigen?" she asked.

Laura shook her head. "We've never crossed paths."

Cress toyed with her salad. "She's rather . . . conservative."

"Does she know about . . ." Laura was going to say "you" but realized it would be a little tacky. ". . . your relationship?"

Cress didn't look up. "So Terryn tells me."

The Inverni were a proud people and a many-times-defeated one. They tended to be suspicious of outsiders, and Cress was about as outside as a fey could get. "Are you worried about something, Cress?"

She pulled her hair back and held it there as she decided what to say. "I'm worried she'll kill me."

Laura struggled for something to say. "That's ridiculous, Cress. Draigen macCullen is not going to kill you. You're not only a *leanansidhe*. You're a person. We know that. Everyone knows that."

"Not everyone."

Laura conceded that—to herself. Cress was right. It was hard to believe that a person whose nature demanded she murder others to survive was anything more than a monster. After all these years, Laura had a hard time putting the thought out of her head. But Cress had moved beyond her nature, figured out a way to control it and become a real person. "Have you talked to Terryn about this?"

She shook her head. "He's worried enough about Draigen's visit. I don't want to add to his stress."

Laura let out an uncomfortable laugh. Cress wasn't joking, though. "Terryn wouldn't let anything happen to you, Cress."

Cress looked away. "He can't be with me all the time."

As regent, Draigen ruled the macCullen clan—and, by virtue of that, all the Inverni. The idea that she might put Cress in danger wasn't far-fetched. Fairies could be vindictive. "Do you seriously think Draigen macCullen is going to kill you?"

She stared. And stared. "No. I think she may want to, but she won't."

Laura pointed at her. "Then you need to stop thinking about it. If you want the rest of the world to believe you're not a danger, you need to stop thinking everyone believes it. You need to live your life, Cress."

She drew her words out with resignation. "You're right. Old habits die hard."

Laura sipped of her iced tea while she considered what further to say. "If you want my advice, you and Terryn both need some time to yourselves and to stop worrying about what everyone else is going to do—including Draigen. I might not know her from a hole in the wall, but Terryn asked her to lead the Inverni because he knew she could handle it. And you have to remember this isn't the sixth century. She's not some warrior queen out to kill a ghostly demon."

Cress bunched her shoulders as she made a decision. "I think Terryn and I need to have a long talk."

Laura grinned. "Good. When you do, tell him if he doesn't want my fragile ego shattered, he needs to knock off the cranky."

Finally, Cress smiled an honest smile. "I've been trying to do that for years."

12
CHAPTER

AS SHE DROVE over the Potomac after lunch, Laura tried to shake off the melancholy from the lunch with Cress. Try as she might, walking in Cress's shoes was not easy to imagine. Laura had been in plenty of situations where she was either not liked or treated with suspicion. But those were for roles she played. At the end of the day, she went home knowing that whatever had happened had been directed against a glamoured persona. Someone who didn't truly exist. Cress was real. Her emotions were real. Whatever her history, it was history. If the fey were going to move forward as a people, they had to let go of the deep past. Convergence had changed everything for them, giving them an opportunity to start over. If they didn't learn anything from Convergence, they might well risk another disaster.

She had to shake it off, though. The afternoon was going to be her first foray into Legacy, and she had to remain focused on impersonating Fallon Moor. Instead of returning to the Guildhouse, she had swapped out the Mariel glamour for the newly created Moor. A short walk up the block to where

InterSec had moved Moor's car, and she was on her way to work, whatever that meant.

The Legacy Foundation occupied offices in a nondescript building in Crystal City, across the river from downtown D.C. Laura drove Moor's car into the building's underground garage and found the section of reserved parking spaces for Legacy. She killed the engine and made a fuss of fixing her hair in the rearview mirror. Watching security tapes of Moor tipped her to the nervous habit. Or vain one. She gathered a bulky purse onto her lap and rummaged through it for Moor's keys and an ID card.

I've arrived, she sent to Terryn.

Reconnaissance only, please, unless a viable opportunity arises, he replied.

Despite the fact that Moor kept few files of interest at home, Terryn wanted Laura to keep a low profile the first day in the office, confirm Moor's data sources, and investigate other avenues to explore. A hard insertion with little prep was risky, but despite Draigen's imminent arrival, they did not want to blow her cover by moving too aggressively the first time out.

As she walked across the garage, she pictured Terryn working in the Guildhouse a few miles away. In the basement holding area, Moor remained in glass-lined enclosures to prevent her from doing sendings. Terryn waited outside her cell so he could relay Laura's questions if necessary to Moor by intercom and send the responses back.

A whistled catcall echoed through the concrete space of the garage. At the far end, men loitered in a service area reserved for limos and black cars. They wore nonchalant smirks as they eyeballed her. With his height, Sinclair stood out from the others. He was smirking, too. She liked to think he was doing it to fit in, but it wouldn't have surprised her if he was the one who'd whistled. Instead of scowling, she smiled self-consciously as she turned away, aware by now that Moor was more than a little vain.

As the elevator doors opened on the twelfth floor, Laura took a deep breath and proceeded down the hall. This moment always gave her a trickle of anxiety. A glamour she created from her own imagination was malleable, with a look, history, and personality able to change according to circumstances. A glamour based on a real person was tougher. She was going to meet people who knew Fallon Moor, and Fallon Moor moved in a high-stakes world. A false step could be deadly.

The hushed quiet of the offices was like other places she had worked—cold, sterile rooms decorated to look fashionable and comfortable but with a manufactured air. No true personality interfered. Over time, the blandness of certain places had become a first indication that something wasn't right, that something other than the stated business at hand was going on. Secrets were about what was revealed as much as what was hidden. On an individual level, hiding one thing among many exposed ones was easy, but that didn't work as well for a corporation. Better to hide everything than risk leaving a clue.

She received mumbled greetings and sideways glances as she made her way to Moor's office. No one stopped her to chat. She worried that she might be doing something wrong, tipping off that something was not right about Moor. But the behavior was consistent with everyone. *I'm getting the sense our informant isn't the most popular kid on the block,* she sent to Terryn.

She's not making many friends here either, he replied.

Laura smiled at his response. Terryn's humor tended to be dry and subtle, but lately it had been missing entirely. It was nice to hear him sound normal.

The windows in Moor's office provided an impressive view of the Potomac and D.C. The river meandered below as if underlining the spread of the city's iconic buildings. While it wasn't the usual coveted corner office, Laura thought it interesting that Moor had achieved some level of importance within Legacy.

She sat at the desk, pulled the computer keyboard closer, and logged on to the network system. So far, so good, she thought. The user ID and password were correct, so Moor hadn't played any petty games on that front. She searched the network, scrolling through directories to note where Moor had open access. Terryn wanted her to use the day for surveillance and not touch anything until they assessed what was interesting and available. Copying and transferring data might be noticed, maybe not right away; but they didn't want to risk it until they had decided what they needed.

At the sound of knock, she lifted her head toward the door. She recognized the dark-haired man standing there as Adam DeWinter from the staff dossiers InterSec had for Legacy. He was listed as the firm's director of technology and president, which was true. What was not on the company letterhead was that he was ex-CIA with extensive security experience.

With a friendly, chastising smile, he leaned against the doorjamb. "You didn't return my phone calls."

Feigning surprise, she picked up her cell phone and scrolled through the messages. Moor wasn't in the habit of logging in her contact names. Few calls came in on the line anyway. The one number that appeared often was a disposable cell, which Laura assumed now must have been DeWinter. "Really? I'm sorry. I had some things to take care of and forgot to check my messages."

DeWinter pushed himself with his shoulder off the doorjamb and sat on the edge of her desk. "More important than talking to me?"

His tone had an undercurrent of seduction. Cocky and self-assured. A little too self-assured. His familiar attitude wasn't simple office banter. Laura twisted her lips in a playful smirk. "Are you feeling neglected?"

He chuckled. "Should I?"

I think Moor held back a relationship with DeWinter. Ask her the status, she sent to Terryn.

Laura leaned back and smiled at DeWinter. "Of course not. I think we both know where things stand."

Amused, he dropped his eyelids half-closed. "I wasn't thinking of standing."

Lovers. We're having a discussion about what else she might have neglected to mention, Terryn sent.

Laura mentally swore. She had no delusion that Moor was being fully cooperative, but risking exposing her like this was skating close to the edge of breaching their deal. She leaned forward and slowly drew her finger across the back of DeWinter's palm. "You'd be surprised what I can do standing."

He playfully tapped her on the nose. "Someone's going to hear us."

She affected an innocent air. "I didn't say anything."

Amused, he moved back to the front of the desk. "I want to go over some financial details before my meeting."

Laura bit her lip and checked her watch. "Can you give me a few minutes? I need to get something out."

A puzzled look came over DeWinter's face. "Sure. I'll be in my office."

He hesitated at the door. Laura threw him a seductive glance as she turned her attention to the computer screen. DeWinter left a moment later. She checked the company calendar to see if his scheduled meeting might give her a clue as to what he wanted. Nothing but his name and a reserved conference room.

She ran through the rest of the network directories, tapping into her mnemonic memory skills as the files scrolled up the screen. Her recall was as much a skill as an ability, honed in her youth as part of her druid training. Nothing out of the ordinary jumped to her attention, typical corporate network setup. She hit a password-protected directory that she wasn't automatically logged in to. She tried the user ID and password Moor had given her, but they were rejected. She didn't try again.

Ask Moor for the password to the V directory, she sent to Terryn.

She glanced at the computer clock in the long pause waiting for response. DeWinter's meeting time was getting near. She had no intention of attending without knowing what it was about, but she didn't want him to come looking for her either.

She doesn't know, he sent.

Laura pursed her lips. Without being present, she couldn't test Moor's truthfulness. *I don't believe her.*

Neither do I, sent Terryn.

She didn't dare guess the password. One failed attempt would be overlooked. Several would be noted—especially if Moor was supposed to have access.

I think we need this, Terryn. A password-protected directory is blood in the water for me, she sent.

He didn't respond. She waited, not dwelling on what she had requested. Terryn was a powerful Inverni, if not the most powerful member of his species. She had seen him do things to wring information out of people that turned her stomach at first. He got results, though, and she had convinced herself the results were more important.

She's going boggie, he sent.

"Dammit," Laura said aloud.

"What's wrong?" DeWinter asked.

She startled at the sound of his voice. *I've got company,* she sent.

She rubbed her forehead in annoyance. "What? Oh, nothing. I forgot a password."

"For what?"

With an air of unconcern, she pushed the keyboard away and straightened papers on her desk. "V-drive stuff."

"Are you nervous about something?"

She shrugged. "No. I wanted to review something. Speaking of which, you said you had something you wanted me to look at?"

"An interesting opportunity has come up that will ease our acquisition. It will cost, though," he said.

She moved some paperwork on the desk. "Okay."

He narrowed his eyes at her. "Okay?"

Situations like this made impersonating someone dicey. She didn't know what he was talking about. Moor had said little about her interaction with DeWinter, an obvious attempt to trip her up. With a distracted air, Laura stood. "I'm sorry, Adam. I've got a lot on my mind. Let's start over."

"We need to move a substantial amount of funds," he said.

"How much?"

"Nine, with three on reserve for contingencies."

She arched an eyebrow. He meant millions of dollars. "That's some ease of acquisition."

He seemed pleased with himself. "It is. Do you think we can find a benefactor?"

She shrugged and took a gamble. "You might have better access to those kinds of benefactors."

"I'll need accounts access for transfers."

She pursed her lips and stared out at the D.C. skyline. His comment seemed off. If he didn't have access—and he was in charge—then Moor or whomever she worked for didn't want to give it. He was testing her. "You find the benefactor, and I'll take care of the rest."

She didn't look at him as he considered her response. "That's fine."

Relief swept over her. Truth. He was fine with her answers. She had bluffed her way through it. DeWinter came around the desk and kissed her on the temple. "You look particularly marvelous today."

She slipped her hand into his. "Thank you. Now I need to get to work before you make me more distracted than I already am."

"Call me when you're ready," he said. He hesitated at the door as if weighing a thought, then smiled and left without speaking.

Laura let out a relieved exhale.

Tell Moor she better not be boggie when I get back, she sent to Terryn.

13
<del>CHAPTER</del>

LAURA STRODE THROUGH the lower corridor of the Guildhouse that led to the InterSec holding rooms. She had switched glamours in the elevator lobby in the garage, shedding Fallon Moor and draping Mariel Tate over her like armor. Angry armor. Her long dark hair brushed from side to side against the back of her black jumpsuit, keeping rhythm with the punctuated staccato of her footsteps. Staffers moved out of her way.

She entered the anteroom to Moor's cell. Arms crossed, Terryn stood at the viewing window, his wings sparking with flashes of indigo and white. Laura stopped beside him. Inside the glass-encased room, Moor prowled, her limbs elongated and bristling with blond hair. She stared back at them, snapping her long-hinged jaws, unable to see through the one-way glass but knowing they were there.

"How long has she been this way?" Laura asked.

"Since I pressed her for the password," Terryn said.

"She doesn't look too far into the boggart mania. Has she spoken?"

He shook his head. "Howled a few times."

Laura grasped the doorknob. "I want answers."

"Do you think that's wise?" Terryn asked her back.

"We'll find out."

She opened the door. Moor lunged as soon as she stepped inside. Laura activated her shields, a hardened layer of essence enveloping her body before Moor made it halfway across the room. As the brownie brought her claws forward, Laura swung an essence-charged fist at her chest and sent her flying into the wall. Moor hit with a loud grunt, then fell to the floor. She scrambled into a crouch, set to leap again.

Thrusting her hand out, Laura stunned her with a blast of essence. Dazed, Moor slumped to the floor. In two long strides, Laura reached her, grabbed her by the hair, and held her up. Biting off the sounds of a binding spell, she sent burning lines of orange essence spiraling out of her free hand and pinned Moor against the wall.

"Drop the act. We need to talk," she said.

Moor threw back her head and howled in pain as the bindings dug into her.

Laura stepped in closer, heedless of Moor's sharp teeth. "Do you think I know nothing about brownies? You're forcing yourself boggie. Knock it off."

Moor thrashed, the bindings pulling tighter with her movements. She howled again. Laura crossed her arms. "You know how the binding works. You move, it burns. You will calm down or stand there until you pass out from exhaustion, and the bindings sear your arms and legs. Your choice. Either way, I'm going to get what I want."

Moor growled in her face.

"Keep it up, Moor. I may not be patient enough to wait for you to pass out." Laura held her hand up and wrenched her fingers closed. The bindings bit in several places, drawing blood.

Moor banged her head back against the wall and screamed. With eyes squeezed shut, she panted, spittle running out of her mouth. Her breathing slowed as her limbs shortened, and her claws retracted. She groaned against the pain of the bindings as her normal brownie shape returned. Still breathing heavily, she glared at Laura through bloodshot eyes.

With a flick of her hand, Laura released the bindings. As Moor fell forward, Laura grabbed her and shoved her onto the metal folding chair. Moor wrapped her arms against her stomach and hunched forward. "I'm going to kill you when I get out of here," she rasped.

Laura crouched so that Moor could watch essence well up in her eyes. "I'll look forward to the attempt."

Moor tried to hold her gaze and failed. "I'm not afraid of you."

Laura stood and paced to the table. "Good. Any damage I do to you will be more pleasurable that way. Tell me the access codes to the V drive."

"That wasn't part of our deal," Moor said.

Laura folded her arms. "Our deal was cooperation. You want to draw a line? Go right ahead. I'll get the information one way or another. You talk, and life will be easier for both of us."

Moor tried to look her in the eye. "It's financial data. You already have it. You showed me."

A waver in her modulation said lie. A partial lie, but still a lie. "I didn't ask what it was. I want access."

Moor did stare then, malice glittering in her eyes. "Do you think I can't take whatever you throw at me? Do you think that after everything I've done to take down the monarchy, a little pain means anything to me? Do you?"

Laura leaned over the table. "Who said anything about a *little* pain?"

Moor laughed. "You're not the Guild. InterSec won't let you go as far as you'll need to. If you think I'll give you the key to bring it all down, you're wrong. Do you hear me? Wrong. I'll die before I tell you."

Truth. Hard, clear truth rang in her words. She wasn't going to tell.

Laura straightened up. "There are all kinds of pain, Moor. I don't have to touch you to start," she said. With the honed skill of years of practice, Laura swapped out the Mariel glamour for the Moor glamour without revealing her true face. Startled, Moor stared at her own image. "Have it your way. I'll fuck the password out of your boyfriend."

Howling screams followed her out the door. Laura stopped short in the anteroom. Sinclair, his face troubled, had joined Terryn while she had been inside. He looked about to say something, then gave her a crooked smile and left without speaking.

"How long was he here?" she asked.

"He saw and heard it all," Terryn said.

Laura didn't speak as she watched Moor's face bulge and contort. She wanted to follow Sinclair and explain. It was the job. Part of the job. Sometimes . . . sometimes things needed to be done. Things she wasn't always proud of.

Terryn interrupted her thoughts. "How did you know she was faking before?"

Laura blinked, stared at her feet. "She agreed to cooperate. She would go boggie only if something kept her from cooperating, and the only thing doing that was herself."

"Unfortunately, we are no closer than before," he said.

Laura shook her head. "Not true. Now we know that drive is important, and we don't need to waste time on other things."

She watched Moor pace back and forth across the room. Trapped. She wondered why Sinclair's watching bothered her. No, why the look on his face bothered her. He knew what she did. He knew the stakes were high. They were always high. She clenched her jaw. She knew why it bothered her and didn't want to admit it. Sinclair was a good guy. Honest. Sincere. Honorable. Things she thought about herself. But in that look he had, she doubted that was what he was thinking. And it bothered her.

Mission after mission, she did what needed to be done. She knew some people believed the ends never justified the means. Those were people who had never walked in her shoes. Sometimes what she did to get results was irrelevant. She would have been dead many times over if she didn't believe that. If she had died, how would that have furthered a greater goal? Or was she being selfish? Did her life matter if her principles were betrayed?

Terryn more often than not held an even harsher view about the brutal necessities of their work. He was immortal. All that time accrued on him made him seem indifferent to the emotion. She knew him, though, knew he had sides he revealed to few. As a druid, she wasn't immortal, but she wasn't human either. She would live a long time. She wondered if the cold precision she brought to the heat of battle was making her lose something intrinsically important about herself.

She closed her eyes. Sinclair didn't have to say anything to make her face herself. She wasn't sure what his look meant, but she knew it wasn't admiration. What was she becoming? And was Sinclair enough reason to change? Did she even want to?

A bang against the glass startled her. Moor scratched with clawed hands against the viewing glass, her face contorting in a snarl. Her eyes blazed yellow as she snapped, her jaw filled with razor-sharp teeth. Frantic, she flipped backward onto her elongated limbs, then scrambled around the room looking for a way out.

"I don't think she's faking it this time," Terryn said.

14
CHAPTER

"YOU LOOK LIKE hell," Laura said.

It had been five days since she had last seen Sinclair. He hadn't called, or, rather, he hadn't called her. He had checked in at InterSec at the prescribed intervals, but he hadn't contacted her even after she left him messages. So she finally called him.

Stretched out on the couch in her Alexandria apartment, Sinclair chuckled with his eyes closed. "I have been awake for almost three days that have included drinking, tramping through the woods, arm wrestling, and drag racing a truck. Then I had to ride here in the trunk of your car. I'm a little tired."

Laura slid a cold bottle of beer into his hand, then dropped into an armchair. Picking up the remote, she lowered the sound on the flat-screen TV above the fireplace but left the news on. "Oh, sure. I'm stressed out undercover with an ex-CIA spook hanging over me, and you're out having fun with the boys."

He levered himself up so he could drink his beer. "I will gladly switch with you. I'm used to arresting rednecks, not hanging with them."

She smiled. "How bad are they?"

He rolled his eyes. "You would not believe the crap these guys are into. The federal government is a criminal organization. The Constitution was dictated by God and must be obeyed, but all the laws that came after are from men and are optional. The fey are dirty scum that need to be wiped out—as well as non-Christians, most everyone darker than an albino, people with college degrees, and anyone who doesn't drive a Chevy."

"A Chevy? That's nuts," she said.

He laughed again. "Yeah. It's a different world."

Laura slumped in her chair, dangling her glass of orange juice and vodka over the armrest. "It sounds like you're in, though."

He held out his beer. "Meet the new freelance consultant for the Legacy Foundation."

She tapped the bottle with her glass. "Let me guess—weapons training at a militia camp?"

"Yeah. They've got several acres up in Virginia where they run around playing guerrilla revolutionary. Now I have to figure out how to teach them enough so they think I know what I'm doing but not enough that they might learn something," he said.

She watched the news anchor Jenna Dahl talking in front of a picture of Draigen macCullen. She was tempted to turn up the volume, but the image was gone before she finished the thought. Terryn would brief her on anything important. She sipped her drink. "That's always the hard part of all this—sometimes helping a cause you don't agree with in the process of getting what you went in for. I try to get in and get out as fast as possible."

He rocked his head. "How far do you go?"

Laura stared down at her drink. How far indeed. She had done things she never thought she would do. Some depressed her, some embarrassed her, and, yes, a couple of things horrified her. She didn't like to think about it. Ever since Sinclair walked away from Fallon Moor's holding cell, she had been expecting his question. "It depends on the stakes, Jono."

Curious, he cocked his head at her. "That sounds intriguing and . . . um, not so good."

"It's not that melodramatic. Sometimes you have to push the envelope. It's the nature of the job." She rose from the chair and freshened her drink at the kitchen counter. More ice and juice. She had rules about alcohol. Living a life with so much solitude and secrets made bottles and pills seductive. She had seen friends and colleagues spiral into despair, then burn out. Burned out of the job. Burned out of their lives. The loneliness of undercover work made them feel trapped, with no one to share their hopes and fears. She knew she wasn't an alcoholic, but she wondered how many people thought about it like she did every time she poured a drink.

"So why are you so secretive?" he asked.

Even Terryn didn't know everything she did to get a job done. Sinclair couldn't see her from this angle. If he thought she was going to bare her soul to him after a few weeks, he was mistaken. Laura returned to the armchair and propped her feet up on the coffee table, something she had never done in the Alexandria apartment. She didn't think she'd ever sat in the armchair before either. She brought the glass to her lips, keeping her expression neutral. "Have I killed people without thinking about it? Have I slept with people I didn't want to? That's what you want to know, isn't it?"

He pursed his lips. "I didn't mean for the conversation to go in this direction."

She let out a mild scoff, not sarcastic, but understanding. "Yeah. That's the thing, isn't it? Things slide in directions you don't expect and don't intend. So you manage it on the fly. Sometimes that means dealing with things you don't want to."

Sinclair focused his attention on his beer bottle. "And sometimes you go over the line?"

She sighed. "The problem with this job, Jono, is that there are no lines except the ones you draw for yourself. And then they move." She took a long sip of her drink. "The answer is 'yes' to both those questions, by the way."

She said it because it needed to be said. If Sinclair ended

up a part of her life—either work or personal—he was going to hear it at some point anyway. When he glanced at her then, she surprised herself by feeling relieved. His face looked reflective rather than disappointed in her.

"When I saw you in the room, like Moor, it scared me a little. We never went that far on the force," he said.

His admission touched her. She doubted Jonathan Sinclair discussed being afraid often. "InterSec has wider parameters for use of force. The situation has to justify it, and we have to answer for it if we're wrong."

"You threatened to kill me the night we met," he said.

She stared. "And the answer to your unspoken question is, yes, I would have if it were necessary."

"But you didn't."

She gestured with her palm up. "Because I had time for alternatives. They weren't great ones for either of us, but you're not dead, and I don't have more blood on my hands. I can live with those results."

He grunted. "Me, too."

"You seem uncomfortable about something," she said.

He pushed his lower lip out, a habit that she thought made him look boyish. "This stuff is a lot less glamorous than I thought it was."

She smirked. "No pun intended?"

He rolled his head toward her. "No, but I guess it's more glamorous for you. I've spent the last few weeks driving businessmen around who spend more time on the phone trying to line up affairs than doing business."

"That's the grunt-work part. It doesn't exactly get the adrenaline flowing," she said.

Sinclair stared at the ceiling. "Exactly."

"But when you do get it going, you realize you can't live on that level all the time, even if it's a welcome rush at the moment."

His eyebrow flicked up. "I hadn't considered that."

The television screen switched to a view of the Key Bridge. The banner crawl along the bottom of the screen announced that Ian Whiting's body still had not been recovered. Footage played from the morning his car was found. The camera zoomed in on his shoes where he left them with a note on the abutment.

"Do you think you could ever do that?" Sinclair asked.

"Suicide?" She shook her head. "Not my nature. Cress doesn't think it was Whiting's either. She thinks he walked away."

Sinclair grunted in surprise. "How about that? Say 'screw it' and walk away?"

"Sure, but I don't think my life's ever been that bad."

"Really?"

"Really." Silence stretched across the room as the news moved on to something else. She wondered if what he had seen in the interrogation room with Fallon Moor was behind that last question.

"I can drive you back if you want," she said.

He didn't speak for the longest moment. "Why did you ask me to come here?"

She shrugged. "Because it's your first real assignment, and whether you thought you needed to or not, it helps to step out of the role. You're going to need to create a safe space in your life, Jono, somewhere you can go and remember who you are."

He grinned. "Is this your way of asking me to move in?"

She laughed. He was changing the subject, or at least lightening it. Whatever he was thinking about what he had seen her do the other day he was letting slide. For now, anyway. "Yeah, that's not going to happen. I thought you might like some dinner."

"Wow. What are you making?" he asked.

She got up and walked back to the kitchen. "A phone call. I'll get the take-out menus."

Sinclair followed her across the room. "You know, for a badass, you're really a big old softy."

She slid folded menus onto the counter. Glancing at him,

she smiled. "Great. Nice to know you think I'm old, fat, and flabby."

He stepped close behind her and spoke into her ear. "You can prove me wrong."

The low resonance of his voice tickled, and she bumped a playful elbow into his stomach. "I don't have to prove anything."

As she turned, he leaned forward with both hands against the counter, pinning her between his arms without touching her. "Maybe I do."

They stared into each other's eyes. This close, she noticed the dark brown and red flecks in his amber irises and wondered about his jotunn heritage. She knew little about the Teutonic giants, less about human/fey hybrids. Jono Sinclair intrigued her on so many levels that warning bells went off in her head. She didn't know why and didn't want to listen to them. He leaned his face closer and closed his eyes. She swept a menu between their lips, and he kissed the other side.

"I'd love a pizza. How about you?" she asked.

Chuckling, he plucked the menu out of her hands and kissed her on the lips. She laughed into the kiss, relieved and happy that he wasn't going to let her work come between them.

Pleased, he leaned his head back and looked down at her. "I get to pick dessert."

15
CHAPTER

LAURA STOPPED AT a traffic light. The building where Legacy had its office glittered in the morning sun. She stared at the building, her eyes scanning the impersonal planes of glass reflecting white and golden light. She wondered what other companies in the building did and what they thought of Legacy, if they thought about it at all. D.C. was filled with people, agencies, and companies with conflicting agendas. They often ended up working near each other cheek by jowl, even in the Guildhouse.

The light turned green, and she pulled into the underground garage. The valet area was crowded with vehicles, more than usual. Their drivers lingered near their cars, smoking and talking. She guessed people from other offices had arrived to attend the same meeting she was going to. An informational update meeting had appeared on the company schedule, and DeWinter was slated to speak. Sinclair was there—she knew he would be—but he gave her no more than a glance as she entered the elevator lobby.

She skipped going to her office, not wanting to get waylaid by anyone. Timing was an issue for what she wanted to do that day, and knowing where DeWinter was at all times was crucial. She strolled the corridor on her floor that led to the elevator. Moor's lack of popularity allowed her to linger without being bothered. People ignored her, as she appeared to be intent on reading a document. She glanced at her watch. DeWinter was running late.

As she neared the elevator, he appeared at the end of the hall. She timed her approach and wandered toward the elevator. Keeping her head down, she bumped into DeWinter. Feigning surprise, she clutched at her papers, using his chest to keep them from falling.

"I'm so sorry!" she said, stepping back.

DeWinter twisted his face away from the fanning pages with an amused smile and lifted his hands to help her. "I didn't think my white paper was that absorbing."

Laura ducked her head. "I've been running late all day and wanted to finish it before your presentation."

They stepped inside the elevator. "Well, you're probably the only one. No one preps for these things as far as I can tell."

She held her folder down out of DeWinter's view. "It's my nature."

When the doors opened, DeWinter held them to let her exit first. "That doesn't sound like a ringing endorsement of how compelling my writing is."

She smiled back. "You're compelling in other ways."

Sinclair walked toward them from the opposite end of the corridor. He passed without making eye contact, brushing against Laura. She slipped him DeWinter's keycard. Picking pockets was an old skill, made easier by the intimate relationship Moor had with DeWinter. He didn't think twice about the contrived physical contact.

In the conference room, DeWinter continued to the front of the room while Laura sat near the rear. People ignored her—or at least pretended to. She sensed more than a little tension from several people who came near her. She didn't know if Fallon Moor was liked, but she was clearly feared. She placed the folder on her lap. DeWinter opened his laptop, and a

PowerPoint presentation flashed onto the room screen as the lights dimmed. He launched into the first set of bullets points. Laura checked her watch. By then Sinclair should have been a few floors away duplicating DeWinter's ID card. She wasn't sure how long it would take.

A chart flashed on the screen. "Year to date, 117 deaths are directly related to the fey," DeWinter said. "With the terrorist attack at the National Archives, the total went to 144, and we're not even close to the end of the calendar year. Of these cases, half remain under investigation and a third are tied up in jurisdictional issues regarding the citizenship of the fey perpetrators."

Laura didn't want to dismiss the numbers, but if someone divided murders by any one criterion—skin color, religion, geography, and, yes, species—the tallied number would look significant. Crime wasn't a trait unique to the fey.

Another slide appeared, listing a series of federal statutes. "The fey, even those considered American citizens, enjoy unprecedented rights and privileges that no other social class enjoys. These rights, in turn, are directly related to undue influence of the fey monarchies in Ireland and Germany."

Laura skimmed the list off her printout of the presentation. DeWinter's argument sounded credible, but he was taking select issues out of context. The politics between the U.S. and the fey monarchies were more complicated than a few statutes that seemed to provide unfair advantages to the fey. It wasn't that he—or Legacy—didn't have a point. Laura wasn't naïve. But the U.S., like any other government, balanced advantages against disadvantages. They wanted to have the fey as allies, both for commercial and military reasons. Sometimes that meant certain leniencies.

"The U.S. government has allowed itself to be seduced by the power of the beneficent fey and nostalgic notions of heroism and chivalry in old tales. These are lies that have no place in modern democracies. The root of the problem is the monarchy system, a dictatorship by another name. If we sever our ties to these monarchies, they will fail. Only when they fail can we hope to negotiate with them on a level playing field. These monarchies must end if humans are to have any chance at a safe future."

Laura surveyed the room. The people in attendance were staffers, rank and file. They weren't the people she was interested in—yet. Some of them might become radicalized, and that was exactly what meetings like this were for. DeWinter used them to garner support for Legacy's goals. Those who believed they could be achieved through government became mouthpieces for Legacy. Those who believed in more violent means were shuttled into Legacy's more covert operations. She had seen the evolution play out in a number of organizations that rallied around radical ideas.

Legacy wanted an end to the monarchies. Given what she had seen of its secret backers, it was about money and power. The more unstable the fey monarchies became, the more opportunities arose for others to take their place. The people in the room might think they were being patriots. Instead, they were becoming pawns to another power structure.

Time dragged as DeWinter droned on about legal initiatives Legacy was involved in. As planned, Laura's cell phone rang. People shifted and heads turned, craning to see who had left a ringer on. Laura hopped up with the phone to her ear, taking her time to ensure that everyone knew it was her causing the interruption as she left the room. Once in the hall, she stayed near the conference room's glass door, fully visible to DeWinter.

Sinclair arrived, but stayed out of view of the conference room. Laura held her hand against the doorjamb as if she were casually leaning on it. Unseen from inside the room, Sinclair slipped two keycards into her hand. He gave her a wink and walked off.

Still pretending to be on a cell call, Laura pushed open the door and resumed her seat. She slipped DeWinter's keycard and a plain white duplicate into her folder. After a brief applause, the lights went up, and the room broke into conversation. As the attendees left, Laura lingered, again making sure to remain in DeWinter's line of sight at all times. If he had noticed his card missing, she didn't want him to think she had gone anywhere with it. When the room emptied, she joined him at the podium, where he packed his materials into folders.

"You were excellent," she said.

He shrugged. "The facts speak for themselves."

She reached out and tugged at his lapel, slipping the key-card back in the inside pocket without him noticing. "You really were good."

He took her hand and kissed it. "Careful. You might make me fall for you."

"You might be worth catching." She let her hand slide seductively down the lapel of his jacket, then left the room. He was good, she thought. Three layers of security good. She held the folder so that the duplicate keycard didn't slip out.

She was better.

16
CHAPTER

OVERLOOKING THE WHITE House, the Hay-Adams
Hotel had an address that demanded high prices of its guests
and the envy of those who wished they could afford it. Laura
had lived undercover at the hotel several times over the years,
and she had never regretted it. While it never felt like home,
the service and atmosphere more than made up for it. For
its location, it could have gone the lazy route, jacked up its
prices, and let the tourists in; but all in all, it had kept its
standards. The restaurants were good, not always spectacu-
lar, but at a place like the Hay-Adams, good was not something to be disappointed in.

When Genda Boone suggested lunch at the Lafayette Room
to Mariel Tate, Laura almost asked to go elsewhere but changed
her mind. After a week of undercover work as Fallon Moor,
juggling plans at the Guild for Draigen's reception, and worrying about Sinclair, she wanted to have a break that did not
involve sleeping in her hidden room at the Guildhouse. The
calm, pale colors of the hotel's restaurant would be a perfect
antidote to her chaotic schedule.

Or so she thought until Genda arrived in a flaming red

dress that moved as much as her undulating wings. As a Danann fairy, she generated an essence field that drew its power from the air around her. Genda let some of her natural body essence emit a static glow that moved her white hair with a languid, mesmerizing motion.

By subtle signs in body language, Laura knew Genda saw her as soon as she entered but pretended to search for her. Otherwise, the turned heads in the room might have missed her entrance. She let her eyes settle on Laura and held her hand out as she crossed the room to the table. "Mariel, sweet, how are you?"

Laura smiled as she half rose from the chair to exchange air kisses. "Perfect, Genda. I love that dress."

Genda's vanity was notorious, and she liked it reinforced. Now that Laura saw the dress—which she did like—she realized the reason for the location. Genda's vibrant slash of color against the pale décor of the Lafayette Room drew stares from all corners. Genda sat with a swirl of material. "Do you? It's a Paul Carroll. Boutique designer out of New York. He dyed this red to perfection for me. You must call him."

Laura sipped some white wine. "You'll have to give me his number." Her Mariel persona liked clothes as much as Laura, though Mariel tended toward more streamlined looks than Laura's feminine tastes. She liked Mariel to project competence with an edge of intimidation. With Mariel's long dark hair, that meant snug business suits in dark shades. It didn't mean dull, though, as she touched her jacket sleeve, dark gray satin with ribbed black pinstripes. The three-quarter-length skirt showed off a sufficient curve of leg. Mariel more than held her own against Genda in the attraction department.

Genda sighed and flicked an imperious hand for the waiter. "I have been swamped this morning. The markets are going insane"—she broke off as the waiter arrived—"springwater, two glasses of the Grüner Veltliner from last week's tasting menu, and have Thomas put together a pâté sampler—tell him it's Genda. Thanks"—she dismissed the waiter with a turn of the head—"you will love this Grüner. Have it with the fish and the asparagus . . . Did you get a chance to see the news?"

Laura twitched her lips to keep from chuckling. "Which?"

Genda leaned forward. "The markets, dear. Chicago is a mess. Commodities are for gamblers, but between you and me, there's a scandal brewing there that is going to embarrass the Teuts, and I can't wait. Interesting times, I tell you, interesting times."

Genda lived and breathed finance. Few people at InterSec understood what she was talking about half the time, but no one rivaled the sharpness of her assessments. In a global economy, the financial ramifications of world events often had an impact on political stability, and InterSec factored that information into whatever missions it undertook. "Teutonic fey? Does it reach to the Elvenking?"

She flipped a dismissive hand. "Oh, Donor is beside the point on this one. No, it'll shake up both U.S. political parties when the money trail is found . . ." Two waiters appeared, one with the water and the appetizer plate and the other with the wine. Genda eyed the bottle label. "Yes, that's the one"—she pointed to the appetizers—"try that crisped foie gras. It's scandalous and delicious." She paused to sip the wine, nodded with a smile to the waiter, and lowered her glass. "Nothing will come of it, of course. The humans will have their hearings and their protestations, and the real money will be avoided so everyone can enjoy St. Bart's this year."

"It's delicious," Laura said.

Genda tapped her hand. "Isn't it? As long as it doesn't affect the equity markets, it will be very entertaining."

Laura smiled and shook her head. "I meant the foie gras."

Genda's eyebrows shot up, then she let out a short, high laugh. "Oh! Gods, listen to me. I have such a one-track mind. Isn't it, though? Thomas is a marvel. So, tell me, dear, where have you been?"

She craned her neck to see beyond Laura and waved to

someone. Laura felt herself begin to relax. She liked Genda. As Mariel, they had shared an office suite together for years. The nature of their responsibilities often kept their conversation on mundane and superficial matters, but that was precisely one of the things Laura liked about it. No InterSec or Guild politics. No guns under the table. Just two office colleagues who shared a similar lifestyle getting together for lunch or dinner. Despite the big personality and need for attention, Genda was a nice contrast to the stoic Terryn and quiet Cress.

She wondered if that was where her attraction for Sinclair was coming from. They had office politics for certain. They'd even had guns under the table a time or two. But Sinclair managed to push all of that aside with an attractive smile, an outgoing personality, and a desire to date. Laura noted how often Sinclair slipped his way into her thoughts. Was she focused on him because she was interested? Intrigued? Or bored by the people around her? Was her recent ambivalence about her job looking for something to pin itself on?

She let Genda interrupt her story about a visit to Paris to tell her own tale about pursuing a German businessman to the observation deck of the Eiffel Tower without using the elevator. Laura laughed. It was a good story.

Genda ran her fingers through her hair. "So, let me be serious and nosy for a moment. Is InterSec looking into the bombing of Kendrick's, or were you there for PR?"

"Kendrick?" Laura asked.

"Hello? The Welsh herbalist? Such a shame about him. He had a flair and a talent. I have some of his hand cream in the office that you must try."

"Oh, um . . ." Laura began, taken off guard. Genda never asked about assignments.

Genda draped a hand on her chest. "I have flustered Mariel Tate! I am sorry. Forget I mentioned it."

Laura tilted her head to the side. She hadn't known the name of the bombing victim. She tried to excuse herself that there hadn't been time, but she knew she hadn't thought to ask. "No, it's okay. You surprised me."

Genda bowed her head and gave her a confidential look. "I know the rules, dear. The written and the unwritten ones, but I saw you on CNN, for Danu's sake. I'm curious because I knew Kendrick through a friend of a friend of a friend. His family must be devastated. I hope you squash whoever is responsible like a bug."

"I do not squash people!" she said. It wasn't true, she thought. She had squashed a few, but she didn't want Genda to know that—or assume it.

Genda let out a burst of her high, fruity laugh. "I never meant to imply! 'Struth!" She leaned in again and winked. "But I'm saying *some*one should squash whoever did it. Kendrick never hurt a soul that I ever heard."

Given the nature of the conversation, Genda was throwing off vibrations of falsity, but she was also exposing to Laura that she hadn't thought about the dead fairy in any other context than as a case victim. "The Guild will take the case. We have a potential terrorist group under surveillance that Rhys should be concerned about," she said.

Genda's hair fluttered on soft currents of essence. "Well, I hope so. The last thing the fey need is bigger businesses becoming targets. We're capitalized better, but that doesn't mean we don't compete with some formidable human firms. Do you like sorbet? The sorbet here is fabulous."

"Sorbet it is," she said.

Laura tried to remain focused as Genda launched into a monologue about vacation spots. Not knowing the bombing victim's name bothered her. "Human" had two meanings in the world—a noun and an adjective. Had she become so self-involved that she was forgetting the human element of what she did? Fey or not, people died, and that meant something. It should. Once upon a time, it had been a primary motivation for her work with InterSec. Maybe that was the attraction to Sinclair. He never seemed to lose sight of the human element.

Sinclair again. She smiled, both at the thought of him and Genda's joke about beaches in Scotland. He was never far from her thoughts these days. She sipped her wine and considered that maybe that wasn't the worst thing in her life.

17
CHAPTER

RETURNING TO THE Guildhouse, Laura and Genda went their separate ways in the suite they shared two flights up from the investigative units. The lunch had had its desired effect, a brief time-out for Laura from the dramas of InterSec and the Guild. It felt normal, something everyone did, catching up with an acquaintance, not getting into the gruesome or tedious details of their lives or feeling obligated to do something out of a sense of duty.

Laura's sense of respite, though, evaporated as she settled behind the desk in the Mariel Tate office. A sealed envelope addressed to her in Terryn's handwriting was centered on her glass-topped desk. The message asked her to meet him on one of the upper floors of the Guildhouse. Terryn rarely left notes. Sending the hard-copy message meant the meeting was about a security issue he didn't want detected by an electronic trail. She swiped a mild charge of essence across the page and obliterated the writing.

The elevator opened on the hushed quiet of a residential floor that Terryn had directed her to. Laura checked her outfit in a large hall mirror as Inverni security guards stationed there examined her ID. Their uniforms—the royal blue tunics with high collars of the Inverni Guardians—confirmed her suspicions. The Guardians were the macCullen clan's official security force, probably Draigen's advance team.

The Guards' sharp, ebony wings glittered with indigo and green spots of essence, a sign of alertness but not alarm. They passed her through without comment. More guards lined the corridor leading to the suite that Draigen macCullen would be occupying the next day. Despite Guildhouse security, it was not unusual for the Guild to allow important public figures to bring their own security with them as long as they remained courteous and cooperative with building staff. By the presence of the Inverni advance staff, Laura assumed Terryn wanted to brief her on last-minute security details.

Laura waited outside the doors to the suite while the guards checked her credentials again. The review was a formality since she had been requested to appear by Terryn, but she didn't object. Rules provided structure, and structure often provided safety to high-level officials exposed to constant death threats.

The doors were opened from within, and Laura entered a large living-room suite. With their backs to the room, Terryn waited with a woman by the large shielded windows that framed a partial view of the Mall. Terryn didn't turn from his position at the window as Laura crossed to the room. "Draigen, let me introduce Mariel Tate, one of my most trusted agents."

The woman shifted toward her, and Laura paused in surprise at her first look at Draigen macCullen in person. Pictures of the Inverni regent didn't do justice to the woman. Most Inverni tended to be shorter in height and stockier than their Danann cousins, but the macCullen clan members were tall. Draigen had her brother's height and dark hair. Her coloring, though, was paler than his, blue tones shadowing the planes of her face. She tilted her head to acknowledge Laura. "Agent Tate, I have heard much about you."

Since Terryn introduced her as an agent, she didn't bow. InterSec agents gave courtesy to everyone but were not required to adhere to royal protocols that appeared to show subservience. "Lady Regent, it is my pleasure. I did not expect you until tomorrow."

I've scanned the room, but I would like you to confirm for me, Terryn sent. His concern about eavesdropping didn't surprise Laura. The Inverni might be part of the Seelie Court, but that didn't mean the clans trusted each other, especially if they were in one of High Queen Maeve's Guildhouses.

Lifting a languid hand, Draigen focused ice blue eyes on Laura. "My brother insisted I arrive with little fanfare to ensure my security."

Rather than touching her forehead to the extended hand, Laura clasped and shook it once. Draigen withdrew, a surprised but unoffended look on her face. "It is a pleasure, as well."

While they spoke, Laura swept the room with her sensing ability, testing for listening wards, but found none. She assumed Terryn had had someone do a sweep for electronics. "The area is clear, Terryn." The oddity of the situation amused Laura. Protocol often conflicted with reality. Terryn, as heir to the macCullen clan leadership, outranked his sister, yet Laura was allowed by the rules to address him by his name while using a formal title for his sister.

Terryn remained focused on the view out the window. "Draigen is settling in, but I wanted you to meet as soon as possible. I've told her she can call upon you at any time in my absence."

Laura had no problem with such assignments, but it was unusual for Terryn to give the "any time" access when she was running an undercover persona. She'd deal with any conflicts it created, but she wasn't thrilled he hadn't informed her beforehand. She would have at least liked some input.

"Why don't we sit?" Draigen gestured to the sitting area. They arranged themselves around a low coffee table, Terryn and Laura in opposite armchairs while Draigen occupied the center of a long sofa.

"Will you have any specific needs from me, Lady Regent?" Laura asked.

Draigen leaned back, her black skirt sliding open to reveal black leggings. Even in a casual posture, she didn't seem relaxed. "Terryn tells me you have insights into the workings of this Guildhouse."

Laura glanced at Terryn, wondering how far he had gone in that telling. She didn't think he had revealed her Guild position as Laura Blackstone. With the heavy warding in the room, Draigen likely would have spoken more openly about it. If she accepted Mariel Tate's bona fides on Terryn's word alone, though, that confidence said much about their relationship. "I've been in Washington a long time, Lady Regent."

"Please, call me Draigen," she said.

"I don't think I can do that, ma'am," said Laura. She meant it. Protocol might justify her not bowing, but that didn't mean she could treat Draigen as a friend. It was one thing to be on a first-name basis with Terryn. His monarchial status was like an entry in a biographical sketch—something that identified him but didn't define him. Draigen, however, was the regent of a major fairy clan. For all practical purposes, she was an acting underQueen, outranked only by Terryn and High Queen Maeve.

Draigen let out a soft laugh, as if she was surprised at the sound she made. "I appreciate that and thank you. I don't often find myself respected for my position these days. If you must, call me Lady, then. If Terryn names you friend, I hope we shall be so as well."

"As you wish, then," Laura said.

A servant entered the room, placed small glasses of whiskey on the table, then slipped out. Among the many traditions some fey liked to keep, toasting to new acquaintances was ritual. They each retrieved a glass and held them out.

"May our meeting grow our shared purposes," said Draigen.

"May our hopes light the way to tomorrow," said Terryn.

"May our hands join in friendship," Laura said.

"*Slainte,*" said Draigen. Terryn and Laura replied the same. They drained their glasses.

Draigen held on to her glass, rolling it in the palm of her

hand. "I have had several assassination threats prior to this journey. I wonder if you believe this Guildhouse would be involved."

Laura debated whether the question revealed a high level of paranoia or a credible assessment of her situation. Someone in Draigen's position always had to be aware of physical threats, but in Laura's experience, some high-level people gave the routine more credence than necessary. "The politics of the Washington Guildhouse can be quite nuanced, Lady. Its mission is to facilitate the High Queen's will with the U.S. government. I'm sure Terryn would agree that destabilizing one of its own constituencies has never been part of its mission."

Draigen set the glass down. "Given his position as heir to the Inverni, we have to assume that Terryn's normal lines of communication may not be as open as usual."

Terryn's earlier words to Sinclair came back to her. As InterSec agents, they considered an array of possibilities, even the unlikely. Draigen's line of inquiry, credible or not, was a fair part of that process, and her suspicion that Terryn might not be privy to a matter close to him wasn't misplaced. "I would be glad to check my resources."

"I was hoping you could work with my own security. My brothers Brinen and Aran are here as well. They lead our Guardian units," said Draigen.

"Of course. Are plans still in place to meet with the U.S. president at the White House?" Laura asked.

Draigen glanced toward Terryn. The look indicated that some matter of discussion had gone on between them that hadn't been settled. "My meeting will be at the White House. As Lord Guardians of the macCullen clan, both Brinen and Aran will accompany me."

"You should take more staff," Terryn said.

Draigen shook her head. "We've discussed this. Having fewer people will send the message that I am not concerned."

"But I am," he said.

"Terryn, dearest, the one thing the human leaders do not

expect is an official who can physically defend herself. Brinen and Aran are macCullens. The White House is a secure setting. In the unlikely event a physical confrontation occurs, three Inverni can hold their own."

Laura had no doubt that was true. She'd seen Terryn's abilities over the years, and each time she wondered if he was holding anything back. The ruling chiefs among the Inverni rivaled the Dananns in power. "I'll review the security arrangements, Terryn. I'm sure it will be fine. We coordinate with the U.S. Secret Service as well. Once Draigen is within the gates, the White House is the safest place in the world."

He grunted. "It's two blocks away."

Draigen gave him a playful smirk. "You don't want to take over if I die."

Terryn glowered. "That's not remotely funny."

Draigen shook her head in amused exasperation. "My older brother never relaxes."

"I have noticed that about him myself, Lady," Laura said. As Draigen murmured in amusement, Terryn glanced at her with feigned insult. She meant her jest to solicit reaction and test the limits of her position. She didn't know the nuances of their sibling relationship and did not want to assume too much familiarity on either side—treating Draigen as less than a royal as she did Terryn or teasing Terryn like his sister often did. Until she understood how the two of them felt about the other personally, she didn't want to expose any perceived weaknesses in Terryn or provoke any irritation in Draigen. "But I've always found him diligent," Laura said.

Draigen sighed. "And it seems he recruits staff as cautious as himself. So be it. If we must be so serious, let's move on to the current situation. The Guildmaster here is going to be a problem, I believe."

Terryn, don't put me in this, Laura sent.

Draigen arched an eyebrow, and Laura swore to herself for being thoughtless. Powerful fey had a sensitivity to sendings. They couldn't eavesdrop on them—no one could—but they could sense when sendings were passed. Sending in such a small setting with such an important figure was outright insulting.

"You're right, Mariel," Terryn said, further exposing that she had done the sending. He shifted his attention to Draigen. "She reminded me that her InterSec position would be compromised if she acted in a political advisory status."

"I mean no disrespect, Lady Regent," Laura said.

"None taken," Draigen said. Truth, Laura sensed. She took what her brother said at face value. So a level of trust existed in both directions between them.

Terryn glanced at Laura. "Perhaps it's best if we continue this conversation alone, Drai. I can advise Mariel of any security-related matters that arise."

Laura stood. "I will leave you to your discussion. It was a pleasure to meet you, Lady Regent."

Draigen bowed her head. "And I, you, Agent Tate. I believe Brinen and Aran are anxious to speak with you. The Guardians will escort you to them."

18
CHAPTER

THE INVERNI GUARDIANS wasted no time escorting Laura to a second suite down the hall. Inside, the furniture had been replaced with conference tables and chairs; more flat-screen TVs had been installed and several telephones. Humans in business suits mingled among the Inverni, security staffers from the Secret Service and Homeland Security. Laura sensed a distinct pause in the room when she entered as people took note of her arrival, some more discreetly than others.

Aran and Brinen macCullen showed little reaction to her presence, proceeding as if she had been expected. On the one hand, she found royalty often acted as if what they wanted to happen would happen. On the other hand, their attitude irritated her a little. Terryn could have at least asked about her schedule before throwing her into a meeting with them. He was as guilty of assuming she would do as she was told as his brothers. Yet there she was.

She saw that all the macCullen brothers resembled one another enough to be mistaken for each other—the height, the dark hair and green eyes, the regal manner—although Aran bore the more stocky body shape familiar among the Inverni.

With Terryn, the royal bearing came off like aloofness. With Brinen and Aran, the attitude exuded much more assumed privilege. She had seen it before—the farther down the line of succession in a monarchial line, the more the person tended to emphasize the blood connection to the ruler.

Their resemblance wasn't confusing for her, though. Their body signatures differed. While family members tended to resonate in a similar manner, the signatures themselves were like fingerprints, distinct and obvious to anyone who had the level of sensing ability to notice.

For all her private grousing, the brothers were courteous and professional. Without argument, they listened to the input of the other security agents who approached, while she facilitated the discussion. Much of the planning was already in place, so it didn't take more than a few hours to review. With Draigen staying at the Guildhouse instead of a nearby hotel, the security plans were long-established procedures for the Guildhouse, leaving the primary focus on travel throughout the city. The macCullens were polite, receptive, and did not argue with her recommendations.

"I think that covers everything," Laura said.

Brinen macCullen frowned as he worked on his laptop. Of the two brothers, he had asked more questions and acted as devil's advocate for the plans. "I'm still not sure I see the need for a personal escort to the car. We'll be operating in a fan pattern with aerial protection."

Laura glanced down at the positioning charts. The escort—her—was unusual, but not unprecedented. "Given the active threat status against the Lady Regent, it seems prudent to have someone beside her."

Aran didn't visibly react to the statement as he shuffled through some folders. "Draigen might think it makes her look weak."

"She might, but I disagree. Caution isn't weakness," said Brinen.

Unconvinced, Aran rocked his head from side to side. "I understand that. Still, she will object."

Laura had noticed that the brothers had a habit of contradicting each other, particularly when it came to their sister. She pursed her lips as she considered how to speak diplomatically. "Gentlemen, I understand that, as Lord Guardians, you are under the direct command of the Lady Regent, but using the protocols for InterSec staff assistance means that InterSec determines the safety of a public figure over any objection of the person being protected."

Brinen and Aran exchanged cryptic expressions. "Have you ever disagreed with our sister, Agent Tate?" Brinen asked.

Laura gave them a small smile to show she knew what they were going to say. "I have not had the pleasure."

Aran pushed his laptop away. "I will ask Draigen for her approval before we can agree to this."

"I am not authorized to agree to that," she said.

He shrugged dismissively. "I can speak with Terryn, if necessary."

Terryn wasn't likely to overrule her assessment; but then, she wondered if he might, given that his family was involved. "I was going to suggest that myself."

Aran glanced around casually before leaning forward and lowering his voice. "Speaking of Terryn, as his counselor, I was wondering if you would provide some insight regarding the *leanansidhe*?"

The last thing Laura expected was to talk about Cress. Considering Cress's fears and concerns, Aran's careful nonchalance with the question made her wary. "Insight?" she asked.

Brinen looked sharply at Aran, annoyance on his face. A long pause hinted that the two of them were conversing through sendings, neither of them happy about the conversation. Aran glared at his brother but directed his comments to Laura. "Yes, insight. How would you characterize its influence on our brother?"

As Cress had suspected, her existence was a problem for the macCullens. That Aran didn't use her name, which he had to know, didn't bode well for the idea she would be accepted by them. Laura kept her tone neutral. "Terryn's personal relationships are not something I feel comfortable discussing without his leave."

Aran smiled. "He names you his counselor, does he not? We are members of his court and also his counselors. It is customary for us to speak openly among ourselves."

Laura almost laughed at the level of false tones in his voice. Whatever information the two shared between them, it was clear it wasn't everything, no matter how openly Aran wanted to imply. "I am an advisor in his role as an InterSec director, Lord Guardian, not his counselor as underKing to the Inverni."

Aran made a dismissive gesture with his hand. "A distinction without a difference. Surely their relationship would be a concern for InterSec as well."

"Not that I am aware."

"Its influence must give you pause," he said.

"Her name is Cress," Laura said, putting a subtle but clear emphasis on the pronoun. "And, no, her influence, as you call it, does not concern me."

Aran arched an eyebrow and glanced at his brother again. "Perhaps I should mention that I am well versed on this subject, Agent Tate. I've met many people over the years who can attest to the rather insidious nature of these creatures. Do not underestimate her. She exerts influence in ways you may not be aware of."

"I do not see the value in this conversation," said Brinen.

Aran pinched his lips. "The clan is at risk, brother. The *leanansidhe* complicates matters of court. I am concerned for our unity."

Brinen smiled tightly. "Which our sister provides unless Terryn decides otherwise. I do not see the need to raise issues that do not need to be raised."

Aran barely hid his disdain. "Need not be raised? Have you any idea of the type of people interested in these monsters? Not all of them have our best interest at heart as you do, dear brother. I do not wish to see the macCullen clan targeted because of it."

"It will only produce tension at a critical time, brother," said Brinen.

"And yet, you are often the first to criticize the underKing about the matter," Aran said.

Brinen drew himself up stiffly. "I have never criticized the underKing. I have merely expressed reservations about his involvement with the *leanansidhe*."

Laura shifted in discomfort at the turn in conversation. Druids had a long history as advisors to rulers, but fairy politics was an area she preferred to avoid. Too many old grievances to track and too much double-dealing. The immortality of faeries made for long-term strategies, and alliances shifted without notice and sometimes without obvious reason. "Perhaps these are issues best left to Terryn."

As if Laura were no longer present, Aran sneered at his brother. "The clan will not accept his leadership as long as he continues to mate with that thing."

Laura stood abruptly, attracting the attention of others in the room. "'That thing' is a friend of mine, sir. Whatever prejudices we have all had against the *leanansidhe* do not apply to Cress. I will thank you to remember that."

Brinen and Aran were taken aback by her tone. She clenched her jaw as she gathered her files. Lord Guardians apparently were not accustomed to being snapped at. Laura didn't care. "I will review the remaining issues with Terryn, gentlemen. Thank you for your time and attention."

Before they could speak again, she walked out. Despite her tone, she showed no further visible indication of her anger. Cress had been with InterSec for decades. If an international agency that dealt with high-level security issues saw fit to keep her on staff, the Inverni had no cause to question her competence. And yet they did, so focused on their own agendas and problems, they couldn't see beyond their limited experience. If they were going to make Cress a problem, Laura was going to make sure it was their problem, not Cress's.

19
CHAPTER

IN ORDER TO gain more time in her day, Laura had spent the night in Mariel Tate's corporate suite a few blocks away. Skipping the commute from Alexandria saved her at least an hour. The elevator arrived blessedly empty in the parking garage. An empty elevator meant no curious stares from other passengers when she got off on the seldom-used back hall of the Guild accounting department. When the doors opened, she crossed the small elevator lobby to the door that led to her private room. She dropped the folders on the bed, making a mental note to retrieve them later. As she shifted out of her glamour, Mariel's long dark hair swirled up and away back to Laura's natural blond. She changed out of her gray suit. Mixing clothing between Mariel and Laura had been one of the ways Saffin pieced together her undercover work. She didn't want to make that mistake again.

She sorted through the ranks of shoes along one wall and caught herself muttering. While the macCullen brothers' demeaning references to Cress justified her anger, she realized she was also angry with herself. She understood their fears. *Leanansidhes* were dangerous. She had seen Cress's power, and, yes, she feared it herself. The only thing keeping Cress from submitting to her inherent nature was force of will and the steadfast support of Terryn. Without both of those, none of them knew what would happen. Despite that, if she could try to put aside her deep-seated fears as she'd told Cress, so could the macCullens.

She slipped on her shoes and checked the outfit in the mirror. As Laura Blackstone, she always looked the consummate businesswoman, stylish and no-nonsense. In control. She had to be to maintain her public personas. Like Cress. But she also knew cracks were forming in the masks she presented to the world. She didn't feel like herself. She didn't know what that meant anymore.

If Cress let herself be herself, she would be draining the living essence from anything she could get her hands on, people in particular. She would be a serial killer, plain and simple. Or she could continue as she was now, keeping focused on assimilating into society without resorting to killing to survive. It wasn't a choice, not for someone with any kind of conscience. And if Laura was feeling the stress of constantly presenting a façade to the world, what did that mean for Cress? What would happen to her if Terryn's love and support were removed?

As she slipped through the closet into her public-relations office, Laura wondered if the situation made Cress more dangerous or less, and maybe Aran macCullen was right to advocate that Terryn move on with his life without a *leanansidhe* as a life mate. And that made her feel angry again, only this time at herself for betraying the best interest of one friend over another.

Laura made herself comfortable in her desk chair and not a moment too soon as Resha Dunne marched into her office. He stopped short in surprise. "Where did you come from?"

She rolled her eyes innocently. "Upstate New York. My father bought a small farm there."

Confusion crossed his face. "What?"

Laura relaxed her face into a natural smile. "It was a joke, Resha. I just got back from a meeting."

She sensed Saffin at her desk outside the door. *How long has Resha been here?* she sent.

How the heck did you get past me? Saffin responded.

The door was locked. I came in the window, Laura sent.

Really?

It was a joke, Saf. What was Resha doing out there?

He was on the phone.

"But I didn't see you," he said.

"You seemed very involved in your phone conversation. I didn't want to interrupt. What's up?"

Resha frowned in deeper confusion, an expression which, on a merrow, tended to look more like anger. "You walked past me?"

Laura drew her eyebrows together in concern. "Are you all right, Resha?"

His eyes shifted in thought as he stared at the floor. He shrugged. "I must have been woolgathering. I stopped by for your advice. The Legacy Foundation rejected our donation."

That surprised and didn't surprise her. Organizations rarely refused unsolicited monies that had no strings attached. In this case, though, Legacy was smart enough to know "no strings" meant "invisible strings," but rejecting it outright was surprising. "Did they say why?"

"He said, and I quote, 'Tell your Guildmaster his guilt money won't pay for the lives lost at the Archives.'"

"Who said?" she asked.

"Adam DeWinter. He's the president of the board."

Laura showed no sign to Resha that she knew DeWinter. She hated when her persona interactions crossed over. It sometimes made things difficult to keep separate. "While not exactly out of character, that's still odd. Why do you think he rejected it?"

Resha eased himself into the guest chair, which was too small for his lanky frame. "I'm not sure. He seemed to be enjoying the reception. Senator Hornbeck introduced me. When I mentioned the Guild's donation, he started lecturing me about the dangers of unchecked power among the fey and said the Archives incident was a major example."

Laura tapped her pen against a pad. "Hmmm. I'm going with Hornbeck set him off. DeWinter used you, Resha. Don't forget—Legacy is an antimonarchial group looking for political favor. DeWinter used you to establish his credentials with Hornbeck."

Resha straightened in surprise. "Well, that was rather rude."

"Didn't you notice any animosity from the other attendees?"

He rolled his claw-tipped hands open on his lap. "Of course. I feel that wherever I go, Laura."

His comment reminded Laura again of the race issues so many solitaries struggled with. On a day-to-day basis, she didn't notice he was a merrow, but when he made a point of saying it, Laura cataloged the characteristics that gave humans pause—the white skin shaded blue and gray, the vertical ridge in his forehead, the sharp predatory teeth, and, of course, those small claws instead of nails on each finger. People who were not fey stared at Resha. He frightened them by existing. Like Cress did to the fey.

Laura softened her tone. "I'm sorry, Resha. I didn't mean to sound like I was faulting you for anything. I'm frustrated because I thought the donation might quiet them down for a bit."

Resha nodded in understanding. "Yes, I can imagine we don't need anyone speaking ill of the fey with the Inverni in town."

"True," said Laura. Resha was no fool. Despite the Guildmaster's contempt, Resha saw more than he let on. That he didn't always exploit those things to the best advantage of the Guild was beside the point. He hadn't gotten to be a Guild director because he was a total fool.

"Rhys will be upset with me. I was hoping you could advise me," he said.

She considered the options. They needed Legacy to back off on criticism of the Guild in the short and long term. The last thing she wanted was the Guild complicating her Inter-Sec investigation. "Does DeWinter work out of Legacy's offices in Crystal City?"

"I believe so," said Resha.

She smiled. "Invite him to the reception for Draigen. Legacy doesn't like the current president. Drop hints that the president might not see the Inverni. DeWinter will like being seen with fey who don't like the president or the Seelie Court. He'll bite."

"How will that play in the media?"

Laura shrugged. "It's a closed reception. We can spin it in our favor."

She watched as Resha let the idea sink in. She wasn't convinced it was the best solution, but DeWinter would have a harder time distancing himself from the Guild while he was sipping champagne. Resha stood. "Thank you, Laura. Your advice is sound as always. I will let you know how things proceed."

"No problem, Resha," she said. She let out a sigh of relief when he left.

A moment later, Saffin walked in, folders clutched to her chest and an avid smile on her face. Her gaze shifted around the room. "I missed you coming in."

"I was in a rush," Laura said.

They faced each other for a pregnant moment. While Saffin knew about Laura's undercover work, she had kept the knowledge to herself for years—not telling Laura she knew. At first, Laura was horrified to have been detected, but after some thought, Saffin's awareness came as a relief. She didn't have to sneak around her anymore, sending her on pointless errands or excusing cryptic phone calls. At the same time, no one at InterSec was aware of Saffin. After Terryn's reaction to Sinclair's knowing about her double life, Laura wanted to keep quiet about Saffin's knowledge. and one way to do that was to keep Saffin on a strictly need-to-know basis. Saffin's obvious curiosity about how Laura had arrived at least confirmed that she didn't know about the hidden room, too.

Saffin dropped the folders in Laura's in-box. "The usual divisions. I'm handling the media inquiries about the reception. The music is all set. One of the flutists asked me out, and the flowers are on order. The Guildmaster wants to meet with you regarding his welcome speech, and I replaced all your office plants because they don't bloom in this light. In case you didn't notice, the old ones were dead, and the new ones are lovely."

Brownies' inherent organizational skills gave them an ability to multitask on a level most people found exhausting. Saffin's launch into the catalog of tasks brought Laura relief. Saffin wasn't going to push the issue and ask too many questions. Laura gave her a sly grin. "A flutist? I didn't know you were such a music enthusiast."

Saffin smirked. "I've been told by credible sources he has a very nice flute."

Laura shook her head. "I don't know how you keep everything together, Saf."

She shrugged. "I decide what's important, keep focused, and make sure everyone around me knows where they stand on the list. Oh! And I cry myself to sleep every night."

"Saf!"

She exaggerated the sway of her shoulders as she left the room. "Just kidding. I don't sleep."

20
CHAPTER

ACROSS THE RIVER in Crystal City, Laura spent the rest of the day impersonating Fallon Moor. DeWinter had an oversight meeting, so she had a full day of uninterrupted time at Legacy trying to gain access to the computer system. Irony frustrated her—that Moor had clearance to look at classified information but Laura was unable to touch it without raising questions. If she asked for help for something as simple as a password, she risked alerting people, particularly DeWinter, that something odd was going on. Moor simply refused to answer any more questions, gambling that InterSec wouldn't make good on its threat to send her to the Seelie Court. Laura didn't fault her strategy. Capital punishment made the member governments of InterSec pause. It didn't mean Moor would go free, but it did mean Laura's threat might be empty. She had warned Terryn that might happen.

She decided to take a different approach to the problem. DeWinter's office was at the end of the corridor, far from others and surrounded by conference rooms. His door was closed, the card-swipe mechanism glowing with its little red light to indicate locked. The mechanism was an extra layer of security on some offices as well as access to entire areas of the floor. Fallon Moor's card let her into some of the latter, but she hadn't lingered in them long enough to figure out what was being hidden. She didn't want to raise suspicions unless absolutely necessary.

She paced in front of the plate-glass wall, aware that a ceiling camera recorded her every move. She looped back and forth, randomly nearing DeWinter's door for a closer look at the card swipe. After a few passes, she made out the style and manufacturer of the unit. If InterSec could hack into the system, they might be able to produce a card that would get her in.

DeWinter's reflection appeared in the window. She cursed to herself. She had hoped he wouldn't stop in the office at the end of the day, and now she had no choice but to talk to him. Sliding his hands in his pockets, he joined her at the window and took in the view. "What are you looking at?"

She ran her hand through her hair, noting its coarseness, so different from her own. Her glamour effects extended beyond the visual, and she made it a point to remember that smells and touch were important to mimicking someone. She wondered what nuances DeWinter might detect that she had missed. Did her hair feel right? Her skin? Did she have a scent he liked that she had missed? He didn't give an indication that something was amiss, but she worried. She jutted her chin toward the view. "I was thinking how new all that is. What is it? A couple of centuries old? That amount of time means nothing to the fey."

"It will when we're done. They need to learn that this is and always has been a human world. Everything else they've touched has been destroyed," he said.

Laura pursed her lips. A philosophical argument on fey versus human goals was something she knew how to play. Over the years, she'd read enough theories and arrested enough radical dissidents to know the thought problems. "Will they learn or fight? Is what we're doing any guarantee of long-term success? The fey held sway in Faerie a long time."

In the reflection of the glass, she saw him cock his head toward her own reflection. "Are you having doubts?"

The response frustrated her. DeWinter's intelligence training meant he wasn't prone to talk. No spontaneous monologues about his master plan were likely. "No. Reflections. The monarchies are formidable opponents. Not to brag or criticize, but I've experienced that more than you have."

He glanced up the corridor, trailing his fingers through the short tufts of hairs along her forearm. "Do you need more convincing?"

She let him touch her, deciding what to push with him and how. His voice reverberated with seductive tones, but whether he meant that as sexual or playful, she couldn't tell. She responded in the same tone but kept the subject on business to see where he would take it. "For twelve million dollars I might."

He glanced up the hall again. "Yes, thank you for your speed on that. I've already put the transaction in motion."

"I know," she said. DeWinter had found his benefactor, and she had routed the money into an offshore account. Everything had been done electronically, and no one had met in person. She kept the accounts flagged to monitor activity. DeWinter had moved half the money as soon as the funds arrived in the account.

"Let's go in my office," he said. He withdrew his ID card from the inside pocket of his suit jacket. She lingered behind him, amazed at her luck. He was going to use the keycard in front of her. She hid her interest by gazing at the view across the Potomac. As he punched the combination into the keypad, the soft tones of his tapping finger, barely audible, tickled her ear.

"Fallon?" he said.

She turned from the plate-glass window, acting like he had prodded her out of a daydream. The access code settled into her mnemonic memory. Six digits. Hit the enter key twice.

The office was utilitarian, made to look more so with hard, modular furniture. DeWinter settled behind his desk. "Let me check my email."

She didn't respond as she draped herself near the end of a low-slung couch upholstered in a stiff orange fabric. The office revealed nothing about the man. The modernist furniture didn't feel personal; the abstract paintings on the walls didn't relate to each other. Everything seemed selected to project an image, but it lacked personality. Either DeWinter decorated it in a deliberate attempt for neutrality, or someone had been given simple instructions to do it.

She eyed his computer setup. His desk was almost a sculpture, all glass and steel, with no drawers. Easy access. She decided to take advantage of the opportunity. "Can I have a drink?" she asked.

He glanced up. "What's your pleasure?"

She grinned seductively. "Give me a drink, and I'll tell you. I think I saw some fruit juice in the kitchen."

He grinned back and rose from his seat. "Don't move. I like seeing you on my couch."

She tossed her hair over her shoulder and chuckled as he left. She waited a heartbeat, then hurried to his desk. She pulled out a memory stick that she had been keeping with her since she arrived at Legacy. Plugging it into the back of his computer, she downloaded a keystroke program onto his system. InterSec had designed it to be small and unobtrusive. She went to the door to check the hall. Empty. She pulled the memory stick out and resumed her position on the couch.

DeWinter returned a few minutes later and handed her a glass of orange juice. He sat on the couch, trailing his hand along her leg. "We haven't had a moment alone in over a week."

"I've been working on something," she said.

He toyed with a strand of her hair. "Can you tell me about it?"

Smiling as she sipped, she shook her head. "Not yet. I'll have to check before I bring you in."

He leaned over and kissed her. She forced herself to return the kiss. He brought his hand to her cheek and pressed against her. Her mind raced for an exit strategy. She didn't want things to go any further. It wasn't necessary for what she needed. As his lips found her neck, she closed her eyes, realizing that she was not going to let anything sexual happen. This time, she thought. Or anytime, she hoped. She didn't want to face Sinclair and admit that, yes, they were sort of seeing each other, and, yes, she'd had sex with someone else. For work. They didn't have any commitment to each other, didn't have any rules or parameters about their relationship. The fey were more open-minded about sexual relationships—even outside committed relationships—but Laura had no idea what Sinclair thought about it. He might have more-human attitudes. There were human words for people who traded sex for things, for money, information, access. She didn't agree with that. Not always. That she worried what Sinclair would think surprised her. Lying on a couch with DeWinter was not the time to sort it out, though.

She draped her hand over the back of the couch and released a small burst of essence at the window. It hit with soft bang, and she pretended to be startled. The juice sloshed onto her dress as DeWinter pulled away. "What was that?"

She stood, brushing at her damp skirt. "I don't know. Something hit the window. A bird maybe."

With his head tilted down, he smiled at her. "Your outfit's a mess. Maybe you should take it off."

She laughed and tousled his hair. "Not here. Let me take care of this before a stain sets."

She strolled away, letting him get a good look at the roll of her hips. At the door, she trailed her hand along the wall as she left the room. "I'll be back as soon as I can."

She left him grinning on the couch. The upside to playing cloak-and-dagger games with people who played cloak-and-dagger games was that when someone disappeared on a moment's notice, no one pushed for explanations unless deep doubts existed. If DeWinter had noticed small clues that something was different about Fallon Moor, Laura's handling of the funds transfer had probably allayed those suspicions for the moment. Rather than risk being alone with him on his own turf, she decided to disappear for a bit. DeWinter was going to find himself waiting for nothing.

21
CHAPTER

A FEW HOURS later, Laura straightened up her desk and returned to her hidden room. As she zipped up the uniform jacket and shifted into the Mariel glamour, she cast a longing glance on the rumpled, unmade bed. The day had been long already, but she had more work to attend to. She checked her Mariel image—this time wearing the standard black uniform rather than the business suit. Cress had left word that she would be working late, so Laura took her usual route through the accounting department, then the elevator to the InterSec unit offices. Once through the locked entrance, she knocked on Cress's office door and leaned in. "You left a message for me?"

From her work counter, Cress cocked her head over her shoulder. "Hello. Let me finish this, and I'll be right with you."

Laura leaned against the counter and watched as Cress used an eyedropper to add a clear fluid to a row of test tubes. "Am I interrupting anything?"

Cress shook her head. "Routine. A team brought in some soiled clothing to test. We're trying to figure out where a murder victim has been." She held up one of the tubes and watched

as the liquids swirled around each other. Replacing the tube
in the tray with the others, she loaded them into a centrifuge
and turned it on.

From her desk, she collected a folder and handed it to Laura.
"I received the results from your gloves."

Laura reviewed the report, skipping over the technical
analysis to the summary section. "The taggant is military?"

Cress tapped at a lined sheet covered with signatures in different hands. "All explosive hardware is inventoried and tagged
by recipient. As it changes hands or locations, the information
is updated."

"The C-4 from the shop bombing was from Fort Bragg,"
Laura read.

Cress placed a manifest in front of Laura. "That's the last
registered location. I've already checked the Department of
Defense database. No C-4 reported used, missing, or stolen
from that shipment."

Laura glanced up. "Could they have not discovered it missing yet?"

"It's possible. I opened channels for a discreet inquiry."

"If it came from Bragg, it will be a bigger problem," Laura
said.

"Why?"

Laura flipped through the data analysis. "Special Forces
train and operate there. It's no secret a lot of black ops recruit
out of training camps."

Cress crossed her arms and leaned back against the counter.
"Are you saying these attacks might have official U.S. sanction?"

Laura dropped the folder on the desk. "Maybe. When military hardware is involved, it usually means two things: official
sanction or rogue operatives. Neither is comforting in my
book."

Cress rubbed at her forehead. "Gods, I'm so sick of all of
this."

Laura reached out and took her by the shoulder. "Have
you talked to Terryn yet?"

Moisture pooled in her eyes, startling Laura. She had never seen such an obvious emotional response from Cress. The *leanansidhe* rubbed at her eyes and slipped onto a stool. "No. We haven't had ten minutes awake together in the last few days. This never ends, does it? If it's not some terrorist, it's a government. Or some fey embezzling from humans. Or some plain-vanilla serial killer—which is more sick that I can call something like that plain vanilla. It never ends. It never ends and he . . ." She grimaced and shook her head. "These things pull at Terryn. He never rests, never lets things be. It's always his responsibility. He never gives himself time for himself. For . . ." She stopped.

Laura's chest felt heavy from the emotion pouring off Cress. "For what? For you?"

Cress dropped her head. "And now I am the cause of more problems."

Laura brushed stray hairs back from Cress's cheek and fixed it over her ear. "Is Rhys still making trouble for you?"

With a stricken look, she stared at the ceiling as if she could see through the floors above to the Guildmaster's office. "I don't know if it's him, but I've been called into several meetings. They're questioning me about the Archives."

"Interrogating, you mean," she said.

"Yes," she whispered.

Laura sensed full truth, but it didn't make her feel better. Cress knew she'd sense a lie if she had said no, so she was honest. But then she would shut down any further conversation. They didn't pry into each other's lives. Laura used to think that was the courtesy of friendship. Now she wondered if that said something about the friendship itself.

"Does Terryn know?"

She went to her desk and straightened some papers. "He's busy with Draigen's visit."

Laura shook her head. "That's not good enough, Cress. You almost died saving all those people at the Archives. You don't deserve this."

She hugged herself. "That was my fault. I was focused on

venting off excess essence. I didn't hold anything back for myself."

Cress's choice not to absorb essence from anyone without invitation made it harder for her to maintain her own essence. Even given that, Laura wanted to shake her for blaming herself for not protecting herself. "That's ridiculous, Cress. Nothing was your fault. Rhys needs to know that, and Terryn should help you."

Cress stared at her. "Is that going to matter in the end? I'm a *leanansidhe*, Laura."

"Terryn—"

"Terryn"—she interrupted—"is one man, who takes on more than he should as it is. He's worried about his family, about his clan. He's worried about the balance of power between governments. Do you think he has the time to do anything about a Guildmaster who is afraid of what everyone else is afraid of?"

Laura shrugged slowly. "He's Terryn macCullen."

Cress's jaw dropped. She snapped her mouth closed, then started laughing. "He's Terryn macCullen. You're right. And that's why I can't ask him, because he will try. And when someone tries to do too many things, nothing gets accomplished."

Laura held her by the shoulders. "You matter, Cress."

She closed her eyes. "I wish I could believe that. I know he loves me. I know I matter to him; but in the big picture, is it fair of me to want to matter more than anything?"

Laura did shake her then, but gently. "Yes. It is."

Cress bowed her head. "Thank you for that."

Laura hugged her. "Life sucks, Cress. You know that. The whole point of finding someone like Terryn is that you have someone to turn to when it really sucks."

She knew she heard herself say it, even believed it. Life was a chain of disappointments, but life itself didn't have to be. There were other chains, other paths, that did not lead to sadness. As she soothed Cress, she thought how tired she was and that the best she had to hope for at the end of the day was an unmade bed in a room with no window. Maybe, she thought, it was time to take her own advice. Maybe she needed to move beyond that and remember what life was like outside the walls of a Guildhouse.

When this job is done, she told herself, change is going to happen.

22
CHAPTER

IN THE EARLY-MORNING hours, Laura drove through a still-slumbering city. She had spent the night at the suite InterSec provided her in a nearby residential building, which she used as Mariel Tate's home address. Already glamoured, she arrived at the Guildhouse as dawn broke, ready to spend the day with the macCullen staff as Mariel.

With Draigen's visit to the White House at midmorning, she had cleared her schedule of anything else. No Legacy stint. No Guild work until late in the day. She didn't want to face any hassles balancing other duties while she worked security. Once she was on the scene with Draigen, she needed to see the operation through to its conclusion, so other personas were out of the question.

While the rest of the city awakened, she had already spent hours within the Guildhouse with the macCullens on a final assessment, the plan review, the staff review, the location review. As the appointed time for Draigen's departure drew near, the security team spread throughout the lobby of the Guildhouse. Business continued as usual, with people arriving and departing as in any other office building. As the base for the Seelie Court's diplomatic missions in the U.S., the Washington Guildhouse attracted a number of fey species rarely seen together.

The short trip to the White House was scripted to the minute. Brinen and Aran remained in charge, responsible for any major decisions that cropped up. She had her own role to fill—show up at the right time in the right place and do the right thing when required. It was the type of work that was second nature to her, an assurance of her skills and abilities that didn't require unnecessarily second-guessing herself.

Today, spies concerned her. Opening the Guild in the 1900s to all fey regardless of their historical affiliations remained one of High Queen Maeve's most shrewd decisions. A significant number of Teutonic fey joined or worked for the Guild, producing unlikely scenarios of elves and dwarves and their allies working closely with Maeve's Celtic supporters. The situation gave Maeve political cover, helping her to appear as a unifier among the fey. In reality, the Teutonic fey were given limited authority and never in an area that would have an impact on Maeve's political agenda. Laura knew many of the Teuts were spies, but it was a situation that surprised no one. Maeve had her own spies at the Elvenking's Consortium consulate across town.

The morning threat assessment gave no clear understanding of the Elvenking's position on the Inverni situation. There were arguments for both sides. On the one hand, turmoil in the Seelie Court worked to his advantage, so encouraging the Inverni opposition also worked in his favor. On the other, provoking the Danann clans to act against the Inverni produced the same result. Donor Elfenkonig was a sharp politician, though. He knew the perception of his own aggressive posturing often made him an easy target for criticism. Under the circumstances, he might sit back and watch how Maeve handled the role for a change. Still, the local Teutonic fey bore watching.

The more subtle threat, in Laura's opinion, were the Celtic fey. Not everyone trusted the Danann. They had come to power centuries ago through war. The fey had long memories. And the Dananns trusted no one. The tension between the Inverni and Danann clans only made matters worse.

The travel plans were checked and double-checked up to the moment when the word came down that Draigen was ready and the president was ready and everything that was supposed to bring the two together either was or wasn't ready, but didn't matter anymore. Things had to happen. Immediately. The show was on. A brownie security guard leaned toward her. "Agent Tate, we have a go out front."

"A minute, please," she said. Laura surveyed the lobby one more time as she smoothed her long dark hair over her ear. The security plan was tight, but it never hurt to have additional measures in place, ones that not everyone knew about. She didn't know Draigen's staff well enough to want to rely solely on them, so she had her own check on the plan. *We've got a go, Jono. What say you?*

"Nice, solid barrier spell across the front. Ends capped. I'm seeing a thin gap on one side." His voice whispered softly in her earpiece as he used a radio link. The shield barrier made it difficult for him to send.

No one else knew Sinclair was out there and that he was checking up on the Inverni security. *What does the closest Inverni Guardian look like?*

"Tall, crabby guy. Dark brown hair braided to the waist," he said.

Aran macCullen. *Lord Guardian, this is Mariel Tate. Tighten up your spell. You've got an opening,* Laura sent.

After a long delay, Aran macCullen's sending drifted across her mind. *Thank you, Agent Tate. I think a streetlamp was warping the line. Where are you? I thought you were inside.*

Jono? she sent.

"It's closing," he said.

Affirmative, Lord Guardian. ETA in one minute, Laura sent.

Nice catch, Jono, she sent.

"Thanks. Did I ever mention how hot your voice sounds in my head?"

She smiled. He couldn't see her yet. *Focus,* she sent hard.

He growled in her ear. "Ouch. Ohhhh . . . I like it when you get rough."

Remembering she was supposed to be a stoic security agent, she dropped the smile. "We're good to go," she said to the brownie beside her.

Draigen emerged from the elevator, and Laura fell in step beside her.

"What was the delay?" Draigen asked.

"Final details, Lady Regent. Nothing to be concerned about," she said.

Laura pushed through the revolving door and into the bright sunlight of late morning. As the door spun behind her, she scanned the area while Draigen waited for the signal to exit. Local police blocked off traffic on the short block, redirecting it to the other side of the park opposite the Guildhouse. The limousine idled at the curb. Brinen macCullen was stationed on the sidewalk to the right near the front of the car while Aran stood by the rear bumper. Both men had their backs to her as they monitored the barrier spell that was intended to block any essence-fire directed at the car or the building. Farther down each end of the block, Inverni Guardians and Guild agents boosted the spell, some on the ground, some in the air.

"Hold," Jono whispered in her ear.

Hold, she sent in a wide broadcast. Laura thrust her hand down in a fist in case someone didn't receive the message. Everyone froze. Body shields flickered on or hardened. She spotted Sinclair on the opposite side of the park, wearing a gray track suit and dark sunglasses. *What have you got?*

"I thought the barrier was going to change. It's okay now," he said.

Laura relaxed her hand. Tension eased, and the revolving door spun behind her. Draigen emerged and paused, despite having been told to keep moving the moment she appeared outside. Terryn wasn't the only macCullen who liked to push against imposed limits, Laura thought. Draigen came even with her on the right, and they moved forward together across the sidewalk. Ten steps to the car, and they would be on their way.

"Gap's back," Jono said in her ear.

Lord Guardian . . . Laura began. Something jumped across her vision, small and light-colored. She heard someone grunt as she looked down at a chip in the sidewalk. A small dark object blurred across her vision. A fragment of the sidewalk cement shot up, deflected by her body shield.

Sniper! she burst in a broadcast sending. Moving too fast for a human to track, Laura gripped Draigen by the shoulder and shoved her back and down. Aran jerked his head toward them for a visual check on Draigen, then spread his wings high and wide, hardening the essence in them. Brinen rushed in front of Laura, and their interacting body shields crackled. Laura perceived the movements as peripheral, instant confirmations of who and what moved in her immediate surroundings as other agents moved in to surround Draigen.

She gauged the trajectory of the gunshot and fired a streak of white-hot essence up the street toward the roofline of a building two blocks away. Aran went airborne, using the shot as a directional marker. In a whirl of color and speed, Brinen and Draigen disappeared into the darkness of the limousine. The door slammed shut, and a hardened essence barrier rippled into place around the car.

Inverni Guardians and Guild security swarmed the sidewalk. Laura pointed as more fairies joined Aran in the air. "Roofline, right side, two blocks down."

She hurried to the car. A slivered gap opened in the protection barrier to let her in. She dove through it as the door opened, pulling it shut behind her. Exuding calm, Draigen sat on the rear seat, hands folded in her lap. Next to her, Brinen angled across the seat, craning his neck for a view out the back window. He held one hand against his chest.

"Are you secure, Lady Regent?" Laura asked.

Draigen shifted her gaze to the sidewalk as if the car had paused for her to admire the view. "Yes, thank you, Agent Tate. My brother has been shot, however."

Sinclair's voice came in low and urgent. "Are you okay, Laura?"

Agent Tate is fine. Radio off, she sent.

Laura peered out the window at the gathering agents on the sidewalk. "We'll have a medic team in a moment."

"They can follow us to the White House," she said. The car started moving.

Startled, Laura arched an eyebrow. "Lady Regent, your brother . . ."

"I am fine," Brinen said. He didn't look fine. He held one wing open along the seat, puncture wounds visible near where it connected to his back. His voice vibrated with truth when he spoke, though. If he wasn't fine, he at least believed he was.

Draigen gave her a cool stare. "Nothing will stop this meeting, Agent Tate."

Laura settled into the seat, eyes on the passing sidewalk. She had to admit, the level of determination in Draigen's voice impressed her. An assassination attempt and a wounded brother did not fluster the woman. Terryn had chosen well when he made his sister regent.

Police motorcycles shadowed them the few short blocks to the White House. At the gatehouse, Secret Service agents allowed them in without pause. Laura stared out the window as the car eased along the drive to the side entrance. She had not been in the Executive Mansion during the current president's administration. The amount of security she was seeing impressed her. She glanced toward Brinen, who held his hand lightly against his chest wound. Times had changed. The security had become a necessary part of life in the capital.

The car stopped, and someone opened the door from the outside. Aran ducked his head in, his gaze first to Draigen, then his brother, then Laura. He held out a hand to Draigen. She took it and eased herself out, her wings unfolding with a sparkle of essence as news photographers jostled nearby.

Attend to my brother, please, Agent Tate, she sent to Laura.

The door closed. Brinen visibly relaxed against the seat. He dropped his hand, blood glistening with a pale red shimmer. He grimaced as he unbuttoned his tunic. "Clavicle is cracked or broken. I believe a bullet is lodged near my shoulder cap. No artery hit."

"Oh, good. I was concerned it might be serious," Laura said.

Brinen shot her an annoyed look, one that looked distinctly familiar from her experience with Terryn. Brinen changed his expression to a pained grin. "Terryn never mentioned you were funny."

Amazed, she shook her head as blood welled out of the dark wound on his chest. "He never mentioned his entire family has balls of steel either."

23
CHAPTER

THREE ANXIOUS HOURS later, Laura flipped through index cards in the room behind the Guildhouse conference room. A press conference had been hastily arranged while she waited for Draigen to conclude business at the White House. Brinen had refused to leave, insisting his wounds could wait until his sister was within the protective walls of the Guildhouse. Security for Draigen had been tripled while she met with the president, and, despite her protests, she was returned to the Guildhouse through the garage entrance.

Laura pushed aside those thoughts as she planned her opening remarks. The noise volume from the next room didn't surprise her. The usual group of media people who showed for briefings had been joined by several more people excited about the assassination attempt. News was news, even when it wasn't good.

Someone fiddled with her hair as she reviewed her agenda. Rhys was furious with her—with Laura Blackstone—for being unreachable during an unfolding crisis. Saffin had assumed—rightly, of course—that Laura was with the Inverni and did everything she could to cover for her. A few minutes' delay was excusable, but Rhys wasn't satisfied with the story that her cell phone had been in a dead zone for over an hour. It was a plausible excuse in D.C., with all the signal-jamming tech in use across town; but reason and reality did not always matter when the Guildmaster was angry.

"They're ready," someone said.

The door to the conference room opened. Laura stacked her notes and entered the room. The attending reporters shifted attention to the front of the room. Conversations died off as the whir of cameras replaced them. Local and national television stations crowded in a corner at the back, their techs adjusting the light and sound instruments.

Laura stepped up to the podium, calm and assured as if the situation were routine.

She arranged her cards as the room settled. When she had full quiet, she raised her head with a practiced face of concern, yet unworried. "Good afternoon. Before we get started, I have a few schedule announcements. The Guildmaster will be participating in a briefing regarding today's events later today. We'll set the time within the hour. New security measures are being implemented in the wake of today's events. My assistant, Saffin Corrill, has handouts for everyone regarding same. The Regent Draigen macCullen sends her regards and thanks all for their concern."

She pushed a set of cards aside. "As you are aware, an attempt on the life of the Inverni regent occurred this morning at approximately 11:40 A.M. The regent was uninjured and continued on to her scheduled meeting with the president of the United States. Lord Guardian Brinen macCullen received non-life-threatening injuries during the attack. He was treated at the White House and has already returned to his duties."

She moved more cards. "At this morning's incident, it appears that at least three gunshots were fired, none of which hit an individual. Lord Guardian macCullen's injury appears at this time to be related to a ricochet from the ground. Preliminary investigation indicates that the shots were fired from an office building on Pennsylvania Avenue. A body has been recovered, and the investigation, of course, is ongoing. My office will be keeping you apprised as more information unfolds."

She stacked the cards and spread more general notes in front of her. "I'll take a few questions now. Saffin will continue to respond to further inquiries. Dave?"

The reporter from the *Washington Post* flipped through his notes. "Can you respond to information being received that the shooter has been identified as a member of the Inverni Guardians and, if so, which agencies are taking the lead in the investigation."

She slid a card across the podium. "I can confirm a tentative identification has been made but is not being released, pending further investigation. At this time, the jurisdictional issues are being discussed and will be resolved by this evening."

"Is there any truth to the rumor that the Guild had received reports that an assassination threat had been received and did not relay that information to the Inverni staff?" he asked.

Laura shook her head. "That's not accurate. Information is freely shared among Guild members. The Inverni, of course, are included in these briefings. Jenna?"

Jenna Dahl covered the Guild for the major local television station. "Do we have a statement from the Seelie Court or the High Queen Maeve personally regarding today's events?"

"The High Queen has not made a public statement as yet, though she has been in direct contact with the Inverni regent to express her relief at her well-being," Laura said.

"But no public statement?" Jenna asked.

Laura doodled on one of the cards as if she needed to remind herself of something. "I do not want to get out ahead of the Guildmaster, but he will be addressing that issue later today." She hoped. She had pressed Rhys for that same information, but he wouldn't answer.

"What about the Guildmaster? Any direct comment from him?" asked Jenna.

"As I said, Jenna, he will be speaking later today. Fionn?"

The dapper brownie from the online fey newsgroup sprang to his feet. "Good day, Ms. Blackstone. Can you comment on the fact that only Inverni were involved in the security of the regent and what that says about the level of security oversight at the Guild?"

"Security is handled as an interagency issue. The on-the-ground staff is selected for personnel appropriate for a given situation. The Guild is involved in all such issues," she said.

She glanced down at the watch she kept on the podium. A few minutes in, and questions about the Guild's attention to the Inverni were causing her to dance. She had warned Rhys that people would notice.

"Will the reception for the regent be canceled as a result of today's assassination attempt?" Fionn asked.

Laura shook her head. "The Guild has always taken the position that violence will not change the way it functions. The reception is proceeding as planned."

"With heightened security?" someone in back called out.

The television lights prevented her from seeing who spoke. "That's a natural consequence. We have no concerns about the event."

Publicly, she thought. The heightened security was going to happen, but any visible increase would pale in comparison to the backroom anxiety. The reaction was natural, as she said, but it did cause headaches as everyone scrambled to ensure a security breach would be someone else's fault.

The questions continued, the same questions couched in different terms. It was only a few hours after the shooting, and everyone in the room was sifting for the right turn of phrase, perhaps the perfect word to expose what was being withheld. The reporters were professionals. They knew they would get only the minimal details until the Guild and the White House had determined the spin they wanted to be broadcast to the mainstream media.

Laura knew she was part of the game. Her job at the moment was to remain calm and confident and relay the barest of details while looking like she was as frustrated by the lack of information as everyone else in the room. She moved the cards around on her podium, a small act that implied to observers that she had important additional facts to be shared if only they asked the right questions. Of course, she knew more than she was telling. That the shooter was Inverni. That he was found dead of an essence wound. That no one on the security teams had admitted to the kill shot. That, that, that.

It was a game. Everyone knew it. At that moment, it was a game she didn't want to play. She had been at the scene and participated in it. Someone under her watch had been shot at and almost killed. She did not want to be standing in a room answering questions. She wanted to be elsewhere, gathering real information to understand what had happened, not answering others' questions with scripted avoidance.

Even when she left the room, she knew she wouldn't be able to do what she wanted. Another question-and-answer session waited for Mariel Tate. *You were there. What went wrong? Who is to blame? Who anticipated this and was ignored? You were there. What did you do? What should you have done?* More questions for her, but at least the answers would be her decisions on what to say and how, not the Guild-master's or the Seelie Court's. At least her answers, yes, but still time away from what mattered, which was ensuring that something like it didn't happen again.

She glanced at the watch again. Thirty minutes had passed, probably twenty-five more than necessary to pass on the only information that was to be shared with the public. Time to tie things up, let people report and speculate while she took care of her next obligation.

Laura neatened the index cards into a stack, the visual cue she had trained people to recognize that she wasn't just pretending to leave. "Thank you, everyone. We'll be providing you with additional updates in memo form as necessary between now and the Guildmaster's briefing."

Without waiting for an interruption, she picked up the cards and walked toward the back room. Saffin waited by the door, her hand on the knob, ready to close it behind Laura.

As their eyes met, Saffin's gaze slid over Laura's shoulder. She furrowed her eyebrow.

Behind you, she sent. She showed no fear or anxiety, so the comment didn't alarm Laura. As she turned, she saw Jenna Dahl approaching. Protocol dictated that no one approach the stage or the podium. It was beyond doubt that no reporter went near the door to the back room. Since it was someone of Jenna's stature, that made it intriguing, so Laura paused.

"Can I have one moment, Laura?" she asked as she neared.

"A moment is all I have, Jenna," Laura replied. She let the oddity of the situation show by being pleasant yet curious.

Jenna had worked her way up to anchor quickly and was known for being fair and firm. People across the political spectrum criticized her for bias, so the joke was that she was doing something right. Not unaware of the public perception of female newscasters, she wore her hair to the shoulder, long enough to appear feminine but short enough to be no-nonsense. Laura thought she was probably the only person in the news business who had darkened her blond hair instead of highlighting it.

Jenna dropped her voice for Laura's hearing alone. "I received a call at about 9 A.M. Someone told me to make sure we had someone at the Guildhouse and not just the White House."

Laura wasn't surprised. "All the stations were there."

"I don't think all of them were told to make sure they filmed continuously," she said.

Laura pursed her lips. "Did you know the caller?"

"No," she said.

Lie, thought Laura, a clear lie. "Do you have something on tape investigators should see?"

"Not that I can tell. We're still reviewing."

Laura smiled with professional detachment in case someone was watching them. "You know telling me this means I will have to inform InterSec. They're gathering evidence."

"Of course. That's not why I am telling you. I'm curious

why someone high-level suspected something, but nothing seems to have been done to prevent it."

"High-level?" Laura said. She had to. Jenna made the slip—claiming she didn't know the caller, then identifying it as someone high-level.

"I'm confirming that. I thought I'd let you know, though. I'd appreciate it if you would provide me with any information when you can," she said.

A deal, Laura thought. Not a deal with the devil that the public might think. Jenna had told her something important, something she hadn't reported and was letting Laura know that a two-way communication might benefit them both. It would, but neither of them could come right out and say that. "Of course, Jenna. I'm sure we're all interested in the truth here."

Jenna nodded. "Of course. It's a question that needs answering."

Laura gave her a brief friendly touch on the arm. "I'll let you know."

She walked into the back room, and Saffin closed the door behind her. "Everything all right?" she asked.

Laura sighed as she removed her wireless microphone. "It was nothing."

Saffin worried enough about her. She didn't need to add to it unnecessarily.

As Laura made her way to the elevator, she wondered who the high-level person was and where. Guild? American government? InterSec? Someone, indeed, knew something and hadn't said anything. Jenna was right to wonder why. It was a good question.

First, she had to face other questions. As she rode up to Draigen's floor, she knew that Mariel Tate's day wasn't going to get better.

24
CHAPTER

LAURA WASTED NO time getting upstairs. Under normal circumstances, she would never risk transitioning personas near a public area, but the macCullens were waiting for Mariel Tate. With no concern for courtesy, she forced two people out of an elevator and activated her glamour. When a failure in security happened, the last place she wanted to be was out of the room while others made their cases.

Draigen stood at the wide window of her suite, looking out across the Mall. Behind her, her brothers' voices rose and fell as each made his points. Since the return from the White House meeting, they had argued over which of them had been in the best position to prevent the assassination attempt. Laura did not miss the subtle criticisms thrown her way as Aran and Brinen bickered. Neither did Terryn.

"Mariel has extensive experience in security, at this building in particular," Terryn said.

"Then how did we become so easily exposed?" Brinen asked.

"I was presented with cleared staff," Laura said. It was a statement that masked her own criticism. The sniper had been

found before Draigen reached the White House. In the attic of
an office building up the street from the Guildhouse, a dead
man had been found with a recently fired rifle. The man—
an Inverni fairy named Sean Carr who had been attached to
Aran's staff—had died from an essence-bolt to the chest.

"A plan destroyed by one man is a poor plan," Aran said.

Laura maintained her composure. Despite her own feelings of doubt, she was not about to take the sole blame for
what had happened. "I recommended an integrated staff con-
sisting of InterSec, Guild, and Guardian officers. I was over-
ruled."

Draigen turned from the window, one eyebrow arched in
threatened insult as she looked at Terryn. "Is she implying a
question of loyalty with respect to our staff prior to this?"

Terryn shook his head. "We prefer to use integrated staff to
keep units on alert. People unfamiliar with each other tend to
be more observant of each other."

"People unfamiliar with each other tend not to work well
together," Brinen said. He had insisted on a Guardian-only
security force.

Draigen turned back to the window. "Interesting."

Laura rubbed her forehead. "If I may, the team composition
was a philosophical and strategic difference of opinion and is
now a moot point. The question isn't so much how it happened
but why. Answering how merely fixes a flaw in procedure.
Answering why might prevent any future attempts."

Terryn craned his head toward Draigen. "Speaking of
which, after what happened today, I would prefer you not
stand at the window like that."

Draigen tilted her head to observe something outside.
"Cities never sleep. Sometimes I think when we moved from
the country to the city, our priorities changed in an unfortunate way. We began thinking less about our homes and
started worrying more about what our neighbors were doing."

"I'd worry more about the lack of security in this building," Aran said.

Draigen chuckled as she withdrew from the window and took a seat on the empty sofa. "Aran, brother, the attack came from outside the building."

Annoyed, Brinen glanced at his brother. "And I'd worry more about who is a friend and who is an enemy."

"Your taunts tire me, Brinen. My people are as loyal as yours," Aran said.

"Except Sean Carr, of course," Brinen said.

Aran glared. Sean Carr had been found and identified within minutes of the attempt on Draigen's life. "I cannot speak for the thoughts of one man, brother, but I will defend my people with every breath."

Brinen grunted. "Yet I am the one with a bullet wound."

"You should be resting," Terryn said.

Brinen shrugged with a slight wince. "The bullet did not cause major damage and was easily removed. The healing spell is working."

"What can you tell us about Sean Carr, Aran? Why would he do this?" Terryn asked.

Aran shook his head. "I don't know. These are troubled times, brother. They breed troubled minds."

"In some more than others," Brinen said.

Aran pushed away from the table and stalked to the door. "There is a reason for what happened, and we will find it. Until that becomes the focus of discussion, I will not hear any more of these accusations."

He slammed the door as he left. A bitter smile curled on Brinen's lips. "I'm sure he'll start with his own staff."

"Enough, Brin," Terryn said.

Draigen sighed. "Yes, enough. Pray, get some rest, Brinen. We have much to do in the next few days, and I would prefer you strong."

Brinen stood and bowed. "As always, sister, I abide by your wishes."

He favored a short bow to Terryn as well, then closed the door quietly behind him as if to distinguish himself from his brother.

Draigen sighed. "They will argue to the ends of the world."

"The fact remains, sister, you were attacked by one of our own, regardless whose subclan he was from," Terryn said.

She poured herself a cup of tea from the service on the low table in front of her. "I was attacked by someone suborned. Aran is correct. Shifting politics make for uncertainties."

"I apologize for my lack of depth on the subject, but are you saying the Inverni are not united in the effort to gain U.S. support?" Laura asked.

Terryn did not change his expression, but amusement flickered across Draigen's face. She lowered her tea and rested her hands in her lap. "And she touches another family dispute."

"Draigen did not want to meet with the president," he said. "She was concerned it would appear as a weakness to solicit human aid."

Vindicated apparently, Draigen smiled a small smile. "I acquiesced to my brother's wishes on the condition I move quickly before political opposition at home solidified."

"Is the opposition coming from within your own clans?" Laura asked.

"Unfortunately, yes," said Terryn.

Draigen waited for him to continue. When he did not, she retrieved her tea and sipped. "The Inverni are a complicated people, Agent Tate. Clan strife defines us. Under the present circumstances, there are clans, such as the Alfreys, who feel that the Seelie Court has already declared war against us. There are also clans who feel the matter can be worked out diplomatically. I believe this trip has found ill favor among the former."

"Aran's people often align themselves with the Alfrey point of view," Terryn said.

"The Seelie Court may be exploiting that," Laura said.

Again, the small smile played on Draigen's lips. "I never discount the hand of High Queen Maeve in matters involving our people."

Terryn favored her with his own smile. "Times have changed, Draigen. This world is not ours. Maeve has done well opposing the Elvenking. That benefits all the Celtic fey."

Draigen frowned. "The Elvenking rules a land while we huddle in pastures."

Terryn shook his head. "Maeve chose the right alliances at the right time. What she did in the Treaty was what she thought she needed to do to protect all our people. She was wrong to do it. I believe she can change her mind."

Draigen glanced down. "Then we must hope she does so quickly, brother, because while she fortifies her front door against the Elvenking, her kitchen garden may be overrun by her own subjects. We may not be able to stop it."

He stood. "I will think on that as always, sister. You, too, need rest now."

Laura stood as well. "I will continue to offer my services, Lady Regent."

Draigen smiled up at her. "My younger brothers may suspect your talents, Agent Tate, but if Terryn has faith in you, so shall I."

Laura followed Terryn into the hallway. Anxious and alert Inverni Guardians watched their every move. Brinen waited in the small elevator lobby and gestured at the Guardians nearby to move out of earshot. "Terryn, we need to talk."

"I'm listening," he said.

Brinen glanced at Laura. "Perhaps we can go to my rooms."

Terryn pressed the elevator call button. "Speak freely, Brinen. I have appointments." A pause followed while Brinen stared at Terryn. "I said speak freely, brother. Sendings are not necessary in front of Mariel."

Brinen compressed his lips. "I am concerned, Terryn. This attack on Draigen exposes a rift in the clan that the Seelie Court will exploit."

Terryn pursed his lips. "The Seelie Court exploits everything to its advantage. You know that."

"I care less about that than the unity of our people, Terryn. They need a strong leader," Brinen said.

"They have one, Brinen. I have faith in Draigen."

"Do you have faith she will survive another attempt on her life, Terryn? Our people want their true underKing. While Draigen leads, they doubt her authority. While Draigen leads, brother, you leave open the door for the unwise to press their case for war."

"And how does goading Aran prevent that, Brinen? You do no good pitting yourself against him."

"I remind him that he and his people are watched, Terryn. I remind him, brother, that we will not allow them to lead us to our destruction," Brinen said.

"We need to be united, Brinen. I would rather persuade Aran and his people to our way of thinking than order them," said Terryn.

Brinen placed a firm hand on Terryn's arm. "You may not have that luxury. Our sister could have been killed today. While you demand from abroad that she stand firm in your resolve, she must face the pressure at home. She may not break from you, Terryn, but she may not survive it. Can you live with that?"

Terryn didn't answer right away. The pain of his brother's words showed on his face. "We will find a way, Brinen. I will find a way."

Brinen brought his face close to Terryn's. "You are our leader, Terryn. Our people will follow you."

"I will think on this, Brinen," he said.

"That's all I ask, as ever," he said. Brinen released his arm. The two brothers faced each other. Laura didn't think they were sending to each other but searching each other's faces for some answer neither knew. Brinen bowed and left the lobby as the elevator arrived.

The elevator doors closed. The turmoil that Terryn projected made Laura uncomfortable. She wanted the calm, secure InterSec leader she had worked for all these years. This troubled Inverni was someone she didn't recognize, and she didn't know what to say. When they reached the InterSec floor, Terryn lingered outside the door, and she looked back at him. "Terryn?"

"What do you make of this?" he asked.

She considered. "Brinen doesn't think Draigen can handle the situation."

"Does he speak true?"

She paused. Asking her what she had sensed revealed a level of suspicion she hadn't expected. "Are you saying you don't trust him?"

Amused, Terryn grunted. "I trust my family to perform their duties. That's not the same as telling me the truth."

Laura took a steadying breath. "Brinen spoke true. He is worried."

"He and I usually agree," he said. "He has been my eyes and ears at court, and I value what he says."

She tilted her head toward him. "Not that I don't want you here, Terryn, but I've never understood why you made Draigen your regent and didn't take the underKing title."

His expression made it obvious that it wasn't the first time someone asked him. "It was well-known that I wasn't in favor of my father challenging Maeve. When he died at her hands, it would have looked like she paved the way for me to take the underKing title because I was less likely to defy her. At least, many of the Inverni would have seen it that way. Draigen, though, was as forceful as my father on the issue. I made her regent to keep the Inverni united when we lost our underKing. I've never regretted that decision, but now I wonder if things should change."

She looked at her feet. "Are you considering leaving?"

He sighed, letting his gaze drift upward. "No. Not yet. Brinen has been advocating I take the crown for decades. I think he sees it as his role at this point. I wonder, though, if he truly believes I am putting Draigen in danger?"

Given the conversation, her first impulse was to say yes, but as she thought about it, Brinen's words didn't ring forcefully true. Her truth sensing often failed when someone spoke in hypothetical tones. Speakers didn't necessarily need to believe in their fears when they were merely articulating them. "Terryn, honestly, I think you're asking me to answer the question for you. To me, any high-profile figure is in danger by default. That's how I look at the world because of my job. That doesn't mean Draigen is in danger. I assume it's a possibility, and maybe so does Brinen. The only real answer is what you think because only you can decide what you will do."

He closed his eyes. "You're right, of course. I think what Brinen means is that one way or another, I may have no choice but to return to Ireland."

His words hung in the air. She didn't want to see him leave, as much for herself as him, but she knew that decision could cost him far more than her. "What about Cress?"

"I will take her with me," he said.

Despite the conviction in his voice, Laura sensed pain. Laura tried to imagine which choice she would make. Cress would not survive long among the Inverni if attitudes like Aran's were any indication. If Terryn's own family did not accept her, Laura didn't believe anyone else would. Yet, if he left her behind, Cress would go mad with grief.

She didn't see a solution.

25
CHAPTER

THE ASSASSINATION ATTEMPT on Draigen domi-
nated the conversation at the Guild staff's weekly meeting
the following morning. Guildhouses focused on local issues,
but a few—as those in Washington, Berlin, and Paris—had
become key strategic locations to further the political agenda
of High Queen Maeve. Her opposition to the Elvenking in
Germany required constant attention—and constant reinforce-
ment of alliances. A change in leadership of a major fairy
clan caused more than one department to consider the political ramifications for the Seelie Court.

Laura shifted her folders on the table for the third or fourth
time. Guildhouse staff meetings were like corporate meetings
everywhere. Sometimes interesting, most times too long. Rhys
ran an efficient meeting. He enjoyed being the center of attention, but he wasn't a rambler. Despite that, the conversation had leaned on speculation more than anything else, and
Laura wanted the meeting to end.

The assassination attempt had thrown the building into a
high security alert, which restricted access to most outsiders.
Laura counted herself lucky that she didn't have outside cli-

ents who needed to allow extra time for clearance—if lucky meant her workload was limited to her public-relations duties in the building and her InterSec mission. Rhys was firing off press releases on a near-hourly basis addressing rumors of anti-Inverni bias at the Guild, failures in security that had almost killed Draigen, demands for more investigations into the terrorist attack at the National Archives, to say nothing of the seemingly random attacks against the fey around the city. Saffin helped Laura manage the changing priorities and ran interference as necessary. The weekly meeting was the last place Laura wanted to be.

Rhys made some final remarks about heightened security and his desire to protect the building staff. Laura wasn't offended by the undercurrent of falsity that ran through his words. She knew he cared about the people who worked in the Guild, but he brought it up in the meeting to give the staff the impression he was actively working on their protection rather than relying on others to handle the nuts and bolts of the details. People in Rhys's position dictated policy. They didn't implement. She jotted down some notes. Some of what Rhys said could be used in more public announcements, too.

Rhys closed his loose-leaf notebook and adjourned the meeting. From her seat at the side of the room, Laura rose to let people pass. She adjusted the stack of folders in her arms when Rhys called her name. "A moment, if you please."

She shifted past the exiting staff and sat next to him. While the room emptied, he checked his PDA. When the last person out of the room closed the door, Rhys placed the PDA on the table. "I need an internal memo, something nuanced but pointed."

His manner intrigued her, cautious yet bemused. She lifted her pen, waiting for him to continue. "I've purged the *lean-ansidhe* from my Guildhouse."

Anger surged through Laura. "What do you mean 'purged'?"

Rhys arched an eyebrow. "Is that essence light I see in your eyes?"

She inhaled sharply, surprised that her emotion had broken through her normal control. She tamped down the essence, drawing it into the core of her being, and relaxed her grip on the chair. "I'm sorry, Guildmaster. The term took me off guard."

Rhys's face relaxed. "Ah, that. It was an ill-chosen word. For a moment, I thought you were going to raise an objection and defend the creature again."

Laura dropped her eyes, not wanting to challenge him. Rhys rarely misspoke. After World War II, solitaries who collaborated with the Elvenking were interned in camps across Europe. Those who escaped found refuge in the U.S. They called it the Purge, and the rise of solitaries as a protected class in the U.S. began. "What's happened?"

"I've barred it from the building. An investigation into its presence will be commencing shortly. I want a notice sent to all staff that this is an isolated instance until we can clarify the situation."

"Where is she?" Laura asked.

"Who?"

She glanced at him sharply. "Cress. The *leanansidhe*."

Rhys pursed his lips. "It apparently lives with Terryn mac-Cullen of all people. I want that mentioned. They've agreed that the *leanansidhe* will submit to Guild authorities and remain under guard in the apartment until the legalities are straightened out."

Kill two birds with one memo, she thought. Demonize Cress and smear an Inverni.

"This isn't Faerie, Orrin," she said.

At the use of his personal name, he cocked his head. "Do you have something to say, Laura?"

She hesitated. It was hard to know when to be frank with him and when to tread carefully. "I don't know the full politics of the Inverni and Danann clan disputes, but I do know American attitudes. What plays well at the Seelie Court may backfire here. We need to maintain the Americans as our allies against the Elvenking."

"Donor Elfenkonig has voiced his support of the Inverni cause. That is enough for our American friends to support us," he replied.

"Support" was too strong a word. Laura had seen the news dispatches. The Elvenking had criticized the Treaty clause as archaic—ironic considering his preferences for old ways. He had not explicitly denounced the Seelie Court. "You know that's posturing on his part, Orrin. I'm concerned about the solitaries as well. They will watch and worry about what Maeve does to a major segment of the fey population. Cress may be a *leanansidhe*, but the solitaries will view her as one of their own even if they fear her kind."

Rhys folded his hands across his chest and leaned back in thought. By the sudden agitation in his wings, she knew she had made a sharp point. "I will bear that in mind. Thank you, Laura. Word will spread quickly about this. I would like a draft memo within the hour."

"What about Resha?" she asked.

"What about him?"

"It might play better coming from him."

Rhys chuckled. "I like that. He won't, but I do. I'll make the call personally."

She hated herself for offering the idea. Putting Resha in a propaganda position against his own people felt worse, but she did hope it would help. He might find a way to present the news without its sounding like Cress was targeted first, investigated second. Solitaries were used to that order of events, and it didn't sit well with them. "Is there anything else?"

"No."

She stood. "I'll write up a draft for Resha to work from that includes your talking points."

Rhys called her when she reached the door. "Laura, I'm concerned you're angry with me."

"I'm concerned we're putting too much pressure on the situation, Orrin, especially in light of the assassination attempt. People are emotional and upset. We've effectively put the fey on notice that any opposition to the Seelie Court will be met with heavy punitive action. Threatening to make the Inverni political prisoners and exiling a solitary because we're afraid of what she might do as opposed to something she's actually done can create an explosive situation. I don't want us to be seen as encouraging that kind of behavior. That's all," she said.

"Sometimes forcing a situation relieves the pressure," he said.

She offered him a troubled smile. "I hope so."

As she waited for the elevator, she did her best to control her breathing. Politics or not, Cress was her friend. So was Terryn. For the first time in a long time, the personal mattered to her more than protecting the Seelie Court and Maeve.

26
CHAPTER

TO COVER HER switch to the Mariel glamour, Laura had to return to the public-relations department, then to her private room, where she made the transition. She refrained from rushing through the accounting department. It was times like this that the necessary secrecy around her competing personas frustrated her. The constant changing of elevators and cutting through other departments to hide her tracks were time sinks she didn't need.

Once through the security locks at the InterSec unit, she registered a jumble of body signatures in the main corridor. Some she recognized as other agents and staffers, but several were unknown. She stopped at Cress's office. Why, she didn't know, maybe to confirm what Rhys had said, maybe to pretend that she had misheard him. Cress kept her office neat and utilitarian, but now it felt more so than usual. Not a book or specimen jar or document was out of place, everything tidy. Cress wasn't there and hadn't been. Others had, though—more strange body signatures.

She strode down the hall to Terryn's office, slowing at the sound of a woman's voice she recognized. Genda Boone spun slowly in Terryn's chair, a cell phone to her ear. She smiled and waved Laura in. Perplexed, she sank into the guest chair.

"No, Damine, it's on the top of my dresser . . . Yes, the blue one. Send it down. I want to wear it this afternoon. Then call Jarnell and tell him I have five more people coming for dinner. No pork and no peppers . . . Yes, she's in town. I have to go." She disconnected.

She pulled the chair closer to the desk, her broad translucent wings flaring out to the sides. "I'm so glad you came in, Mariel. This is all so odd and sudden, and I haven't had time to figure out who's who and what's what."

Laura smiled diplomatically. "I'm a little confused myself. Where's Terryn?"

Genda's thin eyebrows shot up. "You don't know? He took a sudden leave of absence." She leaned forward conspiratorially. "It's related to the *leanansidhe*, I'm sure, but no one's talking. Well, everyone's talking, but I can't get confirmation. Where in Danu's name have you been, dear?"

She tried not to show her surprise. "I was . . . in a closed meeting. When did this happen?"

Genda shuffled papers, her gaze ranging avidly across the desktop. "About an hour ago. I received the call shortly afterward. Where does he keep his calendar? Don't tell me he took it with him."

"Genda, what are you doing here?"

Genda paused, a sympathetic smile on her face as she leaned forward and placed her hands on the desk. "Is this going to be awkward, Mariel? I mean, it *is* awkward, but this kind of thing happens all the time. Besides, it's not like I will be here twenty-four/seven."

Laura hid a sense of dread. Genda had never been a field agent. As far as Laura knew, she had no idea how to run a field operation. "Here? You've been transferred here?"

She tapped the desk. "Yes, dear. I thought you understood. I was asked to be acting director until, well, I don't know when. Like I said, it's all so sudden, I haven't had a chance to tell Damine to order business cards."

Terryn? Laura sent.

I can't talk now, he replied.

Tell me if you are safe, she sent.

Yes. We can discuss it later.

Is Cress?

She's fine at home.

Genda's cell phone vibrated on the desk. She snatched it, holding a hand up to Laura. "Wait, I need to take this . . . Yes, James, I'm here. I need the algorithm this afternoon. Those numbers look suspicious, and I'm positive there's more to it than a little embezzlement . . . Oh, good. Great. Did you get the confections I sent? Aren't they marvelous? It's a shop in the French Quarter I found last week, darling woman runs it. Human, but I can't hold that against her after I tasted that layered pastry . . . Yes, I want Chicago in on this and put a call up to Davis in New York. Tell him it's the real-estate firm I'm interested in, not that silly shell company they have as a front . . . Okay, good. I have to go."

She disconnected. "I'm sorry. Do you see? I have my other duties to attend to as well."

"I'm still confused," Laura said.

Genda nodded vigorously. "I know, I know. Honestly, I'm not going to be looking over your shoulder. I've been asked to assess and reprioritize and keep things running as smoothly as possible."

"You're in charge," Laura said. It wasn't a question as much as a need for her to hear the words aloud.

"Yes, dear, what's wrong? Thank Danu you were in his group. A situation like this is hard enough without knowing whom to trust. I know I can rely on you to do . . . whatever you do." She laughed high and loud. "What do you do? We've never been in the same branch before."

Laura clicked into professional mode—no showing of emotion, no disclosing of true thoughts. Not working for Terryn macCullen was something she had not expected without some kind of warning. "Investigations. Political considerations," she said.

Genda nodded again. "Yes, I've assumed as much for years. You're working on these fey attacks, aren't you? Why isn't Community Liaison handling that? Wait . . . you don't need to answer that. I know, I know. Let's push it back to them anyway. It'll go in their queue, and we can focus on what's important. Who else is on that assignment? I see only your name. You can't be handling it alone." She laughed again. "Oh, that sounded wrong. Of course you can handle it alone. I meant that more as surprise that they would burden you with something like this when you're on the macCullen security detail."

Terryn had said Sinclair was on probation until he proved himself, and he meant it—apparently to the point of not having evidence of his presence in the department if Genda's lack of awareness was any indication. If that was what Terryn wanted, she wasn't about to disclose anything until she understood what the hell was happening. "No one else," she said, glad that Genda didn't have her truth-sensing ability.

"Good. That makes things easier. Why don't you focus on your security detail for now. Send me the file on what you have with the fey attacks, and I'll make sure Community Liaison has everything."

"Community Liaison coming in cold might derail the investigation," Laura said.

Genda's bracelets jingled as she moved Terryn's things off the desk. "I know, it's hard to let go of things, but I'm tasked with straightening out priorities. By the way, can I have a copy of the financial files you acquired during the Archives mission? Terryn sent me macrodata to analyze, and it would help if I had details."

"I gave it all to Terryn," she said.

Genda let out an exaggerated sigh. "I can't speak for his strategy skills, but I do have to say his organizational skills leave a lot to be desired." She shrugged. "Well, it is what it is. I'll have to find where he put them. Anyway, I have a ton to get up to speed on. Can we regroup tomorrow?"

Laura stood. "Okay. I'll send you my security schedule."

Genda was already looking at her PDA. "Great. Your hair looks wonderful, by the way. Are you using a new conditioner?"

"Something like that," she said.

Genda glanced up and smiled. "This is going to be fun working together."

Laura gave her a tight smile as she stepped away. "I can't begin to agree."

She ducked into her office, retrieved an unregistered cell phone, and hurried down the corridor to Sinclair's office. She surveyed the empty room, devoid of personality, as if it had recently been assigned to someone new who hadn't quite moved in. Which was what it was. She dialed Sinclair's direct line.

Sinclair picked up, his voice cautious. "Yes?"

"Jono, it's me. Do you have anything personal in your office?"

"Not really," he said.

She moved behind his desk. "Not 'not really.' I need a yes or no."

"What's going on?"

She pushed papers aside, mostly internal memos that didn't have his name on them. "No time. Is there anything here that can identify you? Anything with your name or personal information?"

"No . . . Oh, wait. Some notes."

"Where?"

He paused. "Top left drawer."

She opened it and found a small stack of pink phone messages and scrap paper. She sorted through them. All in her handwriting. They were nothing important, quick scrawls to meet for lunch or reminders about meetings. "These notes?"

"Yeah."

"What did you keep these for?"

A longer pause. "Because you wrote them."

She started to laugh. In the midst of whatever crisis was

unfolding, she found herself touched by the thought he had saved them.

"Look, throw them away. They don't mean anything," Sinclair said.

His embarrassed tone made her regret the laugh. "No, I'll save them for you. Can you meet me in about an hour at the corner of O and Ninth?"

"Okay."

"Gotta run." She disconnected. She scooped up the notes and shoved them in her pocket. Taking one more look around, she made her way to the service elevator. As she walked through the accounting department, her mind whirled with unanswered questions. Whatever had happened had happened fast. Terryn would have told her his plans otherwise. She wanted to get to Cress and see what she could do to help. But first she had to write a memo justifying kicking her friend out of the building.

27
<del>CHAPTER</del>

A LIGHT DRIZZLE fogged the air as Laura waited for Sinclair. Halfway up the block, two Guild security agents stood in front of Terryn's apartment building. At the far end of the street, she had spotted a brownie watching the street from a car. As the drizzle turned to rain, she moved into the shelter of the awning over a deli door. Sinclair's body signature moved up behind her. Laura wore a long raincoat with a hood, but he didn't need to see her face. He sensed the shape of her essence, something he claimed did not change despite whatever glamour she wore. "Okay, now I'm confused. I thought you would be Mariel, not Laura," he said.

"I was worried someone might be watching for Mariel. Laura Blackstone isn't well-known to the Guild investigative branch," she said.

"What's going on?" he asked.

She watched the street. "I don't know. Cress agreed not to leave her apartment without Guild permission, and Terryn's suddenly out of InterSec on leave."

"What's that got to do with stuff in my office?"

She leaned into the rain. "I don't have a good feeling about it. If Terryn still has you off record, then we should keep it that way until he says otherwise, so I removed any trace of you."

He dropped his voice into a saccharine tone. "You did that for me?"

She glanced at him impatiently. "Why do you read something into everything I do?"

He grinned. "I like to read. So far, you're a good book."

Dumbfounded, she stared. "That has to be the most corny pickup line I've ever heard. I think I'm in pain here."

He pouted playfully. "Can we turn the page? I don't like this chapter."

She resisted the urge to laugh. "Jono, this is all nuts. They put Genda Boone in charge while Terryn's on leave."

He narrowed his eyes. "And, what, you're pissed it wasn't you?"

She poked him in the shoulder. "No. I don't want to be in charge. I'm pissed because Genda has no idea what she's doing, and that's a dangerous thing in our line of work."

"So what are we doing here?"

She turned her attention back to the street. "I have to talk to Terryn or Cress and find out what's going on. Cress isn't responding to my sendings."

Sinclair peered up the sidewalk, rain glistening in his hair and on his face. "I'm getting interference. Probably a shield of some kind."

"You can sense that far?" she asked.

He smiled. "Is that a conversational question, or are you taking notes?"

She elbowed him gently. "No games. I'm worried. You know *leanansidhe* are hated. I want to be sure Cress is safe."

He shook his head. "I can't sense anything beyond the shield. Why is she under guard?"

Laura followed his gaze up the street. "Because she's a *leanansidhe* and an easy target for Rhys to make points. If she hadn't agreed to the guards, he probably would have gotten the feds to detain her for trumped-up national security reasons."

"She saved his life at the Archives," Sinclair said.

"Gratitude isn't one of his strong points," Laura said.

A woman stepped out of the building and opened her umbrella. She hesitated when she saw the Guild agents, then walked between them.

"Why don't we knock on the door and see what happens?" he asked.

She pursed her lips. "Because they might be looking for Mariel Tate to do that. Rhys is intent on discrediting Terryn. If he can take out another member of Terryn's InterSec team for some bogus reason, he'll do it. I don't want to give him an opportunity."

The woman from Terryn's building passed them and continued around the corner. Laura took Sinclair's arm. "Follow me."

She pulled him along the sidewalk, moving fast enough to catch up to the woman. "You dropped something, miss," Laura called. The woman turned and looked down. Laura muttered in Gaelic and tossed a pinpoint of essence at her. "Sleep."

As the woman's eyelids drooped, Laura grabbed her arm to prevent her from falling.

"What the hell are you doing?" Sinclair asked.

Laura cast furtive looks in either direction to see if anyone had seen her. "Take her other arm and help me get her coat off," she said.

Sinclair did as she asked with a concerned look on his face. "This is technically assault and battery, you know."

Laura shrugged out of her raincoat. "Good thing you're not a cop anymore. Put this on her."

She slipped on the woman's coat. It was snug, but it wouldn't matter in a moment. Rummaging in her own pocket, she pulled out a small garnet ring. Touching the woman's cheek, she sampled her body essence. With a brief chant, she wrapped her own signature around it, pushed it into the ring, and slipped the ring onto her finger. Her features blurred and shifted.

Sinclair looked her up and down. "Wow."

"How close am I?" she asked.

"Pretty close. You look like a cross between you and her."

She shifted in the snug coat. "That's good enough. I don't have time for precision. I doubt those agents spent much time looking at her. Keep her out of the rain. I'll be right back."

Without waiting for a reply, she grabbed the woman's umbrella and walked around the corner, lowering the umbrella to obscure her face. The rain accommodated her by falling more heavily. As she reached Terryn's building, she pulled keys from the woman's pocket. One of the security agents tilted his chrome helmet toward her, and she rolled her eyes dramatically. "I forgot my phone."

They gave her room to enter through the unlocked outer door. In the close quarters of the vestibule, she hid her fumbling with the keys behind the open umbrella. She found the right key, closed the umbrella, and let herself in. A static prickle danced on her skin as she walked up the stairs, evidence of the shield spell Sinclair had sensed. She reached Terryn's apartment and listened at the door but heard nothing.

Cress, it's Laura. Are you alone? she sent.

The door opened a few inches, one of Cress's whiteless eyes peering through the gap. She pulled the door open all the way, and Laura hurried inside. "I don't have much time. Are you all right?"

In the dim light of the apartment, Cress looked small and forlorn. "They haven't hurt me."

"Where's Terryn?"

She wrapped her arms around herself. "With Draigen. He'll be back tonight."

"What happened? Why did he take a leave?"

Cress lowered herself on the couch. "He didn't. They suspended him, too. The Guildmaster agreed to say it was a leave because Draigen threatened to accuse him publicly of harassing her family."

"I don't understand what's going on."

Cress lowered her chin and frowned. "The Guildmaster accused InterSec of endangering the Guildhouse by granting me security clearance. I'm suspended while they investigate. I think I'm fired."

Laura hugged her. The *leanansidhe*'s essence flared a moment, purple tendrils flickering out of her skin before she pulled them back in. Suppressing a shudder, Laura released her, trying not to appear as if she were pulling away. She knew the reaction was instinctive, but it made her uncomfortable, even if Cress didn't absorb any essence from the contact. "You're not fired. This is all Rhys's political posturing while Draigen's here."

A sad smile creased Cress's face. "I don't have your confidence in that, Laura."

"The Guild doesn't dictate to InterSec. You'll be cleared. Rhys is going to have to live with the fact that you are a good person."

She compressed her lips. "Thank you for that."

Laura squeezed her arm. "You are, Cress. Don't let what other people think make you feel any different. The only opinions that matter are your friends'."

A smile tweaked at the corner of her mouth. "Do I get to count you as more than one friend?"

Laura laughed. "I'll be as many friends as you need me to be. Right now, though, you need a lawyer."

"Resha is taking care of that," she said.

Laura cocked her head. "Resha? I didn't know you knew him."

"He watches out for all the solitaries in the Guildhouse. He was the first person I called after Terryn," she said.

Impressed, Laura shook her head. The seemingly inept merrow surprised her in interesting ways. "I'll do whatever I can to help him."

"You should go. Your glamour is fading," Cress said.

The body signature was weakening, but she didn't realize Cress could sense it. "Tell Terryn to call me as soon as he can."

Cress placed her small hand on Laura's forearm. "I need you to do something for me, Laura, that has nothing to do with any of this. I finished the autopsy on Draigen's sniper before they escorted me out of the building but didn't have time to write the report. There's residual body essence on the corpse, but I've never met anyone who was at the arrest, so I couldn't identify the signature."

The Inverni Lord Guardian team had made the arrest. "I have."

"That's what I was thinking. You need to examine the body. Without me there, I don't know how long the stasis field will preserve the body signatures. We need an imprint," she said.

"I'll have someone make the imprint, Cress, as soon as I get back," she said.

Cress gripped her arm. "No! You need to do it. I don't think it was a coincidence that I was banned from the building. They didn't bring someone else in when they detained me. Something's wrong there."

Laura leaned forward and kissed Cress on the cheek. "Okay, I will, then. Call me for anything, and tell Terryn I want to see him ASAP."

"I will," said Cress.

Laura pulled the door closed behind her and hurried down the steps. She pushed more essence into the glamoured ring, but without a firm template, she had nothing to anchor the woman's essence. Outside, the rain had turned into a downpour, and she exited the building by opening the umbrella into the nearest security agent's face. "I'm sorry," she called, as he twisted away from it. As she swung the umbrella to hide herself from them, the glamour faded.

Around the corner, Sinclair and the woman waited where she had left them under the awning of a small café. Without speaking, they swapped the raincoats and maneuvered the woman back onto the sidewalk. Wrapping the woman's hand around the umbrella handle, Laura released the sleep spell. Sinclair slipped his hand into the crook of Laura's arm and held his umbrella over them. The woman swayed. Laura steadied her. "Are you okay?"

She startled at the torrential downpour. "Wow, that came up quick."

Laura held out her keys. "You dropped these."

Surprise and relief crossed the woman's face. "Thank God, you saw them. I'm lost without my keys."

"No problem. Have a nice day," said Laura.

"Everything go all right?" Sinclair asked, as they walked the block to Laura's car.

"Yes and no. Cress is okay, but things are moving in directions I don't understand. With any luck, Terryn will be able to clear it up for me. Do you need a ride?"

He shook his head. "I need to get back. I don't think a limo driver showing up in a tricked-out Guild SUV would be good for my image."

She chuckled. "Good point. We'll talk later."

He quirked an eyebrow at her. "Dinner?"

She twisted her lips into an amused smirk. "Okay, dinner. I'll call you."

She leaned toward him on tiptoe and kissed him on the cheek. "Thank you, Jono."

He smiled in surprised. "For what?"

Her hand closed on the notes in her pocket, but she didn't give them to him. "Just thank you."

28
CHAPTER

MORGUES WERE ALWAYS in basements, Laura thought as she stepped out of the elevator. The dead didn't need sunlight. The living didn't want to be disturbed by their presence. Between the InterSec offices and the local Guild crime-liaison department, the Guildhouse's morgue was larger than other fey facilities. The Guild and InterSec used separate staff to perform autopsies and forensics. What redundancies the situation created was balanced by less friction over who had priority on research staff.

Laura Blackstone had never had a reason to be seen in the morgue, which made transitioning to Mariel Tate necessary after returning from seeing Cress. Mariel didn't attract undue attention there by her mere presence. Part of her job was following up on deaths. People did look at her, though. That was one of the points in making the Mariel glamour so attractive—to distract from whatever she was doing. It worked most of the time.

She pushed open the door to the cool room. That late in the day, no one was working, and the lights were dimmed. As she moved toward Sean Carr's locker, she stopped. Her mnemonic memory worked on several levels, recording body signatures, data, events, and places. Things like places logged themselves into her memory like subroutines, something she didn't consciously do and didn't pay attention to most of the time. When she entered the cool room, on a subconscious level, her awareness noted several changes, changes that were filtered as normal and disregarded. Gurneys had been moved. Counters cleared. The lights, of course.

Except one thing flared out in her memory as out of place. In the kick space in front of the cooler sat a small granite plate. To the casual eye, it appeared innocuous, a forgotten piece of discarded stone on the floor and swept out of view. Laura saw it for what it was: a listening ward. Someone was keeping tabs on who entered the room. If that was the case, she didn't want anyone to know she was looking at the body.

She retraced her steps and texted Sinclair to meet her. As she lingered near the elevators, she used her PDA to catch up on public-relations emails until Sinclair arrived. He made a show of looking up and down the hallway. "Not the dinner spot I was hoping for."

"I need your help with something," she said.

He feigned surprise. "My help? Me? If this is about changing a lightbulb because I'm taller than you, I'll be very disappointed."

She led him down the hallway. "Not a lightbulb, but I'll keep that in mind. Follow me."

"Anywhere," he said.

Her fear that he was able to mask his truthfulness through some ability she didn't know warred with her desire to believe him. The desire was winning out over the fear more and more lately. She was starting to think that wasn't a bad thing. She stopped shy of the door to the examining room. *Can you pull out your medallion for me?* she sent.

He waggled his eyebrows. "Is that what we're calling it now?"

Although it wasn't the time for jokes, she realized that it was the perfect time for Sinclair. His joking was a mask, she decided, a way of glossing over the seriousness of a situation. She, of all people, knew about masks. She glowered playfully and held her fingers to his lips. *There's a listening ward in the room,* she sent.

Sinclair threaded his medallion from beneath his shirt. The metal held an odd coolness, unwarmed by his skin. Essence burned both hot and cold depending on how it was used. Laura didn't understand the spell that suppressed Sinclair's fey essence, but she had been able to enhance it before. She pushed essence into the medallion. Her skin prickled as the spell expanded to cover her, too.

Sinclair smirked. "You made it bigger."

Ignoring the comment, she released the medallion. "I need you to stand near the listening ward to dampen it."

She opened a door in the wall of coolers and rolled out a long metal shelf. Sean Carr lay on the shelf, a thin white sheet covering him to the waist. Cress's stasis spell surrounded him, already weakening. Laura estimated it would be gone within a day and with it any trace of essence-related evidence.

The spell prevented his wings from curling inward. They lay flat to either side, a tattered hole in the left one near the shoulder. A cratered burn mark on his chest splayed out like a bloody star against his pale skin. Laura lifted her gaze to see Sinclair's reaction. He leaned against a counter on the opposite side of the table, posture relaxed, arms folded against his chest.

She lifted the shroud, the stark white overhead lamps accentuating Carr's pale skin. Carr might have been a failed assassin, but Laura still respected the dead. Playful banter with Sinclair could wait. She pulled on latex gloves and handed Sinclair a pair. "Can you hold up a wing for me?"

The thin appendage draped over his fingers as Sinclair lifted the soft folds. Laura scanned the drab mauve surface, searching for anomalies. Fairy wings were resilient to incidental injuries, but essence could damage them.

"What are you looking for?" Sinclair asked.

"Cress wanted me to get body-signature imprints before they faded."

The dead man's body signature shone as Inverni a day after

his death. Not a surprise for a member of a powerful group, even if he was from a subclan. She gestured for Sinclair to move closer. "Do you sense anything here?"

"Just the guy's shape. There are layers of other essence on him, but they mean nothing to me."

She moved her hand along Carr's body, sensing residual essence. "They're multiple body signatures, likely contaminants from the way he was brought in."

"Sounds like poor procedure to me," said Sinclair.

Laura sensed her own essence on the body. "Agreed. This wing burn is mine. I'm getting a nice strong tag on the kill shot. That will help identify the killer once we have someone in custody."

As Sinclair released the wing and adjusted it along the rolling slab, Laura started to push the body into the locker but paused. This close to the body, her sensing ability picked up nuances in Carr's body signature. The strength of the field didn't surprise her. As an Inverni, that was a given. She leaned closer. Still nothing. "There's nothing there."

Laura lifted Carr's hands and scanned them. "There's gunshot residue from firing at Draigen, but there's no residual essence concentration in his hands. Essence-fire pools on the skin surface before it discharges. It leaves a ghost image behind, like gunshot residue. There's no afterimage in these hands."

"So?" asked Sinclair.

"He didn't fire essence at whoever killed him, Jono."

Sinclair met her gaze. "Which means he was either surrendering or wasn't expecting to be fired on because he knew the fey who shot him."

Laura pulled the shroud back over Carr and pushed the slab back into the locker. "Either way, Jono, it means he was murdered."

29
CHAPTER

THE SMALL RESTAURANT in Alexandria was not far from Laura's condo. The menu was good enough for repeat visits, but the place had remained under the radar and hadn't been spoiled by popularity yet. Laura had not once recognized someone from in town when she had been there.

She toyed with the straw in her drink. Sinclair picked up the saltshaker and tapped a few grains into his pilsner glass. She chuckled. "I haven't seen someone do that in a long, long time."

Sinclair sipped his beer. "It's an old habit from my grandfather. He said beer used to be better, and the salt made the swill we drink these days taste better."

She gave him a lazy smile. "So why order swill?"

Sinclair shrugged. "It's not. Old habit, like I said. I only do it because it reminds me of him."

"Were you close?" she asked.

"Are you asking me what else a fire giant might have told me?" he said.

She sighed. "Why is it every time I ask a question, you assume I have ulterior motives, but every time you ask one, you get annoyed if I don't answer?"

He grinned. "Because we don't trust each other."

She picked up false tones in his voice and immediately felt ashamed that she was using a fey ability he didn't know about. She tamped it down, shutting off her truth sensitivity.

"What did you just do?" he asked.

She startled. "Are you scanning me?"

He blushed. He actually blushed. "No. It was a latent thing. Your essence shape sort of . . . dimmed."

"I'm trying to relax," she said.

He held his glass up. "Good. To relaxation."

She hesitated, then tapped her glass against his. "With everything going on, it feels wrong, though."

He leaned forward. "Laura, something is always 'going on,' isn't it? There's nothing you can do right now. Your friends are fine for the night. You need to learn to enjoy yourself, I think."

She shifted defensively in her chair. "I just got back from a vacation."

He draped an arm over the back of his chair. "Let me guess: You sat on the beach and read. Got up early, maybe went for a run. Went to bed early. Had room service more than once."

She smiled into her drink. "Did you follow me?"

"Did you laugh?"

She cocked her head. "Excuse me?"

"You were gone for two weeks. How many times did you laugh?" he asked.

Bemused, she played with some bread crumbs on the table. "Okay, I get your point. But in my defense, it was a decompression vacation."

He chuckled. "It doesn't seem to have stuck."

She found herself smiling. "You're analyzing me."

He tilted his head. "A little. When was the last time you went on a date?"

"Does pizza the other night with you count?"

He smiled. "You said it wasn't a date."

"If I say it was, can we change the subject?"

He laughed. "Okay, fine. Let's not talk about work or our pasts. Let's pretend we're not supersecret agents saving the world and talk about stuff like normal people."

She exhaled pleasantly. "I think that's a fine idea."

She did let herself relax then, let the conversation run where it would, not throwing out roadblocks. It was easier than she thought. Sinclair made it easy. She liked the way he focused on her when she spoke yet didn't stare. He seemed to relax, too. It felt comfortable in a way she'd forgotten two people could talk and not have it be concerned about meetings and agendas and threats and, yes, danger. When the check came, it surprised her at how fast the evening had gone.

When they stepped out into the cool evening, Sinclair draped his suit jacket around her shoulders. "That's rather gallant," she said.

He made an amused face. "Oh, gallant? I'm gallant?"

She elbowed him as they waited for the valet to bring her Mercedes. "What?"

He chuckled. "That's a fifty-cent word for a ten-cent guy."

"Well, it's a nice gesture. What would you call it?"

He walked her to the driver's side of the car as it pulled up. "How about a nice gesture?"

She smiled up at him as they stood by the open car door. "It was a nice gesture."

He grinned. "You're welcome."

The moment stretched as they stared at each other. Her heart beat faster as she wondered what to say next. Sinclair turned his head to see if the valet had brought up his car yet. He wrapped his arms around her as he looked back and lowered his face to hers. She closed her eyes as their lips met. His mouth was warm and smooth with a touch of wine. The soft kiss lingered, then he pulled away with a slight tap of his tongue on her lips. "I'm not going to ask you to let me go home with you."

She giggled, then laughed at the giggle. "That's not what I expected you to say."

He brushed her cheek with a gentle hand. "I'm not asking because I don't want you to say no. I want to end the night on the perfect note."

"Jono, we had dinner . . ." she said.

He held his finger against his lips. "See? Don't talk. I want to pretend you didn't humor me."

She slipped off his coat and got in her car as the valet brought Sinclair's car up behind hers. "I didn't humor you, Jono."

"Thanks," he said.

"Now, get in your car and follow me before the valet starts blowing the horn."

Subtle surprise lit his face. He slid his finger along her jaw. "You're sure about that?"

She smiled. "No, but is anyone, ever?"

He leaned down and kissed her again, then went to his car. Her heart racing, she waited until the valet cleared the driveway before pulling onto the street.

I'm insane, she thought as she checked to make sure he was following. Inviting him back to her place went against her rules. She had gotten involved with people she worked with in the past, but not someone in the same unit. Jono was different. He wasn't impressed with her abilities as a druid agent. He didn't care if she screwed up, and he listened when she explained herself. Gods, he listened when she talked. Alone in the car, she laughed. Maybe she wasn't so insane.

After parking his car in front of the condo, he met her at the front door. As they entered the living room, he placed a light hand on her back, as if he were afraid she wasn't there. She glanced over her shoulder, and he kissed her on the cheek. Neither spoke. She slipped her hand into his and led him into the bedroom. They left the lights off, the glow from the living room providing the only illumination.

Laura turned into his arms, and they kissed. His mouth

tasted of subtle mint and wine. She slid her hands inside his suit jacket and helped it slide off him to the floor. He reached behind her and unzipped her dress. Not releasing the kiss, she stepped out of the dress and left it next to his coat on the floor. She pulled herself closer as he lowered them both to the bed.

She rolled on top of him and removed her bra. Sinclair sighed and rubbed his hands up her sides. Her essence sparked with the rush of physical desire coursing through her.

"You're glowing," he whispered.

She leaned forward with a smile, resting her hands against his shoulders and tickling his face with her hair. His body signature smoldered in shades of amber and gold. "You are, too."

He chuckled, warm and deep. "This is what I've hoped for."

She sensed truth in his words and in his essence. He wanted her with no subterfuge. "So have I," she said.

More truth. She pulled him into a seated position as she straddled him and brought her lips to his. He murmured with pleasure, and she let go of any more hesitation.

30
CHAPTER

THE NEXT MORNING, Laura reviewed messages on her PDA in the anteroom to the Guildmaster's office. The text in front of her didn't make much impression as images of the previous night flashed through her mind. She had made a choice that even in the light of day felt like the right one. Getting involved with someone—with Sinclair—didn't frighten her anymore. It was a risk, like all relationships, but she wasn't going to let work take priority over her personal life from now on. Instead, she took the last remaining moments before meeting with Rhys to remember the feel of Sinclair's arms around her, his face nuzzled into her neck as he slept. Near dawn, he eased out of bed trying not to wake her, but she rolled over and smiled up at him, half-dressed in the faint dawnlight. He kissed her good morning with a promise to meet her later in the day.

Laura glanced at Rhys's assistant, a young Danann fairy who was typing with speed. She didn't know the woman's name and tried not to feel guilty about it. The assistant would probably be gone in a month or so. Rhys burned through his help, but he never lacked for interested applicants. Having his name on a résumé looked good and as a reference even better, provided one didn't screw up too badly. Everyone screwed up as far as Rhys was concerned.

"He'll see you now," the assistant said. She hadn't stopped typing or diverted her attention from her computer screen. No phone or intercom rang. Still reading her PDA, Laura entered the office. Rhys spoke quietly on the phone, so she sat and texted Saffin a few details she remembered for Draigen's reception. Rhys hung up as she finished the message. He worked at his computer as if she weren't there. She closed the PDA and folded her hands on her lap. Rhys continued typing.

"I'd like an explanation," she said.

He didn't look up. "Oh, are you ready to see me?"

"Are you?"

He spun slowly in his chair. "I like when you're annoyed, Laura. It means your job is challenging. It's what makes you stay."

She snorted. "Do you want me to leave?"

He smiled. "No, I want you to do what you do best."

"Which I can't do if I don't know what's going," she said.

He sighed. "You seem to be spending time angry with me lately."

She shook her head in exasperation. "Are you trying to provoke me or avoid the subject at hand?"

"Which is?"

"Terryn macCullen, as if you didn't know."

"Ah, I was wondering when he would come up." An obvious lie. Rhys didn't care that she was angry.

"You should have told me he was suspended," she said.

Rhys made a show of surprise. "Is he? I thought he went on leave."

"Orrin, I'm getting very close to losing my temper. There's a difference between being challenged and being antagonized."

He chuckled. "You're right. I'm sorry, Laura. I'm feeling perverse today. Things are going so well, I find myself unable not to gloat and irritate."

"Well, if this is your good mood, warn me when a bad one's coming," she said.

He laughed. "Okay, I should have told you. It was part of the package with getting rid of the *leanansidhe*. I told Inter-Sec that if macCullen didn't accept a suspension, I would publicly accuse them of incompetence and have Maeve allow me to throw them out."

"But you're accusing them anyway," she said.

He shook his head. "Privately, yes. Publicly, I'm letting them save face and claim they initiated their own investigation."

"You should have told me," she said.

"I was going to, but macCullen took me by surprise. I gave them twenty-four hours. He walked out before I knew what happened. I should have anticipated such a move. These mac-Cullens are always working at cross-purposes."

Truth hummed in his words. That did sound like something Terryn would do. He didn't like being given ultimatums any more than anyone else, but if he had to accept one, he'd find a way to do it on his own terms. Rhys's throwaway comment intrigued her, though.

"Cross-purposes?" she asked.

He waved a hand dismissively. "Our Lady Regent gave me the idea to suspend him. When I told her I was getting rid of the *leanansidhe*, she said she understood and that it would be unfortunate for such a fate to befall her brother. I thought the idea intriguing, so I used it."

"But she said . . ." Laura stopped at an exasperated eyebrow lift from Rhys.

"Don't be naïve, Laura. She said it to me with the purpose of putting the idea in my mind. I don't know what her game is, but sidelining Terryn macCullen appealed to her and works fine with me."

Rhys was right, she realized. She wasn't naïve. She knew the nuance of conversations with subtext. But like Rhys said, she didn't understand why having Terryn out of InterSec would benefit the Inverni cause. It surprised her.

"All well and good. In the meantime, I'm getting pressure from the media. They see your hand in this," she said.

He grinned. "Do they?"

She sighed and ran a hand through her hair. He was intent on staying in this mood. "Okay, I get it. You want them to know the Guild is behind it, but you want deniability. Can I ask why?"

He leaned forward. "It sends a message. The Inverni need to know that the Seelie Court will not be passive if they seek allies against it. And the public needs to know the decisions that the Inverni make. Letting a *leanansidhe* into the Guildhouse has upset many people, Laura. That thing was dangerous."

"No, she isn't," she said. As soon as she said it, she bit her lip. It had been an impulsive reaction.

Rhys pulled his chin in, surprised. "How do you know that's true or not?"

She shrugged. "She's a solitary. Resha Dunne would tell us if there was a danger, wouldn't he?"

Rhys scoffed. "Dunne wouldn't know his ass from his back fin."

Laura shook her head. "Still, Orrin, Resha knows how to cover that back fin. If he knew of a danger that might reflect on him, I think he'd do something about it."

He leaned forward again. "How about this, then: I don't like it. I don't like that a *leanansidhe* was free to roam this building. I don't like that it exists. You're young, Laura. Hereborn. You don't know the damage those things have done here and back in Faerie."

She closed her eyes a moment. She hated when an Old One invoked the past in Faerie. She couldn't argue it. Never mind that the fey who did remember Faerie recalled only bits and pieces. That Rhys remembered a *leanansidhe* meant he had experienced them, and by all accounts, the *leanansidhe* did cause havoc. If what she had heard was any indication of the true reality, Cress's sister *leanansidhe*—if not Cress herself—were formidable foes.

Nothing she could say at that point would change Rhys's mind. She heard it in his voice and saw it in his body language. She entertained the idea that he was afraid of what Cress was capable of. He had watched her absorb an enormous amount of essence at the Archives, then destroy the roof of the building. That Cress did it to save lives was beside the point to him. That she could do it at all was the problem.

"Let's let go of this discussion, Orrin. What's done is done, and we need to address the ramifications for the Guild," she said.

He leaned back again. "Good. Put something together that says we are surprised at the recent changes at InterSec and look forward to the release of their findings. Throw in something about regretting that such an esteemed member of the Inverni clan as Terryn macCullen decided to go on leave, and that it is an unfortunate loss at this time because his wisdom will be missed."

His disingenuous tone set her teeth on edge, but she had pushed him as much as she could for one day. "I will. Can I have your word you'll give me more of a heads-up than the day after you do something radical?"

He chuckled. "I will, but you know I won't be able to keep it."

"I know. It would be nice to hear you say it, though," she said.

He tilted his head in a bow. "I shall try not to make your job harder than it is."

She stood. "Thank you. I'll get back to work, then."

"Before you go, Laura, I want to say one more thing. After all these years and all you've seen, I admire your optimism. I hope you aren't sorely disappointed when people turn out exactly as they are."

She paused by the door. "Do you believe in redemption, Orrin?"

He seemed surprised at the question and paused before answering. "I do. But I don't believe that acceptance always follows. Sometimes it shouldn't."

A sad smile slipped across her face as she left. She had to believe in redemption—and forgiveness. She had spent years doing some harsh things in the name of the greater good. She believed that someday she would be called to account for them, and she hoped whoever judged her showed more mercy than Orrin ap Rhys.

31
CHAPTER

INTEL FROM THE assassination attempt had begun to flow into the InterSec unit before Laura had returned from the White House. In two days' time, the volume of material had grown exponentially. Her acting as Mariel Tate for most of the previous day had pushed the public-relations department into critical mode as requests for interviews and statements from the Guildmaster swamped the office. Saffin had done her best— and her best was an understatement—to keep things moving.

With her dual roles slamming into each other, Laura gathered files from InterSec and took them up to public relations. She didn't like mixing the duties of the two offices, but troubleshooting the media had become a nightmare she didn't want to leave Saffin alone with. By late afternoon, the pressure had shifted course, and she had to address the preliminary investigation as Mariel. In a moment of desperation, she flat out told Saffin to keep visitors away while she plunged into the InterSec material.

Saffin took the news as if Laura had told her she was going to lunch. Keeping silent about her double life in front of Rhys and everyone else at the Guild was difficult, and knowing that Saffin could be trusted made life a little easier. A quick knock sounded at the door, and Saffin slipped in. "I'm sorry to bother you, but Resha is on his way up again."

"Again?"

Saffin folded her arms. "Third time. He's getting suspicious about your door being closed. He almost opened it last time."

Laura looked down at her desk. Inverni Guardian schedules and notices were spread everywhere. On her monitor, surveillance video from the assassination attempt played. "I've been trying to find decent footage that shows the location from which Draigen's sniper fired. How much time do I have?"

Saffin raised her eyebrows and twisted her lips. "Minutes."

She jumped up. "Dammit." She stacked papers together and shoved them in folders.

Saffin rushed to the desk. "Yikes. Don't do that in front of me."

Laura paused. "What?"

Saffin neatened the folders. "Make such a mess."

Laura bit her lip as she watched Saffin, then checked her watch. "Saf, I have to take care of something and can't let Resha chew up my time. Can you hide all this stuff and pretend you never saw it?"

She shrugged. "Sure. I do that all the time with crap I don't want to do."

Laura picked up her bag. "You're kidding, right?"

Saffin rolled her eyes. "Yes, Laura. Of course I'm kidding. Get going."

"You're the best, Saf," she said as she rushed out the door.

"I know," Saffin called after her.

Laura took the elevator down to the parking garage. In the lower lobby, she sidled into a blind spot of the security camera and activated the Mariel glamour. It was an old trick, one she used sparingly in case an attentive security guard noticed anything on the monitors in the bowels of the building. Taking a moment to leave her bag in her InterSec SUV, she walked out the exit ramp to the sidewalk.

Barricades along the sidewalk stood like accusations of

failure, the chipped sidewalk a testament that the shooting had not been prevented. Draigen was alive, Laura reminded herself. That was what was important. The regent of the mac-Cullen clan was alive and the only person who had died was the shooter.

Laura didn't think it was over. Despite the failed attempt and the heightened alerts, chatter among security-agency channels had not abated. Rumors abounded of a trial run, that the assassination was meant to fail. The conflicting information came in from disparate sources that had never acted in unison before. Local U.S. interest groups and European political cells were rattled and excited. Yet no one claimed responsibility.

The building Sean Carr had fired on Draigen from was a long two blocks away. The walk was easy but did nothing to set Laura at ease. Bureaucracy had already set in at the building, and she had to work through four lines of security. The D.C. police held the front line, weeding out visitors who did not have legitimate business in the building or who were not law enforcement. After them, the Guild recorded names and photographed any fey who entered. Under the circumstances, that smacked of intimidation of Inverni supporters. The Inverni security staff themselves were next, a suspicious group that acted convinced everyone besides them was interested in destroying evidence. After the twenty minutes it required to meet their approval, Laura was happy to see the familiar black jumpsuits of the InterSec guards who had control of the top floor and attic space of the building. Not all of them knew Mariel Tate on sight, but they knew enough to read a high-level InterSec pass without causing an argument.

Finally alone, she trailed down a dusty hallway on the attic level, sensing body signatures. It was as much exercise as investigation. The hallway wouldn't tell her much—too many people had passed through it since the assassination attempt—but sorting through the different trails helped her calm down and prepare for what she had come for.

Crime-scene tape stretched across an open door. As she

ducked under the tape, the ozonelike odor of essence strikes tickled Laura's nose. At least two major bolts had passed through the space. She wound her way through stacked chairs to a broken window frame with plastic sheeting fixed over it.

She picked up traces of her essence-bolt where Carr must have stood to make his shot at Draigen. Laura's return fire had hit him and wrecked the window casing. She peeled back the sheeting. Without leaning out far, she had a clear view of the plaza in front of the Guildhouse two blocks away. Perfect line of sight. She pressed the sheeting back in place.

Slowly pivoting, she noted the pattern of scattered chairs. Her shot would have thrown Carr left, right where the chairs had been knocked askew. She crouched, sensing his body signature on the floor, but no telltale investigation markers to indicate his body had fallen there. Which meant that wasn't where he died.

She stood. People in a panic used the most direct path available. She paced the open aisle through the stacked chairs to a line of storage boxes against the back wall. With her pocket flashlight, she swept a beam of light along the floor and under the chairs. Crime-scene investigators had been through already, but the chance they had missed something always existed. Maybe not in such a high-profile case, she thought. Before she reached the boxes, someone knocked at the door.

"Hey, someone said there was a crazy lady in the attic, and here you are," Sinclair said.

Laura smirked over her shoulder. "I'm surprised you got through all that security."

He frowned in curiosity. "Why?"

Crouching in front of the boxes, she flicked the light along the floor. "Your security clearance isn't as high as mine."

He tickled her on a shoulder blade, then stepped back, a subtle reminder that he remembered how she felt about mixing work and play. "It was a breeze."

She glanced up, smiling. "Are you kidding me?"

He shook his head. "I knew the D.C. cops at the door. The

Guild guys waved me along because they thought I was human. You left my name with the Inverni guards, and Eldin passed me in down the hall."

"Eldin?"

Sinclair gestured over his shoulder with his thumb. "Skinny elf in the elevator? Works across the hall from us?"

Her eyebrows drew together as she tried to place him. "He does?"

"Yeah. He thinks you're hot, by the way. They all do over there."

She tilted her head up. "They? You know a 'they' over there? How do you know them?"

He shrugged. "Met them in the gym. We shoot hoops."

She brought her attention back to the boxes. "Don't tell me—you play center."

"Nope. Forward. Galt from accounting plays center. He's a frost jotunn. They're kinda short for giants, but he's at least a head taller than me."

She shook her head. "You know someone in accounting, too?"

He peered over her shoulder. "Yeah. He used to give me the hairy eyeball when I picked up my check. I thought he might have been sensing my jotunn essence somehow, but turns out he couldn't figure why Terryn was paying me out of a supplies account. I told him it was top secret, hush-hush."

She smiled. "Paying you out of supplies, Jono, is an example of Terryn's sense of humor."

He leaned against a crate and waggled his eyebrows at her. "You know, I don't mind being used as a tool sometimes."

She leaned down as the light flashed on something. "I'll keep that in mind."

"What are we doing here?" he asked.

"Sean Carr had two major wounds—one to the chest and one to the wing. The chest shot killed him. I'm a good shot, but I fired blind. The wing hit was mine." She walked halfway up the room toward the window. "The essence evidence in here confirms it. My hit knocked him out of the window. Seeing this layout, it would have been virtually impossible for someone to deliver the deathblow from outside."

"Virtually," Sinclair said.

She leaned to the side to see beneath a chair. "Right. It's possible, of course, but I was the only person to react to the gunshots and gauge the direction of their source. We didn't have security this far up the street, so no one could have been on scene fast enough to deliver the shot without Carr's being ready for it."

"You did wound him," Sinclair said.

"He probably couldn't fly with the damage, but it wasn't incapacitating. So he was trapped here on the ground. Which means that whoever killed him did it inside, and if it was done in here, there might be a body signature I can lock on."

Sinclair pursed his lips. "Except probably a hundred people have been through here since the shooting."

Laura stepped around a chair that lay sideways on the floor. She crouched again. The flashlight beam picked up a flash of pale yellow. "Ah, there it is."

She stood next to an index card on the floor. "This marks where Carr's head was when he was found. Judging by the position, I'd guess he got up from beneath the window and made his way down the main aisle. The impact of the kill shot would have thrown him back a few feet"—she shifted away from the index card toward the back of the room again—"which would have put him about here."

Sinclair faced her, holding his hand out as if firing an essence-bolt. "So the shooter would have been about here."

"Lower. You're likely taller," she said.

He dropped his hand a foot. "I don't think the shooter was here. Carr would have been facing him directly and seen he was about to be fired on. He would have tried to defend himself." He stepped to his left behind rows of chairs. "Line of sight is blocked on this side." He moved to the right in front of the boxes, keeping his hand pointing at Laura. "Anywhere along here is possible. Carr wouldn't have necessarily seen it coming from here."

Laura moved along the main aisle. Dozens of body signatures flared in her senses, streaming colors of blue and white, yellow and green, indicating various fey species. She recognized a flash of a signature here and there, people she had known on the InterSec security teams or some she had met on the Inverni Guardian units. Aran macCullen had been in the room, which was no surprise since he had taken the lead in the investigation.

"It's pretty contaminated," she said.

She moved next to Sinclair and immediately registered three or four strong signatures. "Okay, this is interesting. I'm sensing a large pool of Carr's essence, so he must have hung out back here waiting for Draigen's scheduled departure. I recognize a druid from InterSec who works on crime-scene investigations. He must have sensed Carr's essence, too, because he lingered long enough to leave a good imprint. There's also another Inverni essence that shifts back and forth like someone was pacing."

"Aran macCullen?" Sinclair asked.

She shook her head. "Not strong enough. It matches the signature I picked up in the morgue, though. If I know the person, I can gauge how old the signature is by how it's degrading, but without knowing who was here, it could either be someone with Carr or someone watching the investigator work. I've got a good fix on this signature, though."

"So now what?"

She grinned up at him. "We play poker."

32
CHAPTER

LAURA STARED OUT the window of the office at Legacy. The faint reflection of Fallon Moor's face stared back at her as she tapped into her hyper memory recall. Between the research profile compiled by InterSec and her own interview, she processed everything she knew about what Fallon Moor knew. DeWinter had left a message for her—for Fallon— that a project-update meeting was scheduled, and she needed to be there. No other details were given.

She reviewed the list of possibilities. Intelligence reports indicated that Moor was a facilitator of sorts, using her connections within an underground network to make things happen. She also had a keen eye for finances and knowledge of how to move through electronic banking systems without leaving a trace. Legacy had a number of backers with substantial means, but they wanted deniability in the event Legacy's more shady operations became public. Moor's skills provided both sides with satisfaction. Legacy got its fund. Its backers got their anonymity.

Laura checked her watch. *Has she come up with anything else?* she sent to Terryn. Despite being on leave, he had stationed himself outside Moor's holding cell again to relay messages. As long as Genda didn't find out and make an issue of it, they could continue the Legacy investigation.

No, he replied.

They had been trying all morning to get Moor to discuss what she thought the meeting was about. She offered the likelihood that it was about the rocket launchers from the InterSec raid. Laura suspected that was wrong. It didn't tell them anything they already knew. Of course, Legacy wasn't happy about the lost weapons. That was self-evident. But why have a major meeting about it? The email listed a dozen people, none of them on the company directory, all of the addresses false or masked accounts.

Keep at her, Laura sent.

She fixed her hair in the reflection of the window, then picked up a pad and pen and went down to the conference room. The small room had no windows and no telephone. Eight people, including DeWinter, sat in silence, waiting as others arrived. No cell phones or PDAs were out. Laura suspected electronic jamming surrounded the room.

Laura met DeWinter's glance as she sat a few places away from her. The two men to either side did not acknowledge her. She recognized about half the men and women, most businesspeople with strong anti-fey politics. The only other fey person in the room was an elf. Out of habit, she triggered her hyper memory so that she could recall faces in detail later.

"That's everyone. Our other two guests could not attend," said DeWinter.

"Let's move quickly. I have a plane to catch," a plain-faced woman said. Her name floated into Laura's memory: Rosa Lentner, an executive with a major science research firm in the Midwest.

DeWinter reviewed his notes. "Our acquisition is imminent. The funds we provided have enabled us to bypass several security measures."

"I thought we weren't prepared to receive the package?" Lentner asked.

"Yes and no," DeWinter said. "The system is not ready, but we have facilities to contain the acquisition. It's only a matter of a few days."

They're talking about an acquisition and a package, she sent Terryn.

A large, overweight man Laura didn't recognize leaned forward. "I don't like to think that the pod isn't ready."

Ask Moor about the pod, Laura sent.

A tolerant smile creased DeWinter's face. "I assure you, it's fine. The same technology for the pod can be used as a temporary solution in a separate room."

She's being evasive, Terryn sent. *She said it sounds like weapons. Legacy has been interested in military transports.*

That was new, Laura thought. *What about this pod? What is it?*

Please repeat. You're fading, Terryn said.

Laura shot a look at the elf. At close range, she was able to sense his body signature, but she didn't notice that he was using essence. *The pod, Terryn. What is the pod?*

Faint . . . intermittent . . . he sent. The sending sounded broken and weak, as if it had lost its energy.

Terryn? She received no response but hid her frustration. Someone had jammed her sendings. Given the lack of electronics in the room, it didn't surprise her that they employed essence wards, too. Legacy might not like the fey's abilities, but they sure liked the benefits.

The elf moved his head in her direction, and she wondered if he sensed her sending. She could feel flutters in the air when people did sendings. It was an ability that powerful fey tended to have. He didn't look directly at her and didn't say anything, so she didn't think the jamming was coming from him.

"Why the rush? We have more than enough room in the schedule," said Lentner.

"This window of opportunity might close. We've already had one failed attempt. I don't want another," said DeWinter.

Lentner didn't respond, but an older gentleman steepled his fingers together as he shifted in his seat. "Where did these funds come from?" he asked.

DeWinter looked at Laura. With Moor's access codes, she had made the transfer herself. As she had said to Sinclair, she wasn't happy about helping an enemy, even doing their work, without knowing the full extent of what was going on, but sometimes it was necessary to reach the larger goal. "A liquid asset account."

"That's not what I asked," said the man.

Laura glowered at him. "I know. That's all you're getting."

The man clenched his jaw. "The transfer was substantial. I have to make accountings for the funds."

"Please assure our benefactors that the funds came from a new, unexpected source," said DeWinter.

Interesting bit of information to relay to Genda, Laura thought. If a new player was on the scene, it wouldn't be in the data files InterSec had. "Can we expect more?" she asked.

An uncomfortable smile twitched the corner of DeWinter's mouth, and she worried she might have made the wrong move. "Not likely. It appears to be a once-only event," he said.

So, whoever it was wanted this acquisition to happen, then to have nothing more to do with Legacy, she thought, a random variable in the process. That likely meant whatever Legacy was planning would have broader ramifications than its own goals. No one gave away twelve million dollars without a direct, possibly personal, interest.

"Are you saying you've brought someone in without our approval?" Lentner asked.

The woman was vocal and persistent. Laura thought she might bear looking into more closely.

"You misunderstand," said DeWinter. "The benefactor knows nothing of our operations. Our brief association is of mutual but separate benefit."

Definitely meaning the package would have broader impact, Laura thought.

"I still don't like the package being on hand like this. The longer we have it before we are ready to execute, the higher risk for exposure."

DeWinter rested his hands on the table. "I am considering accelerating the timetable. We have a very timely event that might provide greater success than our original plan."

Lentner made a dismissive sound. "You always press like this, DeWinter. You're getting too rash. We need to be fully prepared."

"No names here," he said.

That made her angry. "This isn't a game, DeWinter. We all know each other."

"Security. If you cannot refrain from being careful with your speech, you will have a hard time in front of a Senate hearing," he said.

As Lentner and DeWinter challenged each other with stares, the overweight man turned his attention to Laura. "Your absence from Monday's meeting has caused concern."

Moor hadn't mentioned any Monday meetings, and Laura had no idea who the man was. "I had a more pressing matter to attend to," she said.

His eyebrows arched. "More pressing? What could have possibly had more importance than"—he glanced at DeWinter—"replacement for the lost supplies?"

Laura didn't want to continue the conversation. Unknown territory was dangerous territory. "Are you questioning me?"

The man seemed to gather some courage. "Yes, in fact, I am."

Laura boosted some essence into her ruby and accessed part of her template. She let her hand twitch against the table surface, let the fingers lengthen and her nails shift to claws. She took a calculated risk. "I don't answer to you."

All eyes in the room went to her hand. The threat of going boggart intimidated many people, and having most of the people in the room afraid of the fey in the first place only added to it.

"I have already discussed that with her and approved of her

decision," said DeWinter. He smiled at the man, but Laura knew the look was for Moor.

She sensed the lie, but she didn't need that ability to know they hadn't discussed anything. They hadn't. This sort of situation was the reason personal relationships in an operation were bad. They created competing priorities and loyalties. It was one of the reasons she worried about getting involved with Sinclair. Still, he had made a good case for ignoring that worry, and she was letting him convince her.

"What is this meeting about?" she snapped.

People shifted in their seats, sending furtive looks at DeWinter. He had called the meeting. His level of authority was evident. "To announce the shorter schedule of operation. I will have the precise date in a day or two. In the meantime, it is imperative we use the next few hours to protect our assets. I suggest we all initiate the market-management plans we've discussed."

The overweight man frowned at Laura. "That is precisely one of the items discussed at the meeting you missed."

Laura had nothing to work with to defend herself. She didn't know the plans or the players. DeWinter's answer to her question rang true in her senses. The intent of the meeting was more to inform others that he was speeding up his schedule than anything substantive. The situation had reached the point where the risk of exposing her lack of understanding of what was going on outweighed whatever additional information she gained. She stood, sending her chair skittering back. "You heard what you need to know. We have the funds, the opportunity, and the schedule. Get moving. I don't have time for this."

She stalked out of the room, leaving behind a ring of stunned faces. She had not been in her office more than ten minutes before DeWinter arrived. "That wasn't very diplomatic, love," he said.

With a practiced air of guilt, she smiled. "I'm not much into coddling, Adam."

He chuckled. "True, but some of our relationships are fragile. We need to make them feel part of the process."

She strolled around her desk and caressed his cheek with the back of her hand. "You call the shots, Adam. They needed to be reminded."

He gathered her hand in his and kissed it. "You've been on edge lately the last few days. Not yourself."

She lowered her head against his shoulder. "I know. I have a lot to keep track of. I promise I'll be my normal self again soon."

He held her and kissed her on the forehead. "I love when you allow me to see you like this."

Keeping her head down, she rubbed her hand on his chest. "You make it easy to be myself."

He kissed her again. "I have to go. Some of them want to talk privately."

She broke their embrace. "Okay. Let me know if there's anything I can do to help with the new schedule."

"You'll be the first to know," he said.

Laura breathed a sigh of relief as he left. DeWinter knew how to run a secret operation—no written evidence, no names, coded phrasings. She gathered her things, not wanting to risk getting cornered by any of the other meeting attendees.

She had some good leads. DeWinter's accelerated schedule worried her. Less time to find answers meant the possibility of failure. She refused to accept that as an option.

33
CHAPTER

THROUGHOUT THE FOLLOWING day, dozens of Inverni staff had paraded through the Guildhouse conference room, their faces stoic or apprehensive or annoyed. Laura had forgotten how large entourages could be. At the start of the interviews, she had been cordial and conversational, but that soon fell away in the monotony of reciting the same questions over and over.

Terryn surprised her by walking in with the last person on the list, a male brownie attached to the Inverni administrative staff. She had tried to coordinate a meeting with him throughout the previous day, but he had remained behind closed doors with Draigen and her staff.

The brownie sat with poise, unflustered by the presence of Terryn, whom he had to recognize. Laura picked up the one-sheet survey she had had all the visiting Inverni fill out. "You're Davvi Norrin?"

"Yes, ma'am."

"You're on Draigen's staff?"

The man did not move at all. "Yes, ma'am."

"You wrote down 'assistant.' What do you do?"

Davvi tilted his head. "I assist, ma'am."

Laura didn't sense any sarcasm or guile. "In what respect?"

He lowered his gaze as if trying to read what was in front of Laura. "Schedules, ma'am."

She glanced at him. "For?"

He leaned away, resuming his stiff posture. "The Lady Regent, ma'am."

"Can you be more specific?" she asked.

"No, ma'am," he said.

Caught off guard, Laura chuckled. "Why not?"

He frowned, his thin, pale eyebrows pulling together in sincere puzzlement. "I work for the Lady Regent, ma'am."

Laura pursed her lips. "We've covered that already."

Davvi nodded. "Yes, ma'am."

Laura stared at him, trying not to let her frustration build. He didn't seem to be paying any attention. "What do you schedule for the Lady Regent?"

"Her business, ma'am."

"Can you be more specific on that?"

"No, ma'am."

Laura closed her eyes. She had been at it for hours and had no idea what was going on with the man. She didn't need to continue with the interview anyway. He was a brownie, and the signature she was looking for was fairy. His silence intrigued and annoyed her, as if he had something to hide. "You seem reluctant to answer my questions, Davvi."

He looked surprised. "No, ma'am."

"This agent has my trust, Davvi. You may answer her as you would me," Terryn said.

"Yes, sir," he said.

Laura shot a curious glance at Terryn. "Where were you when the Lady Regent was fired upon?"

"Here, ma'am," he said.

"The Guildhouse?"

"Yes, ma'am," he said.

His abrupt responses baffled her. "Where in the Guildhouse?"

"Here, ma'am," he said.

"Here?"

"Yes, ma'am."

The urge to snap at the brownie welled up within her. He didn't seem to be uninformative on purpose. She reminded herself that she had been asking fruitless questions all day, and he hadn't. She reviewed his answers in her head when realization struck her. "You mean you were in this room at the time of the sniper attack, Davvi?"

"Yes, ma'am. As I said, ma'am." The look on his face seemed puzzled that he needed to clarify.

Truth permeated his words. Davvi Norrin worked in an exacting environment and had learned to be careful, if too precise. She gave up. "I think we're fine, sir. Thank you for your time."

He hesitated, confused perhaps or unsure. He stood and bowed. "Thank you, Agent Tate."

Surprised yet again, she cocked her head. "How do you know my name?"

A subtle shift in his shoulders passed as a shrug. "I schedule the Lady Regent's business, ma'am."

She smiled, sincerely. "Thank you. The Lady Regent is lucky to have you."

He bowed again. "Thank you, ma'am."

Laura swiveled her chair toward Terryn. "I think I was just trumped in an interrogation."

Terryn stared out the window, focusing at something across the way on the Mall. "Davvi's been with my family for as long as I can remember. He wouldn't tell you the time of day if he thought you would use it against a macCullen. We called him the Stone when we were children."

"That's loyalty," she said.

Terryn didn't move from the window. His pointed wings stood straight up from his back, their pale blue translucence flickering with shots of white and indigo. Tension wrapped around him like a veil. "And hard to come by these days."

She pushed her notes aside and joined him by the window. "I've been meaning to talk to you about that. I had Jono stationed in the park as a hidden backup. No one knows that. He noticed the protection barrier weaken before Draigen came out. It was subtle and happened twice. That means the shield wasn't interfered with by natural means."

"What are you suggesting?" Terryn asked.

Laura gave him a significant look. "Someone among the Inverni Guardians might be a traitor. The weakness happened on Aran's end of the barrier. Someone who knows Aran would also know how he builds his spells and be able to interfere with them."

Terryn pursed his lips. "We've already established that Sean Carr was the perpetrator."

Laura crossed her arms. "I've established he wasn't working alone. I have a body signature tag on a possible accomplice."

He narrowed his eyes. "That's why you wanted to do these interviews in person."

She gazed into the distance across the Washington Mall. "It was a bit of a bluff. Davvi was the last on the list. I've eliminated seventy-nine people. We had two no-shows, both Inverni Guardians. Rory Dawson is attached to Draigen's house staff, and Uma macGrath is with Aran. Everyone was told this was mandatory. I'd like to put out a warrant on them if you're okay with that."

A muscle pulsed along his jawline. "Do whatever is necessary, Laura. You don't need my permission."

It struck her that she didn't. Besides the fact that he was on leave, Genda would likely rubber-stamp her request. Terryn's emotions rubbed against her sensitivities. He managed to remain hard for her to read, but she was sensing pain and anger beyond what she would expect from the attempt on Draigen's life. "What's wrong?" she asked.

"Cress's car was set on fire last night," he said.

Laura's chest tightened. "Was she . . ."

"She's safe," he interrupted. "Her house-confinement agreement doesn't allow her to travel. The car was on the street.

The location had been leaked. People have been gathering outside the building, throwing things and yelling."

She placed a hand on his arm. "I'm sorry, Terryn."

Essence flickered in his wings as his anger built. "Someone set her car on fire not thirty feet from my front door in full view of the Guild security agents, and they did nothing."

Anger heated her chest. "Terryn, you have to let me say something to Rhys. This has got to stop before someone gets hurt."

He shook his head. "Your position is too valuable, Laura. I don't want to see us all destroyed because of Rhys's obsession with my clan. I will have Draigen dispatch Inverni Guardians to protect the building."

She moved in front of him, so he wouldn't miss her serious expression. "Don't do that, Terryn. Rhys will exploit it. The last thing you need right now is having the Inverni court seen as protecting Cress."

She regretted saying it as soon as she heard herself. The pained look on Terryn's face struck her in the stomach. She touched his arm again. "Don't misunderstand me. Cress is my friend. I've been arguing her case with Rhys for days."

He closed his eyes. "I know. It's still hard to hear. No one has any idea what she means to me. No one can."

She crossed her arms and stared out the window. "Of course not. That's the nature of any relationship, isn't it?"

"I need to protect her."

"Leave that to me. I'll talk to Genda. InterSec is the most neutral party we have right now," she said.

He managed, if not to smile, at least not to look as upset. "Thank you. I think if we get through the next few days until Draigen leaves, Rhys will move on to something else."

She rubbed his shoulder. "We will. In the meantime, let's not tell anyone I have this body-signature tag."

He lifted an eyebrow. "By which you mean my family?"

She lowered her gaze to lessen the sting of what she had to say. "You have a traitor among your people, Terryn. It's not that I don't trust your family, but they trust someone they shouldn't. We're working a long shot, and the wrong word to the wrong person could ruin the whole thing."

"I know," he said. "It's difficult advising you and my family at the same time."

She murmured a laugh. "Welcome to my world."

His face clouded over as he stared out the window again. "You have my sympathy."

34
CHAPTER

TERRYN'S WORDS DIDN'T change Laura's stress at juggling multiple jobs. She appreciated his sympathy, of course, but she didn't have a choice of skimping on any of her responsibilities. As she worked through the mountain of paper on her public-relations desk, sympathy didn't make things any easier when she was falling behind.

Saffin carried a small lamp into the office and set it on a low filing cabinet. She threaded the cord down, struggled to plug it in between the cabinet and the wall, then switched on the blue-white light to illuminate the new plants. "That should help."

Guilt-stricken, Laura ducked her head. "I'm not very good with plants, am I?"

Saffin made a disappointed face. "It's a crime, really."

"Gee, thanks. On a more sincere note, thanks for taking care of those files the other day."

Saffin's gaze darted to the door as she kneaded her fingers together. She looked at Laura, then nudged the door closed with her foot. "Promise you won't get mad?"

Laura pursed her lips. "I'll promise to listen."

Saffin eased into the guest chair. "When I put away those files, I, um, didn't do it immediately. I read them."

A hot spot formed in Laura's chest, not anger, but disappointment. "Saf, you shouldn't have done that."

She twisted her fingers together. "I know. But you were so stressed for time and have so much going on, I thought I could help."

Laura shook her head. "I'm not mad. It's as much my fault for letting it happen. But I'm serious, Saf; you can't do something like that again."

Crestfallen, she looked down. "I know. I won't." Peering from beneath her brow, she smiled slightly. "I think I found the video you were looking for."

Laura dropped her head in her hands. "Show me. Just . . . show me."

Saffin hustled around to Laura's side of the desk. Opening a drawer, she retrieved a memory stick and plugged it into the computer. When the directory appeared, she scrolled through and opened a file. A black-and-white video started playing. From the movement and angle, Laura guessed it was from a helmet camera worn by a Danann agent in flight.

Saffin was right—the video showed a clear view up Pennsylvania Avenue toward the Capitol. An Inverni Guardian hovered in the background up the street, directly across from where Sean Carr had fired. "Is that what you were looking for?" Saffin asked.

The footage riveted Laura. The Guildhouse was out of view to the left of the frame. The advance guards appeared on the sidewalk on either end of the block. Aran and Brinen entered the scene next, followed by Laura in her Mariel glamour, with Draigen beside her. There was no sound, but the action of the next frames indicated the shots had been fired, with Laura shoving Draigen back and Aran and Brinen reacting. The image became chaotic as the Danann wearing the camera swooped down on the sidewalk and took up a new position. When the view returned to the front of the Guildhouse, Draigen's limo had departed.

The interesting point for Laura was the movement of the unidentified Inverni in the background. As soon as the shots were fired, whoever it was dashed into the building where Sean Carr was found dead. Except she hadn't found anyone mentioning that in any of the reports.

She played the scene back again. "Is that a man or a woman in the background?" she said.

Saffin peered at the screen. "Can't tell. The resolution's not good enough."

Laura made a note to check the security plan in order to see who had been stationed there. "This is exactly what I was looking for, Saf."

Saffin preened as she returned to the front of the desk. "Good. And it won't happen again."

As Laura chuckled at the irony of the statement, her phone lit up. From the caller ID, she saw it was from Rhys's assistant. "He needs to see you immediately," she said, when Laura answered. Then she hung up. Without waiting for a response. Irritated, Laura stared at the phone. She gathered up a pad and pen. "I have to go upstairs. Good work, Saf."

Saffin spun on her heel. "Thank you, and you're very welcome."

When she arrived at Rhys's office, she marched by the assistant without waiting to be announced. Rhys held a phone to his ear as he waved Laura toward a chair. Above the long credenza, a wide-screen television tuned to the local news station played on mute. Curious, Laura took a seat and watched Jenna Dahl, the station's star anchor, while the president's face appeared in an inset. Rhys didn't speak. After several minutes, he set the phone in its cradle and picked up the television remote. "You'll want to hear this."

Dahl's voice filled the room. " . . . an investigation into the hiring of an allegedly dangerous fey staff member by the International Global Security Agency is receiving additional scrutiny today. Our sources indicate that the Washington Guild and the White House pressured InterSec to suspend the personnel involved. Now records are showing that a significant sum of money from an unnamed party was paid to Guildmaster Orrin ap Rhys prior to his contact with the White House, raising questions regarding the motivation for the suspension of Cress Leanansidhe as well as other staff at Inter-Sec. We go now for a live report . . ."

Rhys muted the audio again as the screen changed to a local reporter in front of the Guildhouse. "I'll need a press release within the hour, Laura, denying any bribery took place. I returned the money as soon as I realized it was in my accounts. We can offer to show records, pending approval of legal counsel, of course."

"Returned to whom?" she asked.

"What?"

"To whom did you return the money?"

He smiled with satisfaction. "Let's let that unfold elsewhere."

She felt anger rising. "That's not good enough, Orrin."

Rhys glared. "What is the matter with you lately? This *leanansidhe* business seems to have you unusually upset."

Frustrated, she shook her head. "You know what has me upset? These mind games you keep playing, then dumping in my lap. I can't do my job if you don't give me more warning than thirty seconds before airtime—excuse me, *after* airtime."

He grunted as he pushed out of his chair and went to the credenza. "Ah, so it's procedural, is that it? For a moment, I thought you were going to defend that thing again."

She couldn't help raising her voice. "Cress saved lives at the Archives attack. She saved your life and mine, Orrin."

He poured himself a short glass of brandy. "Twenty-nine people died."

"Not because of Cress," Laura said.

Rhys gestured at her with the glass as he resumed his seat. "Ah, there we have it, don't we? The Inverni were responsible for that. It's all related."

She jabbed her finger on his desk. "*An* Inverni, Orrin. Singular. Simon Alfrey planned and executed the plot and is in custody. You're playing with people's lives."

He'infuriated her more by laughing. "Me? I don't think I'm the one at whom to cast blame, Laura. There are others who are less than pleased with that creature's existence. I cannot be blamed for taking advantage of the situation."

She inhaled deeply to calm down. "Who, Orrin? Who are we talking about?"

He leaned back again. "As I said, that will play out elsewhere. Right now, your primary concern is deflecting any negative perceptions of me and this organization. Start taking notes."

They stared at each other. She wanted to slap the smug look off his face. Whatever happened to Cress, he was making it worse. She knew it, as she knew he didn't care. He raised a single eyebrow. "Shall we begin?"

She wasn't Mariel Tate, not when she was working for the Guild. Laura Blackstone had a job to do. Terryn had told her not to expose herself, not to let Rhys know who she was. She broke eye contact and uncapped her pen. "So, you had no idea the money was in your account."

He smiled. "None."

Lie, she thought.

Liar.

35
CHAPTER

WITHIN HOURS OF sending law-enforcement agencies the names and pictures of the missing guards, a tip call came in on Rory Dawson, one of the missing Inverni guards who hadn't shown up for Laura's staff interviews. A hotel desk attendant thought he recognized the Inverni as the same man who had checked in two days earlier and hadn't left. If there was an upside to human suspicion of the fey, it was that they paid attention when the fey were around.

Laura welcomed the interruption. Sitting in her office crafting press releases and talking points for Rhys made her angry. She had become so accustomed to generating whatever spin he wanted on a given topic, she realized she had stopped thinking about the people involved, the real people who would be affected by the things the Guildmaster said and did. Now, with its happening to Cress and Terryn, she remembered, remembered and felt guilty that she had become so indifferent. Bringing in an AWOL fairy was the perfect antidote to her mood.

She parked her SUV amid a sea of Guild and InterSec vehicles in the fire lane in front of the hotel in the southeast section of the city. The location was convenient, convenient being a matter of perspective. The stadium was not far for those who liked sports and an easy walk. The Washington Navy Yard sat to the south, a warren of naval support offices and a museum. The views left a few things to be desired. A view, for one. Parking lots and nondescript office buildings surrounded the hotel.

Inside the lobby, Aran macCullen worked behind the registration desk with a group of Inverni Guardians. They huddled around computer monitors while the hotel staff stood aside, their faces interested or apprehensive. Laura rested her hands on the counter. "That hardly looks subtle out front, Lord Guardian."

He flashed her a smile. "He's in a room in the back, Mariel. Hasn't left since he checked in."

"Is he alone?" she asked.

Aran shook his head. "We think he has a woman in the room. Human. We're clearing the floor of other guests."

"Has he been ordering room service?" she asked.

Aran looked over at one of the hotel staff. "Three, four times a day," said one of the women.

Laura considered the situation as she surveyed the staff Aran had brought with him. The Inverni had a traitor among them. Sean Carr might have fired the gun at Draigen, but another Inverni had killed him, probably to silence him. Even though Rory Dawson was a suspect, any of the Inverni Guardian staff in the lobby could be allied with him or part of a larger conspiracy to assassinate Draigen. After running through all the macCullens' personnel, she recognized people from subclans who reported to each of the macCullen siblings. Not the best way to isolate the problem, but the missing Guardian was being treated as an internal matter for Draigen. Too much conflict of interest for Laura's taste. "I'm going in. I'd like a hotel staff uniform, please," she said.

Aran arched an eyebrow at her. "He's one of my people, Agent Tate. There's no need for you to take an active role."

She leaned in so that no one else could hear her. "Your

people are trained primarily to engage other fairies, Lord Guardian. He won't expect me."

Subtle body movements among the men around Aran indicated he was conferring with them via sendings. Eyes shifted toward Laura and away, not all of them pleased. She decided to make her next comment private. *If he escapes, it will not look good,* she sent.

Brinen is setting me and my people up, Agent Tate. I will not let that happen, he sent.

Your men are on edge and resentful. I'm concerned they might overreact, she sent.

Aran drew down his eyebrows, not happy at her implication. "Fine. You can take the point."

A Guardian gestured to the same woman from the hotel staff to precede him. Laura skirted the counter and joined them in a back room. The woman glanced at her with an appraising look as she sorted through uniforms on a rack. She handed over a maroon tunic. Laura removed the tight black zippered jacket she wore as part of her InterSec uniform. She slipped on the tunic, smoothing it down over her hips. The woman held out a pair of matching pants, but Laura shook her head. "This is as much polyester as I'm going to wear today."

A nervous smile trembled on the woman's lips as she returned the pants. She rummaged in a drawer in a nearby desk and gave Laura a badge that read ROOM SERVICE. Laura pinned it to her chest and met Aran at the elevator.

On the seventh floor, Guardians filled the elevator alcove, out of sight of the main corridor. "We've got troops outside the windows in case he tries to fly out. I want you to go in with two men as backup," Aran said.

"They take orders from me. The civilian's safety gets top priority," she said.

"They'll do their best," Aran said.

She checked the staff position out on the floor. Guardians lined the corridor, giving Dawson's room a wide berth. "Best isn't what I want to hear, Aran. Unless this guy has skills you haven't mentioned, he's not getting out of here with all this security."

Aran set his jaw. "Securing a threat to Draigen must remain our top priority."

Essence sparked in her eyes. "Then we are in agreement. If a human gets injured in this, you'll have a bigger problem than you have right now. Understood?"

Aran narrowed his eyes at her. "Do you speak this way to my brother?"

"Terryn? If necessary, absolutely," she said.

His face became a mask. "Interesting."

She tugged at the ill-fitting tunic. "Let's get this going."

Two Guardians followed her as she pushed a room-service cart down the hall. She stopped in clear view of the fish-eye lens in Dawson's door while the guards hid to either side. When they charged their hands with essence, pale indigo light welling up from their palms, she knocked on the door. "Room service."

Something fell inside the room. A woman laughed, followed by the sound of a deeper voice speaking, obviously annoyed. Laura tensed when the door shifted in its frame as someone leaned against it from inside the room.

"Did you order?" she heard him say. The woman spoke, but her reply was too muffled to hear.

"You freakin' liar. There's a damned cart out there. Don't tell me you didn't order anything. I'm not made of money."

Louder, he spoke through the door. "Must be a mistake. We didn't order."

Laura made a show of checking an order ticket in case he was watching. "No mistake, sir. The orders are logged off the phone system. Room 734. I took the order myself, sir. It was a woman that called."

Dawson yanked open the door. Wrapped in a towel, he reeked of alcohol. He swayed on his feet, eyes bloodshot, hair disheveled. Pinpoints of deep blue light flickering in his indigo wings. "I said we didn't call."

Laura swept her hands up, charging them with essence. "InterSec, stand down."

Confused, Dawson stumbled back toward the frightened woman huddled on the bed. In the room windows beyond her, Guardian agents descended into view. Dawson hurried toward the bed as the windows shattered. Bolts of essence flashed through the room.

Laura rushed in, shouting, "Hold fire! Hold fire!"

Dawson jumped onto the bed and crouched over the woman. A Guardian raised an essence-charged hand. Dawson flung his hand out, feeble sparks of essence flickering blue around his fingers. Laura leaped forward, jabbing her shoulder into the middle of the Guardian's back. His shot went wild as he lurched forward and fell against the foot of the bed. Still in motion, Laura rolled over him and activated her body shields as she landed on the disheveled bedding.

Dawson struggled to his feet, trying to stabilize his essence charge. "Thanks," he said.

Laura grabbed him by the neck and thrust him facedown on the bed. "I'm not your friend, idiot."

She put her foot on his neck as the Guardians jostled for space. The one who had fallen stood, his face angry as he raised his hands, charging up essence. Laura thrust her fist under his chin, bright gold essence light illuminating his skin. "I said hold your fire."

He set his jaw but didn't extinguish his essence. Laura pressed her fist harder, tilting his head back. "Go ahead. Try me."

He glared, dousing his charge. Laura stared down the half dozen guards beyond her extended body shield. Behind her, the woman's sobbing filled the sudden silence.

Aran entered. "Guardians, attend!"

They fell back to the perimeter of the room. Aran flicked his hand, and they exited. Laura lowered her fist and shot a small burst of essence against Dawson's back. The man shuddered once and passed out. His essence didn't match what she'd found in the morgue. He hadn't killed Sean Carr.

Turning her back on Aran, she stepped off the bed and leaned over the sobbing woman. "Are you okay?" She didn't answer. Laura pulled her to her feet. "Come with me. You're safe."

Wrapping her arm around the woman's shoulder, she guided her around the end of the bed. She would turn the woman over to Guild security for protection. The operation had been a waste of time. Dawson was nothing more than a party boy who skipped out on his job. As she passed Aran, she glared at him. "He's not our guy. I'll be talking to Terryn about what happened here."

She left him in the room to clean up the mess.

36

INTERSEC REPORT FILES surrounded Laura in stacks, dozens from the day of the assassination attempt. As she read through each one, the information became embedded in her memory, years of druidic training enhancing her near-photographic memory. At first, reviewing files had been a welcome relief from the fruitless episode at the hotel the day before. After a while, though, the process became mentally taxing. Coupled with her lack of sleep over the recent days, fatigue was starting to take its toll.

She relaxed the mnemonic spell that boosted her memory retention. The information she had absorbed jumbled in her mind. In a day or two, it would settle into more coherent patterns on its own, but she had keyed her thoughts to focus on the events leading up to the finding of Sean Carr's body in the attic. Report after report of the first responders showed a consistent pattern. Every person on the scene described Carr as dead on the floor upon their arrival. She had found no one who had claimed they fired on him nor anyone who mentioned they saw the strike. She surmised either a report was missing or whoever had done the deed hadn't filed one.

She stared at the paperwork. Terryn's sources claimed Draigen remained a target, but nothing in the data identified a source of the danger or the means. Even the time was vague—sometime before she left the States. Gut instinct told Laura the ideal time would be the reception, the only event left on Draigen's public calendar. Her logical reasoning, though, made the reception seem too obvious. Someone planning an attack of this magnitude would know security had been hardened considerably. No, Laura thought, another assassination attempt would come from an unexpected direction, and an internal threat was much more likely.

She paused as a strong wave of body essence filtered up the hall, then relaxed when she realized it was Genda. Even with the ward dampening in the Guildhouse, a Danann fairy stood out. She scanned her desk to confirm there was nothing she didn't want seen.

Genda stopped at the door. She wore a white dress that shifted on subtle currents of essence, small images of orange flowers shimmering on the fabric. "There you are, love. I saw that you checked in. How is everything going?"

Laura glanced down at the folders. "Slow. I'm trying to get a lead on the assassination attempt."

A guilty look mixed with amusement came over Genda. "That's something I wanted to talk to you about. I found something strange."

She handed Laura a sheet of paper. The lists of numbers were similar to series she had seen for bank-transaction routing numbers. "What's this?"

Genda stepped into the office, the guilt slipping away to satisfaction. "It's my nature to look at the financials of everything. When I got the names of the missing Inverni, the first thing I did was pull bank records. Those are tracking numbers for Uma macGrath. I hope I didn't overstep. Terryn used to provide me with data and access. I assumed that I had the authority to do this."

Laura pursed her lips as she reviewed the numbers. Two substantial lump sums had been deposited into macGrath's account—one before and one after the assassination attempt. "You're clear, Genda. We have pretty broad authority to move quickly on things like this."

Relief swept over her face. "Oh, good. I was afraid we might not be able to use this."

Laura considered the numbers. "I'm not surprised she was paid. Sometimes in these situations, the perpetrator is motivated purely for political reasons, but money isn't far behind."

Genda laughed. "Oh, yes, definitely. Money's behind most things. That's what makes it so fascinating." She leaned across Laura's desk and pointed at a few lines of data near the top of the list. "For instance, look at this."

"The first payment went into her account a day earlier, the second the day of the attempt," Laura said.

Genda tapped the paper. "Exactly, love. But no second payment for Carr. He died, obviously, but it's interesting macGrath was paid despite Draigen's survival. Odd, no?"

"That's a good point," Laura said.

"I traced the wires. The payments came from an old Inverni shadow account in Wales. I haven't figured out whose it was yet. There was some activity in the account prior to the payments, likely a transfer from the Caymans. Have you ever been? The water is amazing, but the clubs are filled with thugs in bad casual wear."

Laura shook her head. "No, not in years. Are you suggesting someone in an Inverni clan hired macGrath to assassinate Draigen?"

Genda sighed dramatically, her hands fluttering to her sides. "I don't know what I'm saying. I'm a numbers person. What do you think it means?"

Laura let the paper fall to the desk. "It could be the Alfreys. They've been rivals for centuries from what I understand."

Genda played her hands through her hair. "Oh, that old feud. What a mess. Draigen should marry . . . What's his name—Simon? The son? Seal the breach, as they say."

"He's in prison, Genda. He was the one who orchestrated the Archives attack."

She tapped her temple. "Oh, right, right. I doubt it was them, though. They love Draigen." She glanced toward the door and lowered her voice. "Don't get me wrong, dear, but she's the real sapling from the tree, you know."

Laura tilted her head. "What do you mean?"

Genda glanced at the door again, her face avid. "You're too young to remember. Draigen's the one who convinced her father to challenge the High Queen, and her politics haven't changed much. It's why the Inverni can't get investors like the rest of the Celtic fey can. Too uncertain politically." She shook her head in memory. "What a dashing man Aubry mac-Cullen was. Very astute financially, too. I would have risked a scandal for a night with him, let me tell you."

"Genda!"

She laughed, high and musical. "Oh, come now, Mariel. Clan rivalries are one thing. Romance is another."

Amused, Laura shook her head. "I'll keep that in mind."

"Anyway, my money's on this whole assassination thing being internal politics. Draigen will probably find a way to blame the High Queen, though."

Laura raised an eyebrow. "That sounds like Rhys talking."

She shrugged. "Another brilliant man. Another man I'd"—she laughed self-consciously—"oh, never mind. So, what's the next step with this information?"

"Can you keep trying to track the original source of funds?" Laura asked.

Genda nodded. "Of course. Absolutely. Shall we inform the macCullens?"

"No!" Laura said. She took a deep breath. "I'm sorry. I didn't mean that to come out so loudly. The Inverni Guardians are on edge as it is with the would-be assassin being one of their own people. Let's wait for confirmed information before we give them more to be paranoid about."

Genda nodded vigorously as she moved toward the door. "As you say, then. I'll get right on it."

"Before you go, Genda, I'd like to recommend InterSec provide security for Cress."

She paused in surprise. "The *leanansidhe*? Are you serious?"

Laura spread her hands. "She's one of our own, Genda, regardless. The Guild is not the best security for her under the circumstances. You have to keep in mind our own morale. If we don't protect her, it's going to cause anxiety for every InterSec agent undercover."

Genda frowned. "Surely they don't want to be seen as supporting her?"

"Not her, per se. The organization." Laura hesitated, steeling herself to speak. "If you end up more than acting director, Genda, internal support from rank and file will be invaluable."

As the thought settled in her mind, Genda's face relaxed. "Interesting. I hadn't thought of that."

Feigning indifference, Laura shrugged. "Think about it, then."

Genda winked. "I will."

Laura took a deep breath. The idea that Terryn could lose his position made her almost feel physically ill. That Genda—with no field experience—might replace him made it worse. That she had encouraged that thinking made it awful.

Her phone chirped as soon as Genda left, and Laura checked the text message. Terryn wanted to meet with her and Sinclair later that night at the Guildhouse. She stared at the files. She didn't think the Guildhouse was a good location under the circumstances. She texted Terryn and told him she'd send him a more secure location. Someone in the Inverni entourage wanted Draigen dead. It was too obvious to consider anything else anymore. She was afraid of where it would lead. And what Terryn would do about it.

37
CHAPTER

LAURA WAITED IN the dark of the Holy Rood Cemetery, old granite tombstones pale and silent around her. Terryn had given her the location in a sending, and she passed it on to Sinclair. In the distance, the Washington Monument glowed like a white spike against the deep azure sky. The graveyard had fallen into disrepair long ago, its occupants ancient and forgotten. No living descendants of the interred had visited in decades. Despite its proximity to Logan Circle, the place wasn't high-profile or likely to draw attention. Which was what made it a convenient meeting place.

Sinclair arrived first, his tall silhouette recognizable as he strode up the hill from the street. Laura lingered in the shadows, watching. He avoided direct lighting and, once in the graveyard proper, moved along the darkened perimeter. His casual gait appeared to be that of a someone out for a late-night walk. She knew the moment he sensed her by a subtle shift in the angle of his path.

"You sensed me from a pretty good distance," she said.

He smiled down at her. "Always checking out my abilities, aren't you?"

She pursed her lips in pleasure. "Always questioning my motives, aren't you?"

He playfully flicked a strand of hair off her cheek. "Hey, I'm not complaining. Anytime you want to check out my abilities, you let me know."

She arched an eyebrow. "Oh, we're calling that 'abilities' now?"

He handed her something small, and said, "Skills, then. I brought you something."

Foil wrapping caught the light. "How'd you know I like dark chocolate?"

"I saw the wrapper in your trash the night we had pizza," he said.

She slipped the candy into her mouth. "Thanks."

He snorted. "What? No 'how dare you look in my trash'? Or where else was I snooping?"

She crumpled the wrapper and poked him in the shoulder. "I'm not that bad."

He leaned closer. "You're badder."

She laughed. "You don't give up."

"Are you telling me to?" he asked.

She pursed her lips through a smile. "I'm not telling you anything."

They stood in amused, almost bashful silence. Laura broke eye contact and glanced down toward the street. As she faced him again, he put his hands on her waist and lowered his lips to hers. She closed her eyes. His lips covered hers, a warm, soft pressure that didn't push for more. She returned the kiss, then eased away. She glanced over his shoulder as a faint dark blue spot appeared in the sky. "He's coming."

They watched as Terryn dropped out of the sky, landing effortlessly next to them. Laura felt uneasy as Terryn's gaze shifted back and forth between them, as if he wasn't approving of something. "My apologies for being late. There were some last-minute details on security for Cress."

"No problem. We were necking while we were waiting," Sinclair said.

In the long pause after he spoke, Laura fought feeling self-conscious. Even though by now Terryn knew he said things to provoke reaction, she knew that Terryn wasn't a fool. He had to know she was interested in Sinclair. "Why are we meeting here, Laura?" he asked.

She looked toward downtown. "Privacy. Too many eyes are on you right now, Terryn. From here, I was able to watch if you were followed."

"And why would that be a concern?"

She hesitated. Coming right out and saying what she was thinking was going to be difficult. She decided to avoid it for the moment. "I'm close to accessing the files at Legacy."

Terryn ignored Sinclair. "Is Genda monitoring the case?"

She shook her head. "She thinks I'm closing it down. She wants me to focus on Draigen."

"Has she made any unusual requests?" he asked.

"Not particularly, although she's complained that you don't keep very good files."

Terryn considered. "We need to keep her distracted until I return."

"How's the vacation going?" Sinclair asked.

Terryn's body signature shifted, a flash of essence that Laura knew meant anger. Terryn leveled a cool gaze at Sinclair. "I begin to tire of your disrespect, Sinclair. Don't push me further."

Sinclair slid his hands in his pockets. "Or what? You'll tell Rhys you're doing an end run around the successor he had them pick for you? Or that you've been employing agents off the books? Or that you're running your own op outside channels?"

Terryn stepped toward Sinclair. Sinclair dropped the cocky grin. "Come on, big guy. Take a shot. Just remember, you'll be looking over your shoulder for the rest of your life."

Laura held her hand on Terryn's chest. "He's immortal, Jono."

Sinclair shifted his eyes toward her, then back at Terryn. "Fine. The rest of my life."

"Are you boys done? Because I have work to do," Laura said.

Terryn moved away. "What's your report, Sinclair?"

Sinclair glowered, not speaking. Laura elbowed him gently. "They have a crew doing urban-assault exercises," he said. "There's an old warehouse complex about fifty miles west of the city. They're training us for something but haven't said what."

"How many?" Terryn asked.

"Several dozen. Maybe a hundred people total."

"Fey or human?"

"All human," he said.

"That doesn't make sense," Laura said.

"Bullets work very well against the fey," Terryn said.

She paced in thought. "Even so, they've got to know we're on high alert. If they're planning another assault against Draigen, men with guns against Inverni Guardians is a big tactical disadvantage. We're missing something."

"I agree. The answer might be in the Legacy files. How soon can you acquire them?" Terryn asked.

She had hoped Moor would come through with the information when she calmed down. She hadn't. An idea drifted through her thoughts, one that she had threatened Fallon Moor with. She had bluffed about seducing the information out of DeWinter. It could be a shortcut, one she didn't want to take. She avoided looking at Sinclair, as if he could read her thoughts. "I'll speed up the timetable as best I can."

"My back channels tell me that whatever they're planning, it will happen soon. Draigen's here for a few more days, then we can relax," he said.

Laura snorted. "Yeah, that happens."

Terryn frowned at her. "Don't let Sinclair rub off on you."

"I'll rub whoever I want, thank you," Sinclair said.

She glared at Sinclair, annoyed as much at herself as at him. Terryn was wound tight. It was bad enough she was about to add to it. She didn't want him to think she was being frivolous. She took a deep breath. "Terryn, the real reason I didn't

want to meet at the Guildhouse is because I'm concerned
something's going on with your family."

He arched an eyebrow. "Such as?"

She steeled herself to say what she had been thinking. "A
cover-up, Terryn. Between Brinen seeming to hide something
and Aran letting his people be overly aggressive at the hotel,
it's almost like they don't want to know what happened."

"The Inverni—and my family in particular—can be . . .
protective of their own," he said.

"How much more 'their own' can Draigen be?" she asked.

"It's not a matter of hiding the truth as much as it is keeping it within the clan. Trust me. They are all concerned about
what happened," he said.

"I'm beginning to think they're obstructing the investigation," she said.

He shook his head. "Whatever the disagreements within
my family, Laura, they do not extend to murder."

Sinclair let out a loud sigh. "Makes you rethink that whole
looking at all the angles thing when it strikes close to home,
doesn't it?"

Terryn glared at him. "I don't believe I said I am making an
excuse to dismiss."

Sinclair didn't react. "You're right. There goes my bad
again."

"I think we should rerun background checks on Aran's
staff. Brinen's, too. Aran thinks he's being set up by Brinen,"
Laura said.

"Run the checks. Tell no one. Is there anything else?" Terryn asked.

Laura crossed her arms. "Anything else? For Danu's sake,
Terryn, Cress is under guard, and you've been suspended.
What the hell is going on?"

"It's all part of Rhys's plan to discredit the Inverni cause.
How better to make people suspect our motives than to point
out that the heir to the clan consorts with a demon fey?"

"I'm going to say something to him," she said.

"I think that's a bad idea," said Sinclair.

Laura whirled toward him. "Really? Since you know nothing about Guild politics, why don't you share your wisdom?"

He narrowed his eyes at her. "I'm only pointing out that if Rhys finds out Laura Blackstone works for Terryn and InterSec, it will look like you're a spy. A spy for an Inverni. Which, frankly, you kinda are, now that I think about it."

She flushed with embarrassed. "I'm sorry. That's a good point."

"Apology accepted." Sensing honest truth, she glanced at him. He wasn't being smug, which made her feel worse for snapping at him.

Terryn made her feel worse when he agreed. "It is an excellent point. This will pass, Laura. It's a skirmish in a very old fight."

"But what about Cress? She thinks she's fired."

Terryn sighed. "What's happening to her is unfortunate. She found a place at InterSec once. She'll find another there or somewhere else. Not everyone is as thickheaded as Rhys. We'll get through this, Laura."

She crossed her arms and hugged them to her chest. "I hope so."

"Thank you. For everything, Laura. I mean that," he said. A mauve light swirled through his wings, and he lifted off the ground. He hovered, staring down at Sinclair, making his annoyance obvious. Sinclair waggled his fingers in a sarcastic wave. Terryn's wings blazed brighter, and he flew off.

Laura placed her hands on her hips. "You have got to stop doing that."

Sinclair walked away. "Yeah, I noticed you telling him the same thing."

She strode after him and grabbed his arm. "What's gotten into you, Jono? With everything going on with him, I thought you agreed to lay off?"

He pulled away. "Lay off? What about him, Laura? Poor, poor Terryn, threatened from every side. What about me? I'm being threatened by one person and one person alone: Terryn macCullen. Do you have any idea what it's been like being told that one wrong move, and you're dead? Or being told everyone else's life is more important than yours? And then being told to put your life in danger to prove you are worthy of the great Terryn macCullen's approval? Am I wrong about who I think you are, or are you just not getting it?"

Stunned, she blinked rapidly, letting what he said sink in. The smug looks he had thrown at Terryn were gone, replaced by utter frustration. "I'm sorry," she said.

He thrust his hands up. "Thank you. And I'm sorry if the only recourse I've had from all this is to break his balls, but too damned bad."

He started down the hill, and she hurried to catch up with his long strides. "Jono, you're right. If this is the way you need to handle it, then go ahead. The only thing I ask is that you don't let it get physical."

"I can't promise that," he said.

She tugged at the lapels of his jacket. "He can kill you without breaking a sweat, Jono. Please be careful."

His face softened. "I think you care about me."

She shoved him lightly and danced away. "Yeah, even when you're impossible."

He sauntered after her. "I think I'm entirely possible."

She slipped her hand into his, but he pretended to shake it off in annoyance. She caught it again and laughed as their fingers struggled against each other. They left the cemetery hand in hand until they reached the edge of the pool of light from a streetlamp. Sinclair lifted her hands and kissed them.

"Be careful walking to your car," he said.

She smirked. "Be careful with the urban-assault training."

He chuckled, the deep chest chuckle she no longer denied liking.

38
CHAPTER

I NEED YOU at my apartment immediately.

Terryn's sending hit her so hard, Laura almost lost control of her car as she maneuvered her way the next day through the morning commute. She slammed on the brakes. Horns blared around her as other drivers swerved and passed. She turned on her siren and dashboard lights and hit the gas. Traffic parted in front of her as she tore up Pennsylvania Avenue. Terryn sounded desperate.

What's wrong? she sent.

Cress is gone, he replied.

I'm ten minutes out, she sent.

Law-enforcement vehicles clogged Terryn's street. Laura pulled onto the corner curb and ran; holding her InterSec badge over her head. A police officer—the only person clueless enough to try to stop her—received a shove in his chest that sent him flying against a car.

People clustered on the sidewalk in front of Terryn's building. Genda Boone, of all people, stood at the door, her white wings flailing with agitation as she pointed a finger in a brownie's face. Essence whirled in the air, disturbed flares of red and orange as the fey on the scene exposed their anger. A thick wall of essence, anchored by a brownie standing in front of the building, blocked the street door.

Laura pushed her way through the crowd to Genda's side. "What the hell is going on?"

Angry, Genda turned as if she were about to argue but calmed when she saw Mariel Tate at her side. "That's what I'd like to know. This brownie is anchoring a shield barrier and won't let me through."

Laura craned her neck to see beyond Genda. "Davvi? It's Mariel Tate. I need to get in to see Terryn."

"I've been waiting for you, miss," he said. He held his hand up. Laura hesitated, then realized what he expected her to do. She pressed her palm against his, and the barrier shivered around her. She stepped through to the vestibule.

"Mariel, tell him to let us in. If something has happened in there, I need to know," Genda said.

Ignore her, Terryn sent.

"Let me see what this is about, Genda," she said. To avoid any argument, she entered the building. Inside, an older woman, conservatively dressed, stood at the open door of her apartment. Another shield barrier blocked her from leaving. "Are you the police? What's going on? Why am I not being allowed to leave?"

Mariel glanced up the stairs as she made a calming gesture. "Please stay inside, ma'am, until we clear up the situation."

"Am I in danger?" she asked.

"Please get inside now, ma'am. This will be over shortly," she said.

She mounted the stairs. The barriers were saturated with Terryn's essence. As she reached his floor, she charged her hands until they glowed white. Pausing on the landing, she listened. On the next floor up, someone shouted to be let out. She stepped to the apartment door.

Terryn? she sent.

He opened the door. Fury flowed off him in waves, his wings glowing dark indigo, with shots of white flashing through them. From the main door, the living room, dining room, and kitchen were visible. Everything was immaculate. Puzzled, she took two steps in and stopped. "What happened?"

He shook his head. "InterSec security called me as soon as they got here. She was gone when they arrived."

"What do you mean 'gone'? Guild security was here."

"They weren't here."

She jerked her head up. "What? They were supposed to transition to our team."

"InterSec took over at nine. The Guild left at eight. Brinen coordinated everything with Aran. The Guild insists they had orders to leave at eight, but Aran says that the security order said nine."

"Well, where's the order?" she asked.

Terryn paced into the room. "Aran said it's blank now. Some kind of safety spell erased it. I don't care about that right now. What infuriates me is that the Guild didn't inquire where the InterSec unit was. They left her here alone. They left her here, and she's gone."

The anguish in his voice tugged at her. Seeing Terryn emotional was a rare event. Seeing him distraught was unheard of. She held her hands out. "Okay, let's step through this. This apartment doesn't look tossed. Did you straighten up?"

"Of course not. Everything remains as it was when I arrived. Her keys are on the counter. Her handbag with all her identification is on the bed."

"We need to get a team in here, Terryn," she said.

He paced beside her. "Not yet. I need you to look at it. I don't trust anyone else."

"Is that why you locked the building down?" she asked.

Terryn glanced sharply at her. "Of course."

She stopped his pacing with a hand on his arm. "Terryn, you're technically holding your neighbors hostage. You need to drop those barriers."

"She could be trapped in the building," he said.

She grabbed him by the arms. "Terryn, calm down and listen to me. You know your neighbors. You'll only bring charges down on yourself if you don't release them. If Cress is in the building, we'll find her, but you have to let those people go."

He stared at her, breathing shallowly, then closed his eyes. Tendrils of blue essence whirled out of him, danced to the floor and out to the hallway. Several doors slammed and footsteps could be heard running. "I've modified the shield so that they can leave through the front door. No one gets in yet."

She was about to argue but decided that was good enough for the moment. "Let me see the bedroom."

He led her through the living room. She had been to dinner at the apartment but had never seen the bedroom. The riot of color on the walls, swirls of red and yellow and orange, surprised her. Every available surface—dresser tops, the headboard, windowsills—was covered with odds and ends—small dolls, teacups, a collection of fabric tassels over the windows, and stacks and stacks of magazines. The contrast to either of their organized offices was startling. As if seeing the room through her eyes, Terryn smiled nervously. "She likes to collect things."

The *leanansidhe* were hoarders, most often of their victims' belongings. Cress might not have acquired her treasures through the same path, but she obviously still had the impulse. Despite all the clutter, the room did not look ransacked.

"I'm getting faint human body signatures in here," she said.

"Human? No humans have been here," he said.

She sharpened her sensing ability. Except near the door, the room read blank, as if all the essence—including the normal ambient residue of a fey dwelling—had been drained from it. A chill went over Laura. "She used her abilities in here, Terryn. For some reason, she absorbed all the essence in the room."

"But she didn't need any. She . . . I give her essence every morning," he said.

Laura averted her gaze from his discomfort at the admission. The nature of their relationship intrigued her. She knew that Cress absorbed essence from Terryn. Cress had done the same thing to her recently. Even though it was to save her life, Laura shivered at the memory. A hunger had lurked behind Cress's touch that had filled her with revulsion.

"Then why would she . . ." Laura stopped and faced the door. A faint pattern of purple essence splattered across the wall by the door. "She fired essence, Terryn. She fired at someone in this doorway."

She stepped closer. "It's so faint, though, as if it was re-absorbed again." She looked at the bed. "But it didn't go back into the room."

She circled the bed, assessing the edges of the essence void. A faint, sickly sweet odor filled her nostrils. "I smell chloroform."

"She was drugged?"

Laura bent closer to the bed. "Looks that way. Someone figured out how to subdue her long enough to use chloroform. I'm not sensing any other essence discharge here."

He narrowed his eyes. "She's alive, then. They wouldn't have gone to all that trouble if they were going to kill her."

Laura examined the area where she smelled the chloroform, but, again, nothing seemed out of place. Her gaze fell to the nearby dresser, covered with stacks of playing cards, and she noticed that while the top surface hadn't been cleaned recently, there were clear spaces in the dust. The spaces caught her eye because they were in distinct stripes, not scattered as if being touched with hands. Visually following the clean lines, she noted several cards had rippled areas. She touched one. "This is damp."

She ran her hand over the quilted bedcover. "More dampness. They stunned her, Terryn. That would be the only explanation. They used a liquid stun gun. Someone tried it on her a few days ago."

"What are you talking about?" Terryn asked.

She compressed her lips. "She thought it was a mugging, but I think it was a failed kidnapping. She didn't want you to worry."

"Worry? Why not? I might have been able to prevent this if she had said something," he said.

Laura gave him a stern look. "No, you couldn't have. We had Guild and InterSec security here, Terryn. They screwed up, but you wouldn't have protected her any better."

"I could have stayed with her . . ." he began.

"Which is exactly why she didn't tell you. She didn't want to disrupt Draigen's visit over a mugging. And at the time, that's what it looked like."

He tried to keep himself under control. "And now she's gone."

"Why would anyone want to kidnap Cress?"

Stricken, Terryn met her gaze. "Because she's dangerous, Laura."

"Terryn, I'm not going to hear . . ."

He held his hand up. "Listen to me. I know what she is. So does she. A *leanansidhe* is dangerous. The only thing that has helped Cress maintain any sense of normalcy is a constant source of essence. Without that . . . without me . . . she's going to become desperate to fill that need. Someone can use that to their advantage. There've been attempts before."

Laura swallowed in a dry throat. The last thing she expected was for Terryn to admit Cress was dangerous. "How much time does she have?"

He ran a frustrated hand into his hair. "If she discharged everything, less than a day. We tried fewer booster sessions, but it didn't work. Without a daily supply of essence, she's going to revert."

Tears edged into his eyes. "We have to find her, Laura, before she kills someone."

39
CHAPTER

AS THE LEGACY offices emptied at the end of the day, Laura allowed herself to relax. Fewer people meant less risk of exposure. Between researching the computer systems and impersonating Fallon Moor, she was mentally tired. Beyond the standard anti-fey rhetoric, she wasn't seeing anything she hadn't seen in other places. The attacks on fey businesses were an obvious concern, but at best those had a tenuous connection to Legacy. Sinclair was having better luck turning up names of the direct perpetrators, if not the planners.

She distracted herself for another thirty minutes by checking InterSec and Guild bulletins. It wasn't much of a distraction. Still no leads on Cress. She put her PDA in her purse and went to the door. She hadn't discovered any essence-dampening wards in the building, but it was possible she might have missed them. A physical check of the hallway confirmed no one nearby. With a casual gait, she moved from empty office to empty office until she reached DeWinter's closed door. She knocked and, as expected, no one answered. With the duplicate keycard, she swiped through the electronic lock and punched in the password. The light on the console turned green.

Inside DeWinter's office, she quick-stepped to the desk and inserted a USB drive into the computer. The keystroke program downloaded to a reviewing pane. She scrolled through the text, skimming for isolated entries until she found entry points to the locked network drive. Finding the password access was a simple matter of backtracking through the text. With a few keystrokes, she scrubbed any trace of the tracking program and accessed the locked directory. The password worked. The screen filled with the file list.

Relieved, she sorted the data to the most recent viewed and started the file download. She checked her watch. Fifteen minutes had passed, longer than she had wanted to be there. File after file copied with frustrating slowness. Another five minutes, and she decided to get out. She paused the copy mode, checked that no trace of her presence remained, and pulled the drive.

She froze as the lock on the door clicked. She glanced around the space for a place to hide, but the stark furniture offered nothing. As the door opened, she strolled unconcerned toward the windows. She turned with a smile that she dropped when she saw a security guard. She had seen him in the building garage with Sinclair. "Oh, I thought you were Adam. Mr. DeWinter."

The guard eyed her neutrally. "Can I ask what you're doing here?"

She frowned as if it was a stupid question. "Waiting for Mr. DeWinter. Is there a problem?"

Without moving, the guard examined the room. "Mr. DeWinter is gone for the day. Mr. DeWinter has orders that no one should be here when he's out. You need to come with me."

Laura walked toward him. "Fine. I was waiting for him. He said he'd be here."

He let her pass into the hall. As she returned to her office, he kept pace a few feet behind her. She sat at her desk. The guard waited at the door. "Is there something else?" she asked.

"You need to come down to security," he said.

"Why?"

"We need to take a report," he said.

She flashed him an annoyed frown. "So go make your report."

He set his jaw. "I'm afraid I'll have to insist."

She released some essence into the Moor template and triggered the boggie characteristics. "And I'll have to insist I'm not going anywhere. I'm having dinner with Adam DeWinter shortly."

The guard stepped in. "It will only take a minute, miss . . ."

She glared as she rose to her feet. "Do you know who I am?"

He hesitated. "Yes, ma'am. Fallon Moor."

She boosted the essence light in her eyes. "Right. A very annoyed Fallon Moor. You have three seconds to get out of my office before I throw you out. Go make your report. I'll be sure to give Mr. DeWinter my own."

"Ma'am . . ." the guard began.

Laura cursed to herself as DeWinter appeared behind him. "What seems to be the problem, Stuart?"

The guard backed down, his expression becoming subservient. "I found Ms. Moor in your office, sir. I was asking her to come help make a report."

DeWinter smiled at Laura. "I'll take care of it. There's no need to make a formal report."

Laura relaxed the boggart aspect as the guard left. She sat with a loud exhale. "Thank you. That was ridiculous."

As DeWinter strolled toward her, she pretended to type an email. "I thought you had an errand?"

She didn't look up. "It took less time than I thought, so I came back here to finish a couple of things."

"In my office?"

She smiled. "We did leave something undone earlier."

He chuckled. "How did you get in?"

She rolled her eyes dismissively. "I wasn't *in* your office, Adam. I was *at* your office checking to see if you were still here. Your friend Stuart is a little overzealous." She could afford the lie. She had what she wanted and had no intention of returning to Legacy.

Suspicion rolled off him as she gathered her things. "Are you ready to go?"

Feigning surprise, she slipped her pocketbook over her shoulder. "Now? I thought we didn't have reservations for an hour?"

He shrugged. "It won't be a problem."

The thumb drive was hidden in her bra, usually a secure place, but with the way she had been teasing DeWinter, that wasn't a given. Hiding it in the office or somewhere else in the building wasn't an option. She didn't want to return to the building after tonight. She decided to play out the situation on the fly. "Great. I'll get my car and meet you around front."

He slipped his hand through her arm. "That won't be necessary. I'll get us a driver."

She smiled through gritted teeth as he flipped open his phone. "That's fine."

"This is Adam DeWinter. Is Burrell on duty?" he said into the phone. He glanced at her and wrinkled his nose affectionately. "Good. Tell him to bring the limo around."

Laura forced a smile. However the evening was going to play out, at least she had Sinclair as undercover backup. "Sounds like we're off," she said.

40
CHAPTER

THE MOMENT SHE walked into the restaurant, Laura knew that Fallon Moor had been there before. The host greeted her by name, and several other staffers offered professional smiles as they passed. Being alert around DeWinter was a given, but now she had to contend with a roomful of people, too.

As they settled in at their table, a waiter poured water. No one spoke during the brief seating ritual as both Laura and DeWinter surveyed the room with vague smiles. She chuckled.

"What?" he asked.

She flipped open the wine menu. "Nothing, really. I was noticing how we both checked out the room with a fake look of enjoyment on our faces in case someone was looking at us looking."

"You're not enjoying yourself?" he asked.

She didn't look up. "That's not what I said, Adam." She put a dismissive, unconcerned tone in her voice. On cue, he chuckled, too. She allowed herself a smile. If there was one thing she had figured out—without Fallon Moor's help—it was that Adam DeWinter liked to play verbal games and did not like a woman who rushed to explain herself. "What about a bottle of the Bogle cabernet with dinner?"

"I didn't know you liked wine," he said.

She laid the wine list down and picked up the dinner menu as another waiter arrived. "We can do shots before dinner if you like."

"The usual, ma'am?" he said.

She grinned up at him. "Of course."

She leaned on her elbows and peered over DeWinter's menu. "What are you having?"

He handed her the menu. "I can't decide. You pick."

She took his menu and scanned the list again. She suspected he was testing her. "What did you have for lunch?"

"Something chicken."

She gave herself a moment to recall the personality profile InterSec had on DeWinter. "The osso bucco. The wine will go nicely with it. They can swap out the salad dressing for something without nuts."

He blinked, still smiling. "When did I mention I didn't eat nuts?"

He had an allergy to nuts according to the profile. She feigned mild irritation. "I've never seen you eat them. I assumed you were allergic."

The waiter returned and served two glasses of whiskey. Laura put in the dinner order for both of them, and the waiter left a bottle of Bushmills on the table.

DeWinter held his glass out. "To the endgame."

Laura hesitated, then toasted. "To success."

"You don't like my toast?" he asked.

She flipped her hair back on one side. "It's not the endgame, is it? It's a step."

DeWinter played with his glass, rolling the bottom edge in a circle on the tablecloth. "You've been acting strange."

She hid her apprehension at the remark by sipping the whiskey. "More than usual?"

He pursed his lips. "How much of that is you and how much is an act?"

"I am exactly what you see," she said.

DeWinter snorted. "Now, that I don't believe."

She lowered her brow to appear concerned. "Something's gnawing at you, Adam. I'm not sure I want to keep dancing like this."

She also wasn't sure if she was pushing something in a direction she didn't want to go. For whatever reason, DeWinter was acting suspicious of her. Her impersonation of Moor on such short notice wasn't the best persona she had ever devised. It had worked so far, but that was because she avoided conversation as much as possible.

DeWinter shrugged. "You haven't been around much lately. It makes me wonder about your commitment."

She narrowed her eyes at him. "Really? After everything I've done, you wonder about my commitment?"

He raised an eyebrow at her. "Tell me about Dublin . . . Allison."

She didn't panic that he had exposed Fallon Moor's past. Given his former life in the CIA, DeWinter's digging into the background of one of his key players didn't surprise her. What she didn't know was if Moor had discussed it with him. She decided to be flip instead of annoyed. "It's the capital of Ireland."

He maintained a pleasant expression, but she noticed a tightening of his jaw. "That's the kind of thing I'm talking about. I understand why you didn't tell me your real name. What I don't understand is why you've become cryptic around me."

She sighed and leaned forward. "Adam, you know how this works. Whatever you know about Dublin is what you know. I've shared what I want to share. If you expect me to confirm or deny things you suspect about me, then someone's going to be asking about twelve million dollars. Do you want to go there with me? I have nothing to hide."

He waited while the waiter placed salads in front each of them. "I needed the money because I saw an opportunity to increase the chances of success with our acquisition," he said.

All that told her was what she had already assumed. DeWinter had bribed someone to do something. He still wasn't tipping what it was for. "The airport bombing was an accident," she said. "The bombs were supposed to end up on planes, but one went off prematurely. I got out in the confusion."

Quid pro quo. Except for the bit about the accident, everything else she said was known to security-industry insiders, and DeWinter had more than a few of them as contacts.

"This isn't what I wanted to talk about," he said.

Laura picked at her salad. "How about lost rocket launchers?"

"Fallon . . ."

"Yes?" She made a show of continuing to eat.

DeWinter lowered his gaze and toyed with his fork. "We haven't been together in over a week."

The comment surprised her. Despite finding out her real identity, DeWinter's real issue was personal. Laura reached forward and caressed his hand. "I'm sorry, Adam. I completely misread what you meant."

He shrugged and smiled. "I was having fun. I thought you were, too."

She grasped his hand. "I was. Am. It's just . . . things have been busy. When things get like this, I prefer to"—she tickled his palm—"heighten the anticipation."

"It's heightened," he said.

She finished her whiskey with a slow slide of her tongue across her lips. "Well, I've accomplished one goal at least."

"Seriously, though, where have you been?" he asked.

She refilled their glasses. Moor liked her whiskey, though Laura didn't care much for it. "Without going into details, I've been putting some plans into place for after . . . ours."

His smile was patient. "We have the same goals, Fallon. I would hope by now you trusted me."

She pursed her lips. Moor continued to refuse to give any more details about her relationship with DeWinter. Laura couldn't be sure if he was baiting her or not. His voice held tones of subterfuge, but that was as much a factor of his cryptic manner of speaking as it was truthfulness. She couldn't risk assuming Moor had told him more about herself and her plans than he was letting on. "Not all our goals are the same, though, are they?"

"I would think taking down the monarchy was a big enough goal for anyone," he said.

This conversation she knew how to have. She had been among antigovernment people in one form or another for most of her career. "What happens to the fey after the monarchy is gone? Not everyone agrees with us, Adam. Even if—when—we succeed, democracy isn't going to break out. There will still be a lot of work to do."

"I might be able to help with that," he said.

She shrugged in a thoughtful manner. "I guess what I'm saying is that even now our goals aren't precisely the same. You want to prevent the monarchy from expanding and infiltrating your government. I'm already living your fear. Eliminating the monarchy solves both our problems, but they're not the same problems."

"Maybe that's when we leave things to someone else," he said.

He surprised her. She felt a sense of honesty in what he said. Moor's silence about him and hearing him talk about her like this made her wonder if they had true feelings for each other and not a relationship of opportunity and convenience. The idea gave her pause, as much for the unexpectedness of it as her cynicism that hadn't even considered it. "And then what? We retire to a nice cottage with a picket fence? We're not the type, Adam."

Still pleasant, he looked resigned. "Why don't we talk about this when the operation is over?"

She slipped a gentle smile over her face and held up her glass. "Let's make a date."

He raised his glass. "Next Tuesday. No excuses. That will give everything a chance to cool down, and we can talk about other things."

She tapped his glass. "Tuesday it is, then."

She leaned back as the waiter arrived with their dinners. At least she had managed to get a time frame out of him. Whatever Legacy was planning would be executed in the next few days. Maybe Terryn was right, and it was about Draigen, who would be gone in the same time frame. Even so, she wanted harder confirmation than intuition. The data drive waited in her bra. With any luck, she would piece together what the plan was and end it before it began.

41
CHAPTER

THE HIGHWAY CURVED around the Pentagon, the Capitol Building rising above the skyline behind it. Laura loved Washington at night. During the day, its iconic buildings had a stiff, formal look of history made. At night, lighting made those same buildings appear dramatic, as if the true work of the government were happening. She spent a lot of time in those offices, but it was in the restaurants and bars and private parties, or, in this case, a limo, that the real work was done. Having dinner with DeWinter was more work than stealing the data. It was almost over. In a few minutes, Sinclair would stop the limo in front of Fallon Moor's apartment, and she would disappear from DeWinter's life.

"You've done phenomenal work, Fallon," DeWinter said.

She lowered her eyes and smiled modestly as she stared at the amber fluid in her glass. "Thanks. It's been a challenge."

She settled herself more comfortably in the darkened limo. The soft red fabric of her dress rode across her lap, exposing her thigh through the short slit on the side of the dress. She crossed her legs, her rising knee catching DeWinter's eye. Placing his hand on her bare skin, he leaned forward to retrieve a decanter from the bar. Laura held her crystal glass steady as he refilled it. Returning the decanter, he settled back, his hand remaining on her thigh.

Dinner had gone more smoothly than Laura anticipated. She had maintained subtle control of the conversation, poking around in his knowledge of Fallon Moor's life. She had made up stories to fit time periods in Moor's life he apparently didn't know about. For all the heated looks and promises of better times the last few days, DeWinter didn't appear to know Moor that well at all.

DeWinter trailed his fingers up and down her thigh, a bemused expression on his face. "Why don't you come work for me full-time? I can make it very attractive."

Laura glanced through the glass panel separating them from the front seat. As if sensing it, which she doubted, Sinclair's eyes flicked to the rearview mirror. Sinclair had hidden any surprise that she had walked out of the Legacy building with DeWinter. He was handling undercover well, though she knew he would complain later about sitting in the car while she had an expensive dinner.

She smiled into her glass. "It's tempting, but I like being free to make my own decisions."

DeWinter shifted his position, one hand on her knee, the other draped along the back of the seat. "You know, as I watched you work, I became fascinated with you."

"I'm flattered," she said with as much meaning as she could muster. DeWinter didn't impress her as much as he impressed himself. He was like so many men who confused money with invincibility. She sensed a warping in his faint human essence that meant he carried a gun. DeWinter was the type who thought he could handle anything thrown at him, so he didn't bother with an entourage or bodyguards. His most visible trappings of wealth were the clothes he wore and the limo service. His CIA service had been administrative. He had probably never fired a gun outside the practice range.

"You know, the article was perfect bait," DeWinter said.

She chuckled. "Bait?"

He nuzzled her ear. "The article in the *Financial Times*. The one discussing polling algorithms that tested global time differences. I found it incredibly timely considering my team was looking into the issue."

She knew the article. It had been in Fallon Moor's file. The brownie had written it before being hired by Legacy. Now Laura realized that was how Moor had ended up at Legacy. She let them think they wanted her, not the other way around. "Timing is everything, Adam. I'm glad I could help."

She leaned forward to retrieve a napkin from the bar setup, forcing DeWinter to remove his hand from her neck. Though she had done such things in the past, romancing him was not going to be a part of the evening no matter what Moor's relationship with him was. The job was over.

She avoided looking at Sinclair. Wherever their relationship was going, it would be going nowhere if she got physical with him watching. She had what InterSec needed. She didn't need DeWinter anymore. Saying no and getting out of the car at the apartment were going to be simple.

"Who do you work for?" he asked.

She feigned confusion, but she didn't like the question. "What do you mean?"

DeWinter's hand slid farther up her thigh. "FBI? InterSec? MI6?"

Sipping her drink, she laughed. "What in the world are you talking about? I think my politics answer for themselves, Adam."

He moved in on her ear again. "Don't take me for a fool, Fallon. I fell for the article, true. Did you think I would let you into our systems unattended? We found the tracking program."

Annoyed, she pursed her lips while he kissed the side of her neck. She had some skill, but the planted software had come from InterSec. Someone was going to get a good reprimand for sloppy work when she returned to the office.

Get ready, Jono. My cover's blown, she sent. Sinclair's gaze wandered to the rearview mirror.

Still, she held out a hope of getting out of the situation unexposed. She sighed. "I'm sorry, Adam. I lied. We thought you might be working for someone else."

He chuckled deep in his throat and pulled back to look at her. "We? That's interesting. Who's 'we,' and why did you need to steal data you had access to?"

Laura compressed her lips. She was going to give the tech team high hell for this. "I didn't steal any data, Adam. I don't understand what you're talking about."

DeWinter continued caressing her. He moved his hand higher, his fingers slipping under the edge of her underwear. "Where's the data drive, Fallon? Did you hide it somewhere you thought I'd never see again?"

She had passed the data drive to Sinclair when he helped her into the car earlier. She didn't know whether to laugh or punch DeWinter. She had no idea where he thought the situation was going. He clearly had no idea she was a druid, never mind his marked indifference to the possibility of her going boggie. Maybe he liked it rough. His hand slid under the fabric of her panties and tickled the front of her hip.

Brace yourself, Sinclair sent.

"What?" she said aloud, startled.

"I said . . ." DeWinter began.

Laura grabbed the door and lurched forward as Sinclair slammed on the brakes. DeWinter flew across the floor and hit the front seat. She called up essence and shot DeWinter in the head before he could recover.

Laura frowned as she got out of the car. "I had the situation under control, Jono."

Sinclair jumped out and peered in the back. "Is he dead?"

"No. I stunned him. What the hell did you hit the brakes for?"

"You looked like you needed help," he said.

She glowered. "Really? Or did it look like someone was

going for my crotch, and you couldn't deal with it? Get this through your head, Sinclair. If we're going to work together, you have to keep your head clear. I am not your damsel in distress."

He grinned. "You're wearing a short skirt and fuck-me pumps. That's damsel wear."

She jabbed him in the chest. "Try femme fatale, you idiot. I've been doing this a lot longer than you have."

He affected surprise. "You speak French, too?"

She rolled her eyes but allowed herself a smile. For some reason, despite calling him on it, he amused her. They stared down at the unconscious DeWinter.

"Now what do we do?" Sinclair asked.

Laura scanned the interior of the car. DeWinter had fallen facedown. Her glass lay on the floor next to him. "Let's keep you in as long as possible. I don't think DeWinter saw me hit him with essence. When he wakes up, tell him something ran in front of the car, and he must have hit his head when you braked. Then tell him I jumped out and ran off."

Sinclair looked dubious. "You think he'll believe that?"

She withdrew from the car. "Play dumb and embarrassed. If he shoots you before you get him home, it'll mean it didn't work."

He raised his eyebrows. "That's reassuring."

She grinned. "Having second thoughts about the job?"

He let the smile slip back on his face. "Not when I get to see you dressed like that."

She held out her hand. "I'll take the data drive back."

He handed it to her, and she slipped it inside her bra again. She leaned forward and pecked him on the cheek. Turning, she walked toward the nearby highway ramp. "Good luck."

"What the hell are you doing?" he called out.

She walked backward. "I'm going to the Guildhouse."

"On foot?"

She shrugged. "It's a nice night. I'll see you at the office. I hope."

He grinned again. "You're crazy, you know."

She pointed at the car. "Keep your eyes in the rearview mirror."

DeWinter wasn't going to shoot Sinclair. For all his swagger, she doubted he had ever been in a physical fight. It was all show, including the gun. He would wake up embarrassed, probably angry, with a nice headache for his trouble.

She withdrew the glamour essence from the stone around her neck. The wispy blond brownie hair faded to her natural softer hue as Fallon's image faded. Her red dress felt shorter now that she had resumed her normal appearance. She felt mildly ridiculous walking down a highway ramp dressed so provocatively, but she had been in worse places with less clothing. When she reached the end of the ramp, she smirked as she pulled out her cell phone and hit speed dial, wondering if Sinclair believed she was going to walk all the way to the Guildhouse.

"This is Laura Blackstone. I need a car, please."

42
CHAPTER

AN HOUR LATER, Sinclair entered Laura's InterSec office and dropped in a chair. He still wore the suit he used for driving the limo. Laura didn't visibly react to his presence as she reviewed DeWinter's files, taking his arrival as a nonevent. "Oh, good. He didn't shoot you," she said.

"Nice to see you, too," he said with a smile.

She leaned back with a chuckle. "I told you it would be fine. What happened?"

He shrugged. "A lot of screaming and swearing. He bought my story. He didn't seem surprised. Fallon Moor apparently has a reputation for being erratic."

"Yeah, well, I played into that the last couple of days."

Sinclair gave her a measured look, one that told her he wanted to know what she meant. She wanted to clarify for him on the one hand that nothing serious happened but on the other hand disliked feeling answerable to him. The pause in conversation lengthened. He didn't say she was answerable. She realized she wanted to tell him, but that didn't mean she had to. Things were too new between them to expose every detail of her life. "Let me show you what I've found so far," she said instead.

The tension broke, and he leaned forward as she turned to her computer. She flashed one document after another onto the screen. "More financial data. More anti-fey rhetoric, and these . . ."

"Blueprints?" Sinclair asked.

She tilted her head from side to side as she looked at the screen. "But of what buildings, I can't tell. I've been in most of the major terrorist targets in the city. I'm not recognizing anything here. This one looks like a lab." She zoomed in on the document.

The page showed a simple building layout. The first floor showed room after room of the same size, plumbing run into all of them for wash stations and complicated tangles of electrical and gas lines. "It looks hardened against the fey," he said.

"What do you mean?"

Sinclair pointed at the blueprint of the basement—no windows, limited access points, fewer but larger rooms with electronic security systems on the doors. "Look at this section. These rooms are lined with glass and stone. Remind you of anything?"

"Holding cells," she said.

He leaned back with a satisfied expression. "Yeah, I've probably had more experience with those lately than you have."

She smiled grudgingly. Terryn had been quick to hold Sinclair in a cell when they met. "I'm not going to argue that. I think you're right. Good call."

She stared at the blueprints, trying to resolve them into something she recognized. "Could be Quantico or Stafford. I haven't been everywhere in either place. Look at this part. It looks like a medical facility."

A large room held an oblong shape that the notes identified as quartz. Smaller round shapes ringed the oblong in a border. "That sort of looks like a healing crèche," she said.

On the rare occasion when the fey fell ill, essence formed a major component of the healing process. The crèche had been developed, stone beds that could be charged to supplement weakened body signatures as well as deliver targeted healing spells. "It's a lot bigger than the ones I've seen," said Sinclair.

Puzzled, Laura shook her head. He was right. Most crèches were not much larger than a standard hospital bed. "Maybe I'm wrong. It struck me as one."

"So, let's play it out. Why would a crèche be that big?" he asked.

"Maybe for someone gravely ill. The more stone you have, the greater the holding capacity for the essence. Maybe whoever it's for is suffering from some kind of severe essence depletion and needs a large field to supplement it."

"There's room in that thing for a couple of people," he said.

She gave him a significant look. "Or one very powerful one."

He pursed his lips. "Draigen? I thought we hadn't found any firm connection between Legacy and the threats against her."

"Not yet, but under the circumstances, I'm not ruling it out until Draigen leaves the country."

"But why a medical facility? She's not ill," he said.

She stared at the blueprint. The crèche had several kinds of quartz, not that unusual when treating an injured fey. Different stones had different properties, and sometimes it was necessary to create buffers between them to prevent interference. Suppressing essence was another form of healing, too. That thought sparked an idea. "What if it's not for healing but modified as a holding cell? We use ward stones all the time in holding cells to prevent someone from using essence to escape."

"You think they're planning on kidnapping her instead of killing her?"

Laura rubbed at her eyes. "I don't know. DeWinter talked about an acquisition, but, as much as I'm worried about it,

Draigen's being the target bothers me, especially after the assassination attempt. She's so high-profile and secured, you'd have to be a genius or a nut to think you could take her out at this point."

Sinclair snorted. "I vote nut. Isn't that the defining characteristic of a terrorist?"

She leaned against her hand and closed her eyes. "Yeah, you're right. I'm so tired I'm not thinking clearly." She stretched. "Let's make copies of this. I'll get the research guys to take a look at it. Can you make a meeting in the morning?"

"I have some kind of training at Legacy tomorrow. No can miss," he said.

She wasn't about to press him on it. He was doing his part. She knew what it was like to get pulled in more than one direction. "That's okay. You need to keep a lower profile around here anyway, Jono. Someone's bound to notice a mysterious tall guy who keeps showing up."

"Now let's get out of here. We both need to get to bed."

His face brightened. "Did you just ask me to go to bed with you again?"

She gave him a long, slow smile as she came around the desk. Bracing her hands on the chair, she leaned down with closed eyes and kissed him on the lips. She opened her eyes, smiling inches away from his face.

"No, I didn't. Work first. Play later," she said.

Sinclair dropped his head back and laughed. "Evil. Pure evil."

43
CHAPTER

AS SHE STEPPED out of her SUV, Laura made no effort to hide her annoyance as she adjusted the jacket on her uniform. It was bad enough that the emergency call had come in as soon as she had gone home to bed after leaving the Guildhouse, but Genda didn't know that an open call to a crime scene was heard by everyone in the city with a gun and a badge. Emergency vehicles and police cars from a number of agencies filled the edge of the park. If Genda had been more low-key, they would have been able to contain notice to the local police and the Guild's Community Liaison department. Factor in the high-profile players in a town like Washington, and more obscure agencies turned out. Some came out of curiosity or political advantage, but most came for the adrenaline rush of being on scene for a crime with international ramifications.

Walking through a gauntlet of law-enforcement personnel, she held out her InterSec badge. They spent their few moments with her staring at her face. The extra care she had given to making Mariel Tate physically attractive paid off in chaotic situations. No one liked to admit it, but something clicked off in people's brains around good-looking people. They trusted them more, liked them more, and believed them more. And let them slide through security without much scrutiny if they flashed a badge.

As she entered the grassy area of the scene, she noted that at least someone had had the common sense to isolate the area around the body. A local police officer lifted a long strip of crime-scene tape to let her pass. Up a short rise, people gathered near the edge of a stand of trees. Out of habit, Laura scanned the ground as she approached. The area hadn't been processed. Someone could have gone across the same grass she was walking on and left a hint of their identity, but she saw nothing out of the ordinary.

Guild security agents and Inverni Guardians stood on opposite sides of another taped-off area. A few human officers hovered on the edges of the group, impotent in jurisdiction against all the high-level agencies on the ground. She made casual note of Sinclair's presence. He wore his InterSec jacket, the hood pulled up and forward to shadow his face. His height might draw attention, but in a group of fey, that was less likely.

Brinen macCullen crouched by the body of a female Inverni. Alive, fairies resonated with power, their bodies naturally cycling essence out of the air. The energy was always there, to the point where Laura didn't notice it any more than she would the fact that someone was breathing. Part of being in the presence of a fairy. Dead, that process stopped, leaving the body a shadow of itself, the lack of intense body signature an oddity that was noticeable by its absence.

The woman hadn't been dead long. Even without sensing her fading essence, Laura knew by the lifeless drape of her wings that death had been within the last few hours. So soft and supple in life, the gossamer appendages shriveled and hardened in death, wrapping the body like a shroud. The woman's wings lay against the ground, dark but not yet curling.

With one hand, Brinen stroked in the air above the body, shy of physically touching. A faint pool of blue light enveloped his fingers. His attention remained on the body as Laura crouched next to him. "I heard about the hotel. Here to threaten more of our people, Agent Tate?"

She kept her voice cool. "Only the ones who don't follow orders, Lord Guardian. Who called it in?"

"A human walking his dog," he said.

Laura spotted a casually dressed older gentleman speaking to a Guild security agent. A small dog on a leash danced around them, excited by all the activity.

Brinen dangled his hands between his knees. "Essence shock."

Odd, Laura thought. Taking out an Inverni fairy in a fight wasn't easy, and the sustained burst necessary for essence shock was difficult to maintain on a moving target. She played the beam of her flashlight over the woman's body. Dark lines crisscrossed her clothing on the sleeves and pants. Burns, the familiar pattern left when someone struggled against a binding spell. Whoever had killed her had bound her before she died. That took ability and power.

Laura recognized the woman's body signature from the attic where the sniper had fired. She sensed Brinen's signature, too, from the residue of his scan. Other signatures were whispers on her, which meant she had had only casual contact. They had their second suspect, which meant two dead ends. Literally.

"Uma macGrath?" Laura asked.

"She was on Draigen's staff," said Aran.

She pivoted to see Aran standing at the edge of her sensing range. She hadn't noticed him arrive. "You knew her?"

Aran moved closed, his face troubled and angry. "She was the missing guard from your interview list. She and Sean Carr were lovers. It was an open secret."

Annoyed, Laura stood. "Why didn't you mention that earlier? We wasted manpower looking for two people when she was the obvious suspect."

"I didn't know. No one told me the other name until after Rory Dawson was caught."

She glanced at Brinen, who remained intent on the body. For all his attitude, he wasn't as thorough as he liked to imply. She sighed. "What's done is done. There's no telling if we would have found her sooner anyway."

Brinen joined them. "I suggest we start interviewing their associates."

Aran cocked his head. "I was under the impression Agent Tate had done that already."

Brinen glowered at his brother. "Yes, but two people from the same subclan bear investigating. We should check their bloodlines as well as their colleagues."

Color rose in Aran's cheeks. He stalked away. Laura noticed that Brinen didn't appear fazed. "What was that about?" she asked.

"An old family disagreement," he said. Without another word, he walked off, too.

Sinclair sidled in closer. "Looks like the macCullens aren't as chummy as they appear."

For once, Laura didn't bristle at one of Sinclair's digs. He was right. Friction among the siblings was apparent. Still, there was enough stress going on to trigger it.

"Did you notice the burns?" he asked.

"Yes."

"She was silenced," he said.

"Someone has a lot to lose," Laura said.

"Like an underKing's realm?"

She compressed her lips. "I don't think Terryn had anything to do with this."

Sinclair shrugged. "I'm looking at all contingencies until they're discredited. Someone told me that's the way we do things at InterSec."

"I trust him, Jono," she said.

"This is older than us, Cuddles. It has nothing to do with you," he said.

They waited as the medical examiner staff gathered around the body. Laura couldn't dismiss what Sinclair said. When Terryn had realized that the Treaty of London made his people an internal class of enemies, he had reacted like a different person, not the man she knew. Whatever was at stake, it was more than the murder of two renegade Inverni.

"I hate fairy politics," she said.

Sinclair murmured agreement. "Now you know why I pretend I'm human."

44
CHAPTER

DAWN BROUGHT LAURA back to her public-relations desk. In the last few days, the Guild work had grown to beyond neglect. Rhys was writing in a flurry of activity she hadn't seen in years—memos, white papers, and speeches—all of which had to be revised and polished. Whenever the subject of Cress—and her species—came up, the Guildmaster found a negative way to associate Terryn with her. Since politically he couldn't outright attack Draigen, smearing Terryn maintained his image as a defender of the Seelie Court. Laura understood the logic of it. That didn't mean she liked it, even had her friends not been involved.

Saffin arrived with more files flagged with her color-coding system for order of importance. The number of blue tags amused Laura. Blue rhymed with boo-hoo, which was Saffin's way of describing minor problems. Without being asked, Saffin straightened up the paperwork on the edge of Laura's desk. Laura pulled the black-tagged—critical priority—and red-tagged—going critical—folders and set them aside. The rest joined the pile of untouched matters. She noticed the untouched stacks remained suspiciously the same height, and suspected Saffin was handling issues she ignored.

"You've been falling behind a lot lately," Saffin said.

"I'm being pulled in too many directions," she said.

Saffin continued organizing without looking up. "You need to say no more often. You can't be everything to everyone."

Startled, Laura snapped her head up. "What's that supposed to mean?"

With a defiant look, Saffin crossed her arms. "Permission to speak freely?"

"Of course," Laura said.

Without looking, Saffin flexed a leg back and kicked the door shut. "I saw you on the news last night."

She thought about the previous night, remembering her movements in relation to the news crews that had shown up at the Uma macGrath crime scene. She had stayed away from cameras. "Saffin, I have no idea what you're talking about."

"The murder in the park. You were in the background of a news shot. Well, Mariel was."

Laura placed her hands on the desk, staring down at them. "Saf, I can't talk about that."

Saffin waved her hand over the stacks of folders. "I know. I'm not asking about that. What I am asking is, how can you deal with all this and a murder investigation? That's two full-time jobs. Hell, this desk is more than a full-time job. The Guildmaster uses you like his personal laptop, for Danu's sake."

Laura slumped back in her chair. "It's . . . my life."

Saffin tapped her index finger on the desk. "I don't know everything, but I do know one thing. This isn't your life, Laura. None of this is. Your life is what you do outside of all this. When's the last time you went on a date with tall and humpy?"

She lifted her chin in timid defiance. "Night before last."

Saffin's eyes sparkled as she leaned on the desk. "Really? Where'd you go?"

"Dinner."

Saffin pursed her lips. "And . . . ?"

"Then home." Saffin squealed.

"Saf!"

She laughed. "Okay. Over the line. None of my business. But if your idea of a date is standing over a dead body and whispering, I know a good therapist."

"There were no dead bodies."

"I was talking about the tall guy with the hoodie on the news standing behind you in the park last night. I thought he was a cop, not InterSec. When did that happen? Oh, wait! Has he been InterSec all along and went undercover as a cop? I just thought of that."

Dumbfounded, Laura stared. "You recognized Jono from a simple flash on the screen?"

Saffin rolled her eyes. "Hello? I watch the news on the Internet. I paused the shot. I couldn't see the dead body very well, though. She looked like she was executed, poor thing."

"What do you mean?"

Saffin shrugged. "She was on her side, and it looked like her arms were bound. Whoever killed her was a coward who she trusted to get that close. If you're going to kill someone, at least have the decency to let them fight back."

"She was bound. You frighten me sometimes, Saffin."

"Me? You're the secret agent."

Laura chuckled. "Not a very good one if you can figure out my personal life from a long shot on the news."

Saffin waved her hand dismissively. "I notice things. You know that. Is the murder related to the assassination attempt on Draigen macCullen? I'm pretty sure it was Brinen mac-Cullen squatting by the body."

Laura put her face into her hands. "Terryn would kill me if he heard this conversation."

Saffin's eyes went wide. "Really?"

Laura dropped her head back on the chair. "Any other time, I would say I'm joking, but lately his patience has been stretched pretty thin."

Saffin held her hands up. "Not another word from me.

You're the greatest boss I've ever had. If you think I'd jeopardize that, you're crazy."

She smiled. "I *am* joking, Saf. I can't stress enough how serious we take secrecy. If Terryn knew that you know about me, he'd . . ." She paused, thinking. "I'm not sure what he would do."

She thought about the corner Terryn had backed Jono into. What would Terryn say about Saffin? She wasn't trained in law enforcement, physical combat, or weapons.

"Well, you have my word not to say anything. I always look at part of my job as making you look good, boss. Is there anything you want me to take off your hands?" Saffin said.

Laura gazed at the paperwork on the desk. A red-tabbed folder caught her eye, and she handed it back to Saffin. "Can you categorize the guest list for Draigen's reception? Resha doesn't think about balance, and I want to make sure that he invited enough people from competing parties so no one will feels isolated. I can't get my head around it right now."

Saffin took the folder. "Do you want me to order lunch in?"

"No. I'll get something myself."

Saffin opened the door. "I'll keep everyone out for about an hour so you can focus."

Laura stared out the window. She made a mental note, the same mental note she had made before, never to underestimate Saffin Corrill. The brownie knack for detail impressed most people, but Saffin was special.

As she slipped papers out of a folder, she paused. Saffin's comment about a fair fight tickled at her. Uma macGrath had been in the attic with Sean Carr. She escaped only to be murdered. Silenced. She thought of the report on Sean Carr's death. He had been killed in self-defense according to the report. The dead woman gave her pause, though. If she had been silenced—murdered—maybe there was more to what had happened in that attic than the report said.

She gathered her purse and keys and went out to Saffin's

desk. "I have an appointment I forgot about. I don't know how long I'll be. Can you cover for me?"

Saffin kept typing. "Leave your PDA on vibe."

She paused at the door to the hallway. "And, Saf? So you know, you're more than the best assistant I've ever had. I couldn't have done this work all this time without you."

Flattered, Saffin ducked her head and grinned. "And you wonder why I put up with you."

45
CHAPTER

LAURA HAD ALL the files for Legacy spread around her on her desk in the InterSec unit. Too much data and too little data caused problems. Too little, and she was reduced to guesswork. Too much, and she risked overlooking something. Since she had left the public-relations department earlier, the volume of paper had increased, but she was no closer to figuring out what Legacy was planning.

Genda Boone sailed into Laura's InterSec office in a rustle of green taffeta. "Ah, good, you're here, Mariel. I'm on the run, but I have some follow-up for you."

She dropped a memo on the desk. Laura stared at yet more series of numbers, financial transactions and dates. "What is it?"

"Remember those accounts I found for the snipers? Dead ends so far. Someone hacked them. The shadow account in Wales is an old Inverni account, and the Caymans account that the funds initially came from? Imagine this, it's a Guild account. Obviously, neither of those entities would be involved with Legacy. I was researching them before Terryn left, and we've found a significant amount of money-laundering. I guess we can add embezzlement to the list now. I have to nail down the intrusion points."

Laura frowned as she lifted the memo. "Terryn showed me that data. Why would they steal funds if they had so much untraceable cash flow?"

Genda tapped the paper dramatically. "Untraceable, dear. That's always the appeal when someone wants to move large funds quickly. Anyway, I can't stay. I have a thing at the Kennedy Center. Opera. Can't bear it myself, but there's a gentleman I need to meet who has interesting connections in Germany. Don't you love this dress? The material's like grass on a sunny day."

"You look smashing, Genda," Laura said.

Coy, Genda shrugged. "The better to distract someone while he whispers sweet financial somethings. I've got to run." She glanced down at the desk, her face becoming reserved. "You should go home, dear. You've been running yourself ragged."

Laura smiled. "I will. And thanks, Genda. Another interesting piece for the puzzle."

She smiled again as she bustled out the door. "I'll bring you the program. Ta!"

Laura leaned her head into her hands. Piles of paper surrounded her, printouts from the Legacy files. She had found little of interest and nothing specifically tying the group to Draigen. A few vague references to the recent attacks on fey businesses were not enough for any sort of legal intervention that would make an impact.

She lifted her head at the sound of a knock. Dressed in jeans and a sweatshirt, Sinclair stood in the door but looked down the hall. "Is she gone?"

"Yes. Believe it or not, I think that was a work outfit."

Sinclair dropped a duffel bag on the floor and sat down. "Any news?"

Laura swept her gaze back and forth at the surface her of desk. "Nothing. No notes. No calls. Whoever took Cress isn't making contact."

"How's Terryn?"

She heard concern in his voice. It pleased her that despite everything between them, Sinclair wasn't being indifferent to Terryn's situation. "He's in lockup. Genda's trying to get him released."

He rocked his head back in surprise. "Trying? I thought they would have cleared everything up by now."

She leaned back with a sigh. "They're holding him for interfering with an investigation. His neighbors are furious, which didn't help."

He shook his head. "I understand why he did that, but it was a mistake."

Laura swiveled her chair in a small arc. "I'm shocked. He's usually so levelheaded."

"Yeah, that's been my experience with him," Sinclair said with sarcasm.

Laura let it slide. After their talk in the cemetery, she understood where it was coming from. She tilted her monitor so he could see it. "I've been watching this surveillance video over and over. Check this out." She played the video. "Notice anything?"

He shook his head. "Looks like I remember it. I couldn't see macGrath from where I was, but obviously that's her."

"No, watch the action on the sidewalk when the shots are fired." She played it again.

"Well, it's kinda fun to watch a macCullen get shot, if that's what you're asking," he said.

She stuck her tongue out, annoyed but playful. "Ha-ha. Watch again in slow motion . . . We come out of the lobby . . . Brinen moves in front of Draigen . . . I react to the ricochet and push Draigen down . . . Brinen gets hit."

He arched his eyebrows. "And?"

"Brinen moves in before the ricochet," she said.

Sinclair squinted at the screen as she played the video again. "You're right." He frowned.

"What are you thinking?" she asked.

Uncertain, he shook his head. "I want to say that implies he knew the shot was coming."

She exhaled forcefully and dropped her head back. "Damn. That's what I'm thinking."

"Why would he plot to kill his own sister?"

Laura shrugged. "Honestly? I thought Aran was involved until I noticed this. Aran's next in line for leadership after Draigen."

"Assuming Terryn doesn't take it back," Sinclair said.

She gazed at the computer. "Assuming. Of the siblings, Brinen is Terryn's biggest supporter. I don't get it."

They stared in silence as the video played again. Sinclair shook his head. "You said it yourself. Fairy politics are crazy."

Laura rubbed her forehead. "I'm going to see Terryn tomorrow and tell him about it. I can't make heads or tails of it."

"Careful he doesn't get all defensive on your butt like he did with me," he said.

She snorted. "He likes me better than you."

Sinclair chuckled as he leaned down and opened the duffel bag. "I brought you something to see."

He lifted a helmet out of the bag and placed it on the desk. "We did training exercises with these today."

"I've seen this." Laura shuffled the stacks on her desk until she found a thick folder. She flipped through the first few pages, then held up a detailed schematic of the helmet. "Tempered glass with a strip of quartz in the back. It looks like it's modeled on a Guild-agent helmet."

Sinclair took the folder. "They told us it would prevent essence attacks."

Laura lifted the helmet. "The glass definitely would dissipate essence, but I'm not sure it would completely eliminate it. It's heavy as hell."

He leaned down and pulled a hardened plastic harness from his bag. "It rests on this to take the weight off the head. Still heavy, though."

Laura ran her hands over the surface. "It's an interesting design. More waved toward the back. Were you doing combat maneuvers?"

He lowered the helmet to the desk. "The usual practice

sessions, only with the helmets and uniforms. I hate to say it, but these guys work really well together. Their coordination is impressive."

She slid her finger down the strip of quartz on the back. A mild static sparked between her skin and stone. "I don't get what the quartz is for. An essence residue came off it, but there wasn't enough for me to figure out what it was supposed to do."

Sinclair flipped through the file. "They didn't say. I don't remember sensing any essence from it."

Laura put her hand inside and propped the helmet on her fingers. "Was there essence involved in the maneuvers?"

He nodded as he read. "Some brownies fired on us. Not very powerful. The helmet did what they claimed. I felt the pressure of the hit, but it flowed over my head." He paused to read. "Lot of stuff in here about conductive and resistance properties."

Laura placed the helmet back on the desk. "Well, that's something out of this junk. We can turn it over to the R and D guys, see if they can make some use of it."

Sinclair frowned. "Hel, is this a medical report? Is this thing doing something to my brain?"

He handed Laura a sheaf of papers from the back of the folder. She rifled through the pages, skimming over dense paragraph discussions on the mechanics of essence flow. "I don't know. It's old, theoretical stuff. It reads like research from the Druidic College."

Another set of documents detailed a medical evaluation. "Hello," she said, holding up the first page. "Look who wrote this."

Sinclair leaned forward. "Ian Whiting? The guy who jumped off the Key Bridge last week?"

Laura continued reading. "This isn't a coincidence, Jono. I'm thinking Whiting might not have gone over the side by his own choice. He worked with Cress back when she was trying to stop absorbing other people's essence."

Sinclair turned the helmet in his hands. "These guys are

into defense against the fey. A *leanansidhe* absorbs essence. It doesn't project it, right?"

A chill ran over her as she read another document. She jumped to her feet. "This is Cress's medical file, Jono." She pawed through the other folders. "Why would Legacy be concerned about the *leanansidhe*? The *leanansidhe* are no one's allies. There must be something more here."

Sinclair grabbed her hands. "Slow down. You're panicking."

She pulled her hands away and slid them up into her hair. "You're right. I am so frustrated right now. Every time I think I have something, it gets messed up."

Sinclair sat against the edge of the desk and pulled her between his thighs. "Not true. You're worried. You've got one friend in a cell and another one missing. You will figure this out. It's what you do."

She rested her hands on his shoulders. "What if I'm too late? What if something happens to Cress before we find her?"

He pulled her closer. "What if you focus instead of thinking of failure?"

She pushed her lower lip out. "I'm surprised you can say that. I screwed things up for you. What makes you think I won't do that to someone else?"

He shook her lightly by the hips. "What makes you think you screwed things up for me? I might not be happy about how Terryn's treating me, but I'm still right where I want to be."

She stared into his eyes. Truth. Everything he said, he believed. He was doing everything he could to help. He had set her thinking in directions that she had not intended—bringing in the helmet, recognizing the crèche as a medical lab, pointing out the dark side of what InterSec did. She was tired of doubting every word he said. Listing those things triggered a cascade of thoughts. "Danu's blood," she whispered.

He smiled. "You can kiss me now."

Caught up in her thought process, she pulled away and

grabbed the medical research again. Pushing stacks of folders out of the way, she found the crèche blueprints. Notes and formulas from the research correlated with the specifications for the crèche. They were connected—the crèche a direct product of the *leanansidhe* research. It was a tool for channeling a powerful fey—but not Draigen. It was specifically tailored for the abilities of a *leanansidhe*. "The crèche fits the description in this research. It's meant for Cress, Jono, not Draigen. Legacy has Cress."

He twisted in place to see what she comparing. "It does look similar."

She grabbed her jacket. "Where do they do your urban-assault training?"

"I told you, about fifty miles due west of here. Front Royal, Virginia," he said.

She kicked off her shoes. "Get that uniform on. We're going in," she said.

Sinclair moved back as she pulled on her work boots. "That's a thin connection. Can we get a warrant with it?" he said.

She stood. "I'm not going to waste the time. It's been over twenty-four hours. Terryn said that means Cress has moved into the danger zone."

"Laura . . ." he said.

She held her hand up. "I know what you're going to say, but right now I don't want to hear it. I'm going, and I'm taking a tactical team. You can stay or come with me."

He smirked. "I was going to say this is the woman I am all hot about."

She paused. Truth. He hadn't made it up on the spot. She smiled. "Just for that, I'm going to let you drive."

46
CHAPTER

FIFTY MILES NORTHWEST of the city, the line of black SUVs drove along the back roads outside Front Royal, Virginia. Laura rode in the passenger seat as Sinclair led the caravan through the gathering dusk. The trip out had taken over an hour, even with using roof lights the first half of the way. Not for the first time did she envy the power of flight. She had four Danann fairies on the tactical team, but they weren't enough to ferry everyone out to the camp.

"Are you sorry you're missing the party?" Sinclair asked.

Laura checked the cars following in the passenger-side mirror. "You're joking, right?"

He draped his hand over the steering wheel. "A little. I'd think with the way you run your life, a party would be a nice change of pace."

She thought about the reception. The planning. The guest lists. The decorations. The politics. "No, Jono. I don't miss it. I can't remember the last party I went to that didn't have to do with work. They're always about work, one way or another."

He pursed his lips and shot her a slow, sly look. "Man, you need fun."

She wasn't sure whether to laugh or not. They were on their way to find a kidnapped friend. "You know, you have an odd sense of timing."

"I do?"

"Do you think I want to talk about having fun right now?"

"Is there ever a right time?" he asked.

"What's that supposed to mean?"

He shrugged, frustration on his face. "We've been in this car for an hour. We covered the layout of the compound. We bitched about traffic. We made note of all the pretty scenery. At some point, the conversation isn't about crap, ya know? At some point, Cuddles, you need to stop thinking every moment of your life about the dire consequences for everyone else and relax."

She flushed with heat. "Are we having an argument? Because it sounds like you want an argument."

"No, I don't. I want to talk about something other than the end of the world," he said.

"It's not the end of the world," she snapped.

He tapped the steering wheel. "Good. We're getting somewhere."

She glared at him. As much as she wanted to hit him, she knew he had a point. She never did relax. She did think only about work. Having a personal life had always meant letting down her guard. Enjoying herself, as Sinclair put it, meant interacting with other people. It meant risking exposing herself—or worse, them. It meant, she had to admit, that she feared those risks so much, she had let her life disappear. Made it disappear.

"You hit all my sore spots, you know that?" she said. She said it quietly, with little emotion. A statement of fact.

Sinclair glanced at her without any sign of smugness. He dropped his hand on hers and squeezed it. "I think that's why you like me."

She did laugh then. "You know, it would be worth dating you if only to deflate that ego of yours."

He tilted his head at her with a boyish smile. "That sounds like a lot of dating."

She shook her head and chuckled. The smile lingered on her face as she stared out her window. Sinclair still held her hand, and she decided she would be damned if she pulled away.

They passed into Front Royal. The town had a quaintness about it that reminded Laura of other times and other places. Antique shops and colonial homes lined the main route. It was a lot like Alexandria must have been before it became the coveted bedroom community it was today.

"We're a mile away," he said.

Terryn, can you hear me? We're almost there, she sent. No reply. She didn't expect a response. The Guild had Terryn in a holding cell that jammed sendings. She thought it might be worth a try to contact him on the off chance he had been allowed to attend Draigen's reception.

On the GPS screen map, a large swathe of land appeared as blank green space along the Shenandoah River. "It takes a lot of money to make something disappear off satellite maps," she said.

"And the contamination is an incentive not to attract attention," he said.

"Contamination?"

He checked his sidearm. "It's an old Superfund site. Lots of buried toxins. Probably why they were able to afford so much land this close to the city."

She hummed in disagreement. "Close? I hate the commute across the river to Alexandria."

"Yeah, well, not everyone can afford that by double-dipping their paychecks," he said.

She shoved him playfully. "I work for two different agencies, so it's not a double-dip."

He pulled off the two-lane road onto grass overhung by tall trees. "It is if you get paid full for half-time work."

She zipped up her uniform jacket. "I wish. Try two salaries for three times the hours."

He grinned as he got out of the car. "And you have, what? Three or four apartments? I feel bad."

"Jerk," she muttered as she joined him on the side of the road. Behind them, more black-uniformed InterSec agents waited, a mix of Danann fairies, Teutonic elves, and druids.

Sinclair surveyed the gathering. "You know, you're looking at these guys' worst nightmare."

Laura assessed the tactical team. They were armed, trained, and willing to follow orders. "I think this would be anyone's worst nightmare."

"Yeah, but we're a bunch of fey about to storm a protected human compound. That's their biggest fear right here," he said.

Laura started walking toward the camp. "You're wrong. If anything has happened to Cress, I'm going to be their biggest fear."

She sent the Dananns ahead for surveillance. They swept in a low formation over the road, their wings a dim glow in the night sky. The rest of the team fell in behind. They jogged up the road until a tall chain-link fence appeared. Laura started to receive sendings from the Dananns as soon as she sighted the guardhouse next to the driveway.

"We've got one guy in the gate," she said.

Sinclair moved in front of her. "I'll take him."

She grabbed his arm. "Let one of the Dananns do it. It'll be quicker."

"And raise an alarm," he said over his shoulder. "This place is warded with essence detectors. They zap him, we lose the element of surprise across a quarter-mile run up to the bunkers."

Laura considered his proposal. "Make it quick."

He stood. "Make sure your buddies remember I'm on their side."

She smiled up at him. "It's okay. I told them not to shoot the tall guy unless I asked them to."

He grinned as he strolled away, staying in the open, his assault rifle slung casually over his shoulder. In the lit gatehouse, the guard's head lifted as Sinclair approached. He came to the door, hand resting on his holstered pistol. Sinclair leaned against the gatehouse door, talking and gesturing up the road. Laura ducked deeper into the weeds as the guard looked in her direction. In a blur, Sinclair spun his rifle off his shoulder and landed the butt in the guard's face. The man fell to the ground.

As Laura ran up, Sinclair was disarming him. "Nice."

She held out her hand to cast a binding spell, but Sinclair grabbed it. "I told you. Essence alarms."

She coiled her fingers closed. "Oh, sure, they don't like the fey, but they have no problem using fey tools."

Sinclair peered into the compound. "We take a straight shot up the driveway, then to the left."

Laura signaled the team behind her, and they quick-stepped across the pavement as she opened the gate. She trailed behind Sinclair. "One guard at the gatehouse concerns me."

"Yeah. There are usually two," he said.

"Great. Now I'm worried."

As the afternoon light faded, white cinder-block buildings loomed in the shadows of tall, mature trees. "I've never seen the place so dark and quiet," Sinclair said.

A lone figure appeared from the back side of the nearest building. He stopped short when he saw Sinclair and Laura, then raised his gun. A burst of green essence sliced through the night air as someone behind them fired elf-shot. Sirens began to wail.

Laura swore as she ran for the nearest building and crouched against it. Rifle in position, Sinclair backpedaled to watch their flank. The essence burst had been elf-shot. She searched among the running team until she spotted the likely perpetrator who had fired without her say-so. He was not going to like his debriefing at the mission review.

"That would be the essence alarm, I take it?" she asked.

"The very one," he said.

She peered around the corner. Someone with an automatic weapon scuttled across the access road. "The med bunker is up and to the left, right?"

"Yeah, but let's go left, then up. Less light," he said.

"Okay, you lead," she said.

"You just want to look at my butt."

"It's a very nice butt," she said. Two could play his game.

She broadcast a sending to the tactical team, directing them up and to the right to draw away as many Legacy guards as possible. Sinclair slipped in front of her and watched the open driveway as she ran for the building across the way.

They hustled down a paved walkway at the rear of a line of buildings. Legacy guards cut across the path ahead, moving to the northeast of the compound. Sinclair paused at the next corner, spying around the building. "Something's not right. This isn't a tenth of the guys that should be here."

"Let's hope they're not staying put at the bunker," Laura said.

Gunfire erupted in the distance to their right, followed by the unmistakable crackle of essence-fire. Sinclair dodged left around a utility shed. He gestured with his rifle across the grassy front of a low building. A door stood open, unguarded, spilling light into the night. "That's the med bunker. We go straight in, stairwell halfway down on the right to the lower level. Doors all the way."

"Take the point," Laura said.

"Sure," Sinclair muttered. "Good enough to take the first hit, but not for health benefits."

"You're wearing their uniform. It's an advantage," Laura said as she chased him across the grass.

Sinclair hit the wall beside the door. He ducked his head out and back. "Clear."

He quick-stepped in, rifle low and pointed at the first door. It remained closed, and they passed it. Step by step, they crept down the empty hallway. No one challenged them. Sinclair peered into the stairwell. "Clear."

With muted steps, they descended. "I've got a bad feeling about this. Why did they abandon their posts?" Sinclair asked.

"You said they look understaffed. Maybe the rest of the tac team is near a more high-profile target," Laura said.

They reached the lower level. "Yeah, that's not helping. It looks like the lab's the next door."

They moved along the corridor, the silence an uncomfortable weight bearing down on them. Sinclair reached for
the door handle. He glanced to check Laura's position, then
ducked as he pushed the door open. No sound came from
within.

"I'm not sensing anyone. In fact, I'm not sensing anything
at all down here," Laura said in a whisper.

In a crouch, Sinclair entered. Laura counted off the seconds until he called out, "Clear."

Inside, as the blueprints indicated, the fifteen-foot granite
crèche stretched down the center of the room. At regular
intervals, shallow bowl-like niches made a double ring around
the circumference. Bands of quartz connected the niches with
the deep bed of the crèche.

Laura didn't sense Cress, or anything else for that matter.
As she approached the crèche, the air deadened, void of a trace
of essence. "Cress was here. The room feels scrubbed, like
there's no essence at all."

Beside her, Sinclair touched the edge of the crèche and
swayed on his feet as his essence dimmed. Laura grabbed his
arm. "You okay?"

He shook his head rapidly as if clearing it. "It's some kind
of essence sink."

Laura examined the hollowed interior without touching
the crèche. "That's what the documents described—the crèche
channels and amplifies abilities. They tuned the crèche to
Cress's abilities. That's why it's trying to absorb our essence.
That also means that Cress was in this thing. From the look
of it, something rested in here like it was a cradle. She was
on or in something."

"Now what?" Sinclair said.

Laura glanced around the room. "We search the complex.
If the crèche is still active, I'm guessing Cress was here recently. She might still be here somewhere."

She moved around to the other side of the crèche. Glass
helmets sat in several of the rounded-out niches. She pulled
one out and held it up. Her body essence flowed down her

arm toward the helmet. With some effort, she pulled the essence back and raised her body shield.

She examined the helmet again and peered into the niche, finding a matching quartz strip. "The stone tabs on these helmets are tuned to the crèche, Jono. They have the same essence warding on them. Mobile essence-draining units. The glass shunts essence over the head to the stone tab, and the tab must send it somewhere. The crèche acts like a charger for the helmets."

She replaced the helmet and froze. Two legs stretched out on the floor at the far end of the crèche. "We've got a body."

She hurried the length of the room as Sinclair circled in from the other side. A man lay facedown on the floor. She pulled him over by the arm, and he rolled on his back. "Danu's blood, this is Ian Whiting."

"The druid suicide?" Sinclair asked.

She applied her fingers to his carotid artery. "I'd recognize him anywhere. Dammit. No pulse. No living body essence. He's drained. Dead."

Sinclair held his hand out. "No, wait. I can see the shape of his essence. It's faint, but it's there."

Laura placed her hand on Whiting's chest. Without any other essence source in the room, she pushed some of her own into him. His body shuddered as a warm yellow light swirled into him. "I'm seeing a body signature now."

She jerked her head up at a sudden intake of breath from Sinclair. He was crouched next to her, but his gaze was toward the crèche. At intervals on the underside of the helmet niches were small bricks of C-4 explosive. Lights flashed from timers on several of them.

Sinclair pulled Whiting into a seated position. With no effort, he lifted the man from the floor. Sinclair grabbed Laura's arm. "We need to get out of here now. Crank your shields all the way up, Cuddles. It might get breezy in here."

They ran for the door, Laura's hardened body shield expanding around them. As they made the outside corridor, the room erupted. The door blew off, slamming into the shield.

Laura stumbled against Sinclair. They hit the wall and fell. Another explosion went off somewhere above them, and the lights flickered.

"Go! Ghost out of here. I'll get Whiting out," Sinclair shouted.

She shoved him forward, almost knocking him to the ground again. "Keep moving. You don't have a shield."

Explosions rocked the end of the corridor as they reached the stairs. Laura swayed under the pressure, dizziness threatening to overwhelm her as the force of the concussion destabilized her shield. Sinclair stumbled on a step, and they fell again. With Whiting draped over his shoulder like a rag doll, he wrapped his arm around Laura as she struggled to get her feet under her. Debris rained down, bouncing off her body shield. The strain of covering all three of them without an external essence source drained her. Black and red spots flashed in her vision as she fought to remain conscious.

Sinclair dragged her down the crumbling upper hall. An explosion on the main floor sent them airborne. They burst through the door, arcing into the air. Laura's shield shredded as she hit the ground.

47
CHAPTER

LAURA WRENCHED HERSELF up into a sitting position, several yards from the burning building. Dazed, she watched as her hands shifted in shape, a brief flutter as the depleted essence in her necklace struggled to maintain the Mariel glamour. Dropping her hands to either side, she drew on the essence in the ground, pulling it in to replenish some of what she had lost. She let her head fall back a moment as the renewed energy surged through her, and the glamour stabilized.

Ian Whiting lay nearby, on his back, unconscious. He appeared dead, his skin leached white, but his signature registered a faint film of yellow light around his body. The boost Laura had given him in the lab had been enough to jump-start his body signature.

Sinclair staggered into her field of vision, his uniform torn and singed. He leaned over Whiting as she shuffled on her knees next to them. "Is he okay?"

Sinclair leaned back on his heals. "I think he got hit with debris. Are you okay?"

Laura pulled her hair back and retied it. "A little rattled, but I'm fine. We need Whiting awake."

She leaned over Whiting and scanned his body signature. She didn't have healing skills, but from what she saw, he wasn't damaged, only drained. He needed rest to replenish what he needed, but she could infuse him with a temporary boost like she had given herself. With one hand on his chest and the other on the ground, she tapped into the organic essence of the soil. The essence flowed through her and into Whiting, using her body as a conduit. It wasn't healing precisely, but enough to jump-start his own essence regeneration. Whiting's chest heaved as his body reacted to the influx. Laura eased him to his side as he started to retch.

She waited until he caught his breath. "Do you know who you are? Can you tell me your name?"

"Ian Whiting," he rasped.

He could hear. He could think. "Mr. Whiting, I'm Mariel Tate with InterSec. What happened here?"

Dazed, he stared at the fire. "Was I in that?"

She helped him sit up. "Where's Cress?"

"She tried to kill me," he said.

"Well, she didn't. Where is she?" Laura asked.

Now that he was awake, he pulled more essence on his own. He shook his head. "She was in the pod."

Laura exchanged glances with Sinclair. "The pod? Is that what was in the crèche?"

Whiting got to his feet. "When I activated the final sequence, they ordered Cress to kill me."

"Sequence for what? What the hell are you talking about?" Laura asked.

He stared into the distance. "We have to stop her."

Laura shook him by the shoulders. "Focus, Whiting. What the hell was going on here?"

Instinctively, he activated his body shield. Rather than struggle with him, Laura let go. "We need a healer, Jono."

Whiting held up his hand. "No, I'm fine. Give me another moment. My head is clearing."

While she waited for him to compose himself, sendings from the rest of the team flowed in. Buildings all over the

compound had been rigged with explosives and were now in
flames. The few Legacy staff remaining had escaped on boats
on the river side of the site. The fighting had been a distraction
until the bombs went off.

Still confused, Whiting's eyes alternately cleared and glazed
over a few times. "We have to get to Washington."

Laura stared at him. "What was going on here?"

Whiting rubbed a hand against his temple. "They stole my
research on Cress and made an amplifier for her abilities.
Amazing work, actually. I hadn't thought through the implications."

"Implications for what?" asked Sinclair.

Whiting tilted his head up. "I proposed the crèche as a way
to dampen the cravings Cress had for essence. These people
inverted my design. They created a pod for Cress's body and
the helmets to expand her abilities. They're using her as a
weapon to deactivate essence. The fey will be helpless against
them."

"Cress would not have agreed to this," Laura said.

Whiting's face became troubled. "She didn't. I created a
ward on the pod that suppressed her consciousness. It's slaved
to a control helmet. A man named DeWinter has it."

Laura swore. "I should have blown his head off in the
limo."

"Hel, that explains it," Sinclair said.

"What?" she asked.

"When I wore the helmet during training, I kept making
moves and decisions that surprised me," he said.

Whiting's face was becoming animated. "It worked, then.
I'd wondered how successful it would be. The crèche is a
ward generator. The modules on the sides synchronize the
helmets to the pod. The stone embedded in the back of the
helmet is an impulse conductor. Put the two together, and
anyone who wears a helmet is under your direct control."

Laura interrupted him. "You said we have to get to Washington."

Whiting became subdued as he remembered something.

"They're going to attack the fey leadership. I don't know the details."

Laura met Sinclair's gaze. "Draigen's reception. She's been a target since she arrived, and the entire fey leadership is there right now. "

Sinclair sighed. "Why did I know this would end up about Terryn?"

Laura frowned. "Terryn's not the point, and you know it."

"They'll need a granite-based structure to create an essence-dampening field," Whiting said.

Sinclair shook his head in feigned annoyance. "Gee, how will we ever find a granite structure in D.C.?"

48
CHAPTER

THREE DANANNS FROM the tactical team raced through the air, carrying Laura, Sinclair, and Whiting. The wind whipping past their ears removed any possibility of audible conversation. Below them, the landscape whirred by in a smear of darkened foliage and intermittent streetlights. Laura didn't want to risk time getting Whiting to a healer by driving, and she wanted to be back in D.C. as soon as possible.

She had already done a sending to Genda Boone about their discovery, which set in motion security protocols across the city. Laura monitored the InterSec alert channels, a constant stream of sendings updating security in real time. Even with the Danann's shield barrier protecting her from wind shear, alerts slammed back at her as agencies scrambled to respond.

The district is in lockdown. The Washington Monument has been taken over by unknown sources, she sent to Sinclair and Whiting.

Sinclair's sending came in with a snide tone. *I wonder who they could be?*

What a brilliant idea. Whoever thought of it is wasted on this, Whiting sent.

Excuse me? Laura sent.

The Monument is perfectly shaped and granite. Remember your fundamental ward skills, he sent.

Laura stared in disbelief at Whiting across the open patch of sky. *Danu's blood, are you kidding me?*

Not at all. It's brilliant, he sent.

The Danann carrying Sinclair was somewhere behind. *I don't get it,* Sinclair sent.

They're going to turn the damned Monument into a giant ward stone to absorb essence, Laura sent.

Is that possible? he asked.

Theoretically. With the right configurations and ability sourcing, sent Whiting.

How big a field will it generate? Laura asked.

Impossible to tell without knowing all the variables. A mile? Two? Simply amazing, Whiting sent.

Well within range of the Guildhouse, she thought. And practically every major government facility. A smudge of light appeared on the horizon, the top of the Monument visible from thirty miles away, the tallest point in the city. As she spotted it, it took on the sharpness of its more recognizable shape. Laura estimated their arrival in fifteen or twenty minutes.

Genda sent a brief mention of shots fired at the Guildhouse and that an evacuation was under way. Laura sorted through the InterSec sendings, creating a picture of the defense forces being set up. Every conceivable branch of law enforcement had been rolled out—Marine units lining the Mall, various police agencies locking down and guarding government buildings, and private security firms rolling out their hardware.

The Coast Guard had units surging up the Potomac. Civilian government staff—including the president and legislators—were being whisked to secure facilities.

As they neared the outskirts of the city, streaks of light

marked the paths of F-16 fighter jets. Blackhawk helicopters hung like dark clouds ready to release a storm. A sudden shimmer in the distance rippled on the horizon, the lights and buildings of downtown blurring out. A confused chatter broke the calm tone of the emergency sendings, then everything went silent.

Laura tried sending to Genda but received no response. She tried tapping any of her regular communication-sending channels to no result. She did a broadcast sending open to anyone who could hear, only to receive the same back from bewildered fey, all of whom were not in the city center.

I lost contact. I think the essence dampening has been activated, she sent. They would have to fly blind the rest of the way in. She hoped all the human forces had been given her heading coordinates before sendings were jammed.

Laura's stomach clenched as a fighter jet soared past them and raced toward the city. In its wake, the three Dananns fought against air turbulence, spreading farther apart. As they regained control, a sudden drop in altitude brought them dangerously close to the rooftops.

Take us in low. You're going to lose your flying abilities when we get closer, she sent.

In unison, the Dananns descended, skimming over the trees of the outer neighborhoods. They passed through an abrupt break in the surrounding air, a space devoid of essence. The Dananns struggled to maintain altitude without essence to use as lift. Banking sharply, they coasted on air currents until they were out of the empty-essence zone, skirting over George Washington University and tacking north of the White House. Laura directed them to set down in Mount Vernon Square, which was outside the dampening field.

The Dananns brought them down onto a clear sidewalk space. Around them, abandoned cars clogged the streets. National Guard troops marched through, moving vehicles and setting up a line of defense to the south in the direction of the Mall. Civilians milled about, most running north and east, while others stood in confusion or fascination. Tanks rumbled into positions throughout the square as emergency vehicles swept south.

Laura held Whiting by the arm while she searched for Sinclair. She spotted him leaning over between two cars. "Jono, what the hell are you doing?" she shouted.

He hurried to them, pale and sweating. "Sorry. I'm not so good with heights."

Surprised, she tried not to smile at the unexpectedness of it. "We need to get down to the Guildhouse."

"No problem," Sinclair said. He stepped into the street as a truck carrying National Guardsmen barreled toward him. The truck screeched to a halt as he held up a hand. Guns appeared out the windows and back of the truck. "Whoa! We're friendlies. We've got intel for command up the street."

"Nice way to almost get shot," Laura said, as she and Whiting joined him in the street. She held up her InterSec badge. "We need to get up there ASAP."

The driver of the truck wasted no time arguing. Sinclair helped Whiting into the back while Laura jumped onto the running board. "If I wasn't going in the same direction, you guys would be roadkill," the driver shouted.

Laura snorted in derision. "If that's what you need to think, go ahead. Get moving."

Once past Franklin Park, the street emptied of civilians. Military personnel drove or marched south, the transport truck weaving through the various contingents. If there was one thing Washington, D.C., had down, it was emergency procedures. As they neared the Guildhouse, the sound of gunfire carried through the engine roar of army vehicles.

Anxiety gripped Laura as the ambient essence around her began to fade. She had never seen such a thing. The bright colors of essence paled the closer they approached the Guildhouse. It was worse than at the med lab. There, it had been one room, something she had experienced from time to time. Out on the street, though, the effect was enormous and widespread.

The dampening field bore down like a layer of heat and humidity. She felt light-headed, as if she had stepped into a different reality and didn't have any ability. She hadn't realized how she had taken for granted the existence of essence, how it energized her. She wondered if that was what it felt like to be human.

Visual chaos confronted them as they reached the back of the Guildhouse. Danann security agents patrolled the surrounding roofs, their black uniforms shadows against the night sky. Brownie guards gathered on the sidewalk—some of them armed with automatic weapons—preventing anyone from approaching within a block. Armored vehicles from the U.S. government blocked the way to the front of the building. Scattered among the security and vehicles, fey of all kinds clustered, coordinating an evacuation. That many of them were dressed in formal attire from the reception added a surreal element.

In a lemon yellow evening gown, Genda Boone stood out like a beacon among the dark security uniforms. She had her cell phone pressed against her ear as they approached. "Yes, Damine, and make sure my upgrade to business class is all set. Last time there was a snafu . . . Of course not, dear. No one in their right mind would think it was your fault. Oh, and can you call Dmitri for me? I've been standing in this wind for over an hour and will need a touch-up tomorrow. Thanks. I have to go. Mariel's here, looking all business."

She closed her cell, grabbed Whiting by the hands, and air-kissed his cheek. "Ian, darling, I'm so glad you're all right even if you ruined my dinner party." Still holding his hand, she stepped off the curb. "Let's go, everyone."

At the corner, she waved at a tall elven woman huddled with a large group near evacuation buses. "Alfra, call me tomorrow. I want to hear all about your bus ride." She snickered as they crossed the sidewalk. "I'm sorry. I'm usually not that catty, but that woman has the biggest ego you can imagine. I'd be surprised if she's ever ridden a bus in her life."

Dubious, Sinclair looked at Laura as they quick-stepped after Genda. "She's in charge?"

Genda called over her shoulder, "Yes, she is. And who might you be?"

Laura's warning look checked his response. "Um . . . Bill," Sinclair said.

Genda led them around to the front. "A good omen. Everyone knows I like big bills." She chuckled at her own joke as they all ducked at the sound of gunfire.

Armed military personnel ran past them toward the Mall. She stopped next to a Stryker, one of the army's armored assault vehicles. "Now, let me bring you up to speed. We're staging a diversion on the other side of the Mall to draw off their forces, but it probably won't work very well. They're intent on the Guildhouse and have already taken over the front of the Hoover Building. That's what all the gunfire is, if you were wondering."

She slipped her arm around Whiting. "I'm sorry, Ian. I tried to get Rhys to release Terryn, but he refuses." She waved her free hand. "I swear, the man sees conspiracies everywhere. Anyway, I'll try to get him to change his mind, but you'll have to go in without him. Everything's nearly in place."

"Genda, you need to slow down. What is the mission plan?" Laura asked.

Genda turned to Whiting. "You haven't told her?"

Whiting looked both embarrassed and baffled. "I thought we were talking theoretically."

Genda patted his arm as if to soothe him. "Ian and I were discussing the situation on your way in. They're using a ring formation around the Monument with the majority of their forces in the outer ring. Their plan appears to be to disable our fey forces, which, frankly, they've done, so we're turning the tables and using mainly human forces and a ground attack to get you to the Monument. Ian thinks he can deactivate the *leanansidhe* pod once you secure it."

Sinclair stared at Laura. "Once we secure it."

"I can't go in without Terryn macCullen. Cress will not be in her right mind. I need someone she trusts," Whiting said.

Genda patted him on the chest. "Oh, Ian, you were her doctor or something, weren't you? Of course she'll trust you."

He shook his head. "That's a huge risk, Genda. We haven't spoken in years."

"I'll go," Laura said. Everyone stared at her. She shrugged. "I'm her friend."

"You're not going in there without me," Sinclair said. Genda turned to him with a frown. Sinclair shrugged. "I'm her friend."

Genda sighed with deep exasperation. "Really, I do not understand how Terryn ran his department with all this . . . this . . . friendship, but we need to get this done. Fine, friends, whatever is necessary. Ian thinks the *leanansidhe* is on the main level of the Washington Monument—don't you, dear?— so we're going to provide air cover while you storm the plaza. This DeWinter fellow is either at the top or the bottom of the Monument or in the Blackhawk."

"Blackhawk?" Laura interrupted.

Tapping her hand off the side of her forehead, Genda shook head. "Yes, sorry. So many details have cropped up. They have a Blackhawk in the air. It's armed with two hellfire missiles, but I don't think we need to worry about it."

"Are you serious?" Sinclair asked, dumbfounded.

She nodded vigorously. "Oh, yes, very. They've had a clear shot of the White House and the Capitol, but haven't fired. The humans are quite nervous about the whole situation, but, really, it's obvious they've been moving in on the Guildhouse for the last thirty minutes. Our analysis is that they're waiting to get their ground force closer before attacking and picking off anyone who tries to escape. They only have two missiles, after all. I don't think they'll waste them on an unidentified truck."

Amazed, Sinclair looked at Laura. "Only two missiles?"

She smoothed her hair back. "You'll be much too busy to worry about them."

Genda gestured to one of her bodyguards, who then banged on the back of the armored truck. The rear door of the Stryker opened to reveal a half dozen military personnel in combat uniform. "They're all Special Forces. I'm told they're very good." She glanced down at her phone. "Oh, the F-16s are turning. With any luck, they'll take out the Blackhawk on their first pass. You'd best get going. Let these boys do their jobs."

They startled at a barrage of gunfire from the park across the street. A line of Legacy fighters was pushing toward them. Bullets whistled through the air, ricocheting off the front of the Guildhouse. Genda peered around the side of the Stryker. "Oh, damn, we've cut it too close. Keep your cell phone on so I can update you as necessary." She backpedaled away from the truck. "Good luck! By the way, cute boots, Mariel. You'll have to tell me where you got them when you get back. Okay, boys, time to get inside."

Her bodyguards fired back up the street as Genda trotted behind them back around the corner. Laura jumped into the Stryker as Sinclair helped Whiting in behind her. The truck pulled out as Sinclair closed the door and moved to the front of the vehicle. He sat and looked at Laura. "Is that woman crazy?"

Laura smirked. "A little, but very efficient. Do you think you can deactivate the pod, Mr. Whiting?"

He shifted on his cramped perch. "That's the one thing I'm sure of. I built in a shutdown."

"Convenient," said Sinclair.

Puzzled, Whiting cocked his head. "No, it isn't. I'm a scientist. The pod is too experimental not to have a built-in failsafe. That would be a foolish risk."

Sinclair grinned. "As opposed to, say, getting hit with a hellfire missile."

"What do you need me to do, Professor?" Laura asked.

"I'll need you to talk to her, persuade her that everything is all right. She's going to be very afraid. Once she's calm, I'll put her into a sleep trance, and this will be over," he said.

Laura leaned forward. "I'm not going into a fire zone unarmed. I'd like a weapon, please."

"Make that two," said Sinclair.

A soldier handed two rifles down the line. "We were told you were cleared for these."

Sinclair whistled as he took one. The rifle weighed almost eight pounds, with an infrared scope mounted on the top rail. "An Mk-16? Can I keep it?"

"No," Laura said. She pocketed an extra magazine of ammunition. She didn't like guns. Guns were meant to produce blood at a minimum, death as a matter of course. She almost never carried one, but under the circumstances, she knew it would be foolish not to. Without being able to tap essence, she was limited to her body's own reserves, and once that was gone, it was gone.

An explosion rocked the truck. Tense silence swept through the back of the truck as everyone became quiet. Two soldiers returned fire through the top port. The longer they drove, the more the Stryker rang with the bullet impacts. Nothing pierced the armoring, but that didn't lower anyone's anxiety. They bounced as the Stryker jumped a curb, then skidded on a soft surface. They had arrived on the Mall.

Another explosion jolted the truck, and it lurched to a stop. The six soldiers around them readied to disembark. The vehicle commander ordered a smoke grenade launched. Someone hit the rear door, and the soldiers jumped out with their weapons primed. Laura slid to the rear, the air filled with gunfire and smoke. They were a lot closer than she had imagined they'd be, barely fifty yards away. She craned her neck out, but the smoke limited her field of vision. Somewhere above, she heard the rotor-blade whir of the Blackhawk.

Soldiers lay on the ground nearby, firing at the main entrance to the Monument. Theirs wasn't the only team. She hadn't expected that, but now she realized taking the Monument with six men wasn't a likely scenario. People ran back and forth through the smoke. Screams reached her ears as the sound of gunfire dissipated.

"We're inside. Still meeting resistance," the vehicle commander called out.

"Why aren't we out there?" Sinclair asked.

Laura kept her eyes on the entrance. "We're here to protect Whiting and get Cress. It's not a war-game exercise."

Sinclair squeezed in next to her to see out. "Yeah, except I'm trained for this."

She glanced at him, impatient. "Good. You can mop up anything these guys miss. Now, pay attention."

"We've got a go. Make it fast," the commander shouted.

Laura popped the door. She and Sinclair hit the ground together and helped Whiting. Aircraft filled the sky, fighter jets and helicopters circling in the distance. A wall of helicopters hung in front of the White House. A staccato burst of gunfire flared across the Ellipse in front of the mansion.

Above, the smoke curled away to reveal the deep black underbelly of a Blackhawk. The helicopter veered to one side and turned. Another smoke grenade launched from the Stryker. "Get moving! We have incoming," the vehicle commander shouted.

They scrambled down the sidewalk, dodging among debris and bodies. A sense of nothingness shimmered over them, a wave in the air with no essence, but they stumbled on. The Monument burned with neon purple light, Cress's body signature permeating the white stone surface. Near the peak, a rainbow slurry of essence revolved as the giant obelisk sucked it in.

A soldier appeared at the main entrance and waved them in. "We've found no one that matches the description of Adam DeWinter," he said.

Laura surveyed the lobby; chipped masonry and dead bodies were scattered about the floor. "DeWinter's not here. There's no way out. He isn't the suicidal type."

"Ma'am, I believe what you are looking for is back here," said the soldier. He led them across the damaged space to the elevators. In a narrow alcove to one side, two long rods of white crystal stretched from one wall to the other. Resting on top, a dark gray lozenge-shaped tube of quartz burned with a deep violet essence.

"Ah, now I see what they wanted those rods for," Whiting said.

They spread out in a loose arc at the foot of the pod. "What do they do?" Sinclair asked.

Whiting grimaced as he ran his hand over one. "They're conduits, tapping into the granite of the structure. It's how Cress is accessing the essence in the Monument stones."

"Can we disconnect them?" Laura asked.

He leaned over the head of the pod. "They're not important now. Getting Cress out of here is."

Outside the main doors, an explosion lit the night sky, followed by the roar of tearing metal. Another explosion erupted, a blinding orange light flashing into the lobby. Laura's cell phone chirped. She found a text message from Genda signed with a smiley face. "They took out the Blackhawk."

Whiting stepped over one of the support rods and leaned over the pod. The air throbbed against Laura's face. Blood pounded in her ears. Until it was missing, she had never noticed how much ambient essence kept her energized. "Why isn't the pod draining our body signatures?"

Whiting crouched to examine the underside of the pod. "The system is designed to facilitate and amplify Cress's abilities. It absorbs local essence but needs to be in direct contact with body signatures to absorb those."

"So we're safe as long as we don't touch that thing?" Sinclair asked.

Whiting hummed to himself. "Yes. Unfortunately, we need to touch it to stop it." He tapped at a strip of red stone embedded on the top of the pod and grimaced. "This is the control ward. It's not responding. Too much interference from the selenite in the pod itself, I think."

Laura stepped over one of the support rods. "What are you saying? You can't stop it?"

Without touching it, Whiting pointed to the red stone. "This ward stone is suppressing Cress's consciousness. It allows

DeWinter to direct her abilities and control his fighters. I keyed a deactivation response to my body signature, but the selenite is draining it off before it can penetrate."

Sinclair lifted his rifle and brought the butt down hard on the red stone. A piece chipped off. He hit it again. A crack formed. He hit it again. And again, until the impact broke the ward crosswise. Whiting grunted in approval. "That works, too."

Whiting pulled out the stone fragments. "The locks should release now. Pull up on the clamps on your side there."

He stooped and yanked at two large stone levers while Laura and Sinclair opened the others. "Now what?" Laura asked.

"The lid's heavy," Whiting said. "I used essence to lower it into place, but now that it's activated, it will drain us the moment we touch the pod. We need to lever it open as quickly as possible."

"You guys are the brains of the operation. I'll do it," said Sinclair. Bracing one foot against the wall, he dug his fingers into the channeled seam that encircled the pod. With a shout, he heaved upward, throwing himself against the opposite wall. The lid pivoted, missing Laura and Whiting by inches. Pale, Sinclair slid to the floor.

Laura rushed to his side, and he smiled up at her. "And before you ask, no, that wasn't an ability. I'm just freaking strong."

Laura didn't answer as she scanned his body signature. His medallion interfered, but as far as she could determine, his contact had been brief enough to cause only a minor dip in his essence levels.

She straightened and froze as she saw inside the pod. Cress lay on her back, unconscious, her body twisted in pain. In the short time she had been missing, every bit of fat had been leeched away beneath her skin. Her head was tilted back, cheekbones prominent, mouth agape as if she were crying out. Her whiteless eyes, though, bulged in their sockets and burned with a dark light.

"Dear Danu . . ." Laura whispered. On impulse, she touched

Cress's cheek. Thick violet tendrils of light slithered out of the *leanansidhe*'s skin and wrapped around Laura's hand, sucking at her body essence. With a startled cry, Laura yanked her hand back, rubbing the skin.

The Monument trembled around them, cracks snaking up the walls.

"I don't think this place is taking the stress," said Sinclair.

Whiting peered into the pod. "She's trapped in a fugue state. Until she regains consciousness, the pod will keep draining essence into the Monument."

"Will it help if we pull her out?" asked Laura.

Whiting scratched at the side of his head. "It should. The warding on the Monument will be disrupted, but I don't know if that will be enough. We're actually inside a stone ward now. Cress might not need to be in the pod anymore for the draining to continue. "

Laura clutched Sinclair's arm as another tremor rocked the building. "Well, let's drag her out of here."

Whiting shook his head. "We won't make the front door with her. Cress herself will keep draining essence until she awakens and stops."

Laura narrowed her eyes in thought. "Then we'll relay her out. Whiting, you get her as far as you can into the lobby. Jono will take her from there, and if he can't make it out the door, I'll finish the final leg."

"He's not fey," Whiting said. "He won't last more than a few moments against her."

Laura made sly eye contact with Sinclair. "He's full of surprises."

Another tremor sent masonry falling from the ceiling. "I don't think we have a choice, folks," said Sinclair. "Let's do this and get out of here."

Whiting activated his body shield and reached into the pod. He pulled Cress by her arms and over the lip of the pod. His shield dimmed as he struggled with her, then faded entirely.

"Faster, Whiting," Laura said.

She watched his body signature fade next. With a last burst of energy, Whiting wrapped his arm around Cress's waist and collapsed, using his weight to take her to the floor. Sinclair darted in and dragged him away from Cress. "He's not dead, but he didn't last long. I don't think this is going to work."

Laura crouched beside Cress. "He was already drained once tonight, Jono. I think we'll last longer. Hand her off to me before she knocks you out."

She met his eyes. "Ready?"

"Ready," he said.

With a deep breath, he hauled Cress off the floor and onto his shoulder. The contact staggered him backward as deep purple tendrils lashed into his body signature. He recovered his balance and charged for the door. His body essence wavered halfway across the lobby. Thicker ropes of essence slithered out of Cress and tangled into his body essence. He fought against the intrusion, forcing himself forward.

Wake up, Cress, Laura sent. The sending shredded in her mind.

Sinclair stumbled, his legs weak beneath him. He wasn't going to make the doors. He pushed forward, his strength slipping away like a receding tide. He pressed on, determined to cover more distance, struggling to within a few feet of the entrance.

"Take her!" he gasped.

He slipped to his knees as he draped the weight of Cress's body over Laura's shoulder. With more essence pouring into Cress from the Monument, purple tendrils of light wound around Laura's body shield as she pressed through the door. Dazed and nauseated, she staggered across the pavement outside. The landscape spun as she fell forward. Cress rolled away from her. Someone helped Laura stand, but she couldn't stay upright.

"I need earth beneath me."

She was dragged out into the hot night air and eased to the ground.

49
CHAPTER

EYES CLOSED, LAURA became aware of darkness first, her sensing ability not registering anything. The dead earth pressed against her back, its inherent essence a bare trickle. The staccato sounds of gunfire reached her next, a distant echo that sounded more harmless than it was. With the shriek of jet engines overhead, she forced her eyes open.

An army officer stood guard over her. Above, essence whirled like a corona around the man's head as it flowed over the top of the Monument. Laura eased into a sitting position. With a short chant, she tapped into the essence in the air. The tenuous connection flared, and she drew strength from the flow, drinking it in like she was parched. As a druid, she needed to touch something to tap its essence, but so much of it gathered in the air around the Monument that she was able to recharge herself.

The Monument glowed with a sickly indigo light. The faint sheen of the dampening field warped and twisted off the peak in a spiraled dome. Without Cress connected to it anymore, the field was collapsing in on itself, its own stolen essence feeding the dampening.

In the strong wind, smoke and the stench of burning wafted across the Mall. Whiting lay not far off, alive but unmoving. Dizzy, Laura let the soldier help her to her feet. The hulk of a Blackhawk helicopter smoldered on the ground on the other side of the Stryker.

"Where is she? Where's Cress?" she asked.

He pointed beyond the burning vehicles. "She went that way."

"She did? She's walking?"

He nodded once. "Yes, ma'am."

She wandered through the haze, soldiers running in the same direction, toward the White House. A pall of smoke rolled across the grass, obscuring her view. The wind shifted, and the smoke billowed up. Sinclair stood in the street beyond the Blackhawk. His body signature registered normal, no fluctuations or reductions. He stood, mesmerized by a thick column of violet essence spiraling into the air.

"Jono?"

He turned, his face stressed with concentration. As if waking, relief swept over him. In long strides, he reached Laura and wrapped her in a hard embrace. "Are you okay?"

He smelled of smoke and gunpowder and sweat. The fear that vibrated off him—fear for her—almost made her cry. The last time someone had worried about her like that was too long ago to think about. Controlling her emotions, she nodded into the crook of his shoulder. As her head finally cleared, she broke the embrace. "Where is she?"

He gestured toward the column of essence moving across the Ellipse. "That's her. She woke up and knocked me on my ass."

Cress? Laura sent. Static filtered through her mind, but no words.

National Guard unit trucks raced toward them. Soldiers jumped out, moving toward the essence column. Gunfire sounded in the distance ahead, oddly muffled.

Laura rushed across the street. "They're firing on her."

Soldiers ringed the edges of the essence column, shooting

into it. The shots sparked in bursts of orange that vanished, snuffed like spent candle flames. Laura ran past the soldiers, plunging into the hazy purple essence. Cress's body signature burned into sight, an incandescent shape moving away from Laura.

Sinclair ran in after her. "Are you crazy? We're going to get shot."

"The bullets aren't penetrating, Jono," she said. "She's deflecting them with the excess essence."

"Where the hell is she going?" he asked.

"I don't know," she said.

Cress spread her arms, as if reaching out for the Monument. The air roared as wind raged around them. The marble facing on the column cascaded down the sides of the Monument, exposing the granite underlayment. The indigo essence contained within the stone burned in a black halo. It spiraled into the air, coiling above Cress like a funnel. With a snake-like strike, it plunged into her chest. A sound came out of her, the screech of metal and fire.

Laura gasped as essence surged into the vacuum left behind. Cress's body flamed violet in the haze. With sharp gestures, she flung cars out of her path, tossing them aside like toys. She approached a long black van and stretched her arm forward. A gout of black essence burst from her palm and slammed into the van. It flipped on its side and spun in a cyclone of sparks.

A wing of Danann fairies swarmed the air with renewed strength. Bolts of searing white essence rained down as they soared and dove around Cress. With little effort, she absorbed the strikes, then knocked the Dananns back.

"I have to help her," Laura said.

Sinclair grabbed her arm. "Do what? Destroy everything in her path? She's out of control, Laura. You can't stop this."

She yanked herself away. "Look around you, Jono. They are going to kill her. DeWinter did this, not her. I can't let them kill her."

Sinclair slipped his hand into hers. "She's fighting every-one who's trying to stop her, Laura. There's no fighting this."

She fought back tears as she followed Cress toward the van. "She saved my life, Jono."

He tugged at her hand. "She's broken, Laura. She doesn't know what's she's doing."

She shook her head. "I have to try. I'm the only one here she can trust."

"She'll kill you," he said.

Something moved within her, a deep moment of recogni-tion. The look of fear in his eyes, the way his voice cracked. He wasn't playing games, wasn't trying to break down her defenses for the challenge of it. He cared. Jono Sinclair cared. And in that same moment, she knew that whatever it was he saw in her, it wasn't someone who would walk away. It wasn't someone who would give up because she was afraid of dying.

If she let Cress die, whatever chance she had with Sinclair would be gone, no matter what he thought right then. Be-cause she wouldn't be true to herself. And if she couldn't be true to herself, she couldn't be true to anyone. On a level that Sinclair didn't realize yet, that was what he was attracted to. Who she was, no matter the consequences. And that was who she was.

She kissed him, a kiss of passion and thanks and realiza-tion. He held her, his essence glowing, breaking open before her, letting down his guard and showing her the man behind the jokes and frustration and anger. She saw him then, a man in fear. And in love.

She broke the embrace and searched his face one more time. "Please, Jono. I need to do this, or nothing else will ever matter."

"I . . ." he began.

Laura touched his lips. "No more. Just be here. I'm going to need that."

He let her slip out of his arms. She ran toward Cress and

slammed into a shield barrier unlike any she had ever encountered. Cress stalked around the wrecked van. She swiped clawed fingers through the air. The rear doors ruptured and fell aside. Ropes of jagged violet essence slithered out of her hands and into the dark interior of the van. With a clenching of her first, the essence ropes tightened and whiplashed out, dangling a body in the air.

DeWinter.

She pounded against the barrier. "Stop, Cress!"

DeWinter struggled as Cress reeled him in. When he reached her hands, she made a sound like a roar, wiry tendrils of intense lavender shooting from her mouth. They burrowed into DeWinter's face. He screamed.

"Don't do this, Cress!" Laura shouted. She attacked the shield barrier with an intense bolt of yellow essence. The barrier rippled as it absorbed the energy, but it held.

"Cress! Listen to me. It's Laura. You know me, Cress. Trust me, Cress, like I trusted you."

Nothing. Cress shook DeWinter, untempered anger and hatred twisting her face.

"I trusted you to let you in, Cress! Let me in now!" Laura remembered the terror of that moment weeks earlier as she lay almost dead, her mind lost, the overwhelming fear as her body essence came under what she thought was an attack. And Cress's voice in her mind, urging her to listen, to let her in. And she let her in. She had stopped fighting and let Cress in.

Laura paused. She had *let* Cress in. She hadn't fought her. Not fighting was what made it work, allowed Cress to reach her and heal her.

DeWinter kicked the air. Blood vessels spiderwebbed across his skin, pulsing with the rhythm of Cress's essence. She was toying with him, torturing him. His cries cycled higher until the sound was a strangled gurgle. His body convulsed violently, then went limp.

Laura dropped her body shield and touched the essence

barrier. Cress's essence tendrils plunged into her. Gasping, Laura fought the urge to resist, to reject the violation. She forced herself forward as the tendrils wound their way into her essence. It felt wrong. Repulsive. A violation.

Cress. It's Laura, Cress. You know me. Her words flew off, spinning away into the tangled indigo web of Cress's body signature. As Cress pulled her in, Laura didn't resist but moved closer on her own. Her vision spotted with flashes of black and red as nausea welled up within her.

You know me, Cress. Laura. You know me.

The tendrils paused in their wavering, trembling as if deciding their next move. Laura reached out and took Cress by the shoulders and . . .

. . . plunged into a maelstrom, mind-tossed, far-flung, essence-spun . . .

. . . falling, falling, falling, through a purple maze of light across a black pit . . .

. . . burning bright, searing thoughts, tearing . . .

then . . .

. . . *wrong it's wrong I know it's wrong is it wrong what he wants I know what he wants what I wanted once he is wrong I was wrong it was long ago I am not that what once was but he wants it he calls himself he calls himself dewinter a name of ice and loneliness he knows what he wants he wants to end it all he wants them to leave him alone leave them all alone his name is dewinter I want them to leave me alone I want him to leave me alone I am not what once I was he is wrong I am not that what I was I won't be that he wants that he makes me want he is wrong it is wrong I will stop this I will stop him I have stopped him I will stop him he is gone* . . .

Laura pulled back, not fighting but relaxing, letting Cress's mind slip past hers. *Cress, it's Laura. It's Laura, Cress. You must let me in. You must listen.*

. . . *laura yes the beautiful light the light so sweet so rich I yearn I yearn I yearn but I won't I am not what I was I am not that I do not need that I touched her she let me in so rich so sweet but I will not I did not . . .*

Yes, Cress. Laura. Listen to my voice. You must hear my voice.

. . . I remember I remember I remember she is scared how scared she is she is right I cannot say she is not right but she is scared but she will try she trusts she will listen she will give me hope . . .

Yes, Cress. I listened. I believed. It's me. It's Laura. Hear me now, Cress.

. . . they are wrong they hate I feel their hate they fear I feel their fear I am their fear they make me fear I fear . . .

They're gone, Cress. You stopped it. You're safe.

. . . he's here I feel him he's here he hates he fears he will hurt us all he is lost . . .

No, Cress. He's gone. DeWinter is gone. You're safe.

. . . no no no he's here I will find him I will show them I will show Terryn he is here . . .

Terryn is safe, Cress.

. . . not safe not safe not safe . . .

Cress . . .

A cascade of images whirled through Laura—events, places, people—a chaotic rush too fast to sort out. Dizziness overwhelmed her as the images poured forth. Terryn flashed into view, then away. Darkness filled her mind, then Terryn again and even Whiting for a moment. The horizon over the ocean. The Washington skyline. Terryn. Then darkness. Terryn. Then herself. Terryn. Then Laura. Then Cress. Then Laura.

Terryn. I want Terryn. I need Terryn. Lies. They lie. They all lie. The Brinen and the Aran and the Draigen. He's here. He was there. Now he is here. I will stop him. I will save Terryn. Lies. They all lie.

I am here, Cress.

The sound was a shock to her. She heard his voice. Terryn's voice. He was safe. He was here.

I am here, Cress. Focus on my voice.

I am here, Terryn. I am here.

Let go, Laura. Let Cress hear me.

We are here, Terryn. You are safe.

Laura, hear my voice. You have done well. Now let go.

. . . Terryn my love my life my hope . . .

A spark glistened, a glimpse of essence deep within the violet haze. A bright pinpoint of warm yellow light. Her light. Her essence. Laura shuddered as she remembered.

Cress's voice pierced through the fog of her mind, and Laura spun away.

Gods! What have I done? Cress screamed across her mind.

Laura latched onto the yellow mote of essence, wrapped her mind around it, and remembered. She remembered who she was. She stumbled as Cress released her. The visible world asserted itself, a jumble of destroyed vehicles and ravaged buildings.

"Laura," someone said.

She stared at the man. Tall. Anxious. His features familiar. She searched her memory, knew him somehow, knew he would be there. His face wavered for a moment, then resolved into someone she recognized. "Jono."

She slumped against Sinclair. A smile broke across his face. His arms came out and around her. Warm. Safe. Terryn knelt in front of them, cradling Cress's still body. Cress was quiet and calm, feeding off his essence.

Orrin ap Rhys strode through the rubble, his wings flared open and burning bright white with essence. He stared down at Cress, then up at Laura. "Good work, Tate."

Rhys leaned down, his hand out in a gesture of aid.

Sinclair shoved Laura aside. "He's going to fire."

Sinclair flung himself forward, his shoulder hitting Rhys in the chest. The bolt of essence released, and Sinclair went airborne. Hands charged with essence again, Rhys swung back toward Cress.

"No!" Laura screamed.

Essence burst out of her, a shock wave of red amber. Fire coursed through her veins as she threw everything she had at him. As if time slowed, she saw the wave arc out of her chest, saw the shock on Rhys's face, saw the wave roll over him, saw him throw his arms up, saw the wave crash against his body shield, saw him tumble away.

Then she saw nothing.

50
CHAPTER

LAURA CAME OUT of the bedroom of Sinclair's apartment already dressed in her InterSec uniform. She hadn't activated the Mariel persona yet, preferring to be Laura Blackstone when she woke Sinclair. Wearing the white T-shirt and sweatpants from the previous night, he slept in the living room and hadn't moved since she had slipped into the bathroom. She picked up the remote and muted the television. Startled by the silence, he woke and sat up. His short hair was pressed flat on one side. "Someone means business," he said.

She perched on the edge of an armchair. "It's not going to be pretty. How are you feeling?"

He rubbed the back of his head. "Bruised. Headache. Sore back."

She twitched her lips. "You didn't have to sleep on the couch."

He slid into a half-seated position. "You were exhausted. I thought you would be more comfortable alone in the bed."

After she had passed out from unleashing essence on Guildmaster Orrin ap Rhys, she had come to in Sinclair's arms on the Mall, his worried face hovering over hers as he stroked her hair. He had carried her away from the chaotic scene. She had wanted to go back, but he wouldn't let her. Too weak to resist, he led her through a haze of smoke until they were beyond the barricaded emergency zone. They had found an abandoned car with the keys in the ignition and gone to his place.

"Thank you," she said.

He smiled. "Anytime."

She stood. "I have no idea what's going to happen. I'll call you later."

Easing up from the couch, he followed her. He leaned against the edge of the open door as she lingered in the hall. "What?" he said.

She shook her head. "Just thanks. Again."

The InterSec car and driver she had called for waited out front and drove her across a city in crisis. Emergency restrictions limited access to downtown, and the government had reduced all staffing to essential personnel only. Her all-level-security InterSec badge got her anywhere she wanted to go. She had never driven so easily through the normally traffic-choked streets of D.C.

In the bright morning light, the damage to the Guildhouse and surrounding building surprised her. It had looked much worse at night, with all the smoke, the soldiers, and the fires. Parts of the façade had fallen away, and bullet holes riddled the walls of the first two levels. Plate-glass windows gaped with jagged edges. Yet the building appeared more forlorn than destroyed.

At the main entrance, Danann security agents stopped her. "Agent Mariel Tate, your credentials are not valid to enter the Guildhouse per order of the Guildmaster."

She chuckled, which seemed to confuse the agents. The banning didn't surprise her. Without a word, she walked away and around the building. As she turned the corner at the rear of the Guildhouse, she deactivated the Mariel glamour and blurred her uniform to look like a blouse and dress pants. She entered the rear door and held up her Guild badge. The Danann agents stepped aside for Laura Blackstone.

As she cut through the first-floor function rooms to reach the main elevators, she reactivated the Mariel persona. The remains of Draigen's reception littered the lobby. Chairs were overturned or pushed to the walls, and debris was scattered in every corner. In the center of the room, tall, beautiful— incongruous—an enormous vase of white flowers remained untouched amid the mess. Cleanup crews loaded broken fixtures into crates or threw out destroyed furniture.

Once through the main-door checkpoint, no one stopped her. Brownie security guards operated the elevators and rode up with the passengers. When the next available elevator arrived, Laura sent the operator notice that no one else was to ride with her. She wanted her destination as little seen as possible.

Since waking, she had gone over the sequence of events until a pattern emerged, a pathetic pattern of twisted motives that had spiraled out of control. She saw it all, tying the threads together, surmising the obvious gaps. It was over, but it was a waste, and she wasn't going to keep silent.

The macCullen residential floor bristled with Inverni security. The scene gave Laura a certain sense of irony, which she hoped would vanish in few minutes. At the conference suite, the brownie Davvi worked at a spare, organized desk. "Good morning, Agent Tate."

She smiled. "Good morning, Davvi. I hope you can help me."

"Yes, miss?"

"I need a copy of the security-shift change orders at Master macCullen's residence from the day Cress was kidnapped. Would you have that?" she asked.

"Yes, miss," he said.

Anticipation prickled up her spine. She had worked with Saffin long enough to know that brownies tried to follow their usual procedures even when they had to make exceptions to them. She waited, but he didn't move. Although she was in no mood for Davvi's literalness, his responses forced her to be more aware of her own language. "Davvi, please give me a copy."

He opened a file drawer behind him. Without needing to search, he retrieved a sheet of paper and dropped it on a compact photocopier behind the desk. He held out the copy to Laura. When she took the end of it, he didn't let go. Curious, Laura met his gaze. "Is there something wrong, Davvi?"

He pinched his lips, then blinked several times. "I am conflicted, Agent Tate. Master macCullen instructed me to respond to you as I would him. I may have erred with respect to this document and am uncertain of my duty."

He released the photocopy. Laura glanced over the sheet, confirming her suspicion. "What is the error?"

Davvi clasped his hands behind his back and bowed his head. "The Lord Guardian expressed fear of a security breach and asked that a copy of the order not be made. I understood his concern, but I had the utmost faith in my abilities to secure the document. Despite his instruction, I made the copy."

"That's an odd request for Terryn to make."

"You mistake me, miss. The Master is not a Lord Guardian," Davvi said.

She couldn't prevent a small smile. "Yes, I'd forgotten. Which Lord Guardian asked you not to make the copy?"

"Lord Aran, miss," he said.

His explanation satisfied her. It made her case all the stronger. "Thank you, Davvi."

He sighed. "I fear I may have been responsible for the schedule error at the Master's residence that resulted in the kidnapping of his concubine. I will accept whatever disciplinary measure the Master demands."

Laura gaped. "What?"

"I may be responsible . . ."

Laughing, she held up her hand. "I'm sorry, Davvi. I wasn't asking you to repeat. I was reacting to what you said. The last thing I expected today was to hear Cress referred to as a concubine."

Davvi tilted his head. "Is it incorrect? I have researched but am at loss for a more accurate term that respects the Master's life decision."

"I'd run it by Terryn," she said. She glanced at the door. "Are they all in there?"

"Yes, miss."

She tugged at her jacket, inhaled deeply, and opened the door. The macCullens sat at a round table covered with paperwork. As one, they looked toward the door, Draigen with a neutral pleasant expression while Aran and Brinen were distracted. She suspected they had been arguing. Terryn, however, smiled.

"Lady Regent, I apologize for the intrusion," Laura said.

"No apologies needed after what you accomplished, Agent Tate. I was hoping we could meet you before I leave. I want to extend my deepest thanks. I believe we all owe you our lives," Draigen said.

Is Cress okay? she sent to Terryn.

I have her in seclusion. Whiting is hopeful for her recovery, he replied.

Laura bowed her head in acknowledgment. "I am not sure you will thank me when I leave here, Lady Regent. I'll get right to the point. Last night happened because of the people in this room. You are to blame. All of you."

The statement had the reaction she expected. The macCullens stared at her, suspicious and calculating, except Terryn, who cocked his head as he waited for her to continue. She knew that look, a patient waiting for facts and explanation. He wasn't going to like it.

She started with Draigen. "Lady Regent, your life was not in danger until last night. Legacy did target you as part of its broader plan to assassinate high-profile fey, but you were never their sole target."

"What in hell are you talking about?" Aran asked.

From her jacket, she produced a folder and data drives. "The assassination attempt was a well-planned and -executed ruse. This documentation shows that funds were transferred into offshore accounts to Sean Carr and Uma macGrath prior to the shooting incident. The funds were traceable to a shadow account in Wales originally set up as a secret fund in case the Seelie Court moved against the Inverni."

"I knew nothing of this account," Draigen said.

Laura was surprised that she was telling the truth, but her ignorance didn't matter on the point. "Your father set it up or, should I say, had it set up. Our sources indicate only two people had access to that account. Your father was one. Brinen macCullen is the other."

Brinen glowered at her. "I have no idea what you are talking about, and I don't like what you are implying."

Laura ignored him and slid one of the data drives to the center of the table. "MacGrath was paid significantly more than Carr, which confused me since Carr was more criminally exposed as the shooter and had the greater risk. Autopsy results demonstrate conclusively that macGrath killed Carr, presumably to silence him, and thus received a bonus. On the day of the assassination attempt, video surveillance shows that Brinen reacted to the shots prior to the actual firing at Draigen. The only explanation is that he knew the shot was coming. Uma macGrath is clearly visible in the surveillance then, reacting to Brinen's injury."

"I will not hear . . ." Brinen began.

Draigen glanced up at him. "Let her finish, brother. I shall be the judge of her words."

Laura sensed the emotion roiling off him but refused to be intimidated into activating her body shield. "I examined macGrath's body. The residue of essence signatures on her indicated she had not been in proximity to anyone from the time of the shooting until her death. All except one person: Brinen macCullen."

Brinen shot to his feet. "I examined her body at the murder scene. You were there."

Terryn's quiet, firm voice cut through the shout. "Sit down, Brin."

Laura clasped her hands behind her back. "Which is why

I dismissed your essence at first. MacGrath was in a binding spell before she died. Someone had to get close to her to do that, and the only person whom she would let close after the assassination attempt was someone she trusted. That person would have left a strong body signature residue on her. The only strong signature on her was yours, Brinen. The logical conclusion is that you anticipated the issue and acted accordingly at her murder scene to camouflage the essence left behind in the shock that killed her."

Brinen glared. "Quite fanciful. Pray, do shout this to the world. We will bring the entire Inverni clan down on you."

Aran glared across the table. "Perhaps not the entire clan."

Brinen scoffed. "What this . . . person . . . fails to realize is that you have access to the clan accounts, and our father was more likely to share such a ridiculous plan with you."

Laura pulled more documents out of the folder. "Indeed. Aran was clearly the likely suspect. He had access to other accounts, so it wasn't out of the realm of possibility he had access to the account in question. MacGrath and Carr were more affiliated with him than with Brinen. And he had motivation since Aran is the more likely successor to Draigen. Exactly what Brinen wanted us to think. Aran suspected the frame-up, and our sources have confirmed that Brinen made the payments."

Terryn stared at Brinen. "Why would you do such a thing, brother?"

"She's lying, Terryn. I would never try to kill our own sister," he said.

"Killing wasn't the plan," Laura continued. "Fear was. Brinen is afraid of where Draigen is taking the Inverni, with Aran's support. As you told me, Terryn, he's pressed you to assume leadership for years. He thought he had found a way to force Draigen out and blame Aran in the process. He hoped your fear of Draigen's being killed would pressure you to take the underKing crown and blame Aran for attempted murder. But you didn't take the bait because of Cress. Brinen never thought you would choose her over Draigen."

Brinen laughed with a sneer. "This is getting more preposterous all the time."

The level of falseness in his voice brought Laura satisfaction. She was right. "It was at that point that I think things truly went out of control because of Cress."

Terryn became still. "What does she have to do with this?"

Laura took a deep breath. She was about to accuse a head of state of attempted murder. "You and Draigen don't agree on how to deal with the Seelie Court over this Treaty mess. Draigen fears you won't stand up to Maeve, so she looked for a way to discredit you to keep her regency. She found an unlikely ally in Orrin ap Rhys. Rhys suspects you might be able to resolve your differences with Maeve, and he doesn't want that to happen. He would rather see the Inverni destroyed, and with Draigen in charge, that's much more likely. Draigen encouraged Orrin ap Rhys to remove Cress from InterSec and have you suspended in order to discredit you among your own people. It fit Rhys's agenda, so he did it. I have confirmed private electronic communications between them that they had to use because the wards in this building blocked sendings."

Draigen did not react. A flutter of sendings passed in the air, and Terryn tilted his head in consideration. "Continue, please."

She dropped the photocopy from Davvi in front of Brinen. "Can you identify that?"

Surprise swept over his face. "It's the security-shift schedule change."

Laura moved the sheet to Draigen and Terryn. "With the correct times. That was the final piece of evidence that convinced me of what happened next. Brinen insisted that he gave Aran the correct time to switch Cress's security. I believed him, and this order shows Brinen was telling the truth. Aran set up the gap to allow Cress's kidnapping. He despises the *leanansidhe*, and when he saw opportunity to rid the clan of Cress, he took it. He was paid well for his efforts by the Legacy group that attacked last night."

She paused, then decided to provide proof that only Terryn would truly understand. "DeWinter asked Fallon Moor to transfer the money into the Inverni account at Aran's direction. I traced the transaction and have confirmed proof."

I'm sorry, Terryn, she sent.

Terryn looked stricken. *You are not to blame.*

Sendings fluttered through the air. Terryn turned to Laura. "Thank you, Mariel. This is now a clan matter."

She hesitated. "I have one more thing to say. While you played games with the leadership of your clan, people have died. If you keep on this course, more will. Find a better way because I think you are all doomed otherwise. If you can't, you deserve to lose everything."

She walked to the door, but Terryn called her name. She turned, expecting an argument.

"Please tell Agent Sinclair I expect to see him report for official duty," he said.

A bittersweet smile crossed her lips. "I will."

You need to make a decision about your own life, too, Terryn. Good luck, she sent.

She didn't look back. Despite everything—Brinen's misguided plans, Rhys's machinations, Terryn's love for Cress—she knew that what she had exposed to the macCullens would probably cause more problems among the Inverni than any of the others.

She had one more stop to make. When the elevator arrived, she held her InterSec badge up and ordered the brownie security guard out. In the long run, it didn't matter who knew she went to the Guildmaster's office, but given that she had attacked him the night before, she wanted as little security around as possible.

As Laura entered the anteroom to Orrin ap Rhys's office suite, it occurred to her that she had never been there before as Mariel. She had a sense of wrongness, as if she had crossed personas, something she avoided at all costs. There was no conflict, though. Her business with him was a personal matter between him and Mariel Tate.

His Danann assistant glanced up and paused at her typing. She placed a trembling hand on the desk blotter near the phone. "Can I help you?"

"Mariel Tate to see the Guildmaster," she said.

The Danann paused, a professional smile on her face. "The Guildmaster says you should coordinate communications through his lawyer. Would you . . ."

Lifting her hand as if she were brushing her hair back, Laura tapped the ambient essence in the air. "Sleep."

The assistant froze in midsentence. Laura opened the office door. In irritation, Rhys turned in his seat at the sound of her entrance. He drew a subtle charge of essence into his hands when he saw her but didn't activate his body shield. She sensed that his body essence was damaged from her blast. Even a short burst of essence without his shields would kill him. She wasn't sorry he was alive, but at that moment, she wished she had put him in the hospital

"Nervous about something, Rhys?" she asked.

"I had you banned from this building," he said.

She stopped in front of his desk. "Indeed. Yet here I am. Keep that in mind for the future."

"Security is on its way," he said.

She withdrew papers from her jacket and dropped them in front of him. "I won't be long."

He glanced at the top sheet, empty except for rows of numbers. "What is this?"

She leaned her hands on the front of his desk. "Financial transactions. InterSec tracked down the original sources of a significant amount of money. Funds moving from you personally to Legacy to fund the kidnapping of Cress Leanansidhe."

He chuckled. "You'll have a hard time proving that."

"And you will have a hard time defending yourself against conspiracy charges as well as attempted murder," she said.

With a smug look, he extinguished the essence in his hands. "Shall I point out the flaw in your amusing little plan, dear? As High Queen Maeve's representative, I have complete diplomatic immunity. You won't be able to file charges on your rather creative claim."

Laura straightened. "That doesn't mean you won't be deported from the U.S. Once the evidence is made public, no government will grant you credentials again. You'll be trapped in Ireland for the rest of your illustrious career . . . dear."

Rhys narrowed his eyes, a feeble light flickering in them. "You don't know what you're doing."

She gave him the coldest smile she knew how. "Oh, it's much worse than that, Rhys. I don't *care* what I'm doing. I'll be watching. Have a nice day."

As she strode through the anteroom, she withdrew the sleep spell on the assistant. ". . . like to make an appointment?"

"That won't be necessary," Laura said.

On the sidewalk in front of the Guildhouse, she paused. She closed her eyes and lifted her face to the sun. The warmth felt good on her skin. She filtered out the traffic noise and focused on the soft sounds of the birds across the street. She could shut things out. She could do it. She had thought she could, but she hadn't given herself a reason to in a long time.

She opened her eyes, the whir of the city reasserting itself around her. She strode up the sidewalk to where a black car waited. The driver opened the door, and she slid into the backseat. As they pulled away from the curb, she opened her cell phone.

"It's me," she said, when Jono answered.

"Who you?" She heard the smile in his voice.

She watched the decimated Mall slip past the window. "Just me. How'd you like to pack your bags and go away with me for the weekend?"

"I'd like that very much," he said.

"I'll be there in twenty minutes," she said.

She disconnected the call and settled back in the seat. She

had done it, said her piece no matter the consequences. She had been honest about what she thought with people who didn't want to hear. A sense of calm satisfaction spread over her, and she smiled. Then she laughed, anxious to see Sinclair.

**Explore the outer reaches
of imagination—don't miss these authors
of dark fantasy and urban noir that take you
to the edge and beyond.**

Patricia Briggs	Karen Chance	Anne Bishop
Simon R. Green	Caitlin R. Kiernan	Janine Cross
Jim Butcher	Rachel Caine	Sarah Monette
Kat Richardson	Glen Cook	Douglas Clegg

penguin.com

M15G0907

THE ULTIMATE IN FANTASY!

From magical tales of distant worlds to stories of those with abilities beyond the ordinary, Ace and Roc have everything you need to stretch your imagination to its limits.

Marion Zimmer Bradley/Diana L. Paxson

Guy Gavriel Kay

Dennis L. McKiernan

Patricia A. McKillip

Robin McKinley

Sharon Shinn

Katherine Kurtz

Barb and J. C. Hendee

Elizabeth Bear

T. A. Barron

Brian Jacques

Robert Asprin

penguin.com

M12G1107

THE ULTIMATE
IN SCIENCE FICTION

From tales of distant worlds to stories of tomorrow's technology, Ace and Roc have everything you need to stretch your imagination to its limits.

Alastair Reynolds

Allen Steele

Charles Stross

Robert Heinlein

Joe Haldeman

Jack McDevitt

John Varley

William C. Dietz

Harry Turtledove

S. M. Stirling

Simon R. Green

Chris Bunch

E. E. Knight

S. L. Viehl

Kristine Kathryn Rusch

penguin.com

RoC ACE

M3G0907

Penguin Group (USA) Online

What will you be reading tomorrow?

Patricia Cornwell, Nora Roberts, Catherine Coulter,
Ken Follett, John Sandford, Clive Cussler,
Tom Clancy, Laurell K. Hamilton, Charlaine Harris,
J. R. Ward, W.E.B. Griffin, William Gibson,
Robin Cook, Brian Jacques, Stephen King,
Dean Koontz, Eric Jerome Dickey, Terry McMillan,
Sue Monk Kidd, Amy Tan, Jayne Ann Krentz,
Daniel Silva, Kate Jacobs...

You'll find them all at
penguin.com

Read excerpts and newsletters,
find tour schedules and reading group guides,
and enter contests.

Subscribe to Penguin Group (USA) newsletters
and get an exclusive inside look
at exciting new titles and the authors you love
long before everyone else does.

PENGUIN GROUP (USA)
penguin.com

M224G0909